PENGUIN CLASSICS

THE PREYING BIRDS

Amado V. Hernandez (1903–70) is one of the most famous nationalist writers in the Philippines. His poetry, fiction and plays stoked the flames against US imperialism, the workers' poverty, and a feudal land tenancy system.

Born in Tondo, Manila, on 13 September 1903, Hernandez began his career in journalism in the 1920s, when the initial massive Filipino resistance against US military rule had declined. He became an editor of the Manila daily *Mabuhay* (*Long Live*) from 1932 to 1934. In 1939, he won the Commonwealth Literary Contest for a nationalist historical epic, *Pilipinas* (*Philippines*); and in 1940, his collection of mainly traditional poems, *Kayumanggi* (*Brown*), won the Commonwealth Award in Literature. During the Japanese occupation of the Philippines (1942–45), Hernandez served as an intelligence officer for the underground guerilla resistance, an experience reflected in his major novel, *Mga Ibong Mandaragit*, which is translated here as *The Preying Birds*.

After the war, Hernandez assumed the role of a public intellectual: he organized the Philippine Newspaper Guild in 1945; and he spoke out on national issues as an appointed councillor of Manila from 1945–46 and again, from 1948–51. It was during his presidency of the Congress of Labour Organizations (1947), the largest federation of militant trade unions in the country, that he moved from the romantic reformism of his early years to militancy.

An allegorical representation of the sociopolitical crisis of the country from the 1930s up to the 1950s can be found in Hernandez's realistic novel, *Luha ng Buwaya* (*Crocodile Tears*), and the epic poem of class struggle, *Bayang Malaya* (*Free Country*), for which he received the prestigious Balagtas Memorial Award.

Tarred and feathered during the Cold War, which also reached the Philippines, Hernandez was arrested on 26 January 1951 and accused of complicity with the Communist-led uprising. While in jail in various military camps for five years and six months, he wrote the satirical poem, *Isang Dipang Langit* (*An Arm's Stretch of Sky*) and the play, *Muntinlupa*.

After his release from prison, Hernandez wrote countless stories under various pseudonyms for the leading weekly magazine, *Liwayway* (*Dawn*). He also wrote columns for the daily newspaper, *Taliba* (*News*), and edited the radical newspapers *Ang Makabayan* (*The Nationalist*) during 1956–58 and *Ang Masa* (*The Masses*) during 1967–70. He participated in the Afro-Asian Writers' Emergency Conference in Beijing, China, in June–July 1966, and at the International War Crimes Tribunal, where he joined the likes of Simone De Beauvoir, Bertrand Russell, and Jean Paul Sartre in November 1966, and became an outspoken voice for freedom of expression and human rights worldwide.

His numerous honours culminated in the Republic Cultural Heritage Award (1962) and National Artist Award, given by a grateful nation in 1973. Up to the day (24 March 1970) he died, Hernandez was still writing a column and giving advice to the leaders of the massive rallies that were rocking the Philippines at that time. In the uncanny situation of a novel being prophetic, this work prefigured the dictatorship that would soon descend upon the land.

Danton Remoto was educated at the University of Stirling (British Council scholar) and Rutgers University (Fulbright scholar) as well as at the Jesuit-run Ateneo de Manila University (Association of South East Nations scholar) and the University of the Philippines. He has worked as a Publishing Director at Ateneo, Head of Communications at the United Nations Development Programme, TV and radio host at TV 5 and Radyo 5, President of The Manila Times College, and Head of School at the University of Nottingham, Malaysia.

He has published a baker's dozen of books in English, including *Riverrun, A Novel* and *Heart of Summer: Selected Stories and Tales*. He also translated the 1906 novel by Lope K. Santos, *Banaag at Sikat,* into English (*Radiance and Sunrise*) for the South East Asian Literary Classics series. His work is cited in the *Oxford Research Encyclopedia of Literature*, *The Princeton Encyclopedia of Poetry and Poetics*, and the *Routledge Encyclopedia of Postcolonial Literature*. He has been a Fellow at the Cambridge University Summer Seminar on Literature, the Bread Loaf Writers' Conference, and most recently, at the MacDowell Arts Residency in New Hampshire, USA. He is now writing his third novel as well as a new collection of essays and poems. He lives in South East Asia and Los Angeles.

Praise for *Mga Ibong Mandaragit*

'*Mga Ibong Mandaragit* by Amado V. Hernandez is a mirror of life and society when individuals are, at the moment of historical crisis, confronted by their collective life and challenges against their freedom. The novel offers a picture of a just society that shall give birth to Filipinos. When that time comes, then the Filipinos' sense of humanity will be complete and they can hold their heads high . . .'
—Citation for the National Artist Award for Literature, 1973

'The Tanglaw ng Lahi (Light of the Race) Award is given to those who have dedicated their lifetime to promote Filipino identity and have succeeded in steering the national consciousness towards a clarification of the Filipino image . . . Amado V. Hernandez avoided the affliction common to most intellectuals known as 'miseducation'. His works reflect the revolutionary consciousness that runs through the Rizal literary tradition.'
—Citation for the *Tanglaw ng Lahi* Award, 1970
Ateneo de Manila University

'The two novels of Amado V. Hernandez are vigorous reflections of the economic troubles of the times . . . *Mga Ibong Mandaragit* is a fiery protest against the domination of Filipinos by American industrialists, morally bankrupt religious leaders and corrupt bureaucrats. For sheer scope alone, the novel qualifies as the most extensive and searching of Philippine society, the pressures that are undermining it, and the forces that are working to change it.'
—Dr Bienvenido Lumbera, Winner of the
Ramon Magsaysay Award for Literature, Asia's Nobel Prize

'*Mga Ibong Mandaragit* is social criticism presented in a vigorous and realistic manner. It is fictional reality in much the same way that the novels of the Philippine national hero and novelist, Jose Rizal, portrayed actual events.'
—Professor Renato Constantino, Author of *The Philippines:
A Past Revisited* and *Neo-Colonial Identity and Counter-Consciousness*

'The creative self of Amado V. Hernandez was forged by more than fifty years of struggle for Philippine nationalism, democracy and social justice. His life and his writings seem to be one, both marked by deep love of country and the possibilities of hope.'

—Dr Rosario Torres-Yu, Critic and Former Dean of the College of Arts and Letters, University of the Philippines

'Amado V. Hernandez is the grand old man of Philippine literature at whatever age.'

—Ninotchka Rosca, Author of *State of War* and *Twice Blessed*, Winner of the American Book Award

'Like his fellow anti-colonial writer James Joyce, Amado V. Hernandez forged the uncreated conscience of the race . . . The movement of his writing was from an arm's stretch of sky, as seen from his prison cell, to the vast hopes of a free country.'

—Dr Epifanio San Juan, Winner of the Asian American Studies, Outstanding Book Award; Emeritus Professor, University of Connecticut

'Perhaps, the broadest analysis of the different aspects of life from the Second World War until the 1960s can be found in *Mga Ibong Mandaragit*, with Mando Plaridel as its central sensibility. The qualities of [Jose Rizal's] Ibarra and Simoun are combined in Mando, the passive and active protagonist who will wake the Filipinos from their sleep.'

—Dr Soledad S. Reyes, *Nobelang Tagalog 1905–1975: Tradisyon at Modernismo*

'Amado V. Hernandez is both a creator and a destroyer. His writings recorded the heroism of the race . . . He gave words to the poor and the voiceless, and his works awakened the indifferent. His life was a testament to the Filipino genius.'

—Andres Cristobal Cruz, Novelist and Winner of the Carlos Palanca Prize for Literature

'The novel illustrates the constant Filipino theme, which is a continuation in contemporary times of the so-called 'propaganda' tradition that began in 1872. This tradition should perhaps really be called the tradition of social awareness and commitment . . . The theme and structure of the novel is unified by the monomythic pattern of separation-initiation-return . . . The novel escapes the faults of the earlier Tagalog novels by the sheer force of its language and its narrative scope.'

——Dr Patricia Melendrez-Cruz, Critic and Professor,
University of the Philippines

'A highly imaginative novel that is a fusion of fantasy and politics. A watershed in Philippine writing in Tagalog.'

—Edgar Maranan, Poet and Critic; Winner of the
Carlos Palanca Prize in Literature

'The novel is heir to the 'Rizal' tradition of literary realism by virtue of its careful attempt to provide a description and an account of postwar, formally independent Philippine society, its conditions, and its prospects. The imperatives for moral training and knowledge come together in the novel, not only as the content of the novel or what *Mga Ibong Mandaragit* is about, but as the defining parameters of the novel's conception of its own status as a work of literature.'

—Dr Caroline S. Hau, *Necessary Fictions: Philippine Literature and the Nation, 1946–1980*

'Some Tagalog novels, notably Amado V. Hernandez's *Mga Ibong Mandaragit,* were serious works that dealt with socio-political themes. As such, they departed from the long-established formula behind every popular or commercially successful Tagalog novel . . . While this novel was no bestseller in its day, it received critical acclaim and eventually found its way into the reading lists of schools and universities. For this reason, the novel has remained in print.'

—Dr Patricia May B. Jurilla, *Tagalog Bestsellers of the Twentieth Century: A History of the Book in the Philippines*

Praise for Danton Remoto

'Lush, limpid and lean, Danton Remoto is a stylist of the English language. Read him.'
—Bernice Reubens, Winner of the Man Booker Prize for the novel, *The Elected Member*

'I am a fan of the works of Danton Remoto.'
—Junot Diaz, Winner of the Pulitzer Prize and the National Book Critics Circle Prize for the novel, *The Brief Wondrous Life of Oscar Wao*

'Danton Remoto is an accomplished writer whose fiction is marked by elegant and intense language. I am also impressed by the social concern in his language, wrought well in images so clear it is like seeing pebbles at the bottom of a pond.'
—Sir Stephen Spender, Winner of the Golden PEN Award; Poet Laureate of the United States

'Danton Remoto's books are vivid, well-written and enthralling. He is an adroit writer: his works form part of the Philippines' new heart.'
—James Hamilton-Paterson, Winner of the Whitbread Prize for the novel, *Gerontion*

'Danton Remoto is one of the Philippines' best writers.'
—*The Age of Melbourne*

'Danton Remoto is a smart and sensitive writer whose works ask many questions about our complex and colourful country.'
— Jessica Hagedorn, Shortlisted for the National Book Award for the novel, *Dogeaters*

'Danton Remoto is such a wonderful writer. In *Riverrun: A Novel*, he writes about the tropical Catholic magic that saves and destroys.'
—Tiphanie Yanique, Winner of the American Academy Arts and Letters Award, for the novel, *Love and Drowning*

'Danton Remoto's *Riverrun: A Novel* is one of the most anticipated books by an Asian writer in the year 2020.'

—Book Riot, USA

'The works of Danton Remoto are like the quick strokes of calligraphy. The meanings are not just found in the words but also in the white spaces, the silences between.'

—Edwin Morgan, OBE, Lifetime Awardee for Literature,
Scottish Arts Council

'Danton Remoto is a noted poet, fiction writer and newspaper columnist whose books have reached a wide audience in the Philippines and in South East Asia. Self-affirmation is highlighted in many of his writings.'

—*Routledge International Encyclopedia of Literature*

Mga Ibong Mandaragit
The Preying Birds
A Socio-Political Novel

Amado V. Hernandez

Translated by Danton Remoto
Authorized English Translation

PENGUIN BOOKS

An imprint of Penguin Random House

PENGUIN CLASSICS

USA | Canada | UK | Ireland | Australia
New Zealand | India | South Africa | China | Southeast Asia

Penguin Classics is part of the Penguin Random House group of companies
whose addresses can be found at global.penguinrandomhouse.com

Published by Penguin Random House SEA Pte Ltd
9, Changi South Street 3, Level 08-01,
Singapore 486361

First published in Penguin Classics by Penguin Random House SEA 2022

ISBN 9789815017847

Typeset in Adobe Garamond Pro by MAP Systems, Bangalore, India

www.penguin.sg

This translation is dedicated to
the late National Artist for Literature, Dr Bienvenido Lumbera, as well
as to Emmanuel A.F. Lacaba and Alfredo Navarro Salanga

who taught us all
that roots can give us wings,
and that memory is the mother of all writing.

Contents

Author's Preface

In the last days of March 1952, I was sentenced by the lower court to life imprisonment for the charge of 'complex rebellion'. Thus, from the first day of January 1951, the Army threw me into jail at Camp Murphy (now Camp Aguinaldo) incommunicado. But the charges against me were only brought to the proper court in August 1951.

I was brought to the Muntinlupa Penitentiary after the jail sentence had been given to me. One day, the writer Magtanggol Asa (the pen name of Aurelio Alvero) visited my cell. He was also imprisoned in another cell at Muntinlupa. He told me: 'You are innocent of the charges being levelled against you, but you are guilty of something against our language and literature. Since you joined the labour rights movement and became involved in politics, your pen has dried up. So while you're here, I think you should take up your pen again and write.'

But Magtanggol Asa was wrong. My involvement in the labour movement and political work just fulfilled my beliefs in life. I did not want to write from the heights of the ivory tower. I believe that the writer is not just a passive viewer watching the spectacle of democracy.

From my conversation with Magtanggol Asa came *Isang Dipang Langit*, a book of poems that won the Republic Cultural Heritage Award for Literature in 1962. I also finished an epic poem, *Bayang Malaya*, which consisted of 5,000 lines. It was three times longer than Francisco Balagtas' epic poem, *Florante at Laura*, which had 1,700 lines.

My frequent visitors included Attorney Juan T. David and the 'battlehorses' that composed my panel of lawyers: Senator Laurel, Senator Recto, Claudio Teehankee Jr., Enrique Fernando, Antonio Barredo, Manuel Chan and the aforementioned Juan T. David. Juaning David advised me that 'there's no certainty how long you will stay in jail. Therefore, you should write. Many masterworks in literature were written behind bars.'

Juaning David seemed to have spoken with the tongues of angels. For in my isolation cell, I wrote the outline and the first draft of *Mga Ibong Mandaragit*. I was finally freed on 20 July 1956. I continued writing and revising my novel, and in the early months of 1959, *Liwayway* magazine began publishing some of its chapters in serial form.

After several years, I returned to the novel, revised it and finally finished it in July 1964. I was invigorated by the final decision of the Supreme Court, which found Amado V. Hernandez completely innocent of the charges against him on 31 May 1964.

Again, Juaning David's words were prophetic. The charges against me had dragged on for twelve years. Perhaps, my works *Isang Dipang Langit*, *Bayang Malaya* and *Mga Ibong Mandaragit* have also 'absolved' me from Magtanggol Asa's accusations against me for my sins against Philippine language and literature.

This is the first publication of *Mga Ibong Mandaragit* in book form. The only people who have read the complete manuscript in its present form and content are the critic and historian Renato Constantino, Dr Epifanio San Juan of Harvard University and Dr Patricia Melendrez of the University of the Philippines.

My good friend, Indo B. Ayuda, typed the final manuscript of the novel. I would like to thank everyone who made *Mga Ibong Mandaragit* possible.

Amado V. Hernandez
Manila
December 1968

Translator's Introduction

Like Praomedya Ananta Toer's *This Earth of Mankind*, Amado V. Hernandez wrote the outline and first draft of *Mga Ibong Mandaragit* while in jail. Hernandez was charged with the alleged crime of 'complex rebellion', which was primarily rebellion against the state, along with arson and robbery. He was shunted off to various military camps and detention centres for five years. If Oscar Wilde said that 'writing well is the best revenge', then Hernandez did just that. He wrote three books while in detention at the National Penitentiary: an epic poem, a play and the novel whose English translation you now hold in your hands.

Several chapters from the novel were published in serialized form in the highly popular weekly *Liwayway* magazine. While official figures pegged its highest circulation at 200,000 in the 1960s, weekly Tagalog magazines and comics were passed on from hand to hand: from grandmothers to the parents to the children to the house help and the neighbours as well. There were also *sari-sari* stores (variety stores) that rented these weekly reading fares. Thus, the pass-on readership of every weekly issue of *Liwayway* could reach as many as 1,000,000 readers a week.

Hernandez catered to this massive readership by writing a novel that commingled many genres and forms. It is a love story, a war story, a fantasy story, and as the subtitle calls it, also a socio-political story. It obviously recalls Jose Rizal's *El Filibusterismo*, whose last part ends with Father Florentino throwing Simoun's treasure chest of jewellery into the bottom of the sea, to surface only at the proper time. It also recalls Alexander Dumas' *The Count of Monte Cristo*, with its theme of the downtrodden returning as the avenging angel. But it's also firmly rooted in the Philippine literature of protest that started with the Propaganda Movement in 1872 against the Spanish colonizers, flamed in 1890s by the publication of Rizal's *Noli Me Tangere* and *El Filbusterismo*, and continued to rage well into the twentieth century.

Lope K. Santos, who was the teacher of Hernandez and also a newspaperman and fiction writer like him, published *Banaag at Sikat* in 1906. *Radiance and Sunrise*, my English translation of this novel, was published as part of the South East Asia Literary Classics series by Penguin Random House in December 2021. Nationalist feelings still ran high in the early twentieth century, and poetry and fiction was being published in the daily newspapers. They were frankly anti-American, and the new colonizers stemmed these sentiments by passing anti-subversive measures into law—and calling those who opposed them 'bandits' and 'outlaws', words that would later morph into 'Communists'.

Hernandez was born on 13 September 1903, in Tondo, Manila, the cradle of heroes and revolutionaries. His birth seemed propitious, for the Americans were then just beginning their 'benevolent assimilation' of the Philippines, in the words of President William McKinley. Hernandez was hurtled immediately into the vortex of the times. Listen to him talk briefly about his education:

> 'I studied in Gagalangin, Tondo, at the Manila High School and the American Correspondence School, where I finished the third year of my Bachelor of Arts. I wanted to be a lawyer and a defender of the working class at one time, and I almost became a painter. But I turned into a poet instead, because my aunt hit me on the head for painting a portrait of her with horns.'

The worlds of poetry and images led him to work as a reporter for the *Watawat* (*Flag*) newspaper, a columnist at *Pagkakaisa* (*Unity*) newspaper, and editor of *Mabuhay* (*Long Live*) at the age of thirty-two. In his long and storied career as a journalist, he also edited the following newspapers: *Pilipino, Ang Makabayan (The Nationalist), Sampaguita (Jasmine) Weekly* and *Mabuhay Extra.* Alongside editing news and features and writing editorials, he was also crafting his poems and short stories.

When the Japanese came, he went underground and worked as an intelligence officer for the resistance movement. But he was disillusioned after the war. He said:

> 'I saw the rapacious self-interest of those around me, people switching their allegiance. What happened here was a contrast to an English bakery incident I read about, where the bakery was turned over to the community. If you go to the Quinta Market now, you will see food rotting in the stalls, and yet, the people are hungry.'

After the war, he resumed his newspaper work, where he helped organize the Philippine Newspaper Guild in 1945. This paved the way for his work with the labour movement. He later helped found the Congress of Labour Organizations (CLO), which was suspected of being a 'Communist front'.

He was tarred and feathered in a Philippines that was also part of the Cold War in the 1950s. He was thrown in prison, and from the depths of that prison came *Mga Ibong Mandaragit.*

While still in prison, he sent an essay to the 1952 *Yearbook of the International Longshoremen and Warehousemen's Union* (Local 37) edited by the Filipino expatriate writer, Carlos Bulosan. Hernandez wrote:

> 'During the dark days of the enemy occupation, the Filipino workingman realized that labour must speak only one universal language. It has to rise above national and racial barriers, that labour everywhere has one common struggle, and that it must march toward one goal: the liberation of all the peoples from the chains of tyranny, fascism and imperialism.'

When he was released from prison, he published the novel in serial form and rejoined the labour movement. He was also appointed for two terms as City Councillor of Manila on a pro-labour platform.

From 1962 to 1967, he also worked for *Taliba* and *Ang Masa*, while continuing his work with the labour movement.

During the last years of the 1960s, which happened to be the last years of his life, Hernandez revised the serialized 1959 version of *Mga Ibong Mandaragit* and finally published it in book form. Shorn of some of the romantic and touristic asides that catered to the weekly *Liwayway* audience, the revised version was leaner and bolder. Hernandez also updated the novel to include the latest shenanigans of the corrupt powers-that-be, true to his training as a journalist, whose job was 'to hurry history'.

The novel begins with Andoy, a guerrilla fighter during the Japanese occupation recovering from the bottom of the sea the wealth in jewellery that Father Florentino had thrown away after the death of the subversive Simoun in Rizal's *El Filibusterismo*. With this wealth, the former servant in the household of Don Segundo Montero, a wealthy landlord, has now taken the name of Mando Plaridel. He plots the revolutionary changes that will bring about a just society.

After the war, he found a crusading newspaper called *Kampilan* (literally meaning 'cutlass') and whose slogan was 'Truth, Reason and Justice'. He also builds a progressive educational institution called Freedom University. Hernandez seems to say that in the first part of liberation, a free press and a progressive education can help change the status quo. The characters in the novel can still work within the system to alter it. Having known the degradation of the oppressed, Mando also helps the peasants in organizing themselves and labourers strengthen their unions. For these activities, he incurs the fear and wrath of the capitalists, landlords, churchmen and high government officials, who use bribery and terrorism to stall Mando's projects.

Because Mando has the people with him, he wages his battle against the oppressors with a relentlessness that seems unstoppable. Even the President of the Philippines calls on him and his associates to pacify the inflamed people. This chapter runs on parallel tracks to a chapter in Rizal's *El Filibusterismo*, when the Spanish Governor-General invites Simoun to the Palace for a discussion on the affairs of the state. In both cases, the talks fail to arrive at a consensus. A threat of arrest on charges of rebellion is dangled above their heads. Then, soldiers and goons break up a peasants' rally and kill their leader, Pastor. The novel closes with a scene in which Mando (the editor of the *Kampilan*), a labour organizer and a peasant leader, resolve to struggle together to form a truly democratic society. Finally, the unholy trinity of the intelligentsia, labour and peasantry are one.

Dr Bienvenido Lumbera, winner of the Ramon Magsaysay Award (Asia's Nobel Prize), said: '*Mga Ibong Mandaragit*, like [Hernandez's poem] *Bayang Malaya*, gathers together strands of literary traditions in order to create magnitude . . . The result is a book that recalls the epic scope of *Noli Me Tangere* and *El Filibusterismo,* together with the allegorical method of the "seditious" playwrights of the early American period and the primer-like discursiveness of *Banaag at Sikat* . . .'

For her part, the literary scholar Dr Soledad S. Reyes said that for Hernandez, paternalism is not the answer to the problem of a feudal land-tenancy system. The novel emphasizes that the landlord still owns the land, and the peasants will continue to work under unjust conditions. The ideal situation, according to Freedom University President Dr Sabio ('*Sabio*' is Spanish for 'learned'), is for the peasants to own the land they till, or failing that, to get a higher share of profits from the harvest. The latter could be done within the context of a farmers' cooperative. Only the alliance of the awakened peasants and the progressive intellectuals could see if this would work out. But by the end of *Mga Ibong Mandaragit*, the novel seems to show that the birth of a new system is close at hand.

In *Necessary Fictions*, the expatriate scholar Dr Caroline S. Hau says likewise. 'A crucial component of the "lessons" in the novel deals with the characters' attempts to determine just what course of action is available and must be taken in the present situation. The "answer" lies in education. The novel's emphasis on Mando's subsequent involvement in the establishment of a periodical and university conceives of postwar Philippines' immediate problem to be one of transforming individual (and by extension, collective) consciousness. That is, the novel holds that society can be changed for the better by a national subject whose ability to act depends on the full development of her potential as a human being, and on her acquisition of knowledge about her country's "true" history, situation, and putative course of development . . .'

Let us give the last word to the poet and critic Dr Epifanio San Juan, who has devoted a whole lifetime championing the cause and the writings of Amado V. Hernandez. In his epilogue to the first printing of *Mga Ibong Mandaragit* in 1969, he said: 'In this novel, Hernandez has given the country his vision of the *good* in life, in the human community, so that from this example, at once a mirror and a symbol, may be born a future in which every Filipino can realize his full personality face to face with his fellow men, no longer darkly but luminously with his god.'

When all is said and done, there is in Amado V. Hernandez a repetition of Rizal's imaginative act: a Western form (the novel) has been made part of the native landscape and infused with 'a local habitation and name.' It also offers us a glimpse into a brave new world without horizons.

A Note on the Translation

The translation is based on the 1969 edition of *Mga Ibong Mandaragit*, the publication of which was personally supervised by Amado V. Hernandez. The book has become part of required reading in high schools and colleges, and is still in print until today.

When I began translating this novel, I followed the principles that I employed when I translated *Banaag at Sikat*, the 1906 novel by Lope K. Santos, who was the teacher of Hernandez. I was keenly aware that I would be translating for a reader of the twenty-first century.

Therefore, I edited the repetitious lines and phrases that are found in the novel, especially in the latter parts. Please remember that Hernandez wrote this in jail, the way Pramoedya Ananta Toer of Indonesia also wrote his novels while incarcerated by another oppressive regime. Thus, he must have forgotten that he had already introduced a character in a much earlier chapter, or he had already described him or her on an earlier page. I decided to cut these superfluous parts to ensure smoother reading and to make the pages turn.

Aside from being a journalist, Amado V. Hernandez was also a novelist. He was a journalist writing a novel, which was both a boon and a bane. It was a boon because he employed the sometimes staccato style of writing the news and features in magazines, and this made for easier reading. He also had an eye for human interest in the news. It was a bane in the sense that he sometimes assumed that the readers knew the background (economic, cultural, social, political) of the issues in the story. What I did was flesh out some details, adding a phrase here or there, that I thought would clarify the expression of an idea.

It was also clear in my mind that I was writing a translation that would try to approximate the way the characters spoke—*if* they had spoken in English. Thus, I avoided the wooden, textbook prose that passed for the translation of some 'classic' works of literature. I also used a brisk late twentieth-century prose style, which I thought would be appropriate for the readers of this translation.

Moreover, I used the English equivalents of words ('jasmine' for *sampaguita*). I directly translated the words, phrases and sentences from Spanish to English. I have also retained the 'pidgin English' used in the satirical chapter on the lawmakers debating in the smoke-filled Philippine Senate, certainly a sly allusion to one day in hell.

In many cases, I have retained the names of places and proper names (*Señorita, Doña*). I also retained the original spellings that the author used.

I called my English translation *The Preying Birds* because of the play of words. It is also an allusion to the novel *The Praying Man* by the late Bienvenido N. Santos, who like Hernandez, was also born in Tondo, Manila. Coincidentally, Santos's novel was also banned during the early years of the Marcos military dictatorship in 1972.

I would like to thank the family of the late Amado V. Hernandez for giving us permission to translate this novel.

I wrote this translation in the silence and solitude of the COVID-19 lockdowns in Kuala Lumpur and Manila. I could hear the ambulance sirens wailing around me and people I knew were dropping dead like flies, but I kept on writing.

Final revision and proofreading for this translation were done at the MacDowell Artists' Residency in New Hampshire, USA, where I spent six weeks in the summer of 2022 among the world's best artists. Thank you for the blue skies and the green trees, the astonishing atmosphere, that made revising this novel such a joy. Special mention goes to Peng Zuqiang for the great company and warm conversations at MacDowell. The words floated, whether the sky was pitch-black or sown with stars.

I would also like to thank Nora Nazerene Abu Bakar, the Associate Publisher at Penguin Random House South East Asia, for entrusting the English translation of the Philippine literary classics to my hands.

As with *Banaag at Sikat* (*Radiance and Sunrise*) by Lope K. Santos, I would sometimes have vivid dreams about some scenes in *Mga Ibong Mandaragit* when I was translating it. Even if I was, in another wit's words, 'a mere translator', I also lived inside the world of the novel I was working on. It also happened to me when I was writing my book *Riverrun, A Novel* at Hawthornden Castle in Scotland, many years ago. I guess you have to *dream* it, so you can write it.

World, please welcome Amado V. Hernandez, the Philippine National Artist for Literature.

'For the gifts of the earth are meant for all.'

—*Ecclesiastes*

I

It was late in 1944. The Japanese Imperial Army in the Philippines was about to crumble. The strength of the Filipino guerrillas' resistance was growing with each passing day. The people steeled their resolve not to help the enemy and survive the scarcity of food and basic necessities. But twenty million unarmed people, their energies sapped by three years of hunger, sickness and maltreatment, remained defeated by half a million rifles and bayonets. The situation only proved the saying that a hero becomes braver when wounded.

The rosy promises of President Roosevelt and General MacArthur were not fulfilled. Other than the occasional raids by a few American planes, the Philippines was still under the hobnailed boots of the cruel and bow-legged conquerors. But the country did not give up hope. So when Bataan and Corregidor fell in April and May 1942, respectively, the people's resistance flamed throughout the land, all the way from the Sierra Madre Mountains in Luzon, to the forests of Mindanao and to the shores of the Visayas: the hills, the plains, the fields, the rivers, the lakes, and the caves of the archipelago. Volcanoes smouldered in the hearts of the descendants of Lapu-Lapu, Rajah Soliman and Andres Bonifacio.

One September afternoon, three men limped their way to a hut in a secluded spot at the foot of the Sierra Madre. Darkness had already smothered the last rays of the sun, and the hut seemed to melt into the mountain and the woods. Like a big nest embraced by the dense trees leaning against a hill, it overlooked the vast Pacific Ocean, up to the pencil line where the sea met the sky.

It was already twilight and a deep darkness had fallen upon the forest. It had rained the whole day, and on that cloudy afternoon, the sun rarely peeped beneath the clouds. From noon to dusk, the three men had difficulty walking the fifteen kilometres in the wilderness. They crossed rivers, cut their way through thorny vines and stepped on stones. Leeches attached themselves to their bodies and sucked the blood from their legs and arms.

After their second call, a voice answered.

'Friends,' the leader answered for the group. Then they climbed the stairs of the shack without waiting to be asked.

'Tata Matias,' the leader warmly greeted the old man who was peering through the door.

The lips of Tata Matias were parted; he was trying to place the visitor's voice. He looked closer, and upon recognizing Mando, welcomed him.

The young man stood at five feet, ten inches tall. He was indeed tired, but still, the muscles of his arms and neck looked like raw rubber. He had shiny bronzed skin and several days' growth of beard.

'It's me, Tatang,' Mando answered with respect, wiping his right hand over his dirty face.

'When was the last time you came here, Mando?' asked the old man, glancing briefly at the two companions.

'About four months ago,' Mando recalled. He introduced Karyo and Martin, his guerrilla comrades.

'Please come in,' said Tata Matias.

The three slumped on the bamboo floor of the bare, narrow room. Tata Matias lit the wick of an oil lamp made from a halved coconut shell. The light warmed the faded pictures of Jose Rizal and Andres Bonifacio, the two foremost Filipino heroes.

'You're tired,' the old man said. 'You must have walked far.'

'Indeed, sir,' agreed Mando, adding, 'the Japs had attacked Sampitan.'

The news surprised Tata Matias. He could only stare, and then he waited for further explanation.

'They surprised us,' added Mando, 'We were almost wiped out.'

The old man was keenly aware of the implications. Sampitan was the last headquarters of the Filipino guerrillas in that part of the Luzon mountains, in southwestern Tayabas (now Quezon Province), north of the Bicol Region. It shielded anyone who wanted to attack the general headquarters in Infanta. The attack on Sampitan showed that the Japanese wanted to take Infanta, where the Allied submarines had lain since the middle of 1943. Firearms, medicines and other war supplies were discreetly loaded in this rendezvous. From Infanta, the supplies were then sent to the guerrillas in southern and central Luzon, and even to some places in the Visayas.

Mando described the bloody encounter. The Japanese not only surprised them; they were also clearly outnumbered.

He said that he carried his rifle, sought cover and then fired back. But he ran out of bullets and had to escape. Staying there meant certain death. Martin and Kario, who had already retreated unarmed, later met up with Mando in the forest.

From his hiding place, Mando saw some guerrillas board two motor boats. They had not gone far when the bullets rained on them. Many fell, but some dove into the sea. Mando could not find out what happened to them, since he had to move when he ran out of bullets.

The sudden rain saved the three guerrillas. The Japanese seemed to have let them go and returned to the siege of the headquarters. The guerrillas decided to walk down a path and seemed to have been lost in the labyrinth of the wilderness. But Mando led them through a path where the trees and vines seemed thickest. They walked slowly, freighted danger.

'You must be hungry,' said Tata Matias after Mando had recalled the event.

'When have guerrillas not been hungry?' the young man asked. The old man quickly understood, for he knew that the guerrillas were lucky to have even one square meal a day.

'I've cooked the rice, but I should cook some more and fry some dried fish.'

'Salt will be all right,' said Mando.

'Dried fish!' Martin clucked and gulped. 'How much rice did you cook?' he teased the old man.

'With my appetite, fish would taste better than roasted pig,' Karyo said.

'We're lucky you have dried fish,' added Mando.

Tata Matias said that he had caught two large fish and some mudfish with his traps in the rice fields below. He had been eating his catch for several days.

'We'll eat in a while,' he said, then disappeared into the kitchen.

The small house was divided into two. The door led to the kitchen, which was split from the rest of the house by a wall of dried leaves and woven bamboo slats.

Ten rough-hewn but strong wooden posts supported the hut, and the roof was made of cogon.

The old man himself had built the house many years before the war, and he lived there alone. Before, he could be seen going down to the village to buy his provisions, but lately, the vendors from town brought him what he needed.

People visited the house in the midst of the war. Many of them were guerrillas who knew that the safest path wound through the thick forest.

The hut served as a temporary haven from the law or from the enemies of freedom. The refugees rested here, and the old man kindly shared his provisions with them. Before they left, some people gave donations, while others left with gratitude, having nothing but the clothes on their backs. Tata Matias showed the same hospitality to everyone who sought his help. He would give his last cup of rice to anyone who needed it. Or, if there was no rice, he always had a supply of cassava for times like these.

Mando had already visited the hut of Tata Matias several times before. The first was more than a year earlier, when he was climbing the Sierra Madre mountains from a town that lay south of Manila. He went with a group, and they had a guide, who told them that the old man was a revolutionary. He had fought against Spain and the United States, but he chose to stay in the mountains after Americans came to power. While some leaders of the revolutionary republic at Barasoain surrendered and others became outlaws, Tata Matias stayed in a secluded town at the mountain's toenail. When those who refused to fight any more were hunted down, he simply vanished, as if the caves had swallowed him up, leaving no trace of him whatsoever. However, after many years, when he was almost forgotten by everyone, the people who wandered in the wilderness of Sierra Madre brought back the news that the old man was indeed alive and well. The name of Tata Matias spread by word of mouth, and he became known as the 'old man of the mountains'.

Mando's second and third visits happened only four months ago, when he carried a message to the guerrillas in the plains and later climbed the Sierra Madre mountains. He was alone then. He and Tata Matias quickly became friends. Mando opened his heart to the old man and told him his life's story. He was an orphan who worked for a rich family in Manila. He was sent to school in payment for his services. His studies stopped when the Japanese came. He fled and joined the outlaws in the forests when his master betrayed him to the Japanese.

The two men talked about many things: the meagre help from the sympathizers; the widespread poverty that stalked the land; and the wealth of the collaborators, which was growing immensely by the day.

'If I were your age . . .' Tata Matias said with a deep sigh that made his stooped shoulders rise and fall, and then he looked into the distance. 'In my youth, I joined two struggles,' he recalled. 'Now in my old age, this is all I can do.' And a cloud of sadness covered his face.

He was referring to the hospitality that he offered to the guerrillas who were either climbing or going down the mountains of the Sierra Madre.

'If I were you, I'd look for ways to support the national movement without counting on the unreliable supporters.' He sighed and continued, 'People have become greedy and focus only on themselves. They give only when they get something in return. In a conflict, they usually side with the winner, even if that person is wrong and even when the victim is their relative.' He shook his head, sadness clouding his eyes. 'Ah, if I were your age, Mando.' Mando couldn't help asking why.

'What would you do then if you were me?'

Tata Matias didn't answer at once. Instead, he walked over to an old chest made of hardwood, sitting in a corner of the room. Slowly, he opened it and from its bottom, retrieved an ordinary, woven valise.

It contained three or four books, a few pamphlets and papers that had turned yellow with age, a machete, and a dagger.

Tata Matias chose a book, closed the valise, and returned it to the bottom of the wooden chest. Then he went back to Mando.

'*El Filibusterismo!*' said Mando, surprise written all over his face.

'Yes,' the old man said, 'the second novel of our national hero, Dr Jose Rizal, that was printed in Ghent, Belgium, in 1891.' He looked at the eyes of the astonished guerrilla before he spoke again. 'Here, in this book, is what I'd do if I were your age. How old are you now, Mando?'

'Twenty-four, sir.'

'You're in your prime,' said the old man, as if admiring a rare thing, 'a beacon for those who are now lost in the darkness. You're older than I was when I joined the revolution.'

When Mando kept quiet, the old man asked, 'Have you read this book?'

'Yes, sir. I've also read the *Noli Me Tangere*,' Mando replied, the words tumbling out of his mouth in a rush. 'Yes, the *Noli* was published in Berlin, Germany, in 1887. It was Dr Jose Rizal's first novel.'

The young man's eyes glistened with pride.

'What did you read in those two books?' Tata Matias' voice was suddenly alive.

Mando thought briefly before answering. He had read the two famous novels of Dr Rizal more than once, and he knew the plots and the main characters by heart. But the question surprised him. He felt like an unprepared student being cross-examined by a teacher, but he rarely faltered when he spoke.

He spoke slowly and quietly when he saw the old man looking at him in earnest. 'I've read about the illness of a nation and the instability of the government during Rizal's time—the leaders' corruption and the masses' oppression.'

'You're right!' said Tata Matias. 'You have read them, indeed.' Then he asked, 'Do you still remember Simoun?'

'The new Machiavelli,' Mando answered, 'Yes, Simoun—Juan Crisostomo Ibarra in the *Noli* who became Simoun in the *Fili*.'

'What else do you remember about Simoun?'

'From his adventures in foreign lands, Ibarra—now Simoun—returned as a rich and powerful man. He brought an iron chest full of priceless jewellery.'

The old man opened the book and scanned it. He was looking for several passages about Simoun. Then he said, 'Here is Simoun', and he asked Mando to read. Mando read the words aloud, as if he were just talking to someone in front of him.

Simoun told his sad story. He had returned from Europe thirteen years ago, filled with hope and happy illusions. He was to marry the girl he loved. He was prepared to do well and forgive those who had wronged him, as long as they left him in peace. But this was not meant to be. Vicious, anonymous hands grabbed him from behind and threw him into the whirlpool of an uprising that his enemies had schemed. He lost everything: his reputation, position, love, prospects, freedom, everything! And he only escaped certain death because of a friend's heroic gesture. Then he swore revenge, which grew inside him like a caged beast. With the ancestral wealth that had been buried in a forest, he fled overseas. He went into trade, took part in the Cuban War, helping now one side and now the other, but always doing everything to his profit. One day, he met the general, who was only a major at that time. He won him over by lending him money. Later, they became close friends because of certain crimes, the dark secrets of which were known only to the jeweller. Simoun bribed people and secured for the general an assignment to the Philippines. And once in the country, Simoun used the general as a tool, pushing him through his greed to commit all manner of injustice.

He then asked Mando to continue.

I returned to our islands summoned by the vices of the rulers. Disguised as a merchant, I've gone from town to town, opening locked doors with my money. Everywhere, I've seen greed in its terrible forms—hypocritical one time, shameless the next, but always cruel to the bone, fattening on a dead social system like a vulture on a corpse. I asked myself why the corpse didn't contain in its entrails some deadly virus that would kill the bird. But the corpse let itself be torn to pieces, limb by limb, and the vulture had its fill. I couldn't bring this corpse back to life and turn it against its oppressor.

On the other hand, its decay was taking too long. So I stoked even greater greed; hence, injustices and abuses grew. I encouraged crime and cruelty to accustom people to death. I fostered insecurity to push them to seek desperate solutions. I crippled business so that the country, now ruined, would no longer have anything to fear. I whetted appetites for public funds. But when this still didn't prove enough to make the people rise in revolt, I wounded them in their most sensitive spot: I made the vulture pollute the very corpse on which it fed.

Mando's throat had turned dry when he stopped reading. Tata Matias said in a victorious voice: 'Simoun failed because he was driven by revenge, as Father Florentino said. Sin and evil can't be cleansed by other sins and evil deeds. The country was not yet prepared; besides, a country gets the government it deserves.'

'The government can be changed,' Mando said, 'but the nation goes on. Oppression often rouses a country to turn and break its chains. That's what happened in the Philippines, and it will surely happen to the Japanese as well.'

Tata Matias agreed, but then he added with a hint of caution, '*Only* if we don't make the same mistakes and if the young people become our real hope. These are my thoughts about Simoun's wealth, which Father Florentino had thrown into the bottom of the sea.'

Mando reflected and then said, 'But I thought that Simoun was just a figment of Rizal's imagination?'

Tata Matias smiled and shook his head. 'Everything that Rizal wrote was true,' he finally said. 'Although Rizal didn't call them by their real names, his characters were drawn from actual people who lived and breathed, not just mere figments of his fantastic imagination.' He added, 'Don't you believe that Captain Tiago, Fray Damaso, Cabesang Tales, Sisa, Huli, Maria Clara, Elias, Tasio the Philosopher, Isagani, Basilio, and Ibarra or Simoun were real people who lived during Rizal's time?'

'I do,' Mando said, noting that the old man was getting a bit annoyed. 'Otherwise, why should he have stoked the hatred of his enemies? Besides, this usually happens in a country that has been colonized. Its story is forgotten, its lovely folklore and its heroes erased from memory. Later, they become only myths like Bernardo Carpio, Mariang Makiling, and many others. How many still know the heroism of Lapu-Lapu, Soliman, Dagohoy, Diego Silang, and his wife, Gabriela?'

'That's true,' said Tata Matias, and then he repeated, 'Everything that Rizal wrote was true. We saw it then; now you, the young people, are seeing it as well.' He added, 'Nature is taking care not only of Simoun's wealth. Where is the money from the Revolution of 1896 and 1898? It has vanished, as if swallowed up by the earth, since the Barasoain Republic fell. Perhaps all those riches are buried in secret in the heart of the wilderness. Look at what happened to the silver money of the Commonwealth Republic before Manila was left to the Japanese. That wealth was thrown between Manila Bay and Corregidor. You must have heard that, with the Japanese position being unwieldy, Yamashita thought of stashing away the wealth he had stolen from the Philippines. That is similar to the situation of Simoun's jewels. If our history were to be written later on, it would be considered fiction.'

Mando stared at Tata Matias, thinking: is this old man, who is now in his seventies, already senile? But he saw not a trace of senility in him. The revolutionary was in full control of his mind. Tata Matias continued: 'Truly Mando, if I were your age, I would not hesitate . . .'

'To do what, sir?'

'Dive into the sea to look for Simoun's wealth.'

The young man was stunned.

'I would dive for it,' the old man repeated.

'But Tatang,' Mando groped for words. 'Do you . . ?'

'What?'

'Do you believe that Simoun's wealth was really thrown into the sea by a foreign priest?'

Tata Matias smiled, and then he answered.

'Father Florentino wasn't a foreign priest,' he explained. 'He was a holy Filipino priest. My grandparents knew him. My father told us the story he heard from his father even before the troubles in Cavite that led to the death of the three Filipino priests . . .'

Briefly, Tata Matias recalled the story of the good priest, who was the son of a rich and famous family. 'He didn't want to be a priest. He had planned to marry his lovely sweetheart. However, he had to follow his mother's wishes. She had promised the archbishop that her son would be a priest. As a priest, he was respected and liked by everyone. He decided to retire to avoid being suspected along with the other Filipino priests in the Cavite uprising of 1872. He lived in a house where Simoun later went to hide, and to die. Unlike many Spanish friars, Father Florentino did not care for money nor for the things of this world,' the old man said.

Mando told the old man that Elias and Simoun were among his idols. He rued the fact that people seemed to have forgotten them, the way they had erased from their memories Rajah Soliman, the leader of pre-Hispanic Manila, and other early heroes.

'That is the conqueror's usual ploy, as you would say,' said Tata Matias. 'They erase all proof, even traces and memories, if possible, of the noble children of the country they had conquered. They want the newly subjugated people to get used to the slavers' condition and ways.'

Mando promised to study and prepare to dive for Simoun's jewels. 'I need to know more about this,' he said.

That night, the old revolutionary and the young guerrilla recalled their conversation as if it had only happened yesterday. But that conversation had taken place four months ago.

II

The rice and fried fish vanished from their plates in no time at all. The meal was already both lunch and supper for Mando and his companions.

The old man cleared the table and then asked his guests if they wished to rest now. It had been a long and tiring day.

'We have mats and pillows here. You can unroll the mats and rest.'

Mando got the rolled mat near the old chest and spread it on the floor. Right away, Mando and Karyo lay down. They stretched and yawned, and were soon fast asleep and even snoring.

But Mando didn't immediately go to sleep. He went outside, as if drawn by an irresistible force. He inhaled the fresh cool breeze of the mountain. From the branches of a tree, the full moon cast a silver glow on everything it touched.

'Why don't you sleep, Mando?' Tata Matias said from the door of the hut.

'I'm just enjoying the beauty of the night. Who would have guessed that such bad weather would be followed by a night like this?'

'The darkest night gives birth to the brightest dawn.'

Mando looked at the sea. It was so silent and so vast. The sky mirrored the silver greyness of the water. Yet the sea was bright green, like a carpet of melted emeralds. Every time a fish jumped, a chunk of the emerald would break into a thousand small diamonds, which were swallowed up by the giant darkness.

Suddenly, the moon hid behind the clouds, as if shivering. Mando returned to the hut and saw Tata Matias sitting by the doorway.

'I recall the jewels whenever I see the silver moonlight and the sea's diamonds and emeralds,' Mando said. 'I remember our long chat about the *Fili* four months ago.'

'Ah, Simoun's jewels,' sighed Tata Matias. 'The only difference is that you see only an illusion, whereas Simoun's jewels are real . . .'

'Buried at the bottom of the sea,' whispered Mando.

'No sea is too deep to dive in,' said the old man.

Mando stood on a wide rock that served as a stairway to the hut. But the old revolutionary did not budge from the narrow doorway. It seemed that he did not want to end the conversation with the young guerrilla.

'When you were my age,' Mando spoke with calmness, so that the old man would not think him disrespectful, 'why didn't you dive for Simoun's jewellery?'

The old man just smiled bitterly. But when he spoke, there was no trace of bitterness in his voice.

'I'm glad you asked that,' he said. 'You should know why I didn't do in my prime what I'm now asking other people to do.'

'But I didn't mean that,' Mando protested.

'Your question was valid, don't take it back,' Tata Matias. 'Diving for Simoun's treasure has been on my mind since 1898. That is the real reason I settled here. But I gave up my plan when I saw the revolution being betrayed by the very people who should have supported it, when surrender became a mark of patriotism, and to continue the struggle was called treason. I told myself it was better to keep the treasure safe at the bottom of the sea.'

The old man stood up to let Mando pass. 'So, you think it's time to recover the wealth and use it?'

'More than ever.'

'Why?'

'Because the enemy is more heartless now. The country has suffered from poverty and conquest. And there are good men—you, loyal guerrillas—who should use this wealth.'

'But Simoun's wealth is big for one person, but it's too small to save a country that's the victim of war,' Mando said. 'How much would this wealth be? A few million pesos in cash. It's not even enough for a warship and a few fighter planes.'

'I didn't say it was enough to fund the war or to win it. Money and firearms alone don't win a war. More important is the courage of a nation that refuses to kneel and bow before the conqueror. I meant that Simoun's wealth is important, since it can be used to build—or destroy. If it goes in the hands of your movement, it would be used not for this war, but afterwards, in times of peace. The Japs won't last much longer . . .'

Tata Matias stopped when Mando aired his doubts. 'Our headquarters were destroyed and the three of us barely escaped. Perhaps the Japs are on their way to the guerrillas' general headquarters at Infanta. I'm afraid that . . .'

'Yes, the headquarters were destroyed,' Tata Matias cut in, 'but you and the others are alive. Losing one battle doesn't mean total defeat. Didn't the enemy occupy Manila, snatch Bataan and Corregidor? They've been here for three years. But isn't our resistance more spirited now than when the war began? When the United States Armed Forces in the Far East surrendered, we had to defend ourselves, and we did so with uncommon courage. During Napoleon's time, he attacked Spain and Russia and occupied a large territory. But he didn't really win even for a day. This is what is happening to Japan in the Philippines: the clock is ticking and her days are numbered.'

'Unfortunately, some of the Filipinos have sided with the enemy,' Mando said, gritting his teeth.

He was thinking that if he had not escaped, Don Segundo Montero would have had him killed by the dreaded Japanese military.

'Don't think too much of cowards and traitors,' said the old revolutionary. 'Why grieve over the water's ebb and flow, the falling of the leaves, the flight of summer birds when winter comes? That's nature, my son.'

'Is treachery natural?' asked Mando, with loathing on his tongue.

'It's one of man's weaknesses. Remember that there are always chameleons in any group of people, across time. Jesus Christ had only twelve apostles, yet Judas Iscariot was among them. Even this chosen disciple denied him three times. Certainly, major events are like floods: they sweep everything that is frail and weak along the way, but the strong posts and trees remain. As long as a nation has people ready to kill or be killed to preserve her freedom and honour, that nation won't become a slave, even if occupied by a stronger force.'

'But these traitors should be killed, for they're like snakes and other poisonous creatures,' Mando said.

'They're digging their own graves with their treachery,' said Tata Matias. 'Besides, circumstances make the traitor, just as the occasion makes the hero. You should not think that anyone is born a traitor or that one starts out as a hero. Many who have turned traitors in difficult times were considered patriots in better times.' He paused, trying to recall something before he continued.

'That happened to us during the Philippine–American War. When they saw that the tide was turning against the republic, some of Aguinaldo's own ministers jumped ship. They said they only wanted to save the country and return peace to the land. Naturally, the new white masters called them patriotic, and even rewarded them with high positions, vast lands and other opportunities. Those who didn't surrender were called traitors and outlaws. They were blamed for various offences. Those who fled to the mountains or refused to bow before the American flag were either jailed or exiled, like Apolinario Mabini, Artemio Ricarte, and our other heroes. Others were hanged, like Macario Sakay and his companions.'

His face was lined with bitterness as he recalled an ugly chapter in the Philippine–American War, something that was repeated during the Japanese War against the Americans and the Filipinos.

'That's why I didn't return to the town and lived like a hermit here in the mountains,' said Tata Matias. 'History has failed me. But you . . .'

'That might happen to me, too.'

'No, Mando. You're young, and your path is still clear. You can avenge the victims, the slain. You'll be the hope and wellspring of a new life . . . You, the young people . . .'

'Tata Matias, who among our heroes are your models and idols?' Mando asked. 'Is it Jose Rizal or Andres Bonifacio? It might be Rizal because . . .'

The old man quickly answered.

'All heroes deserve to be honoured equally: Bonifacio and Rizal; also Burgos, Plaridel, Mabini, Jacinto, Luna; also Aguinaldo, for some of his qualities. Everyone was noble, and all of them served the country. But of course, one is better than the other. The bedrock of Filipino heroism consists of Rizal, Bonifacio and Mabini. Rizal was the lodestar who raised the prestige of the Malay race. Bonifacio was the brave man who broke our chains and forged the people into a nation. Mabini was the brains who built the First Republic and proved that Filipino leaders could equal anyone. Plaridel and Jacinto also had rare qualities, but these were also possessed by Bonifacio and Rizal.'

'Then, sir . . .'

Tata Matias made a sign that he was not yet through.

'But a hero's nobility is not his alone,' the old revolutionary went on. 'I'll repeat what I had said earlier—that the circumstances create the traitor just as the situation shapes the hero. For example, the treacherous killing of Bonifacio and the attempts to shame him lessened his glory. If Plaridel had returned to the Philippines before the revolution and had led the revolutionaries, he would have been our main hero. But unfortunately, he died of tuberculosis in Barcelona. Look at Rizal; he knew that the uprising was already near, because Bonifacio had sent Dr Valenzuela to him in Dapitan. But he refused to join. Instead, to prove to Spain that he had nothing to do with the revolution, he wanted to go to Cuba and serve as a surgeon with the Spanish medical team. Was he not on his way to Havana when he was seized in the dead of night and returned to Manila? The friars and the Spanish authorities refused to forgive him for the blistering attacks he launched in his novels. Besides, they were afraid of intellectuals. They expected to defeat Bonifacio, but the ideas of Rizal's two novels would blaze like fire, not only in the Philippines but also in Spain and Europe. Thus, Rizal was lucky even in death. If he had not been shot at Bagumbayan and had not become a real martyr, he might have ended up just as quislings like Trinidad Pardo de Tavera, Fernando Canon and other learned Filipinos. Look at our first President, Emilio Aguinaldo. If he had been killed at Palanan and not captured by General Funston with the help of the Macabebe Scouts, he would be above Rizal and Bonifacio. The nation would forget the killing of Bonifacio and General Antonio Luna. Someday, I will tell you of the nobility and tragedy of Macario Sakay.'

Tata Matias unravelled his thought as if he had been reading from the pages of history. Mando admired and respected the old man all the more, a man so well-informed and noble, despite his secluded life in the Sierra Madre. Why, he thought, Tata Matias should be the model for the New Filipino.

'I've reached life's sunset, my son,' Tata Matias said to the young man and held his arm. The young man's arm felt as hard as steel. 'Yes, I'm old, while you're in the prime of life. You're a newly risen sun. You weren't wrong to think I'm counting on you to realize my dream. But I don't talk like this to everyone. I've faith in you. I believe the noble priest meant the wealth is not for my time, but yours.'

'What do you want me to do?' asked Mando, his eyes fixed on the old man. It seemed that he had been swayed to follow the wishes of the old revolutionary.

'I've already told you what I'd do,' said Tata Matias, 'if I were your age and in the face of what's happening to the country.'

'Ah, yes, Simoun's jewellery!' Mando said, guessing what was in the old man's mind.

'No other,' said the old man.

Tata Matias walked away and moved carefully between the two sleeping men. He opened the old trunk and retrieved the native suitcase. Karyo and Martin just slept on. Tata Matias returned to Mando, who was leaning against the wall. Tata Matias opened the book to its last pages. When he found what he was looking for, he gave the book to Mando.

'The last time you came, you read about Simoun, his desire and plans, and why he failed. This time, please read the part about his death and how Father Florentino threw the treasure chest into the sea.'

Mando looked at the passage and read. His voice was soft and clear.

The patient was already dead when the priest came. He knelt and prayed.
When he stood up and gazed at the corpse, he saw extreme grief,
the result of a life without purpose, which he would bring beyond death.

The old priest was shaken, and he muttered. 'May God have mercy on those who led him away from the right path.'

Mando paused, but Tata Matias urged him to go on.

Meanwhile, the servants whom he had called were praying the requiem. From its hiding place, Father Florentino took the iron chest containing Simoun's fabulous wealth. He hesitated for a while, then he calmly went down the steps with the iron chest, towards the cliff where Isagani often sat, gazing at the ocean.

Mando took a deep breath before going on. Karyo moved but he did not awaken. Martin continued to snore loudly. Tata Matias fixed his gaze at the young man who was reading.

Father Florentino looked below. He saw the waves of the Pacific Ocean kissing the rocks, shining like fire in the moonlight. They looked like diamonds scattered by a genie from the depths. Father Florentino looked around. He was alone. Then he threw Simoun's iron chest into the ocean. It turned several times before it hit the water. The water splashed, and a sound gurgled. Then just as quickly, the water closed and swallowed up the treasure. He waited a while to see if the water would throw it out, but the waves just moved on, as if nothing but a small stone had fallen into its depths.

Tata Matias cleared his throat, and Mando read up to the end.

'May nature keep you in its depths, together with the beautiful corals and pearls of the boundless seas,' said the priest, stretching forth his arms. 'If you should be needed for a noble purpose, may God suffer you to be taken from the depths of the sea. Meanwhile, you shall not cause evil, you won't buy injustice, or stoke further greed.'

It was already late when Tata Matias and Mando ended their talk. When the morning dawned, the three guerrillas said goodbye to the old hermit of the mountain.

III

The three didn't know where to go when they left Tata Matias's hut. In the meantime, they would go wherever their feet led them. Just the same, they followed the serpentine path leading them away from Sampitan.

They wanted to reach the guerrillas' general headquarters at Infanta. From where they were, the shortest way would be to cut through Sampitan. But because of what had happened the day before, returning to that garrison meant certain death.

Mando told Martin and Karyo that they had to go down to Laguna or cross over to Rizal. From there, they could move slowly to Infanta. There was another way from Bulacan, but it was already too far from southern Luzon. In Laguna, they could travel through hills and forests once they had reached Longos or Santa Maria. In Rizal, they could also make their way to Infanta from Baras and Tanay. The guerrillas and outlaws had already made footpaths in these towns.

On the other hand, they didn't know which places were held by the Japanese and which were in the hands of Filipinos, who had refused to surrender. They would just sniff their way and be cautious, for the situation was fluid and changed from day to day.

So they stopped from time to time, for there was no need to hurry. It would be impossible to reach Infanta in less than a week, not even if they would walk from sunup to sundown.

Food was their first problem. For several miles around, there was no house or people. That was why Mando was surprised when he suddenly tripped on a stone marker. It was engraved with the initials of the proprietor.

'So someone owns this place,' he said.

'Really?' Karyo was also puzzled.

'There are lands registered in the name of every big shot,' said Martin. 'The only land we own is the mud on our bodies.' And he looked down at the mud that had dried up on his feet and arms.

'But I'm sure,' said Mando, 'that the surveyor was the only one who reached this place. The man with the initials on the marker can't come here; it can't be reached by car.'

'If he tries to climb this height, he'll surely roll straight down the ravine,' said Martin, and then he laughed.

'But they don't have to come here. They've many servants from among small people like us,' answered Karyo.

'And where are those rich people?' Mando asked. 'I bet most of them are in Manila, enjoying themselves with the Japanese. While we are here . . .'

'Because we don't like the Japanese,' said Karyo.

'Because we're not turncoats,' Mando said in anger. 'We don't want to act like slaves.'

'The chameleons want to stay in power forever,' said Martin.

'Everything has to end,' answered Mando.

'But after the war, they'll surely be in power again.' Martin spat out. 'Pwe!'

'Over my dead body,' Karyo said.

'The nation can't be fooled all the time,' answered Mando. 'We were fooled by the Spaniards for four centuries, but this won't happen again . . . no more.' There was a hard edge to his voice and then he sighed. 'But now powerful Filipinos are the ones fooling the country.'

'If a dog has gotten used to being muzzled . . .' said Martin.

'But once the muzzle is removed, the first to be bitten would be the one who put it on,' said Mando.

'But in times like these,' said Karyo, 'the chained dog is lucky because it's fed. Friends, if you're not yet hungry . . .' And he got up from the rock on which he was seated. The three walked silently in a single file. Suddenly, Karyo stopped at the mouth of a riverbank and . . .

'There!' He pointed to the guava trees luxuriant with fruit.

Karyo and Martin raced to climb the trees. They perched on the branches of the trees and ate there. They threw some guavas to Mando. Then they picked the ripe and half-ripe ones, and placed them in their pockets. They had their fill of the guavas.

'We'll have food till tomorrow,' Karyo said happily.

'Yes, until you've a stomach ache,' said Martin.

In reply, Karyo twirled a large ripe guava around his fingers.

'One guava with seven holes.' Then he finished it off in two bites.

After they were full, they looked for a waterfall and drank the clear water, and then they walked on.

Darkness deepened in the forest. They walked faster to reach the plains before night fell. It would be hard to pass the night up there, without shelter, because of danger from the snakes. The leeches also crawled and sucked on their bodies, causing wounds and bleeding.

The moonlight was already tearing away the night's veil when they reached a riverbank. The river was swollen and the currents were swift.

The three decided to stay there until morning. They sat on the ground and continued eating the guavas.

'Even dried-up guavas could satisfy me,' said Karyo as the seeds of the guavas made a grinding sound between his teeth.

'Now all I ask for is a whole fried chicken,' Martin said before biting into a half-ripe guava.

'All I ask for is a bed without pests,' said Mando, and he stretched on the ground with his head pillowed by his palms.

Then he got up hastily, rubbing his hard legs, shoulders and nape. Insects had swarmed upon him as soon as he lay down.

Martin and Karyo sat restlessly because insects also crawled all over their feet wherever their bodies touched the ground.

After gathering bamboo twigs and dried leaves, Mando took a box of matches wrapped in cellophane from his shirt pocket, and then he made a bonfire.

'It's all right to make a fire,' he said, remembering one guerrilla rule. 'There are no Japs here anyway.'

'If only we had dried fish,' said Martin, 'It would be delicious roasted over that fire.'

'Roast the guavas then,' Karyo suggested.

'See, the insects are now gone,' Mando said happily, lying down again near the bonfire.

But as he looked up at the moon, he saw how quickly it had been covered by the clouds. Darkness spread swiftly, like a black veil thrown by a giant in the forest. In a short while, Mando felt the raindrops, slowly at first, then suddenly thick and fast, and soon rain was falling in torrents.

The three squatted with their backs to each other. They were soaked to the skin and suffered in the intense cold. They were tired from walking the whole day long, eating nothing except guavas. And now they would be wet the whole night and would not be able to sleep. This was not the first time they had endured such hardship.

'It's hard to love one's country,' sighed Mando when the rain had stopped. 'If I'd known that life in the mountains would be like this, I wouldn't have left the stone house.'

'Stone house?' asked Karyo.

'Jail house,' said Martin.

'You were jailed?' Karyo asked.

'Yes, more than once! First, I wounded someone; next, I was accused of stealing,' Martin said. 'But what's wrong with that? I had a debt; I paid for it. The horrible ones are the shameless people who commit grave crimes daily against their fellow men, society and the government. Yet, they are called honourable!' Martin said in anger.

'Indeed, Rizal's prophecy has come true,' Mando said. 'To be honourable, one has to go to jail first.'

'The way I see it,' said Karyo, 'bad and good depends on whether one is caught or not. You're bad when you get caught; you're good as long as you don't get caught.'

Martin protested. 'One should be judged according to his true self, not according to the externals, just as a fish is judged by its flesh and not by its scales.'

'I wish it were so,' said Karyo, 'but this is not what happens. Because the skin and scales are exposed and seen. But even if the flesh is rotten, it's not easily noticed.'

'I'm bad, I admit,' said Martin, 'but I'm not a hypocrite. I joined the guerrillas to save myself. Is there a safer place for an escaped convict than here? You can find all sorts of people, both good and bad, among the guerrillas. No one will scrutinize you. No one will ask where you came from. As long as you're ready to fight, you'll be accepted and you'll get your arms. If they don't have weapons, it's up to you to get them. But it's always better if you bring your arms.'

Karyo, a country boy, told them a different tale. 'I became a guerrilla,' he said, 'because the Japs raided our town. My pregnant wife was killed when they sprayed the place with machine guns. I'm an unschooled labourer, but I love my wife and I love our country.'

The two asked why Mando became a guerrilla. He was young and intelligent. Surely, the Japanese would want someone like him to be a collaborator. But why did he go to the mountains? Why did he join the fight?

'I'm a Filipino,' Mando said simply. 'Isn't that enough reason?' he asked. He did not relate how he had barely escaped from the anger of the Japanese military when they raided the meeting place of a group of students who had gathered together to relay the real news about the war. These contradicted the reports in the papers hawked by the newsboys, and they were called 'newspapers with fake news'.

In their minds rose the bitter truth that many Filipinos were helping the enemy in various ways. Mando would not forget that his own master had reported him to curry favour from the Japanese.

The three men huddled back-to-back, patiently enduring the torrential downpour, which finally subsided to a shower.

All of them were wet, but they received some warmth from each other. For a while, they forgot their discomfort during the lively exchange of stories.

When the moon peeped out again, the only sounds in the surrounding stillness were of the flow of the water and the wind rising among the leaves. After a while, they dozed off. Their drooping heads rested on their knees.

The first shafts of sunlight woke them up. The sky was already bright and clear. The weather had turned and the river receded. No trace of last night's ugly weather remained.

They shook off their fatigue in different ways. Mando ran backwards, shadow-boxing. Then he lifted the rocks with his outstretched arms. Mando had boosted his unusual inborn strength with exercise and karate.

Along the river bank, they found some coconuts left by the rising waters the night before.

'God's gift,' Karyo remarked happily and he began picking up the scattered coconuts. They broke open the coconuts with sharp stones and then sipped the water.

'Sweet,' commended Martin. 'Good! We'll have "rancho" for two days.'

'Who says anyone will starve on this land?' Mando said mockingly.

'They did in the city,' said Karyo, 'for they've no coconuts or guavas to pick.'

Then they split the coconuts, scraped off the white flesh and ate it.

'Before I left Manila,' Mando told them, 'small pieces of coconut meat were being roasted like corn by the roadside and sold at twenty pesos per piece. Many people even ate them for breakfast.'

'Coconut is an excellent product. It's even called the tree of life,' boasted Karyo, who was from a region that produced lots of coconuts. 'Aside from food, it is also a source of many things.'

'It's truly wonderful,' said Mando, nodding. 'Just look at this coconut. Its meat is better than the contents of the heads of many Filipino leaders.'

'Our leaders' heads are not empty,' objected Martin. 'They're just filled with ashes.'

Karyo said, 'A leader should not lose his balls. A leader without balls is not a man.'

Mando and Martin agreed. Then, Martin added: 'If you want, let's see who has the biggest,' he challenged, and the three laughed. 'Let's see who is the most manly.'

Then, they saw two monkeys masturbating. 'There's your cousin,' Karyo said to Martin in jest, and the three of them roared with laughter.

'Do you know what I'll do when the Americans return?' asked Martin.

'What else? Clean their shoes, of course,' Karyo said in a teasing tone.

'That's where you're wrong, my friend,' declared Martin and flexed his arms. 'I'll grab two American girls and get both of them pregnant in a month.'

'Would they pay attention to a dark person like you?' mocked Karyo.

'Oy, American girls are crazy over Filipino men. Just ask the Filipinos in California. That's why there are frequent fights between Americans and Filipinos. The moment the white woman has a taste of the Filipino man, she says goodbye to her damned white boyfriend.'

'That might just be a tall tale,' said Karyo.

'No kidding. Do you know why the American girl likes the Filipino?'

'Why?'

'Because he's circumcised, smooth like the head of a top,' said Martin in a boasting manner. 'The white men are not. They've raincoats like the monkeys.'

Mando and Karyo laughed at Martin's comparison.

'But among our fellow Filipinos, there are also many who aren't circumcised,' said Karyo. 'How many did I operate on at the guerrilla headquarters? Some of them were even married. The Visayans and the Bicolanos envied the Tagalogs, so they also got circumcised.'

'Maybe the whites think it's all right to be uncut as long as their children's noses are pointed,' said Martin.

'Once, I saw a picture of the statue of Hercules, the strongest man, and just think about it . . . he's also uncircumcised,' said Mando. 'But Jesus Christ was circumcised.'

'Maybe that's why Magdalena liked him and jilted Judas,' said Karyo.

Their jesting stopped when they saw the clear water of a spring. They ran and dived to slake their thirst.

IV

The river, which last night had been a fierce, forbidding monster, was now like a tame water buffalo, quiet and just calmly waiting for its owner.

After breakfast of coconut meat, they took the leftovers and crossed the river. They faced another day of walking.

The place they passed was like a door that closed behind them. To the left before them were the hills and forests, and to the right were thick vines, which were shaped like prison bars. Above, the clouds were turning red like fire, emitting burning arrows. Mando thought of the gap between those who helped the enemy and those who not only refused to help but also fought back. He saw the image of resistance in himself, Martin and Karyo; in Tata Matias; in the guerrillas whom he saw swimming in the sea, while being chased by Japanese bullets; and in the corpses of those slain in the garrison at Sampitan. On the other hand, there were the collaborators, one of whom was Don Segundo Montero, the haughty Monte of Manila and Nueva Ecija.

Monte was among the first to welcome the Japanese Imperial Army when their hobnailed boots began to march in the suburbs. In front of his car, a huge flag with the rising sun waved in the wind. He quickly greeted the head of the occupying troops with respect, and declared that he was ready to serve and obey. The same subservience was also found in his family. His wife, Doña Julia, and his daughter, Dolly, made no objections. The spring of memory was bitter and Mando

25

recalled it now. He had just turned twenty-one, living as a servant in the Monteros' grand residence. He was nicknamed Andoy. He had no salary, except for his food and a small allowance. He served Don Segundo and the whole family, and often, the little time he had for his studies was still spent doing errands. Some days, he was a servant; on other days, he was a gardener. Sometimes, he was sent to buy household items; at times, he drove for Doña Julia, or cleaned Dolly's room. Dolly, the couple's only child, was about to graduate from an exclusive girls' school when the war broke out. Andoy was often slapped and abused by the family, even when he was already grown up.

The day before, when Mando was asked why he had fled to the mountains, he said that he was a Filipino and that was enough reason to do so. But in his heart, Mando knew that there was a reason deeper than he had cared to let on. Andoy, or Alejandro Pamintuan, who later became Mando Plaridel, had driven Don Segundo's car outside the city to the temporary headquarters of the commander of the Japanese Army. The American Armed Forces had already left Manila. When they arrived at the headquarters, Don Segundo leant back in his car and asked Andoy to go down and enquire.

A mean-looking soldier with a rifle stood at the gate. Quietly, Andoy approached and greeted the soldier in English. He was startled when the soldier slapped him twice. Then, shouting 'kura, kura', he was about to hit Andoy again. Andoy nearly lost his composure and was about to use his strength and knowledge of karate. Fortunately, a Japanese civilian arrived and intervened. He asked the soldier what happened, then he explained to Andoy why he was ill-treated. The soldier was angry because Andoy did not salute him and also spoke in English, which the soldier deemed as a challenge.

Afterwards, the civilian approached Don Segundo's car and accompanied him inside. After fifteen minutes, Don Segundo came out looking pleased.

Apparently, Don Segundo's trip was successful; he won over the Japanese officer. However, he could not forgive Andoy for the incident at the gate, which had almost ruined his mission. All the way home, he heaped abuses on Andoy, calling him a fool for not bowing before the Japanese. He said that Andoy was a slowpoke for not studying Nihongo as soon as the war broke out. He regretted spending on Andoy's education for he was dumb, surely inheriting this trait from his stupid ancestors and his peasant parents.

Andoy was furious, but he controlled himself. He was patient by nature and not used to talking back. Then, he had no idea that he would ever kill anyone. He remembered how Don Segundo had also abused his late father, who was then Montero's driver. Andoy's mother was the laundry woman until she fell ill and became bedridden.

Such heartlessness and abuse naturally aroused similar feelings, or caused festering wounds that cried out for a cure. Certainly, there were enough reasons to drive Andoy, more than the soldier's slap, to leave the Monteros and join the outlaws, but there was a deeper cause. He learnt that Don Segundo had reported him to the Japanese military as a guerrilla spy. He was tempted to kill the Don, but thought the better of it and just escaped instead.

He was disgusted when he saw how slave-like the couple was. He felt that even in his poverty, he could never do such things. He did not realize then that the Monteros were not moved by admiration, a liking or affection for the new master. Rather, they feared losing their wealth and living a life of discomfort. Thus, they debased themselves, because they wanted to maintain their place in society.

When he joined the outlaws, he changed his nickname from Andoy to Mando. The former Alejandro Pamintuan had become Mando Plaridel. And as Mando he had remained all these years.

These sad and angry memories burnt in Mando's mind as the shadow cast by the sun's rays on the branches and leaves fell on their path.

He told himself that while it was hard for a person with a conscience to help the Japanese, living in the mountains was harder. He was like a hunted beast without shelter from sun or rain, not knowing when or where he would eat. The only certainty was sharp hunger and the uncertain hours of rest.

Climbing up and down the steep inclines, with no foothold except sharp stones and thorny vines that jutted from nowhere, when a slight misstep could plunge him into the deep ravine. Bravely crossing wide rivers and being borne away by the strong current. Or walking on the slippery trunks of palm trees bridging the river. Wading across marshes and being sucked with each step as by quicksand. Cutting across the tall cogon whose sharp leaves bit one's flesh. In the afternoon, finding one's body covered by land and water leeches, clinging until they drowned in the blood they had sucked from your body. Tired from walking the whole day, and wet as well, for in that section of the mountain range and the forest, there was hardly a day when it did not rain, even when the August sun shone fiercely on the plain.

If no one offered them rice, eaten with rock salt or cooking oil for viand, one made do with guavas or coconuts picked along the way. And if one were truly unlucky, for many days, not even an unripe guava or a fallen coconut could be seen in the forest.

Luckily, Mando and his companions saw smoke as the sun leant towards the west. They walked towards the small hut. A couple lived there, and an iron kettle was set on four stones.

After Mando had introduced themselves, the old couple invited them inside the hut. After a while, they went to a stream nearby to wash up. The old man lent them clothes so they could wash their own.

On their return to the hut, some pieces of cassava were already smoking. This was what the old woman had been cooking. In the city, cassava became the food of the poor during the war. One only stuck it in the ground in the backyard and it quickly grew and bore tubers without much tending. Its flesh was similar to that of sweet potatoes, which was soft and delicious when boiled. During the war, it took the place of rice and bread on the tables of both the poor and the rich.

The old woman also served them ginger tea that had been sweetened with honey. They drank this from the smooth halves of coconut shells.

'This is the first time I've tasted this,' said Mando. 'Coffee and tea are nothing compared to this.'

'We lack many things here,' said the old man. 'But we've got some things not found in town.'

According to the old man, the town capital of Diliman, which lay ten miles away, was held by the Japanese. They built a strong garrison there. Soldiers from this garrison raided the nearby towns to make the townsfolk feel their presence. Then, the phrase 'There are Japs' meant bad news for the townsfolk. It was like saying, 'There are evil spirits,' or 'There are bandits'.

'Do the Japs come here?' asked Mando.

'They seldom do,' answered the old man. 'Sometimes, they order us to cut the trees, or they ask for wood, stone, or lumber. But they leave before darkness falls.'

The old man added that the Japanese had recently been sent to the town from the provincial capital. Reports had reached them that guerrillas were using the town as a passage to the mountains, so they decided to post a watch.

'But the townsfolk are the ones burdened,' explained the old man. 'So they evacuated here. Many moved to other towns. The Japs would vent their anger at their failure to catch the guerrillas on the peaceful civilians.'

'There are really guerrillas in town, aren't there?' asked Mando.

'Yes,' said the old man. 'But how can the Japs tell who the guerrillas are? Anyone who arouses their anger is caught, beaten up and forced to plead guilty. Once they admit their guilt, they are made to squeal; anyone whose name is mentioned also suffers. In the end, the stool pigeons and those whom they reported are all beheaded. It's just like killing chickens.'

'Poor folks,' Mando shuddered.

'There seems to be a sword hanging over everyone's head,' said Martin.

'Perhaps they had divided the towns into no-visitors zones,' said Karyo.

'They often do that in some towns,' said the old man. 'Once, some Japanese soldiers got drunk and had a brawl. They reported that the outlaws attacked them. The next day, the area where the fight had taken place became a no-visitors zone. Everyone was herded to the old schoolhouse and locked up without food or drink the whole day. The Japs searched their houses and took anything they wanted. Machetes, axes, knives, daggers, scissors, clocks, money, jugs, goats, chickens, eggs, rice, bananas and other things.'

'After robbing every house in the area—for this was robbery, pure and simple—they turned to the people in the schoolhouse. There was a man who was supposed to be from the place, was said to be a spy for the Japanese. He had a woven bag over his face, with holes over the eyes. He pointed out the supposed guerrillas,' the old man sighed.

'That's the "evil eye",' said Martin.

'Everyone pointed out by the traitor was separated from the group,' the old man continued, 'and beaten up without question. Afterwards, they were moved to the garrison. It has been said that they were all taken in a truck at nightfall. They were never seen again.'

The old man covered his mouth to stifle a cough, then he continued.

'The rest were not released until the next day. But many, especially the women and children, could hardly walk any more from hunger and sickness. More died from being cooped up than those pointed out by the spies.'

'Not one tried to hit back?' Mando's eyes flashed with anger. 'Weren't there many guerrillas in the towns nearby, at the foot of the mountains?'

'One night, two guerrillas went to the garrison and shot the guard at the gate,' answered the old man, 'but they were chased and caught. In the morning, they were brought to the plaza and were beheaded right there before the onlookers. Their heads were put on bamboo stakes that were displayed in the town square. The headless bodies were hung upside down from a tree. For a long time, the crows flew and feasted on the rotting corpses. That's what happens to those who try to avenge the Japs' cruelty against the people.'

That night, Mando could hardly sleep. In his mind's eye, he could see the corpses of the two brave guerrillas, who had proved to the Japanese that the Filipinos were not afraid to die.

V

Mando and his two companions followed the rough, winding and rocky pathway that led to the town of Kalayaan. According to the old man, no Japanese boots had been seen in this town.

The disciplined guerrillas were firmly established there. After several attempts, the Japanese realized that they suffered more losses than gains every time they tried to run over the place.

Next to the capital, Diliman was the strongest fort in the province. The old man said that the garrison had several hundred soldiers, who also went back and forth to the nearby towns of Buhangin and Mabato. Sometimes, the enemy would visit Saga-Saga, a town that lay between Kalayaan and Kalumpang, which were both controlled by the guerrillas. But the Japanese seldom ventured beyond Saga-Saga.

Kalayaan lay on the other side of the river. Within whistling distance was the forest's edge. In fact, the entire group of guerrillas gathered in the forest; besides, they also had many followers in town. They practically ran the town, for the puppet mayor had promised to obey the guerrilla leader after he was threatened. He never broke his promise. So he remained in good health and a mayor, even if only in name.

On the other hand, the town of Kalumpang was also controlled by the guerrillas who belonged to a different group. The two groups did not get along.

The Kalayaan guerrillas called the other group the 'Kalampag guerrillas', or 'The Noisemakers'. It was said that they fought each other more often than they fought the Japanese. Between them lay Saga-Saga, which was often the arena to prove the manhood of the guerrillas from the two nearby towns.

Mando was aware that this troop in Sampitan, with a large fort at Infanta, was independent from both groups. But they were not foes; rather, they would join forces when the occasion called for it. In fact, this was one of his aims—a closer union among the guerrilla groups. He had sent a message to the guerrillas in Diliman and other nearby places, a few months earlier. His aim was to motivate the guerrillas on the plains. Unfortunately, the Japanese answered the message by taking over Diliman.

The three walked slowly, but they were alert as soon as they saw Kalayaan. Almost at once, two armed men rushed towards them. In a loud voice, they accosted the three.

'Halt! Identify yourselves,' ordered one.

The three stopped, but they were not alarmed. Mando briefly explained that they had come from the Sierra Madre mountains.

'Are you pro-Jap or pro-American?' asked the man who had spoken first.

'We are pro-Filipino,' Mando answered promptly. Martin and Karyo nodded.

'Hmm . . .You haven't answered the question. Pro-Filipino. What do you mean? Some side with the Japs because they're pro-Filipino. Some side with the Americans because they're pro-Filipino as well. It's not clear.'

'Our being pro-Filipino has nothing to do with the Japs or the Americans,' said Mando. 'We're Filipino above everything else. The Filipinos and the Americans happened to join forces because they were attacked and had to defend themselves. Therefore, we stand according to justice, not for the colour of the skin or shape of the nose.'

Thus mollified, the two let Mando's group enter the town. One even offered to go with them. He said that their leader was in town, and he was the person they should see.

The guerrilla head received them graciously. Mando and Magat were about the same height, but the latter's complexion was darker. He moved quickly, and his eyes were as sharp as an eagle's. Mando and Magat had a long meeting, while Martin and Karyo were busy eating. It was rare for Mando to discuss important matters with a dedicated guerrilla who had solid principles. On the other hand, Martin and Karyo rarely had the chance to taste food such as was served to them. Therefore, the three were equally delighted with how the day had turned out.

Mando learnt that Magat was also in Manila when the war broke out. His guerrilla activities brought him to Kalayaan. When they were already seated at the table, Magat spoke. 'Comrades, we're pleased with your pro-Filipino stand. We're of one heart. My grandparents were followers of the revolution. They fought against the Spaniards, then against the Americans. Now I'm fighting the Japanese.'

Magat paused; the others listened in rapt attention.

'The Philippines is our country,' he continued. 'The side of the true Filipino is the Philippines, always. On the one hand, he should oppose anyone—Spaniard, American, Chinese, Japanese—when they try to invade us. An invader is an invader, in any shape or manner. He could also come through force of arms, commerce, or religion. Let us check closely whether their aim is to conquer and exploit us.'

'And often that is their real aim,' said Mando.

'That's why,' added Magat, 'we can't judge evil by the colour of the skin. There are also serpents among our own race.'

Mando then related his mission the past summer as ordered by the commander at Infanta. He was supposed to unite the guerrillas, for they all had the same goal—to take down the Japanese in the land. He also related what happened at Sampitan. It was borne by the lack of coordination amongst the guerrillas, those in the mountains of Sierra Madre and those on the plains.

'What is happening is disgraceful and dangerous, and an utter waste of lives,' said Magat, who was not hiding any more how bad he felt. 'But how could oil mix with water, sheep with wolves? Some guerrillas pretend to be enemies of the Japs, but they are worse enemies of the people.'

'Those are the treacherous guards,' explained Karyo.

'Worse,' corrected Magat. 'Look, first they set up a reign of terror through violence and cruelty. They enter a town where there are no Japs and run it with an iron fist. Whatever they like—livelihood, tools, utensils, houses, women—they snatch without permission! Any protest will surely lead to something worse. These atrocities are also committed by the Japs, yes, but they are enemies, while the fake guerrillas pretend to be defenders. Now, could you blame us that between this town and the other, which they command, there should be a barrier higher than a mountain?'

When no one answered, Magat continued.

'Why did we become guerrillas when the Americans surrendered? Because we can't condone the enemy's inhumanity. The Japs are enemies not simply because they're Japs, but because of their acts as soon as they arrived. If this is so, can we not consider our countrymen, our supposed brothers, who commit crimes against their people, crimes that cry to heaven for justice, our enemies? Burglary, rape, senseless killings. From the time of Cain to the time of Hitler and Yamashita, such atrocities cry out for punishment. Now tell me,' he asked again, not bothering to conceal his anger, 'how can one bring harmony, not to mention unity, among such groups? That would be like a conspiracy between the devil and the Archangel Gabriel.'

'The guerrilla movement should have its roots among the people,' Magat said, 'otherwise, we won't succeed. Here in Kalayaan, the townsfolk and the guerrillas are one. The townsfolk support whatever the guerrillas do, and any act done by the town's authorities receives our support. We organize groups made up of these three—the town's authorities, townsfolk and guerrillas. So we have no problem of food, clothing, work, defence, enemy attack, etc., that isn't resolved to everyone's satisfaction and for the good of the struggle.'

'I wish this were true of all places under guerrillas,' said Mando.

'Here, there is no theft or looting,' Magat pointed out. 'No profiteering, no tyrannical leader, no raping of women, no Japs with their bold spies. Our principle is one for all and all for one.'

Magat showed them how such a good programme was carried out. Mando remarked that if this were true all over the whole country, the Japanese should have been defeated even without the Americans. He mentioned that arms were needed, but in any fight, the will and morale of the nation are much more important than guns and bullets.

There was a room to store the objects that Magat's men had taken from the enemy—rifles, sabres, daggers, flags, uniform, shoes (for the forest and for the water), tents, rope, preserved food, medicine, books, documents, watches, pens, underwear and more.

'We got their radio sets and bicycles, which we are now using,' Magat told them, pride gleaming in his eyes.

Mando noticed a few helmets and visors for diving. A rubber hose, several yards long and two inches in diameter, was attached to every visor. Likewise, an oxygen tank was part of the contraption. There were also rubber boots. Mando asked Magat if those were instruments for skin diving.

'I don't know if these are for skin diving, but I'm sure they're for diving. The Japs are expert divers, whether for fish, pearls or wrecked ships.'

'Aren't you using them?' asked Mando.

'What shall we dive for here?' teased Magat. 'We just dive into that river. Take them if you need them,' he graciously offered.

'We're returning to the shores of the Pacific,' said Mando. 'They might be useful to us, or to the others.'

Mando chose two visors, together with the attached equipment, and two pairs of rubber boots.

He dusted a visor and tried it on. Karyo attached the cylinder with the rubber shoes.

'It fits,' Mando said with a smile.

'It's easy to adjust those,' said Magat. 'What's hard is diving to the bottom of the sea.'

Mando was relieved to find that he could breathe easily.

I'll try this, he told himself. 'How long can this last?' he asked Magat.

'Up to one hour or more with the oxygen, according to the old diver living here. He says it's better than the old equipment. This one is simpler and lighter.'

Aside from the diving gear, the three guerrillas were given clothes, food and medicine when they left the next day.

'When do we meet again?' Magat asked.

'Perhaps after the war,' said Mando. 'The days of the Japs are numbered.'

'Here, they were done for a long time ago,' Magat said, and then he laughed.

Mando decided not to pass by the plains any more, since they would go through Saga-Saga and Kalumpang. The last was under the 'Kalampag Guerrillas'. They turned back instead.

VI

Christmas, 1944. But Manila, the modern city usually gregarious and noisy, was as sombre as the pallid days of the Holy Week. Bare, orphaned and bleached of life. A ghost of its former self.

By daytime, only a few people roamed the streets. The city was gripped by a blackout every night. Japanese sentries stood on the street corners. One could count on one's fingers, the vehicles passing by.

In business areas, the bazaars didn't have their usual Christmas decorations. In fact, many big stores had long been closed, for there was nothing to sell and few customers bought merchandise. Only a few restaurants and bars in Santa Cruz and Escolta stayed open, to cater to the Japanese soldiers and civilians.

In a few places, the black market had sprouted. It was no different from the small markets on the squares and sidewalks. The goods were held in the hands, or laid on the ground. Everything was mixed up; there was no organization or plan. Haggling was the order of the day, and everything was paid for in cash. All the items being sold were slightly used.

A large area was filled with rows of vendors selling used items. The pickings were very slim. The vendors sold only one or two pieces: a stove, a meat grinder, a clock with broken springs, a radio with broken tubes, old shoes, trousers mended at the knees and seats, old dresses, faded hats and ties, one or two charcoal flat irons, a few dirty cots, rusty scissors, used toothbrushes, mirrors, old umbrellas, frames with saints' pictures, a bust of Rizal, old fountain pens, law and medicine books without covers, and a thousand and one odds and ends. Every item that one needed could be found in the black market. Surprisingly, the quoted price was several times higher than the original price when the item was still new.

'Fixed price' was the usual, scornful expression of the vendors. 'You can find these nowhere else. Also, these items are imported, sir.'

If there seemed to be fewer people roaming the streets of Manila, then most of them could be found in the black market.

Vegetables and fruits were sold in one corner. Watercress and the leaves of sweet potatoes were heaped together with the other food for the poor, like kidney peas, winged beans and eggplants. A small bundle of watercress cost ten pesos; so did a handful of winged beans. A ripe papaya could cost anywhere from fifty to seventy-five pesos. Bananas were sold for three pesos each, and even at that price, they were hard to find. A coconut was not sold whole. It was cut up into pieces at ten pesos a piece. Roasted pieces of coconut meat were sold at twenty pesos each.

Along the row of vegetable vendors was cooked food that was placed in flat baskets or iron pots. They were all for sale and included boiled cassava and plantains, boiled corn, rice cakes, cassava sweet meat but without sugar and as tasteless as the host given at Communion. Also for sale were viands—vats of mussel soup cooked with ginger and pepper. Occasionally, there was spicy goat's meat stewed in tomatoes, and even cooked dog dishes, every day. Many customers came for these last two dishes.

The skulls of the dog and the goat were set on tin plates, while the vendors shouted, 'Goat's meat stewed in tomatoes. Newly cooked dog dishes. *Azucena*. Well-spiced. Genuine. You can even see the skull on the plate.'

The buyers scrambled for the tempting dishes. Right there and then, using their fingers, they devoured the food that they had bought for twenty-five pesos a piece.

'So, you love dog's meat,' one customer nudged an acquaintance who was greedily chewing his food.

'What did you say?' asked the other in the Kapampangan language. 'Who cares for roasted pig?' And he continued chewing.

Not only did the people show extreme hunger, flies also swarmed on the exposed food.

But no one could ask for rice, beef or pork, chicken or fresh fish. These were only for the Japanese and the few Filipinos close to them. In a secret black market, a sack of rice cost as much as 20,000 pesos. Very few families had 20,000 pesos, even the 'Mickey Mouse' money that the Japanese government issued and had practically no value at all.

In one section was medicine of all kinds. Some of them were in bottles while the others were in small, tin cans. Most lay exposed on the flat baskets. Various fruits, roots, bark, seeds, grass and dried or fresh leaves were also sold. They were to be drunk, rubbed, applied as compress, or used for cleaning wounds. According to the vendors, there was no illness that these medicines could not cure—from headaches to toothaches, chest pains, pimples or boils, to smallpox, malaria, and even cholera.

No longer were these miracle cures for all human ailments sold by old women or bearded herbalists, but by young men with glib tongues. A few of them were former magicians and fortune-tellers who claimed to have studied medicine, massage and palm-reading in India and Arabia.

There were also those who sold the real medicine, but only in secret. They had medicines known before the war; some medicines were newly arrived and were 'Made in the USA'. The last were brought by submarines for the soldiers and the guerrillas, but they somehow found their way into the black market. Potent pills and tablets could be bought. Aspirin, atabrin, sulphathiazole, sulphanilamide, sulphaguanidine and others were also available. There were also medicines for injections. But the trading was done in whispers and, if necessary, the medicines were sold at astronomical prices.

The medicine dealers were unknown, for those roaming the black market were agents working on commission basis. But it was rumoured that some of them were doctors and honourable government officials. These traders in contraband medicine grew rich overnight, while all around them, the sick dropped dead like flies. They could have been saved by those medicines.

On the other hand, the poverty during the three years of the Japanese occupation purified the soul and strengthened the common people. Some learnt to make shoes from old ones. Others made alcohol from coconut milk to use as a substitute for gasoline. Tasty biscuits were produced from cassava flour. Cigarettes came from grated tobacco leaves wrapped in ordinary paper, among many other items, showing the resourcefulness of the Filipino.

Now was the time to topple the centuries-old barriers that split the people before the war. In the face of widespread want, the wealthy stepped down from their pedestals and mixed with the ordinary people. The power of money and property had lessened; occasionally, the physical strength and daring of some adventurers were more effective. They looted, hoarded goods, amassed wealth and dictated prices.

Both the poor and the now-impoverished rich could be seen carrying bags, rubbing elbows while shopping for their daily needs. They walked from their homes to the marketplace.

'Now, this is the *real* democracy,' one observer said to himself.

Once, a former Cabinet member could not afford to buy a ripe papaya. A former judge was given a pack of cigarettes by the vendor who had been the judge's former driver. The driver now made cigarettes, and the judge had no means of earning a living. 'God bless you, Rubio,' said the judge. Thus the other vendors would remember the name of the kind man later on.

Meanwhile, the collaborators could be seen driving in cars, and the newly rich put on airs as they rode in handsome carriages drawn by magnificent horses. As they sped by, people in the city threw dirty looks at them and muttered curses. They also caught the attention of the bearded, dirty Japanese soldiers pushing carts. Gone was their arrogance when they first occupied Manila after New Year's Day in 1942.

On such a black market and other gathering places would swoop down a group of Japanese dressed as civilians, with one or two Filipinos dressed as soldiers, down to their caps and boots. From the crowd, they would snatch one or two whom they sought. Should the one caught protest or ask questions, he would be mauled without mercy.

One day, Rubio, the judge's former driver, was taken by the Japanese military police. He was carrying cigarettes, which the Japanese snatched; then they twisted his arms behind him. Another hit him with his fists, grabbed and tore his clothes, then kicked him on the legs. Only when he fell almost unconscious to the ground did the Japanese let him go.

The thick crowd moved back, forming a wary circle while they watched the scene unfolding before them. But everyone seemed paralysed and were like deaf-mutes who had lost all their senses. They could not intervene or even protest.

When the cigarette vendor's body was swollen from the beating, he was left almost lifeless in the middle of the square. Only then did someone come and help him. One of the vendors took him home.

For the next day and the succeeding ones, Rubio, the former driver and cigarette vendor, did not show up. No one could tell why he was maltreated by the Japanese military police. According to some, he was probably suspected of helping the guerrillas. Some thought that he had been reported by the Filipinos who tagged along after the civilian-clad Japanese.

When the former driver disappeared, the incident became cloaked in mystery. Some said he was taken from his home by the Japanese, some believed that he was taken by his family to the province, where he then joined the outlaws.

Once, an unknown man rushed into a restaurant, shot two men drinking beer, and swiftly escaped. No one recognized him. The slain men were Japanese spies and were the companions of the military police who had mauled the driver at the black market. Someone recognized Rubio, but he would not talk. When the military police came, there was no one in the restaurant, only the two corpses and the owner. The frightened owner was arrested.

But more often encountered in public, near markets and eateries, were corpses not caused by the Japanese, or the guerrillas or criminals, but by starvation and sickness. When found, the dead were mere skin and bones, their eyes deep-set, cheeks sunken, but their legs and feet were swollen.

The public was so used to such sights that they hardly paid attention to them, or seemed to see only a dead dog or cat. And the authorities did not pick them up and bury them right away.

The seeming languor of Christmas in 1944 lay only on the surface. In fact, something was seething. Even the Japanese knew that their days were already numbered. This was no secret to many Filipinos. That October, the American liberation forces had already landed in Leyte and were pounding the shores of Pangasinan, to prepare for the landing of US troops in Luzon. Because of this, the Japanese—who were at the end of their rope—had prepared to carry out their final plans to halt the Americans. They would do everything to turn back the Americans and seek revenge on the Filipinos, and if all else failed, they would escape. The Filipinos were also planning to carry out their own revenge and to meet the Allied Forces who would help them win back the freedoms they had lost.

The Filipinos were on the lookout for the fleet of modern aeroplanes, which, like giant eagles with stars on their wings, flew and dove with grace. From the air above the Japanese forts and installations, they would suddenly drop bombs that exploded and burst into flames that spread swiftly and melted everything in their path. While the Japanese were like a pack of rats, hiding and dodging, the Filipinos gleefully watched and rejoiced as if they were just watching fireworks on a holiday.

The Japanese knew they had reached the end of a gamble. The Filipinos awaited a glorious day, more blessed than any Christmas or New Year.

But then, the scarcity, violence, and terror worsened. There was no more rice, no meat, no milk and no sugar for much of the country. No Christmas tree, no Santa Claus, no ham, no wine and no Christmas gifts reminded one of the holiday season.

'Never mind, children,' a mother consoled her two children who remembered it was Christmas. 'In a few days, the Americans will return, and your father will come down from the mountains. And we'll have bread, canned goods, candy, apples and grapes.'

On the faces of the children shone the joy of innocent cherubs, in the hope that the poverty of this Christmas would surely be followed by prosperity.

The mother and her children retired early on the dark and moonless night. Several times, the siren signalled the oncoming attack of the fighter planes, but the three good souls just slept soundly, dreaming of the day when 'Glory to God in the highest, and peace on earth to men of goodwill' would be fulfilled.

VII

The horse-drawn carriage had been waiting for some time to take Pastor to town. Last night, he had arranged for Tano, the driver, to pick him up. He was going to Manila.

From the town, Pastor would take a truck up to Azcarraga near Divisoria Market. From there, he would hire a cart to carry his pieces of baggage. He would then walk or, if needed, push the cart to reach the Monteros' house that stood on the other side of the Pasig River.

In those days, the buses could no longer travel. One was lucky to find space even in those that were packed with people like sardines in a tin. The countless passengers carried all sorts of baggage.

Once a month, Pastor went to Manila to bring rice and other farm produce for the Montero family. Pastor was the overseer of Don Segundo's vast landholding. He was a former tenant; he had replaced Don Segundo's overseer who had been kidnapped by the outlaws. A year had passed, and the land was spared from any more troubles. However, Don Segundo was not as pleased with Pastor as he had been with his former overseer, who was loyal to the bone. Apparently, Pastor got along swimmingly with the tenants—and with the outlaws as well.

Pastor and Tano loaded the two sacks of rice and some chickens on the carriage. Pastor could lift them by himself, for at forty-one years old, he was still strong, but it was just in Tano's nature to be helpful.

Puri, Pastor's daughter, brought a small basket of fresh eggs, a bamboo container of carabao's milk, and a large squash. Puri had served as her father's housekeeper since her mother had died.

Tano teased Puri, whom he had known as a child.

'Oh, look! Puri is getting prettier every day,' the old driver said, then he clucked his tongue. 'I wonder who is making you pretty?' And he looked her over.

'No, sir,' she protested.

'Who?' insisted Tano.

'What can make a girl pretty other than a clean and quiet life?' Puri said.

'That's true,' Tano said, then he turned to Pastor. 'You're lucky to have such a daughter. How many young girls nowadays, even those brought up in the village, like to have a clean and quiet life?'

Tano was not the only one fascinated with Puri. Everyone admired her, especially the young men. She had done only basic schooling, but her beauty, her refined manners, and sense of dignity were indeed rare for a nineteen-year-old.

When Pastor was made an overseer, Don Segundo was startled upon seeing Puri. He offered to bring her to Manila, promising to send her to a girls' convent school, where she would learn to play the piano. He also promised to provide for all of her needs. However, Pastor did not give his consent, and Puri also refused the offer.

'Mother told me to look after Father, sir,' she had told Don Segundo.

Pastor had greater difficulty on this trip compared to the earlier ones. Several times, they were detained and searched by the guerrillas, by the Japanese, by the town police. Of course, Pastor had a secret pass for the guerrillas and a printed pass for the Japanese Army. But the police search was more thorough, especially in the towns near Manila.

The Japanese were strict about the presence of guns and other deadly weapons, but not about food. The guerrillas, on the other hand, made sure that the passenger was not a Japanese spy and that the food, if in large amounts, was not for the Japanese but for the people. But the police were worse than the Japanese until they got what they needed. They always snared their share of the ordinary citizens' food.

Pastor passed a veritable cavalry of travellers from the province to Manila during the last days of 1944. As in the past, the Montero couple greeted him, not with pleasure or thanks, but with reproach and utter blame.

'Why did you bring only this?' grumbled Don Segundo.

'Why are there no peanuts, sugar apple and rice crispies?' Doña Julia said with a pout.

'If I make the trip myself, I'll get everything I need from the landholding,' Montero said with a sneer.

'It's dangerous to travel,' Pastor said.

'Suppose I bring a Japanese soldier, then?' the landlord answered in a bragging tone.

'That would be more dangerous, sir.'

Doña Julia called a servant to bring in the goods brought by Pastor.

Don Segundo went to his office on the first floor, followed by the farmer. 'What the devil is this?' the Don roared. 'Is this my share of the harvest? Why, I don't seem to be the proprietor any more!'

'When there's a war,' Pastor answered in a calm tone, 'values change; customs change.'

'What do you mean?' demanded the landlord, his eyebrows raised.

'Look at what happened to our former overseer. He insisted on following the old policy at the landholding or dividing the expenses and the harvest. He wanted to collect all the debts at once. He wished to bring all the rice to your warehouse in Manila. But what happened to him and to your interests?'

Don Segundo grunted, before asking another question. 'And my sacks of rice, where are they? Surely not these two sacks only, Pastor?'

'Your rice is stored at the warehouse in the landholding. I can only bring you two sacks a month. The outlaws won't allow more than that. They say that is enough for you. If the food is brought to Manila all at once, it might even fall into the hands of the Japs or the black market, which they don't want to happen.'

Don Segundo rose in a rage and almost shouted, 'My rice is mine and I didn't steal it! It's up to me to do as I wish. Does an owner have no more right to his property?'

'Their reason is that each one should not have more than what he needs,' Pastor answered in his calm and collected tone. 'In war, everyone suffers, so everyone should be helped. In short, they want to put human life above property.'

'Oh, I see,' said Don Segundo with a sneer. 'And who will enforce that? The outlaws? The enemies of the law are now the ones making the law. If that is the case, then indeed, the world has turned upside down.'

'In their opinion, even if they're called enemies of the law, those who take advantage of the war are the enemies. They are trying to stop such acts.'

'And what are the leaders doing? Those who were put in their positions by the Japanese?'

'The leaders are scared.'

'And the Japanese?'

'The Japs don't want to die, either.'

With such an answer, Don Segundo could not follow through with his questions any more. Then he said in a torrent of rage: 'I thought the war ended with the fall of Corregidor. It seems that disorder just followed. What's wrong is when the poor people begin to meddle. Everything then becomes mixed up. Anarchy and banditry reign. This is what happens. People have no more respect for the law. They're not even afraid of God. Where is this country going?'

'It seems that,' Pastor spoke slowly, 'the defeat of the American Armed Forces led to a revolution.'

'What revolution?'

'Just like Japan, Germany and Italy,' answered Pastor, aware that he was treading on delicate ground. 'They say that the war came here because they rose against the wealthy nations like England and the United States. Now, with the defeat of the American Armed Forces, the poor are rising against the rich.'

This only stoked further Don Segundo's anger. 'What fools!' he exploded. 'And where did you get such foolish ideas?'

'This is what the outlaws say when they try to get followers.'

'Pastor, remember that those people are a mere pack of bandits. They want to grab other people's property, take what others have worked hard and saved for.'

Don Segundo was panting. He poured water into a glass, finished it in one gulp, and slumped on a chair while Pastor remained standing.

Pastor's eyes were fixed on a picture on the opposite wall, showing Don Segundo and a Japanese official. Below it stood a small flag of the Rising Sun, still in the dry wind. Pastor thought that this must be the powerful military officer who was said to be the Monteros' friend. It was rumoured that Dolly was his girlfriend, and that he helped Don Segundo make his pile of money. Pastor stared long and hard at the picture.

His thoughts were cut short by the landlord.

'I want to know how much rice I have in your charge,' he said. 'Before the war, for every hectare at 50 per cent, my share was . . .'

'You may no longer use that as a basis, sir,' Pastor interrupted him, 'whether in harvesting or in sharing. For almost two years, from the start of the war, the land has lain idle. Many tenants moved away, and some have sought refuge in the mountains. Only since I took over have things improved. But the harvest is barely enough for the tenants' needs and for yourself, besides the amount demanded by the outlaws. I always set aside your share. You still have about a hundred sacks.'

Pastor was saved from the impending storm when Doña Julia entered, followed by the Japanese in the picture. Like a mask, Don Segundo's sharp look and set jaw immediately altered. A glad and gracious smile softened the outlines of his face. He stood up right away and shook hands with the officer.

'Colonel Moto, please sit down. How are you? What do you want to drink?' Without waiting for an answer, he told his wife, 'Julia, send for whiskey, soda and ice.'

No one noticed Pastor quietly walk away from the office into the yard. He had travelled from a far place and had been there for some time, had brought rice and other provisions for the Monteros, yet no one asked if he was hungry or even offered him water. But the thought passed quickly, for he was used to the shabby treatment that the rich meted out to the poor, as well as their grovelling before more important persons.

After a few minutes, Pastor saw Dolly all dressed up, going to her father's office. Then, she came out with the colonel holding her around the waist. The two got into his car.

Pastor then thought of his daughter Puri. He recalled that he used to envy the Montero girl in secret; how he used to wish his daughter would grow up like Dolly, with her education and her charm. Now he saw how the officer held Dolly and how closely they sat in the car, with no chaperone except her own conscience. Then his eyes seemed to burn, and he thanked God for his only child. If Puri ever acted like Dolly, Pastor resolved that he would either strangle her or challenge the colonel to a duel. But, perhaps, Dolly's parents approved of this relationship.

All of a sudden, Pastor heard Don Segundo's voice calling for him. The colonel and Dolly had already left.

'Our talk was cut short,' said the landlord. 'So, there's no remedy for this situation at the landholding?'

'If we don't agree,' said Pastor, 'we'll just lose more.'

Don Segundo's ears turned red, but he realized he should not blame the overseer.

'Very well then,' he said, 'do whatever you think is best under the circumstances. But as soon as conditions improve, I'll fix the way things are. I'll not allow people to be ungrateful. We shall bring back the way things used to be,' he stressed.

He gave Pastor a small sum for expenses and told him to bring four sacks of rice on the next trip.

When Pastor was about to leave, he stopped, remembering something.

'Don Segundo,' said the farmer, 'where is Andoy?'

'Andoy?' repeated the rich man, as if the name did not ring a bell.

'Ah, Andoy,' Don Segundo said after a while. 'Yes, the son of your sister who used to work here. He's bad, a barbarian, an ingrate. He left without a word.'

'He left?' Pastor was surprised.

'Yes, he just vanished,' said Don Segundo. 'You're aware that he grew up in my care. I treated him like a son and even sent him to school. Imagine, he was about to graduate when the war broke out. And how did he repay me?'

'Where could he be?' asked Pastor, worry evident on his face. He was thinking how, after the death of his only sister, Andoy was his last close relative.

'Don't bother to look for him,' said the landlord. 'I heard that the Japanese police caught him for joining some deviltry. If I had not been Don Segundo Montero, I might have become involved because he was my ward.'

Pastor's eyes nearly popped out. In a shaken voice, he asked again, 'What do you think, sir? Did they kill him?'

'How should I know? And I don't want to meddle,' Don Segundo answered in a brusque manner. 'He dug his own grave. This is what happens to the bad ones, to people who are ungrateful.'

Pastor left the yard with a heavy heart. He wanted to blame himself for what happened to his nephew. He should have looked after the boy when his sister had died, the sister who had raised him. But he had been negligent and did not even ask after Andoy. If he were alive and they ever met again, they might not even recognize each other.

But what Pastor minded the most was the heap of insults from Don Segundo. Pastor did not believe that Andoy could have turned out to be a bad or ungrateful person. Andoy's father, Montero's houseboy and driver, and his mother, Pastor's older sister, were both models of virtue. And Andoy was their only child. Pastor felt that the fruit would not fall far from the tree.

VIII

Don Segundo Montero felt sad when his friend Colonel Moto of the Japanese Imperial Army finally said goodbye.

A few days before, the colonel had revealed that he was preparing to leave, following an order from Tokyo. Montero wanted to give a grand party to bid him farewell, but the Japanese commander was against it. As much as possible, it was best to keep his departure low key. He would have to act on a new mission, which was a military secret, he said.

And so that afternoon, the Monteros had no guest besides Colonel Moto and his aide. Both were in their clean, dashing uniforms.

Nevertheless, Doña Julia and Dolly prepared special afternoon snacks. Although it was hard to buy delicious food, the Monteros could afford the food in the black market and so did not lack anything.

They also prepared gifts for the colonel as a token of their friendship. Don Segundo owed much to his friend. When he went to greet the Japanese forces, a few hours before the occupation of Manila as an 'Open City', it was Colonel Moto who met him. The colonel was pleased with the landlord's gesture and assured him he would not regret helping Japan.

When the colonel was assigned to Manila, he became a close friend of Montero family. Hardly a week passed without a grand reception at Montero's home, with high Japanese and Filipino officials attending.

The friendship between the officer and the businessman did not bloom naturally. Rather, it was simple arithmetic, where two and two make four. They both understood that their collaboration would bring them huge profits.

The colonel was assigned to look for funds for army expenses in the area under him. Montero was a businessman and, therefore, could be useful. Meanwhile, the colonel enjoyed the pleasures of the conqueror. He was single and in his prime. Fortune smiled upon him. The Montero family belonged to the upper crust of society. Doña Julia was still youthful, and even his almond-shaped eyes could not miss the beauty of her only child, Dolly. Through Montero, he hoped to be accepted not only as an officer but also as a gentleman who mingled with the upper crust, a group of people who only wanted pomp and pleasure.

On the other hand, Don Segundo was entertaining similar thoughts. He was thinking of how to get close to the Japanese officer and the rewards he would get.

'They need funds; well, I'll take care of that,' Montero said to himself. 'They need cars, dynamos, machines, tires, rope; very well then, I'll hold Aladdin's lamp for them. The colonel likes wine and women? Well, he's in luck. Montero will just be a fool if he doesn't become a millionaire many times over.' He smiled, and then he patted his left shoulder with his right hand.

A kind of Monte-Moto partnership was soon formed.

Before long, the colonel became practically a member of the Montero household. In fact, he had his own room that he could use anytime. During his stay, he was served not by the servants, but either by Doña Julia or Dolly.

He was often alone with Dolly, and they talked of topics other than the war. The colonel enjoyed looking at Dolly; he loved her bearing. He was taller than most Japanese, amiable, and he obviously came from a good family.

Don Segundo supplied the needs of Colonel Moto. He gave him the use of his own office and depot. Because of this arrangement, all bids for the Japanese forces were coursed through Montero. And that was how money, loads of it, simply flowed into his hands.

Such good fortune, of course, was not for free. He repaid the colonel not with money—for what would the latter do with Mickey Mouse money that he printed himself?—but by being his slave.

Aside from the frequent receptions, banquets and dances for the Japanese officers in the Montero gardens or at the grand Manila Hotel, Montero and Moto had their own outings almost every night. By day, Montero reaped huge profits. By night, Moto gathered the perfumed flowers of pleasure.

They became regular customers of the first-class hostesses of well-known nightclubs. Whenever they appeared at any amusement place, the orchestra greeted them with a special piece. The manager would greet and lead them to a reserved room. The top hostesses would enter; three waiters would serve them. Two bottles of wine would be immediately uncorked—wine that was available only to them.

Sometimes, they would dance. Often, they would just drink and talk. After an hour, they would leave with the hostesses, although no entertainer was allowed to leave before the orchestra had played 'Home, Sweet Home' in the wee hours of the morning. But for Monte and the colonel, such rules did not apply. The manager himself saw them to their car.

This happened everywhere. Anything—or anyone—they desired, was given to them; neither the manager nor the owner could refuse, because they could order them to close down, and that would be the end of their businesses. It was even harder for any hostess to say 'no'. That would be disobedience to the boss. She knew on which side her bread was buttered. She was in the nightclub to make a living, not to become a holy person. Anyone in her place who pretended to be clean in such surroundings was a just crow flapping its wings and bragging about its black feathers.

But Colonel Moto was not satisfied with the hostesses and the other birds of the night. Lilibeth, his secretary, was prettier. He met her through Dolly at a party. Lilibeth was an American *mestiza*: her father was American, and her mother was from Zamboanga. She was Dolly's schoolmate before the war. She was fair, shapely and fond of comfort and pleasure.

Lilibeth had stopped studying a few months before the war and had married an American pilot who had just arrived in Manila. The pilot joined the American Armed Forces in Bataan. The colonel hit two birds with one shot. First, he had captured the wife of an enemy. Second, he had a lovely secretary, a rare doll he might have anytime. If Lilibeth was not aware of this yet, he would soon let her know. He would take his chances.

The colonel would not remain guessing for long, however. He guessed right. One afternoon, he asked his secretary to stay under the pretext that he had urgent work to do. When the others had left, the colonel and Lilibeth prepared some unimportant papers. Then they had dinner and went to a nightclub that he did not usually visit. He took her home after midnight. Lilibeth had drunk too much and had to be helped by the colonel, who had drunk just enough to keep his steps and arms steady as he held the lovely woman.

Colonel Moto beat his superior, General Homma, in Bataan at reaching their respective 'objectives'. The amorous Japanese official thought Lilibeth was more attractive than any heiress or woman from the upper crust of society.

One day, the office phone rang. Colonel Moto recognized Dolly's voice.

'I know why you haven't been around,' she told him.

'I've been very busy,' said the colonel.

'Yes, indeed, very busy with Lilibeth.' A tinge of jealousy sounded in Dolly's voice. That afternoon, Lilibeth went home alone. Before dark, Colonel Moto's car could be seen speeding toward the grand house of the Monteros.

Dolly greeted him with affection. She was perfumed and wore a dress of sheer material that showed the outlines of her lithe body. Colonel Moto asked about Don Segundo and Doña Julia.

'They went up to Baguio this morning,' Dolly told him. 'No one was left except my housemaid and I. They also took the other servants,' she added.

'And why did you stay behind?'

'I told them we'd go together.' Dolly looked straight into the eyes of the Japanese officer.

'Oh?'

'Don't you want to take me to Baguio? Or can you not get away from Lilibeth?' she asked.

Colonel Moto merely smiled, pinched Dolly's cheek and went to his room.

'I'll just take a shower,' he said.

After ten minutes, Dolly brought snacks to the colonel's room. He had finished his shower and was wearing a colourful kimono.

'Why do you always mention Lilibeth?' he asked after he had eaten.

'She told me about you.'

'Are you jealous?' The colonel's voice was gentle.

'What right have I?' Dolly said. 'I'm not your . . .'

The colonel quickly stood up, held the girl by the shoulders, and looked at her blushing face.

'Dolly,' he said, 'don't compare yourself to Lilibeth. I've a special regard for you. Here in my locket, on my breast, is your picture. I planned to ask you to marry me after the war.'

Lovingly, he stroked her hair, her breasts. Slowly, he raised her face and gave burning kisses to her lips.

He imprisoned her in his arms. Dolly was a willing captive. For a long time, their bodies seemed welded together. Their kisses seemed endless.

Without speaking, as if unaware of what they were doing, they moved to the bed and sat on the edge. Moto's fingers were kept busy, and he slowly pushed her down, but she suddenly drew away.

'Wait, my housemaid might enter,' she said. She got up and locked the door.

When she came back, the colonel had already removed his kimono and was just in shorts. She saw his well-built body. He seized and crushed her with desire. Dolly did not protest, for he made her feel the same eagerness. The blood in her veins was filled with craving. She was drunk on the wine of anticipation.

Slowly, she lay down. Then she freed her lips from his kisses and asked, 'Truly, am I your only love, darling?'

'You and you alone.'

'Even in Tokyo?'

'Anywhere.' With this, Dolly embraced him tightly. Calmly, Moto removed her dress, followed by her underwear. Dolly felt no shyness in baring herself before him while his eyes narrowed seeing her white skin, her swelling breasts.

When the colonel claimed her as he would snatch a rare gem, Dolly sobbed, 'You are the first . . .'

'I'll make you happy, Dolly.'

'Is this our . . . our honeymoon?'

'Here and in Baguio. And all the days to come.'

There was silence. After an hour, when the housemaid knocked, the lovers were already sound asleep. Dolly's head was pillowed on Moto's right arm. His left hand was on Dolly's front, which looked like a coat of arms as it caught the light. The housemaid wanted to ask if she should bring them supper, but there was no answer. So she just left, shaking her head.

'These two might just die from sheer happiness,' the maid muttered to herself.

In the morning, the colonel and Dolly joined the Montero couple in their rest house in the cold mountain city of Baguio. As Moto had promised, that night they had their honeymoon, a privilege that no Filipina ever enjoyed outside of marriage.

Life afterwards was like a chain of happy moments, which time could not ruin in their memory.

Until that afternoon, when he said goodbye.

Once more, he visited his room and Dolly followed. They recalled their happy moments.

'I've to go, but I leave you my heart,' he whispered.

'You take my love with you,' said Dolly. And she hung a gold locket containing her picture around his neck.

The sun had almost set when Colonel Moto and his aide went down the steps of the house that they would never see again. Dolly was crying as she watched the colonel go.

To Colonel Moto, who did not conceal his sorrow, it was not the sun that was setting but the hope of his proud empire. Their defeat in the last stages of the war in the Philippines was already written large on the horizon.

After a few days, the Montero family received the sad news that Colonel Moto was dead. He had committed harakiri at his house on Daytona Avenue.

IX

Back from the town of Kalayaan, Mando's group spent the night at the house of the same couple, the house where they had stayed before. They continued their journey in the morning.

They followed the path that wound through the mountain and led to the seashore.

While resting on rocks under the shade of the big trees, Mando took out a folded piece of paper from his pocket, then he opened and read it. On this paper, he had written down the various references in the *Fili* about the house of Father Florentino and the place where he had thrown Simoun's treasure chest. On the same paper, Tata Matias had also sketched directions in the form of a map.

Tata Matias figured out it must be a remote barrio outside a town in Quezon, most likely in Atimonan or a nearby town. Therefore, it was within forty kilometres from his hut in the mountains of Sierra Madre. This was how he explained his past search when he was fired with the desire to dive for the lost treasure.

Tata Matias told Mando about the probable place where Father Florentino lived after he retired.

Mando read Isagani's description of his town in the *Fili* and the
house of his priest-uncle:

> It was surrounded by forests at the foot of the mountain and near the
> shore . . . There, far from civilization, there in the midst of nature's
> plenty, inside the forest and at the seashore . . .

Mando went on reading until . . .

> From its hiding place, Father Florentino took the famous iron chest
> with the great wealth of Simoun, firmly went down the steps carrying it
> and went to the ravine to gaze on the depths of the ocean. He saw the
> waves of the Pacific kissing the rocks . . . He was alone . . . Then, he
> threw Simoun's iron chest into the ocean . . . The water swallowed the
> great treasure and closed over it.

The place was supposed to be frightening, and it was said that ghosts
appeared during the unholy hours of the night. After Father Florentino
died, the house was neglected and went to seed until it just crumbled
to the ground. After a long time, the forest completely covered its traces
just as the sea had hidden the wealth of the mysterious guest.

His companions noticed that Mando was engrossed with the paper.
'What's that, Mando? It looks like a map, right?' asked Martin. Mando
told them what it meant and what he thought they should do. At first,
the two merely laughed. Karyo said it would be better to dive for fish
so they could have something to eat. Martin was lazy by nature and just
asked how he could dive when he could not even swim.

But after Mando explained everything to them, they agreed with
his plans. First, they had nothing to lose even if they did not find
the treasure chest; but if they succeeded, they would be the luckiest.
Second, they had the time and the equipment.

All they had to do was look for the area where Father Florentino
had thrown the iron chest. This, they could do with the help of the
map and by observing and searching. They needed food for a few days,
a small boat, rope, an axe, and a few other items. It was not hard to find

such equipment in any town near the seashore between Mauban and Atimonan, which was just a day's walk from where they were.

The three finalized their plans. They decided to walk towards Atimonan. In three days, they had prepared their supplies and equipment with Mando's wise management. But they kept their secret; they simply introduced themselves as guerrillas out on a mission. Right there and then, they received all the help they needed from the people, as if a door had been opened.

They started by looking for a ravine at the foot of the mountain, surrounded by forests and near the shore. They went to within five to six kilometres from the next town after leaving their small boat and equipment with one of the people who had helped them.

At first, they seemed to be hunting for a flea among the shaves of rice stalks. Everywhere they looked, they only found trees, vines, stones, shore and sand. They suffered from hunger, fatigue, and boredom.

'Of all the jobs I've done, this is the most exasperating,' Martin grumbled. 'We seem to be looking for nothing.'

'I got it,' Karyo shouted all of a sudden. When the others came, he showed them five iguana eggs.

They slept on broad stones after eating their ration and the boiled iguana eggs. The moon was bright and round as a coin, and the night was calm and beautiful. The slight cloud in the east was driven away by a strong wind rising from the sea.

'I think that we won't fail,' Mando said before they lay down on the rocks.

'If we should be lucky, how do we divide it?' asked Karyo.

'We are three; therefore, three partitions,' promptly answered Martin. 'Is that right, Chief?' He turned to Mando for support for his opinion.

'It could benefit not only three, but many others, should we wish it; one gem alone is enough wealth. My plan,' he said gently, sizing up their reaction, 'if we should find the chest, is to go to Tata Matias to consult him.'

'What for?' asked Karyo.

'What has the old man got to do with the iron chest?' said Martin. 'Aren't we the ones going through all the difficulties?'

'We owe a lot to Tata Matias,' Mando said. 'He thought of this, he prepared the map and studied what should be done.'

'Then let's give him a fourth share,' suggested Karyo.

'Comrades, we should not think only of the partitioning,' Mando explained. 'What's more important is what we shall do with the wealth.'

'What else, but divide it?' Martin said. 'You get your share, and I get mine. Isn't that right?'

'But of course,' said Karyo.

'Simoun's wealth isn't mine alone,' said Mando. 'Wealth kept in the ocean's womb, with a history, with a purpose. So, we can't just . . .'

Martin and Karyo showed impatience at the direction of Mando's words.

'If it won't be ours, even if we get it, count me out,' Martin said.

'Me too,' Karyo backed up Martin.

'You won't be on the losing end,' Mando calmed down their fears. 'Didn't I tell you that one gem alone is already worth a fortune?'

'I ask only for my share,' Martin said.

'Same here,' Karyo repeated.

'Well, if that's your wish, then you're the majority,' Mando ended their argument.

The next day, Mando found what might be part of the stone steps of Father Florentino's former home. He could no longer see the ravine, but he saw a jutting part that hardly rose above the water and was covered by the big waves. It was clear that the ravine near the stone steps of the house had been swallowed up by the ocean. It could only be reached by swimming, or by travelling on a small boat.

When they saw it, the three marked the place. They went back for their small boat and equipment. They took the small boat to the supposed site of Father Florentino's home a hundred years ago. It closely resembled the sketch on the map.

They cut down some trees, branches, and wide palm leaves. And then, they built a shed on the stone steps for their shelter.

They carefully studied the best way to look for the treasure chest. Because Martin could not swim, he would just stay in the small boat. Mando and Karyo would dive. On the first day, they would dive to know how deep the ocean was. They had also brought a piece of rope to secure them.

Then, they would dive to test the equipment that they got from the guerrillas' headquarters in Kalayaan and look around to check if it was the right place.

They decided to dive only in the daytime. If anyone noticed them, they could just pretend to be fishing. Diving at night would arouse suspicions; besides, they had no flashlight. It would be dangerous, especially at night because of the sharks, who would just suddenly come gliding out of nowhere.

They found the visors and other equipment useful. With the first trial, they stayed underwater for an hour. The plateau under the sea was thick with moss, and it was around five yards deep. Its bottom was sheer wilderness, a tangle of beautiful corals.

On the second day, the sky had cleared up, and the sea was smooth as a wide mat. The fine weather seemed to be a sign of good fortune.

Together, they carried the banca from the shore and laid it on the water. Mando and Karyo put on their rubber boots. Martin fixed the brass cylinder on the backs of the two with the help of canvas belts. Then the visors to which were attached the oxygen tanks.

Martin tied a long piece of rope to a horizontal piece of wood in the middle of the small boat. The other end was tied to Mando's belt. Thus, if anything untoward happened, they could signal underwater to Martin, who would stay in the small boat. They felt that the rope could keep them from going too far, for the length of the rope would mark their movements.

They went into the water one by one. Mando went first, carrying a spear. Karyo followed with a machete. After about fifteen minutes, Martin was startled by a strong yank at the rope, causing the small boat to tilt. He had not recovered from his surprise when he saw bubbles rising to the surface.

'Blood.' Martin was alarmed.

Suddenly, Mando surfaced, supporting Karyo. At first, Martin could not tell who was hurt, but Mando shouted.

'Get Karyo,' he said when they were near the small boat. Martin supported Karyo, whom Mando raised by the shoulders up onto the small boat.

Martin immediately rowed ashore. The moment they landed, they ran to their shed, carrying their wounded companion.

Mando quickly treated their wounded comrade, but he failed. Karyo died from loss of blood.

Mando told Martin what had happened underwater. They had just reached bottom when a shark glided by, facing Karyo. Mando speared the shark and hit it on the side while Karyo hit it in the throat with his machete.

Mando thought that Karyo was unhurt; however, he had been wounded by the shark's teeth. After the wounded shark swam away, Mando noticed that Karyo staggered and then clung to him.

With sadness, the two buried their slain comrade that same afternoon. Then they found the shark that had been washed ashore. They slaughtered it without speaking to each other. The beast that had killed Karyo was now ironically saving them from hunger, they thought.

X

For two days, Mando and Martin mourned in silence. Grief was like a black curtain that had fallen around them, shutting them off from the rest of the world. They hardly spoke, their minds filled only with their own thoughts.

Mando grieved hard over Karyo's death, for he was a loyal comrade and a courageous fighter. He might not be clever, but he had a good heart. He was ready to help and worked with daring and strength. Being a peasant, he was also helpful and obedient.

Although it was an accident, Mando blamed himself. Was he not the brains and the leader of the enterprise that took Karyo's life?

In truth, he liked and trusted Karyo more than Martin. Even if Martin was as manly, his ways, manners and speech did not inspire confidence. He had been jailed several times, he admitted. While going to jail was not enough to condemn a man, but the kind of person he had been—still, Martin himself confessed, 'I joined the guerrillas to save myself.'

Mando felt that Martin was brave, but unreasonable, greedy and unreliable. However, as he had said, in times of crisis, people are thrown together so that one cannot be choosy about one's friends or foes. In buying milkfish wholesale, one accepts both big and small milkfish.

On the other hand, Martin was more regretful than grief-stricken. He wished it had been Mando who was slain. Karyo was more forgiving of Martin's frailties. Mando would make a fuss about everything. He could beat Karyo, physically or mentally; he could probably best Mando physically—although he had never tried it. Sure, Mando had more brains, but Martin knew that he was more scheming.

Mando was aware that his relationship with Martin from Sampitan was a necessary evil. Martin, on the other hand, thought that they were like the monkey and the turtle.

It seemed that Karyo had been their bridge or bond; with Karyo now gone, they felt the void caused by his absence.

'Let's continue tomorrow,' said Mando on the second day after Karyo's death.

'I've lost interest,' answered Martin coldly. 'I didn't know this would be very dangerous.'

'Dangerous for the one underwater,' Mando answered, 'but you're in the boat. What should you fear?'

'Besides, I think we're just wasting our time.' Martin ignored Mando's words and just shook his head.

'I'm sure we won't fail,' said Mando.

For a long while, neither spoke, each one deep in his own thoughts. 'There are only two of us left,' Martin said after some time.

'The two of us can do the work of three.'

'You mean, only two will divide the wealth?' Martin wanted to make sure. 'Is that it?'

Mando barely nodded.

The weather the next day was inviting. The wind was mild, and the sea was calm. The horizon was clear; there was not a single boat as far as the eyes could see.

Mando put on his diving gear. They pushed their small boat into the water. Martin helped Mando fix the oxygen tank on his back. When everything was already set, Martin rowed past the plateau's bend.

Mando went in. One end of the rope was tied to his belt. He held a spear, and at his waist hung the machete. When his feet touched the sand, he looked around. There might be another shark hiding in the depths, but he saw none. He was not afraid, but he had to be careful, especially now that he was alone.

He noticed the seaweeds waving gracefully and the corals aflame with colours. He had thought that the place was shaped like a hill, but after being swallowed up by the ocean, the pounding of the waves had broken it up. Large boulders lay scattered on the sand.

Slowly, he walked around, using his machete to cut away the tangled undergrowth. After half an hour, he felt like yanking the rope.

Martin is probably right, he thought. *It's been a long time, more than half a century, maybe a century*, he told himself. However, he remembered the faith of Tata Matias. Their discovery of the stone steps and this smooth plateau, which appeared to have bent over the former ravine. He remembered Karyo's sacrifice.

'Ah, this is the place where it was thrown,' he reassured himself. 'So it must be here. Gold and gems do not melt at the bottom of the sea. I won't rest until I have found it.'

And he swam back and forth like a strange creature of fantasy.

Martin, who was reclining at one end of the small boat, was already getting impatient, especially with the intense heat of the sun.

Suddenly, Mando noticed something between a large stone and the corals. He was attracted by the red colour, which was different from the black stones and the corals around it. He nudged it with his foot, but it did not budge. He looked closer and saw that the red was rust. It was a box, with the bigger portion buried in the sand, snagged between the stone and the corals. His chest heaved, and he felt his heart beating faster than the waves. Breathing was becoming harder. He had forgotten that he had been underwater for more than an hour. He jerked on the rope; Martin pulled him up.

'I'll rest a while, then dive again,' he told Martin.

'Why?' Martin asked.

'I think this is it.'

'Fortune . . . or false hopes?' Martin said in a mocking tone. But Mando just kept his peace.

After resting for a while, Mando dove again. The sun was now at its zenith, but Martin did not mind the intense heat. He was almost tempted to put on Karyo's diving gear, now that he had heard the good news.

An hour passed before Martin felt a pull at the ropes. It seemed heavier than before. Then, Mando's visor appeared above the water. He quickly climbed on to the small boat and helped Martin pull the rope. He tied the rope around the iron chest after loosening it from the stone. That made it easier for them to hoist it up to the boat.

The two did not feel hungry, although it was almost two o'clock in the afternoon. They ate little, but Martin was agitated.

'Tomorrow is ours,' Mando said and went near the iron chest. 'Let's open it and see if this is it.'

The chest was shaped like a valise with a handle of first-class steel. Even though it was already rusty from lying for a long time in the sand and salt water, it had remained intact. It appeared watertight. Still legible near the handles were the engraved figures stating that the chest was made in England in the early nineteenth century. Also engraved above were the large letters of a name: SIMOUN.

The lid had to be pried open, for there was no more key and the keyhole was rusty. They removed the rust until the iron shone again. Then they inserted the machete's sharp point through a slit under the lid. At first, it would not budge. But they kept at it and inserted a thicker part of the machete. They pounded it with a stone and kept on wedging it. They could hear the grating of the machete as it rubbed mightily against the iron. Suddenly, the lid gave way, and the chest was finally open.

They removed the glass on top. Arrayed before them and glinting in the light of day, were the fabulous jewellery of the *Fili*. It seemed that such wealth could exist only in the world of dreams, as if the genie of Aladdin's lamp had scooped them from the famous jewellery shops of Paris, London, India, Egypt and Arabia, and offered them here, in this part of the forest of the Sierra Madre mountains. What an astonishing find it was!

The iron chest was divided into several partitions. Each partition contained the same kind of gems—rings, earrings, bracelets, necklaces in one container; loose stones, diamonds, emeralds, sapphires, pearls in the second container; watches, gold medals, crosses, brooches, cuff links, purses in the third; old gold coins and rare relics in the fourth. They seemed countless and hard to assess.

'The war is over for us,' Martin exclaimed with joy. 'What more do we need?'

'We have to plan, Martin.'

'I know what I'll do. It's hard only if one has no money. Now that I'm rich, I'll enjoy myself. Who and what can I not buy?'

'Go slowly, friend,' said Mando. 'After deciding what to do, we need to be very careful. There is the iron chest filled with treasure. Should the Japs or a band come upon us, we're lost. They will surely take it all; we'll be lucky if they don't cut off our heads.'

Only then did Martin calm down, but he insisted on dividing the treasure. He planned to return to Manila at once. Finally, he was persuaded to wait until the morning, for night had almost fallen.

They hid the treasure under some bushes and retired early.

At midnight, Mando was awakened by a sharp noise. He looked around; Martin was gone. Mando left the shelter, crouched, and listened.

He did not have long to wait. Suddenly, he saw a shadow moving away, carrying the iron chest. He ran after the figure and recognized that it was Martin.

'Martin!' called out Mando. His voice rang out like a bullet.

Martin stopped at once, put down the chest and went back. When he was near, he lashed at Mando with a machete. In the darkness, Mando felt the sharp edge of the machete hit his left cheek. Mando clung to Martin and they wrestled. It seemed that Mando was losing. He could feel the blood flowing down his face. When Mando fell back, Martin was about to hit him with the machete, but he swiftly bent his knees and kicked Martin with all his strength. Martin was hit full on the chin and thrown back. He fell and hit his head on a large rock.

When Mando got up, he saw Martin slumped over. Blood was spurting from the wound in his head. Mando tried to give him first aid, but Martin was already dead before the day broke.

XI

The past few days had been a whirlwind for Mando: his two companions died; fabulous wealth fell into his hands; and on his face was left a long and ugly scar.

When he was struggling with Martin, he hardly noticed his wound, although the blood flowed down his mouth, lips and neck. But when he saw Martin lying dead atop the boulder, he suddenly felt faint. All at once, he felt the sharp pain of his wound. The bleeding had stopped but the pain still flamed inside him.

He took the iron chest from where Martin had left it and carried it to the shed.

Then he covered Martin's corpse with some broad palm leaves.

Before sunrise, he buried Martin beside the grave where they had buried Karyo only four days before. He offered a short prayer for his two dead companions.

He had no mirror, but he could feel his face was swelling. His eyes and head were aching as well, and his tongue was numb. His throat was parched, although he was quite calm. After his nap, he felt very weak indeed. His heart throbbed, as if the beast of a nightmare was hounding him.

Mando removed the temporary shelter and put the iron chest in the small boat. He was careful to cover it with some equipment. Then he pushed the small boat, climbed aboard and began rowing. The small boat was gliding northwards, towards the home of Tata Matias.

He still felt weak, but he could not afford to lose time. He travelled by water and expected to make the trip in one day. It would take two and a half days if he travelled by foot.

Luck was on his side and the wind favoured him. The sea was calm. But darkness later caught up with Mando, and he had no choice but to pull ashore. He ate a little and rested for a while. For a half hour, he just stretched on the dry sand and closed his eyes. His wound was throbbing with pain.

Then he continued rowing. The soft glow of the new moon helped him along. Fortunately, that part of the water was clear as dark glass. He knew it was safe to sail, even without any lamp.

The whole night, the lone rower didn't stop. The rooster was crowing and the birds were singing when Mando saw, in the pale shadow of night, the shoulder of the hill where Tata Matias's hut leaned. Although he could not see the hut, he was sure that this was the place. Only then could he begin to breathe easily.

He pulled the small boat towards the sand, where it would be safe from the pounding of the waves. He carried the iron chest and climbed the stony path towards the hut.

It was very still; not even the sound of crickets broke through the silence. He stood on the stone that served as a ladder and peeped inside. Then he climbed the ladder without a sound. He could see the figure of Tata Matias sleeping alone. Mando did not wake up the old man. Instead, he just slept outside with his hand on the iron chest, which he had covered with some clothes.

Although he was very tired, sleep would not come to him. When Tata Matias got up to fetch water, he saw that Mando was already sitting in the kitchen. The young man greeted him.

'Good morning, Tata Matias,' he said. 'It's Mando, sir.' He spoke in a loud voice, knowing that in the half-light, it would be easier to recognize his voice.

'Oh, Mando!' The old man was surprised. 'What brings you at this hour? When did you arrive? Why didn't you wake me up? Are you alone?' His host plied Mando with questions.

He struck a match and lit the oil lamp of half a coconut shell. He went to Mando and looked at him slowly.

'What is that bandage on your face?' he asked. 'Are you wounded? Where are your companions? Where have you been? What happened?'

When the old man stepped towards the door, he almost stumbled on the iron chest.

'What's this? Why didn't you bring it in?'

'I've many things to tell you,' Mando began. 'Many important things.'

'You haven't slept, probably,' the old man cut in. 'Go to sleep while I prepare breakfast. I'll wake you up when it's ready.'

Mando took a nap. He was strong, but the series of shocking events could weaken even a man seemingly made of iron.

Mando took the iron chest inside, covered it with a pillow, and lay on the mat.

Tata Matias let him rest. When Mando was awakened, the table was already set for lunch, not breakfast.

After the meal, Tata Matias dressed the wound on the guerrilla's face. On removing the bandage, he exclaimed, 'Jesus!' It was followed by an 'ouch!' from the wounded man.

'If it had been any higher, you would've lost your eye. You're lucky to be alive. Who the devil did this?'

Mando told the old man all his experiences up to the time that Martin attacked him. 'That will leave a big, ugly scar,' said Tata Matias. 'It will change the way you look. Even your own friends won't know you.'

'That would be fine,' Mando said, seemingly consoling himself.

Tata Matias treated the wound with herbs gathered from the mountains and dressed it.

The two went inside, and Mando continued his story. Then he pulled the iron chest and said, 'This, Tatang, is Simoun's wealth.'

Tata Matias rushed to Mando, grasping the arms of the young man.

'At last,' he said, clasping his hands.

Mando removed the rope around the chest and opened the lid. Tata Matias could only utter an exclamation. Mando gaped. Was this a tale or a dream?

Slowly, Mando spread a mat, and one by one he took out the gems from the first partition.

Tata Matias held a few gems that had caught his attention. He looked intently and repeated what Simoun had once said. 'Just like a medical kit, here is both life and death, healing and poison. With a handful of these gems, the people in the Philippines could be drowned in tears.'

'And these could also be used to help them,' added Mando.

'That is true,' said Tata Matias. 'That should be our concern. For if there is anything more precious than wealth, it's how to use it.'

Tata Matias took out a marvellous necklace, the likes of which he had not seen before. It was shaped like a half-moon and made of different gold pendants shaped like miniature figures of gods in green and blue. At the centre, between two outspread wings, was a vulture's head cut from a precious gem.

'This must be the famous collar of Cleopatra found in an Egyptian pyramid after 2,000 years,' said Tata Matias.

'How much would this cost now?' Mando asked.

'No one can tell,' said the old man. 'Even during Simoun's time, its price could not be assessed. Only a rich government could afford it as a relic in a museum.'

Mando's eyes widened. Then it dawned on him that it might not have been just Cleopatra's beauty that captured the interest of Julius Caesar and Mark Antony, the foremost warriors of their time. Most likely, this collar and the other fantastic riches of Egypt helped ensnare their hearts. They were the first imperialists.

'Look at these earrings. How lovely!' said Mando.

The old man took the pair of earrings, and after looking closely, he said, 'Yes, these are the earrings of Princess Lamballe.'

He looked at another earring and said, 'These were given by Marie Antoinette, the consort of Louis XVI of France, to one of her ladies-in-waiting before she was beheaded.'

Mando was impressed not only by the jewels but also by Tata Matias' vast store of knowledge and memory. He knew the back story behind every jewel that glittered before their eyes.

He picked up a large ring. 'I think this was one of the rings of the senators and Roman nobles said to have been found among the ruins of

Carthage,' he told Mando. 'If you offered this to our lawmakers, they would fight over it, and they could certainly afford it.'

Then he noted a large, thick gold ring with a seal. He tried it on, but the ring was still loose around his combined forefinger and middle finger.

'A giant must have first worn this,' he said. 'This might be Sulla's ring, and this seal was likely used to put the final stamp on many death sentences.'

Then Mando brought out a handful of loose stones from the second partition. They looked like tiny stars and a rainbow ablaze in the light for the first time, since they had long been hidden at the bottom of the sea. Aside from the diamonds, there were also emeralds from Peru and other Latin American mines; rubies, the pride of India; sapphires from Ceylon; turquoise from Persia; and all shapes and colours of pearls from the Eastern seas.

'Those are antique diamonds and other gems,' said Tata Matias. 'They're gifts for queens and gems for the Virgin's image during the holy processions.'

'These . . .' Mando shook in his right hand three diamonds. They were not too big, but they were cut with precision and perfection.

'Ah, those are probably the gems for which the Viceroy of India offered 2,000 pounds sterling,' Tata Matias said. 'Now these should cost 100,000 pesos.'

Mando chose two gems that looked like twin blackbirds.

'Black diamonds!' exclaimed the old man. 'They're very large and very hard. Priceless, and without any equal in the world.'

He stared at the pink and emerald green diamonds. 'For this green one, the rich Chinese Quiroga offered 1,000 pesos, but Simoun considered it too cheap. Quiroga wanted to give it to a Spanish-English woman, who was said to be a close friend of the Captain-General.'

Then among the precious gems, Tata Matias noticed a relic, a well-wrought gold medallion aglitter with diamonds and emeralds. On one side was a figure of a fishing boat used by the Apostle Peter where Jesus rode. The two men stared at it.

'This is Maria Clara's medallion,' said Tata Matias slowly after a while. 'This was Captain Tiago's gift to his daughter on the feast day of San Diego. But on the same day, while Maria Clara was taking a stroll with her friends, she gave it as alms to a leper who couldn't make use of it. What he needed instead were food and medicine. The leper couldn't sell it, for no one wanted to touch anything that he had touched,' said the revolutionary.

'That's right,' said Mando, continuing the story. 'The leper gave it to Basilio for treating him, who then gave it to his sweetheart Huli, the daughter of Cabesang Tales.'

Mando looked again at the medallion; he examined its front and back. The gold had already tarnished a little. He said, 'This is the famous medallion, indeed. Once Simoun offered to buy it from Cabesang Tales at any price or to trade any of his jewels for it. Huli's father refused. But one night, Cabesang Tales left this medallion with Simoun in exchange for a gun that he took when he decided to join the outlaws. His land had been grabbed by the friars.'

The two agreed that among Simoun's jewels, the medallion had one of the most colourful histories. It was not among the original jewels of Simoun (for it was not said that Captain Tiago had bought it from him). However, they did not try to look for the medallion's symbolism, which is mentioned in the two novels of Rizal and which passed through the hands of several important characters.

The young man returned the medallion. He was about to bring out the rest, but Tata Matias stopped him.

'We've already seen enough,' he said. 'Now we'll return them all to their container.' He thought for a while, then he asked Mando, 'What do you plan to do with this wealth?'

'Tatang,' said Mando, 'that is the question I want to ask you. This wealth isn't mine.'

'As I have said, how to use it is more important than the wealth itself,' the old man said. 'Fate decided, Mando, that this should be in your hands. It's yours and yet, not yours. So, use it for good and not in the way that brought misfortune to Simoun. What did Father Florentino say? He prayed, "If for a holy and noble cause you'll be needed, may God permit this after a century . . ." And you, Mando, you're the chosen one.'

'I'm ready,' Mando answered. He felt like a knight errant being blest by the king himself. 'I said this wealth isn't mine, because I won't use this for myself.'

XII

For almost a year, all sorts of rumours flew thick and fast in Manila. Some were shocking, others horrifying, but most of them filled the Filipinos' hearts with joy.

It was almost the end of January 1945.

A guerrilla from Northern Luzon brought some news to Manila that the liberation forces brought freedom. But ironically, they also carried fire and swords. Every place that was freed was first left wounded and bleeding.

Every town had a Japanese fort, and each of their headquarters had to be destroyed. But in destroying forts, the Americans could not spare the buildings and the churches, the private houses and the citizens. Bullets brought swift and certain death, but the names of the targets were not written on them.

The guerrillas said that the threat to the city was indeed serious. The Americans would not stop hitting a target as long as one building stood and one enemy was hiding, no matter who got hurt. This was what the white leaders had allegedly warned a guerilla about. When he asked what would happen to the citizens who could not leave the city, the officer said they should leave as soon as they could. It was their duty to leave right away. When told that some could not leave because they had no other place to go, and that the others could not leave their houses and properties, unlike banana plants that could be uprooted and transferred suddenly, he answered that if they loved their houses and properties more than their lives, then they only had themselves to blame for what might happen.

The guerrilla double-checked if the rumours were true. But he had seen the situation with his very own eyes. Before the Japanese would retreat, they would turn their anger and frustration on the common people by burning their houses and killing them. Countless citizens would suffer.

Naturally, there was great rejoicing over the daily news that the 'liberation forces' (according to American propaganda) were coming nearer. There were no more obstacles except the bridges that had been blown up by the Japanese and the felled trees placed across the roads. The enemy no longer fought back, except for the slew of snipers hiding atop the buildings and trees. Every liberated place was assured of safety from Japanese atrocity and from hunger. The liberation forces had hardly put up their headquarters when they began giving away food, medicine and clothes to the hapless survivors. Many of them had been reduced to skin and bones.

The days were filled with joy! It became customary to compare the meanness of the conquerors with the kindness of the liberators.

For two days in the first week of February, the B-29s of the Americans bombed the remaining installations around Manila without a break. Like giant hawks, they would appear from behind the clouds, flying in a V formation—the Victory sign—dive swiftly above the target, then together drop the bombs that reverberated upon explosion, followed by the spread of fire.

Those two days became days in hell for the Japanese. They could neither fight nor escape. But there is no hell without a corresponding heaven. It was bliss for the Filipinos to watch such an effective, if hasty, offensive.

Before sunset on 2 February, the liberation forces had opened the shut gates of the University of Santo Tomas. The Americans and other foreign prisoners were saved. Hardly anyone in the city slept that night. They watched with glee as the fire caused by the bombs of the liberation forces flamed towards the north. And with anxiety, they watched the flames in the south caused by the enemy.

The remaining citizens in the city were shocked when dynamites exploded under the bridges spanning the Pasig River. The north was completely cut off from the south.

The next day, as most of the victorious soldiers were entering Santa Cruz and Sampaloc, the remaining Japanese forces on the other side of the river intensified their massacre of the civilians. They showed no mercy for their victims, be they women, the aged, or the children.

For about a week, no one could cross the Pasig River. The narrow ribbon of water that peacefully ebbed and flowed between Manila and Laguna Bay had become like the mythical river that separated the land of the living from the dead. The north rejoiced while the south wept.

The heartlessness of the Japanese soldiers during their three years was nothing compared to their atrocities during that week when their defeat was at hand. They burnt, raped and killed. They spared no one, not even innocent babies, holy nuns, families and groups. They used fire, bayonets, bullets and grenades to decimate the people. From places in the south—Intramuros, Ermita, Malate, Paco—blood flowed thickly into the Pasig River and stained its waters.

That was a long week, but it finally ended. Every last Japanese straggler was killed in the hole in the concrete buildings—the Post Office, Congress, City Hall—but only after they had gone insane and erased the lives and properties of innocent civilians.

In the end, the whole of Manila was free, but it was a freedom dearly bought.

The capital city looked like a skeleton. Ruins and charcoal, posts that looked like burnt firewood, burnt aluminium, broken glass, potholed streets, felled posts and cut electric wires. In some streets lay the corpses—of people and beasts, of Filipinos and Japanese.

According to reports, only two cities in the world had suffered such horrible destruction: Warsaw in Europe and Manila in the East. Not even Paris or London, Rome or Berlin, or Tokyo—the capital cities of the five countries that started the Second World War—suffered as much. They only suffered scratches compared to the destruction of Manila after its occupation by the Japanese and, three years later, by the Americans.

The ugly rumours at the end of January had come true: The Japanese would rape and destroy the city before leaving it. The American cannons would destroy every building that harboured even one Japanese soldier who had refused to raise the white flag.

How sad that together with the death of many civilians and the destruction of cultural monuments, noble Filipinos also died. Teachers, doctors, scientists, writers and leaders of a society were caught in the crossfire, senseless deaths that were a far greater loss than monuments and buildings and other property that could be replaced someday.

But the nation had no time to grieve in the face of life's new challenges, which could only be met by strong resolve, hard work, and greater struggle. When the guns had stopped firing, another struggle followed, one that was no less intense or significant: the restoration of peace. Mistakes, neglect and indifference had reversed the outcomes of the war. The defeated reaped the fruit of victory, or the wheels of change were blocked in spite of the people's untold sacrifices.

On the other hand, victory caused not only intoxication but also a kind of insanity. Some felt that victory was sweet, but revenge was sweeter.

From all sides mushroomed the quarters of so many guerrilla units. Formerly hidden and moving in secret, they suddenly came forth when the American military police had replaced the Japanese sentries.

They searched whole areas for any Japanese. Like noisy bands hunting for witches, if they could not find their original quarry, they would grab any suspicious-looking person.

Once, an unfortunate Japanese fell into their hands. He knelt with raised hands. He was like a sheep about to be slaughtered; he was very scared. But each one hit or kicked him. No one heard or pitied his plea for mercy. While the rest swooped down on the captive, a guerrilla twisted his neck; another hit his mouth with an iron pipe. His teeth fell off like kernels from a cob of corn. He fainted. Yet another guerrilla got a dagger and cut off his ear. When he regained consciousness, he was forced to chew his ear. But how could he do that, since he had already lost his teeth and blood spurted from the fresh wounds on his lips and gums? He was then hit several times with the iron pipe. When he was dead, his corpse was flung into a dirty canal, and his ear was tossed to a dog.

Two men who were reportedly spies for the enemy were also captured. Without any trial, the eyes of one were gouged out, and the tongue of the other cut off. Then they were strung together with a rope back-to-back and tied to an anthill filled with ants. Some spat on their faces; others stoned them while watching them die a slow death.

Many guerrillas seemed to have been blinded by their thirst for blood and violence. They sought to better the beastliness of the enemy. On the other hand, the nation showed profuse and endless gratitude to the American liberators.

'Hello, Joe,' was everyone's happy greeting.

The newcomers captured not only the Japanese but also the heart of the nation. Some offered them bouquets of fresh flowers; others gave drinks and fruits. Everywhere they went, a long procession of children followed them.

And the Filipino women, who had been snobbish and cold to the Japanese, except for a few who had sold themselves for Mickey Mouse money, now became gracious to all. Everyone was grateful. In countless hearts blossomed the dream of going to America and having the famous 'American way of life' through an American husband. A lucky few were successful, but many were just left behind at the pier, waving a handkerchief at a departing ship bearing their American boyfriend away.

This attraction of the American soldier for the women did not pass unobserved. Every man enjoyed the rewards of the Allied victory. Ten years before the war, the Americans in the Philippines were just content to mine the mountains and have a woman from a cheap cabaret for his mistress. After the Second World War, when they were like magnets, the Americans combined their search for gold with hunting for a wife among the heiresses and choice ladies of the upper crust of society.

The Philippines became independent in July. On 10 August 1945, the first atomic bombs were dropped on the cities of Nagasaki and Hiroshima. The Imperial Japanese Army had no other choice but to surrender without condition to the Allies. The war was over. The bells of peace began to toll again.

With the tolling of the church bells and the sound of the sirens, the nation rejoiced, believing that peace had finally returned. The common man rejoiced, thinking that peace would bring a new life for everyone. The guerrillas rejoiced, thinking that they would receive recognition at last, along with their backpay, which the Americans had promised repeatedly when they needed the Filipinos to sacrifice their lives.

Weeks passed, and then months and years. Long gone were the pealing of the bells and the sound of the sirens, the blare of trumpets and the burst of fireworks, the ringing shouts of '*Mabuhay!*' to send good wishes of long life to everyone. But still, the public could see the unhealed wounds of the war: the ruins, charcoal, and ashes; the unemployed and the homeless; the lack of money and the barbed-wire prices.

The Four Horsemen of the Apocalypse had departed, indeed, but they had left behind four armies, just as dangerous and devastating: the army of the wounded, the army of the beggars, the army of the mountain bandits, and the army of the town bandits.

XIII

Faster than fire among the thatched huts in summer spread the news of Manila's liberation. The wind blew it in all directions. The evacuees rushed back to the city and other centres of population. All roads led to the city and other places, which had been left in haste months, even years, before. Now the people had returned. All vehicles entering the boundaries of Manila were filled with passengers and baggage.

But in the few towns surrounding Kalayaan, no one bothered to return to the capital city, for they were not in evacuation centres. Fighting the hated Japanese and capturing the despised collaborators had kept the guerrillas and townsfolk busy during the war.

The guerrilla headquarters under Magat was moved to the municipal building. They lowered and burnt the Japanese flag and raised, side by side, the American and Philippine flags, for the Filipinos had not yet won independence. They formed a temporary government.

Magat invited the public to a gathering in the town square and informed them about the latest news. He gave instructions. Avoid vandalism, abuses and looting; bring the captured Japanese and Filipino spies to the town hall.

'Let's give them a chance,' said the guerrilla leader. 'Let's show them that we understand what justice means.'

Magat's instructions had the force of law. All citizens suspected of helping the Japanese were brought to the municipal hall and investigated. But those who were found innocent were released at once.

One afternoon, Magat's men brought a known collaborator from a town formerly held by the Japanese. He and his companions were placed in a cell in the municipal building.

'Give them food,' said Magat. 'And don't hurt them.'

He allowed the captives to rest for the day. The next day, he sent for their leader. Magat offered him a seat facing himself.

Magat looked closely at the collaborator. He was about fifty years old. His hair was dark and streaked with grey. He was poorly dressed and barefoot. He was a bit pale and tired, but his eyes showed no fear.

'You are the head of the Japanese collaborators in the town of A,' Magat began.

'Yes, I am, sir,' was the prompt and firm answer. Magat was taken aback, for he had expected a denial.

'Therefore, you admit, Mister . . .'

'Andres, sir.'

'Therefore, Mr Andres,' continued Magat, 'you admit that you were an enemy of our country?'

'No,' answered Andres in a steady tone of voice.

'You admitted you are a Makapili leader, didn't you?' Magat asked.

'That's true, sir.'

'How can you deny being an enemy of our country?'

'The name Makapili, sir, comes from the words "Makabayang Pilipino" (Nationalistic Filipinos),' Andres explained. 'How could nationalistic Filipinos be enemies of the country?'

'A name often serves as a cover for the real nature or purpose of a movement,' Magat answered. 'Hitler called Fascism "National Socialism". The Japanese justified their conquest in the name of Asia's Co-Prosperity Sphere. Slogans are part of propaganda. Not the name, but the deeds should be judged. You Makapilis helped the Japs during the war, and that is treason against our nation.' Magat stressed his last words.

Andres smiled bitterly. 'Maybe we can be accused of treason against America, but not against our country,' said the Makapili.

'What's the difference?'

'Between heaven and earth,' declared Andres. 'Our country is not America, but the Philippines. American power was just imposed on the Filipinos.'

'But America is a democracy,' said Magat.

'A democracy in its own land and for its own people,' said Andres, 'but a colonizer in the Philippines.'

'America saved us from Spanish oppression,' reminded the guerrilla leader.

'And at the same time, they crushed our new and young republic,' the Makapili said in a loud voice. 'You have read our history.'

'Would you deny the good done by America?' Magat asked with some heat.

'Ah, sir,' said Andres, drawing a deep sigh, 'we can't close our eyes to the truth. Let us admit that white is white, and black is black . . .' He paused, looked steadily at Magat. Then he asked, 'Do you believe, sir, that a big power will go to a small nation to help it?'

Magat was surprised and groped for an answer. Slowly, he changed his opinion of this man, a Makapili, whom he had regarded a fool for following the Japanese, a traitor, and an enemy of his own country. By Andres's logic, he was obviously neither a fool nor a traitor.

Magat chose his words carefully. 'The American administration in the Philippines is a cooperative effort of two nations under a peaceful regime. It aims to establish an independent republic. Unfortunately, the Japanese attacked us.'

'Do you think we would be attacked if the Americans weren't here?'

'The Philippines is the only bridge in Japan's goals in the southwest Pacific, just like Indonesia and Australia,' said Magat. 'The Axis Powers began the war of expansion; Germany wanted to occupy Europe; Italy, half of Africa, and Japan, the rich lands of Asia, including China and India. So whether the Americans were here or not, the islands would have been snatched away like roasted corn.'

'Perhaps, we would have been left alone in peace,' Andres said. 'It would have been better for Japan to be a friend to twenty million Filipinos rather than an enemy.'

'That would not be likely,' said Magat. 'Japan attacked and grabbed a part of China even before the Second World War began.'

'Don't forget,' Andres pointed out, 'that China had already been cut up by the white people before Japan came. We've to admit that Japan had a greater cause, in the face of what was happening. It wanted a share of the vast Chinese mainland because its small territory isn't enough for its people.'

Magat lit a cigarette and offered one to Andres. The other man declined. 'I have no vice,' he said.

'You have a rare intelligence,' Magat noted. 'What did you do before the war?'

'I was a village teacher,' Andres answered. 'I supplemented my little learning by reading books on history and sociology.'

'Why did you become pro-Jap?'

'I am pro-Filipino, like most of the Makapilis,' answered Andres. 'We helped the Japanese because we wanted reform. The Japanese promised change. So did the Americans, true, but in fifty years, life in this poor country remained like before.'

'Are there not schools, hospitals, good roads?'

'In the cities, yes. But look around the provinces. Maybe you often go to the villages. In the town, you can find an old church and government buildings constructed during Spanish times. Two or three mansions of the rich families who practically own the town. In the village, you can find a small chapel and a clump of thatched huts. No electricity or running water. No passable road. The rural folk use footpaths. Drinking water is fetched from the river where they also bathe and wash their dirty clothes.'

Magat listened, fascinated. Andres continued.

'It may be said that God willed this situation, which is the lot of the poor,' the former Makapili said in a sad voice, 'but we were oppressed before the war. You're the son of a farmer, so you must have seen the brutality of the constabulary. They attacked the villages while hunting for the so-called bandits. They treated all the village folk like accomplices of the outlaws. They would ransack every house, grab and hurt the innocent, destroy the furniture, steal property, pigs and chickens. It happened so often that it became obvious that hunting for bandits was only an excuse for looting. Who would defend the unfortunate peasants if the supposed law enforcer is the crime leader?'

'Therefore, you sided with the Japs,' Magat concluded, 'because you were dissatisfied with life under the Americans.'

'Because of oppression that cries to the heavens,' Andres said. 'We have not tasted the so-called progress and prosperity, which are said to be the blessings of American democracy. These gifts are only for the owners of vast landholdings and their friends. We've remained in want, sick, deep in debt, unable to send our children to school. Our families die without seeing a doctor or having a drop of medicine. What do we owe a government that's blind to our sufferings? Why should we be one with a society that drinks wine while we drink our tears? The discontentment of the poor isn't their fault. This is the work of the oppressors.'

Magat observed that Andres' right fist was clenched as he recited the litany of abuses against the workers. The guerrilla leader raised his hand to show it was his turn to speak.

'The nation is not made up of a bunch of the opportunists you spoke of. The nation is all of us: you, me and the others. It's the duty of every good citizen to help the motherland in times of danger, like war. The Makapilis went to the other . . .'

'Good you mentioned that,' remarked Andres. 'True, our country includes all. On the one hand, the country is divided into different parties, beliefs, and philosophies. But the majority are the workers, the poor. They make up 85 per cent of the whole. If democracy is the government of the nation, as we believe it is, what is the life of the 85 per cent? What and who are the 15 per cent? Such a government is not a democracy but a closed circle of personal relationships. Naturally, the families and the minions of the powerful help themselves to the bounty.'

The Makapili leader had pressed his hand on top of the table.

'For me,' he stressed, 'the opportunists shouldn't be counted as part of the nation. They are real enemies. Just as microbes and parasites should not be counted as part of a person's body.'

When Magat kept silent, Andres went on. 'But in times of danger and when their own interests are at stake, those in power should ask everyone to help, to make sacrifices. Those who don't follow them because of past disappointments and loss of faith are called traitors. But remember, Mr Magat, now that the war is over, they and the rest of the country will go back to their old paths, like flood waters. The big fish will return to power, the small fry to their small pond, and they will barely remember those like you who suffered . . .'

Magat pointed out that everything had settled down. 'There are national elections,' he said. 'Everyone is free to vote and run. A bad government can be overthrown and should be overthrown.'

'What you say sounds good to the ears.' Andres smiled with bitterness. 'But in our elections, have you seen a candidate who didn't spend money? Have you seen a rich candidate who didn't buy leaders and votes? And how many use their right to vote? Of the twenty million citizens, we would be lucky if even five million go to the polls.'

'Then neither the party nor the candidate should be blamed,' said Magat. 'The one at fault is the nation and those whom you call the "small fry". A country only gets the government it deserves.'

'The greater blame belongs to the leaders who want the people to remain ignorant. For otherwise . . .'

'Has it not occurred to you that the leaders of the Makapilis are among what you call the 15 per cent?' Magat asked.

Andres gaped, then he closed his eyes and placed his hand on his forehead. He seemed to have been cornered by the guerrilla chief.

'We're aware that many of those who helped the Japanese are opportunists,' he said. 'They only love themselves. Just the same, we know that in supporting a good cause, not the leaders, but the members count.'

'Your unity is good, but your approach is wrong,' Magat said. 'The Japanese had evil aims, so helping them cannot be good.'

'Our only interest is our country,' Andres argued. 'In every period, from the Spanish to the American regime, we have seen uprisings. At first, they were called *colorums*—fanatics, bandits, killers. Later appeared the Tanggulan, followed by the Sakdal, and during the last war, Makapili and Hukbalahap, whom you are now accusing of collaboration. All of them are poor and discontented. They are just like clay moulded into cooking pots, stones, flower pots and jars. The only difference lies in the leaders who guide them.'

'There's the rub,' Magat said. 'They're like a flock of meek sheep.'

'If the sheep falls off a cliff, it is not the fault of the flock, but of the shepherd,' said Andres. 'The poor crave for reform.'

'Because of this belief, you helped Japan and fought against the guerrillas, who also came from the masses like you. Look at my face and hands.' Magat raised his hands. 'I'm also a farmer's son, and I went to school as a working student.'

'We oppose the return of the old ways,' said the Makapili leader. 'All our sacrifices would be in vain if we would just restore the pre-war system. For if America wins, as it has, we'll just become captives of the dollar. It is possible that if Japan wins, we might still be slaves, but it has promised reforms needed by 85 per cent of our country.'

'Then you aren't happy about the end of the war, because Japan lost?' Magat asked slowly.

'Magat, we had nothing to do with the outbreak of the war,' said Andres. 'Like any peace-loving Filipino, we want peace.'

'Even if America won?'

'We hope that the victors and losers will learn their lessons from the war. May they learn to correct their errors. Let justice prevail. In truth'—Andres looked in the distance,—'the importance of history isn't in memorizing dates and events, but in learning from them.'

'That's how it should be,' nodded Magat.

After their long and fruitful meeting, Magat began to respect Andres. No matter how he looked at it, there seemed to be little difference between their beliefs about many things. What a pity this unusual man turned out to be a Makapili and not a guerrilla! Nevertheless, he told himself, even if Andres had chosen the wrong path, his spirit was still more noble than those of the Kalumpang guerrillas.

Magat told Andres and his companions that they would be detained in a cell in the municipal building until it was shown that they had not killed people, burnt houses, robbed, or committed other crimes against the people when they were still with the Makapili.

'There are many ways of serving the country,' Andres said. 'All we want is justice.'

Magat was silent for a while. Then he called an aide to bring Andres back to his cell. As the collaborator leader walked away, the guerrilla leader told himself that justice would not mean certain punishment for the admirable Makapili.

XIV

When the Americans came, Don Segundo used again his glib technique for winning friends and influencing people. If he could succeed with the dour Japanese, then it would be easier with these friendly Americans, he thought, with their love for banter and the good life.

However, he could not welcome them immediately, as he had planned. The guerrillas were still hunting for collaborators, and they could be harsh and unreasonable. So he hid for a while in the home of a close friend, who had managed to be in the good graces of both sides.

Don Segundo's friend approached the head of a guerrilla group that had set up headquarters the day after the Americans liberated Manila.

Some of these guerrilla leaders were former American Armed Forces members, who became collaborators after leaving Capas. But they could not pass up a good chance. So the collaborators became instant guerrillas. And who would say that they were, indeed, genuine? Did they not take up arms and fight in Bataan? Weren't they in the long Death March from Bataan to Capas? Weren't they also thrown into jail in Capas? They only worked for the Japanese as a ruse, they explained. They agreed to accept important positions so they could spy for the Americans and sabotage the work of the Japanese.

Many birds of the same feather flocked together in this guerrilla unit. It was not a surprise that they would be recognized and that they would recognize other guerrillas as well, after February 1945.

Don Segundo's friend had only to ask, and he immediately got his impeccable credentials. When Don Segundo came out of his temporary refuge, he was arm-in-arm with a high-ranking guerrilla who called him 'Monty'. In the pocket of his khaki shirt were his credentials, emblazoned with the rank of lieutenant colonel.

This friend and the guerrilla leader brought some American officers to the house of the Monteros. All of the Americans' doubts about Don Segundo vanished when they saw the beautiful Dolly and the alluring Lilibeth.

Dolly was wearing a red dress, and Lilibeth was in mourning. Lilibeth's pilot husband had reportedly been killed in Bataan.

But all of them received the Americans with the traditional Filipino hospitality—and more. Because of the warm reception of the rich landlord-businessman and the American belief in living in the present, everyone easily became friends.

Monty brought out his hoarded alcohol. And the officials, who were always full but still thirsty for a good bottle of alcohol, got engrossed in more drinking.

Montero bragged about a radio hidden in a secret panel in his room. He claimed he would listen every night via shortwave to the news about the war.

'That's why I knew about the trend of the fight up to the end,' he said in a bragging tone.

And he poured more Scotch into the glasses of the Americans.

His friend then related how he and the rich businessman had helped the guerrillas in secret. They claimed to have delivered food, clothes, medicine and money to the guerrillas. 'But we got no receipts,' he explained, 'because receipts would have given us away and led to our capture. During those times, your left hand should not have known what the right hand was doing.'

The guerrilla leader embroidered the stories that Monty and his friend narrated to everyone. He vividly described his own hardships: from the uneven combat in Bataan to the Death March, then to Capas. He forgot his record of collaboration but boasted instead about his work as a spy against the Japanese.

'We've a complete roster of our members and our supporters, who helped us behind the scenes,' he said, pointing to Don Segundo and his friend. 'Have you kept your credentials, Monty?' he asked.

Montero smiled, then he stood up. He went to his room and returned holding a card wrapped in cellophane.

'Now, I'll have the time to frame this,' he said in a boasting manner.

The guerrilla leader took it, glanced at it, and then passed it on to the officer beside him. 'That,' he said, 'are the credentials of a genuine guerrilla,' he said.

The officer looked at the card, nodded, and said, 'This must be a passport to hell when the Japs were around, wasn't it?'

'Indeed it was,' promptly answered the 'guerrilla' leader. 'But I had to take that risk.'

He explained that not all the members of the underground movement knew each other. However, anyone with genuine credentials was left undisturbed. Of course, they would not admit that the credentials of Don Segundo Montero were bought just two weeks after the liberation forces had barged through Manila.

The guerrilla leader also related how he was tricked, threatened and forced by the Japanese to help them, more than once. He claimed that his hard-headedness almost put his family in the cross-hairs of the Japanese.

'But I always outwitted them,' he said. 'The Japs, they're just a bunch of fools.'

Swiftly, Don Segundo shed the scales of a pro-Japanese to become a fanatical pro-American. If one would believe his bluster, it would seem that his loyalty to the US was greater than that of the American Forces itself, for he never surrendered to the Japanese.

'And what about the women?' asked an ageing officer. 'Weren't they molested by the brutes?' The eyes of the group quickly turned to Dolly and Lilibeth.

'Oh, we always outwitted the damned fools,' was Lilibeth's swift reply.

'I salute you,' the American shook hands with her.

Their talk drifted from one topic to another, and the air was filled with levity and happiness. The American praised the bravery of Filipinos like Segundo Montero. In turn, the Filipinos had only the deepest admiration for the noble Americans. They also talked of the Filipinos' impatience over General MacArthur's promise, 'I shall return.' Well, everyone seemed to agree that it's better late than never. Some of the American officers smirked because MacArthur said 'I'. They resented the suggestion that he would save the Philippines by himself.

But the captain and the lieutenant only had eyes for Dolly and her friend, Lilibeth. Their rivalry over the unfortunate Colonel Moto had not dented their friendship.

Both had grown lovelier. The wounds inflicted by recent events on their hearts left no traces on their faces and figures. They were radiant and fresh. They were certainly attractive, especially to men who had just come from the battlefield. Their smiles proved the saying that a stain on a woman's honour could be washed away by a shower. No one could tell that Lilibeth had borne a child while her husband was fighting the enemy in Bataan. No one would guess that Dolly had carried the child of Moto, which had died in her womb.

Lieutenant Whitey was crazy over Dolly, while Captain Green fell hard after his first date with Lilibeth. After a few drinks, both seemed more drunk than the others.

Whitey was an electrician at an industrial firm in Chicago before he signed up for the war. He was twenty-three years old and single. Dolly looked him over carefully. At almost six feet tall, Whitey cut an impressive figure with his reddish hair and light-blue eyes. His accent was that of an educated American who grew up in the city. He also had a pleasant and friendly smile. He spent his time talking to Dolly instead of joining the others in drinking whiskey.

On the other hand, Captain Green was a professional soldier. He had spent twelve of his thirty-four years in the US Army, with the last three in the Air Force. He was five foot seven, strong, and with a robust physique. He had thin, brown hair and a moustache.

Green told Lilibeth that he was already divorced. He and his wife had separated months before the war. Before he was sent to Southeast

Asia, the former Mrs Green started dating someone else. They had no children.

Whitey told Dolly that he planned to go home as soon as he could. In fact, he was just waiting for his superiors' orders for him to go back to the United States. He was planning on taking a break before going back to his old job.

'But now that I've met you,' he whispered to Dolly, 'my plans will probably change.'

Dolly was thrilled by his words. She raised her eyes to his face as if to ask about his new plans.

'I'll ask for an extension of my assignment here, because . . .' He pressed Dolly's hand, which Dolly did not withdraw. They remained silent, aware of the quickening of each other's pulse.

'What's your hobby?' Whitey asked after a while.

'Oh,' Dolly said, 'I seemed to have forgotten my hobbies when the Japs were here. I really enjoy swimming and dancing. But during the war, I only went to church. Those Japs! No one could dance because of them.'

'Then, we'll get along fine. When can we go swimming?'

'It's up to you. But you might be busy.'

'Where do you prefer to swim—in a pool or at the beach?'

'Anywhere.'

'Perfect!'

Captain Green and Lilibeth got along well. Their conversation was similar to what Whitey and Dolly talked about, although Lilibeth was more boastful.

'My father and my late husband were Americans, so I'm an American citizen, but I haven't been to the States.'

'Do you want to go there?' Green asked.

'If my husband were alive,' Lilibeth sighed, 'perhaps we would've gone. But now . . .'

'Will no one ever take your husband's place in your heart?'

At this question, Lilibeth bowed her head.

'Lilibeth?' Green waited for her answer. The young widow raised her face and looked at him with a steady gaze.

'You haven't answered my question,' said the captain. 'Can anyone replace your pilot?' he asked again.

'Only time will tell,' Lilibeth answered, pretending to dodge the question.

'Perhaps I can take his place?' Green said in a gentle tone. 'Anyway, I'm also a pilot.'

Lilibeth decided to let go of her coyness. 'What I want,' she said without blushing, 'isn't a pilot, a captain, or a general. All I want is a man who will love me as much as my late husband did.'

'Then you don't have to search for long.'

'Oh?' she said archly.

Like duelists, they fenced with double-talk, but deep within, they understood each other. Green said he had cigarettes in the Jeep's locker. Would she go with him to get them?

They went down together, and he helped her get in the Jeep.

'I've never tried riding in this,' she said.

The captain took two cartons of cigarettes and handed them to Lilibeth. When their hands touched, the American pressed her arm. Green drew her close and kissed her lips. She neither protested nor drew away.

'What's on your mind?' Lilibeth asked when they finally separated.

'I love you, honey,' Green whispered. Then he embraced and showered her with many kisses. He was like a gamecock that had cornered its foe. Lilibeth closed her eyes in abandon and moaned.

In the days that followed, the two pairs were often seen passing happy hours on the beaches near Baclaran in the morning and later, in the nightclubs. They would swim or go boating, drink and dance the whole night.

One morning, Whitey and Dolly left Manila in a Jeep. The lieutenant sought permission from Doña Julia to take Dolly out for the whole day, since there was a gathering at Nichols Field. He also invited Doña Julia, but she declined. She knew that a chaperone was not in the plans of young American men.

Actually, the two were not going to Nichols Field. They had agreed the day before to go to a place where they could be alone.

'Even for a day?' asked Whitey. Dolly nodded and smiled.

They passed Las Piñas, turned left at the crossroad in Zapote, straight along the long plain to Biñan, and stopped at a restaurant in Calamba. Then they went to Pansol, but seeing the place full, they decided to go to Los Baños.

Los Baños was one of the first towns in southern Luzon that the Americans had liberated. A group of Americans and other foreigners were imprisoned there during the Japanese occupation. Fortunately, the town's swimming places were not damaged. After the war, two or three rest houses were built and they served as hotels.

Whitey took a secluded room with a private swimming pool. It was only ten in the morning but it was already very hot. From the window, they could see the bronze-coloured bay on the left and the green Mount Makiling on the right.

'Now we're here, and the world is ours,' said Whitey as he drew Dolly towards the sofa. In one part of the room stood a wide bed, which seemed to invite them.

Dolly sat on her lover's lap, and he kissed her.

'Are you happy, my darling?' Whitey asked as he stroked her breasts.

Dolly said she was happy but tired from the one-and-a-half-hour trip. 'Let's go then and swim in the pool,' she said.

They changed into their swimming attires. Whitey removed his khaki shirt and pants, leaving nothing but his shorts on. His chest was hairy. Dolly had a pink robe over her bikini. Her breasts spilt over her bra.

The private pool was below their room, and it could be reached by a secret ladder. It was five by three metres, and the water was waist-deep. The water was warm and clear; at its bottom, rested small, white stones.

Whitey went in first and helped Dolly down the stone steps. They tested the water, got themselves wet, and swam slowly. Then he dove and grabbed her thigh. Dolly wriggled free and threw water at Whitey; he did the same to her. They laughed and then embraced tightly like a pair of wrestlers.

'You're crushing me,' Dolly said, feigning a complaint. Without letting her go, Whitey kissed her. Suddenly, Dolly's bra was undone and over her breasts roamed the hands of the American. Dolly shivered.

'Please don't,' she pleaded, but soon, her protests stopped. Whitey proved that he was not only a good pilot but also a good diver.

Not long after, they seemed to have turned into Adam and Eve, like twin fish playing, now chasing each other, now entwining their legs and arms, while around them, the bubbles floated.

It was high noon when they climbed out of the pool and went to their room. After changing, they went down to the restaurant and ate rice and seafood; a salad of young coconut meat, avocado and tomatoes; and sweet coconut meat for dessert.

There were other guests at the other tables, but everyone was engrossed only in themselves. Their purpose in coming to the place was obvious.

After lunch, Dolly suggested that they should go.

'It's still a little too early and the road is an oven,' said Whitey. 'Let's take a little nap.'

'Well, if you say so,' she agreed.

As they lay together, Dolly reminded him that they might get home late.

'But why should you worry when we're together?'

Dolly did not answer. Her lips were sealed by her lover.

'I'll sleep like a dead log,' he said, pressing her hand over the mattress. He closed his eyes, but his hands were busy. Twice, they repeated what they had done in the warm water of the swimming pool. Now, it was more pleasurable as their bodies melted together. Later, the two fell fast asleep, drunk on the wine of love.

XV

After several months, Dolly and Doña Julia suddenly went to Hong Kong. Before leaving Manila, there had been a change in Dolly's looks and disposition. She had lost weight, and blue rings sat under her eyes. Contrary to what she did before, she avoided social gatherings. She did not eat her favourite dishes but only craved unripe fruits. She also lost all interest in swimming and dancing; instead, she spent the day in bed.

Doña Julia noticed her daughter's unusual behaviour.

When she asked, Dolly was evasive. 'Nothing, Mama.'

'Tell me the truth, my daughter,' she said gently. 'I won't be angry, because I just want to help you.'

'Ah, I'm just fed up.' Dolly made a move to leave, but Doña Julia held her back.

'Don't keep secrets from me,' she said. 'I'm your mother, and I'm a woman like you.'

'I'm tired of life.' And tears began to well in Dolly's eyes.

Through her mother's gentle coaxing, Dolly admitted what Doña Julia had already guessed.

'This has happened to many girls your age,' she said to her daughter, who had flung herself into her mother's arms. She did not scold Dolly. There was one change in the tone of her voice when she spoke again.

'Before I got married, I, too, had a similar experience.'

Dolly raised her head and their eyes met. Dolly's eyes wandered, while Doña Julia's were closed. Doña Julia spoke softly, as if she were in the confessional room, before a priest. 'Yes, your father wasn't my boyfriend. I was engaged to another man.' She swallowed hard before going on. 'I also did what you've done,' she admitted. 'But his parents sent him away to finish his studies.'

'And Papa?'

'Your father was courting me, but I didn't care for him. Then, your father would bring goods to the province and exchange them with goods to be sold in Manila. My father liked him and made me marry him.'

'Therefore, Mama, you didn't love Papa?'

'Not at first. But time heals all wounds. Your father is a good man. I learnt to love him later. If I hadn't, would you have been born?' Doña Julia said.

'And where is your first boyfriend?'

'He finished his studies, got married, and is now a governor.'

'Is it Governor Doblado, Papa's friend?'

'Indeed, he is,' admitted Doña Julia. 'He may be a governor, but your father is a millionaire.'

They were silent for some time. 'Does Papa know?'

'He knows that Osky was my boyfriend. But he doesn't know that we had gone that far,' said Doña Julia. 'And why should he know? In the first place, that happened before I met him. Second, I don't want him to think less of me.'

'That's your luck,' Dolly said softly.

'You see,' answered Doña Julia, 'you've to believe in luck. I told you my story so you can see how fate works. What is not meant to be, won't be. Moto was not fated for you. Neither was Whitey. Why get depressed over what happened? Are they the only men in the world? You're young, beautiful and rich. You have many suitors.'

Dolly felt relieved. She was afraid her parents would get mad, although they were also to blame, especially Don Segundo, for what happened to her. But seeing that her mother was not angry and was even consoling her, made her feel better.

'Look at Minnie,' said Doña Julia. Minnie was a prominent society figure who always attended the parties at the Malacañang Palace,

Manila Hotel, and other places frequented by the upper crust. 'She's old enough to be your mother,' she added, 'but she acts as if she were your age. And really, she doesn't seem to grow old. Actually, she has shed her skin several times. Before the war, she was the mistress of an American; afterwards, she became attached to a Spaniard; then, she lived with a Japanese officer during the war. Now, she has an American lover and a sugar daddy at the same time. See how much more popular she is now? And she is still beautiful, she's always in the newspapers, taking trips overseas, living the life of those in the upper crust of society.'

Doña Julia mentioned other famous names.

'But I don't envy those women, Ma,' Dolly said in protest.

'I didn't say you should envy or imitate them,' said her mother. 'I'm only giving their example to show that you should not think that this is the end of the world.

Their conversation happened two months after Whitey had left for Iwo Jima. This sudden departure was his head officer's answer to his request to extend his stay in Manila. He bade Dolly a quick goodbye. He was afraid to be sent to Tokyo and stay there for a long time, because the American forces had so much to do there after Japan had surrendered. If assigned to Japan, everyone from MacArthur down to the last soldier had to stay long in the Empire of the Rising Sun.

Whitey promised to return to Manila, but he could not say when. He also vowed that he would not forget his promise to marry Dolly, but could not say when, either. After all, he was a soldier. It was not for him to decide where he would be assigned, Whitey said.

Dolly grieved for many days and nights, her thoughts lost among the shadows. But what could she do but wait? But her condition could not wait. It was then that her mother noticed it. No doubt her father would notice it too, one of these days. Right now, he was always busy with his many businesses and was seldom at home between breakfast and supper.

Even before her conversation with her mother, Dolly told herself that this was not her first disappointment. She still remembered Colonel Moto, but he was already dead. Besides, even then, she considered that affair merely a way of whiling away the terrible boredom of the Japanese occupation.

But with Whitey, Dolly did not plan to take a chance or while away the hours. Whatever losses she suffered with Moto, she planned to recoup with Lieutenant Whitey, plus interest. Moto was Japanese. What Filipina would have a serious relationship with a non-Christian, even if he had a prominent position? Whitey was American, a member of the liberation forces who came to Manila at a time when every American was deemed an angel descended straight from heaven. The public deeply admired people like him; even their conversation was limited only to wine, canned goods and comics.

Dolly gambled for the high stakes, and she thought she would win. Only a few Filipinas had the good fortune of being wanted by a white man with a high rank and a bright future. However . . .

Doña Julia and Dolly didn't let anyone else know the real reason for their visit to Hong Kong. They only said it was a vacation. Doña Julia was not afraid of Don Segundo, because she could also accuse him of encouraging his daughters' affair. But Doña Julia did not want to upset her husband with women's affairs. If he would know about this, Don Segundo would certainly burn like wild grass set on fire.

And neither did Doña Julia tell Dolly what she had planned.

But in their conversations, she gradually prepared her daughter to accept her plan.

They took nearby rooms in an expensive hotel. Back then, only a few Filipinos made regular trips to Hong Kong. The Philippine peso was stable, and the dollar was not too expensive. Smuggled coins and jewellery had not yet made their way to Hong Kong's black market. Neither had the greedy wives of high government officials. For a few days, the two women toured the well-known places in Hong Kong and Kowloon, ate at popular restaurants, bought clothes and souvenirs, crossed the ferry to Macau, and returned by train to the New Territories.

One day, Dolly was too sick to get up. Doña Julia made enquiries and got the address of a Portuguese doctor, a known specialist for women's illnesses. Why, his name was even known in Manila!

The next day, the two women went to his clinic. The doctor examined Dolly and confirmed that she was, indeed, pregnant.

He said that something could still be done. He could perform a safe and effective operation, and he guaranteed complete secrecy. His clinic did not keep records of such operations.

Doña Julia bit her lower lip when she heard the astronomical fee, but she had no choice. She promised to return as soon as possible. At first, Dolly protested; she raged and cried. She had sinned in the eyes of people; she did not wish to sin in the eyes of God. But Doña Julia said that it was not a sin, for this was just a blob, still incomplete and shapeless. It was more likely to wither than to grow, and should it live, it would probably be stunted because of her ill feelings. Doña Julia reminded her of the scandal, the stain on the family's honour, and her uncertain future. An abortion would be easy; nothing would change. She would keep her figure, no marks would show on her body, and she would continue to have many suitors. Not even her father would know about it.

Dolly was finally persuaded. Whitey did not know that she was pregnant. Besides, she was not the first or the last angel to burn her wings. Why should she bear the burden of their sin alone? What right had she to bring a fatherless baby into the world?

For two days, Dolly stayed at the clinic. On the third day, Doña Julia took her back to the hotel.

'You look the same as before,' said the doctor when they said goodbye.

Her mother helped Dolly in front of a large mirror in their dressing room.

'Look at yourself; you haven't changed a bit.'

Dolly smiled bitterly and shook her head. 'Mama,' she said, 'what you don't see in my face is impressed in my soul.' She felt weak.

'You'll get over it, now that you're back to your old self.' Doña Julia comforted her. 'Believe me, time heals everything.'

Within a week, Dolly's ringing laughter was already being heard again at a rousing grand party in Hong Kong.

XVI

The so-called liberation became like a noisy town fiesta in honour of a patron saint. Bands of musicians played, fireworks burst, and there was feasting in every house, whether it was the house of the rich or of the poor. But what came in the wake of the feasts? Litter, disorder, debts, fatigue, ill feelings and massive migraines.

There were more than 400 small feasts in the Philippines. The rejoicing over liberation was added to such an array of feasts.

The bowlegged Japanese had been wiped out, and the Americans had returned. The drunken soldiers in the bases and streets grew in number.

On the surface, peace had returned, for the booming of cannons and the firing of guns had stopped. But after the initial wave of peace and contentment, the noise and anxiety had moved into the minds and hearts of the people. The struggle continued but not with weapons. It moved to the arena of civil rights and how to make a living. And the opponents were no longer Americans and Filipinos against the Japanese, but the powerful against the weak, the real guerrillas against the fake, the capitalists against the labourers, the landlords against the tenants, the vendors against the buyers, the suffering people pummelled by the high cost of prime commodities.

After the war, the first step was to restore conditions to normal. It was easy to erase the dividing line between the loyal and the disloyal, even though such a dividing line was drawn in blood. Once again, the old markers and signs of rights, of property, of the words 'legitimate' and 'legal' began to appear.

Without warning, the landlords immediately got back their lands, which they had abandoned and left idle during times of trouble. They threatened and evicted those who had tilled these lands and kept them from being swallowed up by the forests or eaten up by the river currents. The owners employed the so-called civilian guards, many of whom had been Japanese collaborators. The guards were given arms and money so they would protect the owners' properties with their own lives.

Naturally, these became the fuse of a new disorder. The farmers were mostly patriotic guerrillas, so it was inevitable for bad blood to rise between them and the collaborators. And the latter were itching for revenge against the guerrillas, who were tougher than the real soldiers. Both believed in the proverbial saying of 'a tooth for a tooth'.

Seemingly, the government was neutral, but because the rich had returned to power, the balance of the scale had tilted heavily in their favour. Just as it was before the war, the weak were oppressed again.

The fake guerrillas were recognized and rewarded, while the real ones remained only on the rosters of their units, or were even removed, because they had no money for bribes.

Naturally, their frustration worked like poison in their minds and hearts. They felt that the new order did not aim to give justice to all, but to favour only a few.

During the first year of liberation, the workers and employees received pre-war wages. All knew that the cost of living had multiplied four times. Prices of goods and services had spiralled, while money was short. However, the goods were scarce not because of high prices but because of the middlemen's greed.

The labourers formed unions to protect themselves. Meanwhile, the farmers' groups were beginning to spread throughout the land. The labourer had not forgotten the lessons gleaned from the war. He felt that he should not always remain fodder for the cannon, especially during peaceful times.

He decided to fight for his rightful share. He knew that he would not get this if he was satisfied with just grovelling. The labour union was his strength; if he learnt to use it wisely and well, it would bring him justice. It would not turn the miserly master generous, but he would have to sit up—and listen. In the labourer's hands rested his own freedom.

From all sides could be heard voices in protest against the greed of those who controlled the economy. Town meetings lambasted the sharks, many of whom were foreigners who had come to the Philippines with nothing but a shirt and a pair of trousers. Unbelievably, at the end of a war that had cost millions of Filipino lives, those foreigners began to own factories and warehouses. What made them influential with the government? Why did the leaders always follow them? And why was the nation like the Arab who was kicked out of his tent by the camel whom he had charitably sheltered from the cold wind?

Meanwhile, the country realized that politicians were not angels. Rather, they were a flock of preying birds. They were not content to snatch and kill the living; they would also feed on the corpses with neither mercy nor horror. 'What are we in power for?' was the common expression. And when one was still in power, why not then feather one's nest?

Rizal's remark was once more proven true: that what was long, was extended and the short, further shortened. Those at the top cared only about making themselves filthy rich through graft and corruption.

Two contrasting views could be seen developing inside and outside Manila. On one side were the jobless and thousands of families living in hovels. Children thin and dirty, mostly orphans of the prisoners of Fort Santiago or the casualties of Bataan. Women sick and emaciated, many of whom were the mothers of these children.

There were also armies of guerrillas waiting for backpay for their services, or for any job. Armies of the wounded with no hospital to admit them nor medicine to heal them. The youth with no school buildings to house them without a politician's recommendation. Infants with swollen heads and deformed bodies because of malnutrition, since the areas meant for puericulture centres had been occupied by petrol stations. No milk for the children of the poor, but plenty of petrol for the long cars of the rich.

On the other side, a different picture could be seen.

As if by magic stood the grand palaces of steel, marble and crystal sitting on land, each of which could hold a hundred shanties of the poor. In every yard, surrounded by thick and forbidding walls, sat the admirable gardens, a garage wide enough for half a dozen cars, and a swimming pool as big and as elegant as the private baths of the Roman nobles in the time of Caesar.

In the modern palaces, the lucky residents lived happily day and night. Ten days a week. From the time they rose until they slept, they hardly took a break between breakfast, lunch, snacks, dinner; dancing, mah-jongg, poker, bingo, and all sorts of gatherings for all sorts of reasons. Birthdays, weddings, baptisms, confirmation parties, wedding anniversaries, farewell parties, welcome parties, graduation, house blessing, fashion shows, garden shows, benefits of all kinds, contests to choose Miss Philippines, Miss Galaxy, or whatever, often without any excuse except the desire to show off.

The creatures in those two opposite scenes—in the hovels and in the palaces—seemed to have nothing in common. There was a great gap between them—blood, condition, and citizenship. But that was only on the surface.

Actually, many in the palaces were high government officials, capitalists, proprietors, businessmen, their ilk. In the hovels lived the humble employees, the labourers, the jobless. The former had reached the top by stepping on those below.

There was no love lost between these two worlds spawned by conditions after the war—conditions that had already existed for centuries. Abuse and insult, envy and hate. Like heaven and earth, they were linked together, but they were always apart. One wanted to keep the status quo; the other was impatient for the change coming, like the swinging of a pendulum.

When the public learnt of the move for Philippine Independence on 13 August 1945, instead of 4 July 1946, a large gathering was held to support it. Their resolution said, 'Independence is the only solution to our problems. We should learn to swim—swim by ourselves and overcome life's waves.'

But the leading politicians, the capitalists like Segundo Montero, vigorously opposed the move. They claimed that staying under the wings of America would make for a stable future. They asked, 'Would we have been freed from the iron heel of Japan without America's power? Could we stay in the vast Pacific in the face of the great threats of Communist Russia and Red China? How could the Philippines survive now that cities, ports, streets, buildings, railways and communications are wrecked? Now that her fields are laid to waste, her animals and farms have gone? How can she get back on her feet again without leaning on American support?'

And they answered their own stream of questions. 'We need America's care and protection. We have to build our cities and towns; repair roads, bridges and ports; repair wrecked buildings; accept American aid and expertise. We need new trucks and gasoline. We need new machines, aeroplanes, tanks, guns, bullets and the technological knowledge of modern warfare.' It seemed they never wanted to cut themselves off from Uncle Sam's apron strings.

'If we should have a plebiscite now,' Don Segundo said loudly at a gathering, 'the country will vote against independence.' Then he added, 'Unless the country has gone to the dogs.'

'What the country needs is not independence but food,' said a reporter. 'The only meaning of freedom these days is the freedom to starve.'

'Hear! Hear!' agreed a few.

Independence would mean change, sacrifice and risks. There was always a certain disappointment before victory; one lost one's way first before finding the right path. But those who lived in comfort did not want any of this. Why should the fortunate still look for other fortunes? Why lie on the cold ground when there is already a soft and warm bed?

Thus, for many days after the war, the spirit of real liberation, the settled feeling of peace, and the joy of victory were denied to many people. Everything lay in disarray.

Many asked if their sacrifice had been in vain—the loss of lives, the blood that was spilt, the young lives snuffed out. But there was no answer.

Many more asked if the Filipinos—the hardy tree and the solid rock that refused to surrender but fought with uncommon courage—had really won the war. But there was no clear answer to that query either.

XVII

When Mando descended from the Sierra Madre mountains, he did not go to Manila right away. He went to Kalayaan to see Magat, the chief of the guerrillas. Although they had not yet seen each other again, that one meeting had deepened the bond between them.

Magat did not recognize Mando because of the large scar on his left cheek. But the man had the same physique—although he had lost weight—the same eyes, mouth and voice. The same grip and warmth in his handshake.

Magat searched Mando's face. 'What happened to you, brother?' he asked with concern.

Smiling, Mando embraced his friend and said, 'Not all wounds are marks of misfortune.'

Mando told Magat briefly of his experiences since their last meeting. But he did not relate how Karyo and Martin had died, only that the Japanese had killed them and that he had barely escaped. He made up a story of an encounter with the Japanese a few days after leaving Kalayaan. Fortunately, he killed his Japanese opponent and escaped from the others who had run after him. He said that the wound on his face came from a bayonet wielded by a Japanese soldier. He related how he was nursed by an old man in a secluded place at the foot of the Sierra Madre.

He had gone afterwards to some places near the shore and met some evacuees from Manila. Mando mentioned Dr Sabio, one of his former professors in college and a renowned Filipino scientist.

It was there that Mando heard the news about the surrender of the Japanese in Manila.

Magat told him of his own plans to return to Manila. 'I've finished my mission here,' said the guerrilla head.

Mando enquired about Magat's plan. He confessed that there was nothing definite, but he would surely look for work.

'What was your job?'

'Copyreader and proofreader,' said Magat, laughing softly. 'A lowly position, but I learnt a lot. Imagine reading the whole day. Different topics. And I learnt to write. Before the war, I was able to publish several articles in the weekly newspaper, and I would have been promoted to copy editor.'

'Then,' said Mando, 'it won't probably be hard to change from proofreader to editor.'

'Editor of what?'

'Of a newspaper.'

Magat looked at Mando, wondering if he was just joking, but Mando looked serious.

'Some of my friends I met at the evacuation place want to start a newspaper in Manila. They also want to set up a school. They've asked me to manage the newspaper, but I've no time. They assigned me to look for trustworthy men who can help.'

'I lack the knowledge,' Magat said humbly. 'That is a big leap from my former job. And that was in a printing press, not a real newspaper.'

'It's the same thing,' Mando said. 'What we need is not so much a vast knowledge of topics but character, courage and honesty. Dr Sabio and I agree that a newspaperman is different from a literary writer. Many can write well, but they are timid and easily scared by power or could be bought. They're also afraid of the truth.'

'If it were only leading guerrillas in battle . . .' said Magat.

'Managing a newspaper and leading a fight aren't too different,' said Mando. 'I also lack experience. But the real mission of a newspaper is to reveal the truth, without fear or favour. Therefore, what's needed is a newspaperman who can't be bullied or bought. As for experience, isn't that a part of daily work? Did you and I experience life in the mountains before we became guerrillas?'

'Well, that's true.'

'Get ready, then,' said Mando. 'We'll discuss this again in Manila.'

'I'll agree on one condition,' Magat said, smiling.

'What?'

'That if I won't do as editor, you'll demote me to proofreader.' With a hearty laugh, the two shook hands.

'Why don't you come with me to Manila?' Mando said.

Magat answered that he had to attend to some things in Kalayaan. They agreed to meet later.

Mando returned to Manila after being gone for three years. Just as he could not be recognized by his former acquaintances, he also failed to recognize Manila under the heap of charcoal and ruins.

Mando spent a few days looking over various places north and south of the Pasig River. What he saw was far worse than the news that had reached them in the mountains.

One morning, he went to the old Montero home in Singalong. Mando was amazed to see a large concrete house. With its surrounding walls and tall trees, it looked like a green isle in the middle of the black ruins left by the war. He thought Don Segundo was not only clever but lucky as well. Almost all the buildings nearby were razed, but the Montero house was left standing. It had been hardly torched by fire or dented by steel. It looked like a proud boxer with his right hand raised above its enemy lying on the ground.

'Weeds don't easily die,' he told himself.

As he wondered at the strangeness of it all, he saw cars coming and going through the gate. Some were American military men, and some looked like businessmen or gamblers who had won the grand prize in a lottery.

The operation continues, he told himself.

For half an hour, Mando observed the vicinity without being noticed. He left after finding out everything that he wanted to know—

that Don Segundo and his family were alive, that they still lived there, that the Don was richer than ever before, that he was still close to those in power.

After a month, Mando bought a printing press on Azcarraga Street. It was a two-storey building with a printing press on the ground floor and the offices and copy room upstairs.

He also rented a house in the suburbs. One day, he returned to the Sierra Madre mountains and asked Tata Matias to live with him in the city. At first, the old man refused, saying it would be hard at his age to change the way he lived. But Mando said that he needed to consult the old man often about his plans. Should they not work together to put to use the great wealth and power that had come to him through Tata Matias? No other living person knew Mando's secret, and the old revolutionary had no one else but Mando. He had touched the right chord in Tata Matias' heart, and the old man finally agreed.

So Tata Matias and a young orphan boy, their former courier who lived near the sea shore, came to live with Mando in a Manila suburb.

By then, Magat was already in Manila. He brought Andres, the former Makapili leader, with him. After a rigid investigation, it was proven that Andres did not commit any crime, for his aid to the Japanese was only in cultural matters. Having committed no abuses, his hands were not stained with blood, nor was his name under a cloud. Magat persuaded Andres to come, believing him to be a man of principle and ability. He wanted Andres to help with the work offered by Mando.

Mando had no objections. He trusted his friend's judgement and was satisfied with his brief talk with the former Makapili.

'I've no experience in this line of work,' said Andres. 'I plan to go back to teaching.'

'Sometimes, we give too much importance to experience,' said Mando. 'I think it's enough to have the ability and the desire to learn. Some of our experiences are changed by what we learn.'

Magat knew a young man named Iman, who had stopped studying a year before graduation. Magat offered him a job, and the young man was delighted to accept it.

Iman then brought along Santillan, a newspaperman who had served in a daily newspaper that was shut down during the Japanese occupation. He had gone home to the province, raised chickens and planted sweet potatoes. He did not use his pen any more. He would have liked to fetch his wife if only he could find a permanent job in Manila. When offered the job, he was happy to work again at a newspaper.

'Santi, why didn't you write during the Japanese times?' asked Magat.

'I preferred to live by selling eggs and sweet potatoes,' he answered, 'than to use my pen to weave lies. I've a son whom I'd like to become a writer someday.'

'Once we start our paper, you won't have to sell eggs and sweet potatoes any more. Count on it,' promised Magat.

'Thank you, sir. I'll tell my wife.'

Mando invited the staff to dinner. The newsmen under Magat, the printers, and the employees were present. Mando left the talking to Magat.

'You already know that we will publish a newspaper,' Magat began. 'Some progressive people backing up our friend, Mando, will put up the capital. We will put in our skills and effort. It will belong to us all. We will receive a just salary, a share in the profits, if any, but not in the losses. But probably, we will suffer losses at the start.'

Everyone laughed when he mentioned the losses. They knew that in the history of journalism, none made a profit at once and countless more threw away money like water down a rat hole.

Magat continued.

'Our newspaper will be named *Kampilan* and will be published in Filipino. We want to address the nation, and we should not use another language. The *Kampilan* will stand for truth, reason and justice. This is our slogan and our pledge—truth, reason, justice. We will have enemies and friends. For sure, we will have more enemies than friends.' More laughter. 'The time will come when those who tell the truth will be branded subversives, and there will also be times when defending reason and justice will be tantamount to rebellion. We shall not be scared or bullied.

'We will accept ads, surely, but the advertisers won't be our masters. We won't become tools of any political party, nor of the people who run the government. Our only guide will be our honest view of truth. We shall defend the freedom of every individual from the establishment. The essence of democracy is not only the right of the majority to govern, but also the equal right of the minority to dissent. This is our principle, and this is also our policy. If anyone is opposed, let us clear the air before we start our first issue.'

No one raised his hand. Everyone agreed; everyone was ready. They happily raised a toast to the success of *Kampilan*.

Mando told Magat that he would ask him to run the newspaper. After a few weeks, Mando would travel abroad and be away for some years. He would go to Europe and then to the United States. Nevertheless, he would be in touch by cable or overseas telephone.

Mando asked Magat not to tell anyone that the corporation had asked him to look for a good rotary press to replace the old one. Should they buy the nearby lots, their present site would be big enough for a building. There would also be space for two or three newspapers, as well as a radio station and a TV station.

'So we'll fight big!' Magat was awed by Mando's plans.

'How can we win the case for the nation—I mean, truth and justice for the nation,' Mando explained, 'if we lack the courage and sincerity that we ask of our helpers? Our weapons should be as efficient as that of the enemy's. Was this not our problem in the mountains of the Sierra Madre?'

'But I thought the war was over,' Magat said with some degree of satisfaction, and he winked.

'Oh, it's just beginning,' Mando laughed.

The following week, the newsboys began selling the first issue of the *Kampilan*. It was a newspaper of eight pages, almost bare of ads, with few pictures, no comics page, no news about social and personal gossip, but full of information not found in commercial newspapers and the mouthpieces of vested interests.

When Mando gave Tata Matias the first issue of *Kampilan*, the old man quickly grabbed the copy, which still smelt of printer's ink. He eagerly read the headline news about prominent men involved in graft and corruption. Then he read the front-page editorial lashing at the threat to deny freedom of speech and assembly to groups that refuse to bow before the administration.

'If Father Florentino could only read this,' Tata Matias said, filled with happiness, 'then he'd know that his prayers for Simoun's treasure did not go in vain.'

XVIII

Everywhere, a terrible heat filled the air. The countryside and the city seemed to be roasting. The heat was not only because of the season but also because of current problems, especially the spiralling cost of living.

In the fields, the situation was explosive in the face of growing discontent among the farmers. The city labourers were also restless because of the lack of jobs. Those who had work lived only from hand to mouth, from pay cheque to pay cheque.

Soon after the war, Don Segundo Montero carried out his threat. He would restore the old ways of doing things in his vast landholding. He directed Pastor to carry out his orders: start collecting old debts and deduct them from the shares of the ne'er do well.

Pastor hesitated, pointing out that the tenants were even asking for better conditions. They said that the landlord should bear all the expenses, since this is part of capital. They also wanted the harvest to be divided equally. Pastor also informed him of the tenants' claim that they had no more debts, for the amounts in Don Segundo's list were merely interest.

Montero's thick eyebrows flew to his forehead. His nostrils flared like a bear who had smelt gunpowder. He got up from his seat with such vehemence that Pastor, who was standing before him, had to step back.

'I said I won't put up any more with their shamelessness,' he shouted. 'I kept silent during the war. But now, cold reason should prevail.'

'But they feel they're not getting a fair deal,' said Pastor.

'Because they wear their conscience on their ass,' Montero exploded. With a voice like thunder, he added an ultimatum, 'Those who don't like my terms should leave. I would rather that my land become a jungle than harbour those snakes.'

Pastor said he could not carry out Don Segundo's orders. He did not want trouble if he could help it. Besides, he also believed the farmers deserved some relief.

Don Segundo turned on Pastor.

'On whose side are you, then?' he asked in a fierce tone. 'Mine or theirs? Well, if you can't do what I order you to do, it's up to you. You have one month.'

Pastor left. In his heart, he felt that the one-month period had ended that same day. But he was neither angry nor sad because of his own situation. He was more worried about the possible effect on the peace at the landholding.

He returned to the province at once. Puri was waiting for him. 'How was your trip, Tatang?' she greeted him.

'Not too good,' he answered without energy.

While Puri was setting the table, Pastor told her what Don Segundo had ordered him to do. Puri then answered that some tenants had come earlier, for an important purpose.

'When they learnt that Don Segundo called for you, they said they'd come back tonight.'

'Who were they?'

'They were five of them, including Mang Tomas and Danoy.'

* * *

That night, Puri had just finished washing the dishes when they heard someone calling at the gate.

Pastor met them.

'Come in, come in.'

Inside, Pastor asked them to sit down and if they had already finished supper.

'Yes, we have, thank you,' Mang Tomas said in thanks. He was the oldest of the group and just a little older than Pastor. Danoy was the youngest. All of them were tenants of Don Segundo.

'We heard that you went to Manila,' said Mang Tomas as Puri entered. She had come in to greet the guests.

'Yes, Don Segundo called for me. Even if you hadn't come, I would've come to see you.'

Pastor then told them of the landlord's decision. Before they could speak, he added, 'But if thinks he'll wait for me to carry out his orders, then he'll just be waiting for the Day of Judgement.' Pastor's voice was firm.

'And if he tries to do it himself, he might hasten his Day of Judgement,' said Danoy.

'Let's not do it standing, if we can do it sitting down,' said one tenant.

'Whoever thought of that saying is not a friend of the poor,' objected Danoy. 'That is the same as "those who tread softly don't get hurt much" and "count up to ten before raising your hand in anger".'

Pastor ended the argument by informing them that Don Segundo had given him a month to carry out the orders and find out who did not agree.

'Even now, we can tell you not even one would agree,' Mang Tomas said.

'That's what I thought,' said Pastor. 'But besides your refusal, what other terms do you want? I know more or less about the expenses and the harvest. But you haven't told me what you've agreed on, lately.'

Mang Tomas spoke, 'We've never considered you an outsider. You're also a farmer like us, and perhaps our parents have the same story. This landholding used to be a vast wilderness. Our ancestors cleared it; our parents tilled and planted on it. But we only inherited this serfdom. Meanwhile, the owners of this land, from the friars down to Don Segundo, have profited from the fruits of this land. But only those who have sweated blood remain poor. Now, is it too much to wish for freedom?'

'Then . . .' Pastor said.

'What we want isn't just land but also justice. In a farmer's life, land is the symbol of justice. You know that we've already formed a union. Its aim is to ask the government to buy this landholding and other agricultural lands, and divide these among the farmers at a cost. We'll pay by instalment, with our harvest as collateral. If we have our own farm to till, then the fruits of our labour won't be snatched by those who live by extorting from us. Is it clear?'

'And if the government has no money?' asked Pastor.

'The government cannot lack funds,' declared Mang Tomas. 'In fact, we can all see that it often throws away money on useless things. And the land need not be paid for in cash. First, the land should be assessed. This will be the basis for computing annual earnings. And this amount will then be paid to the landowner, until the full amount has been paid.'

'In this case,' Pastor noted, 'you'll still be tenants, instead of the landowner.'

'That is only at the start, until the land becomes ours,' said Mang Tomas.

'Is that not like the saying, "same dog with a new collar"?' asked the overseer.

'There is no similarity,' the old man said. 'An individual owner like Don Segundo has no interest but profit. His concern for a tenant is just like a rig driver's for his horse. On the other hand, the government is concerned with public welfare. Even if the programme that will do that means losing money.'

'Your reasoning and proposal are good,' said Pastor. 'However, and I'm sorry I have to say this, I don't see it being fulfilled. First, Don Segundo will oppose it unless he gets the price he wants. Second, the government is different from the heads of government. The officials will listen to the more influential voice of Don Segundo.'

'That, we have to see,' challenged Mang Tomas. 'The tinkle of silver won't always be the master. In a confrontation, silver can't win over iron.'

'Tomas . . .'

'I don't mean anything wrong. But if the humble people join hands, their voice will be louder than several Segundo Monteros.'

Such heated air rose from the fields, spread far and wide, and singed the skin of labourers in the city.

Later, representatives gathered in different factories, business firms and offices, and decided to form a federation. They published a resolution on just wages, hours of work and the relationship between capital and government, the cost of living, houses, clothes, medicine and other needs of the family. They complained loudly about the miserable conditions of the jobless.

Iman, who wrote for *Kampilan*, interviewed the union leader, Rubio. In his thirties, Rubio was well-built and well-dressed. He was like a dynamo. He moved fast and spoke even faster. He could be mistaken for a member of the Lions or Jaycees, or any other civic organization of the upper crust. But Rubio was a real labourer: there were callouses on his hands, his chest was thick, and his skull was even thicker. Iman learnt that Rubio never knew his parents. He was only seven years old when he began selling newspapers and magazines in the streets of Manila. He lived with an uncle who depended on Rubio's earnings. After his uncle's death, he worked as an office janitor for a pittance, with free meals and a chance to attend night school. After high school, he sold medicines for a drug company. But in a stroke of irony, when he became sick and had no money, he could not afford his medicines. For a long time, he roamed the streets without work. Then he played small roles in the movies, but his wages were not even enough to pay the tailor for the suit he used. He later became the bodyguard of a politician, an experience that only made him hate politics and politicians.

Iman smiled while listening to Rubio's experiences as they sipped coffee in a restaurant.

'Oh, yes, I became a driver for a judge for a short time,' Rubio continued. 'This lowly judge was kind, honourable and poor. During the war, I made and sold cigarettes. One day, I saw the judge had no money even for a cigarette, so I gave him a few packs.'

Rubio even told Iman how the Japanese military police beat him up while he was selling cigarettes at a market. His body was almost torn apart. But he told Iman not to put that in his article any more.

'Two spies reported me. I didn't know for what crime,' said Rubio. 'I was left crippled by the Japanese military police; my face was left swollen by their fists. But not one of the thousand witnesses could speak out, or help me. After a few days, I killed the two spies, went into hiding, and soon fled to the hills.'

Rubio left his sickly wife in a safe refuge, but when he returned, she could not be found anywhere. Even the house where she had stayed was gone. Such colourful experiences completely opened Rubio's eyes, especially when he joined the outlaws during the war. He realized that, alone, the common man is like a stone that will only be kicked around or swept by the tide. But when the stones are put together and welded by a meaningful cause, they become sturdy posts supporting large buildings or a strong fort.

'Like the jobless,' he said. 'For their own sake and for that of the organization, it's a crime for them not to have a chance. They were educated and trained; they've honed their skills, physically and mentally. Now, they're just like unused tools lying under the shade. The voice of two million people unemployed people should not be left for lost in the middle of the desert.'

Iman agreed.

The labourer also explained the justness of his cause of labour and why they should succeed.

'The fruits of the land should be for all,' he said. 'That is according to the Bible. But has this ever been realized at all? Is not the Filipino worker until this time still oppressed in the economy, in society, and in citizenship? Does a labourer's wife play mah-jongg by day and dance all night long in a nightclub? Or is she not tied down by washing and ironing? Do the children of labourers come to school in a Cadillac? Do labourer's families live in the palaces at Forbes Park? Do they spend monthly vacations in the mountain city Baguio, or go back and forth to Hong Kong and Tokyo, or visit New York and Paris frequently?'

Rubio paused. His lower lip jutted, then he continued, 'So, if in spite of all these facts, the labourer's cause is lost, it won't be for lack of merit. The fault would lie in the skewed rules of society and the cross-eyed vision of the judges.'

One day, with Iman's help, the farmer's federation and the worker's union joined forces. Rubio, Mang Tomas, Danoy, and others of the same persuasion had a long conference. They realized that they had the same problems—and the same enemy. They realized they should pool all their efforts to fight social injustice as well as the monster of their oppression.

Some farmers recalled that during the war, their paths had already often crossed, since Rubio was a patriotic guerrilla.

Soon, the farmers' and labourers' groups presented their petitions. The landlords, the businessmen, and the government were all shocked, their furrows knitted in grave anxiety.

XIX

Mando's preparations for his trip went without a hitch. He told only a few about his trip overseas, including Magat, Tata Matias and Dr Sabio.

Mando told Magat, his trusted right hand in the *Kampilan*, that he would be gone for some time. In addition to his other plans, Mando was asked by the corporation to buy a modern rotary press. He assured Magat that the needs of the newspaper were taken care of. He had already deposited a sum in the bank, in the name of the paper. Magat could then just deposit and withdraw from these funds.

Tata Matias knew the real reason for Mando's trip. They had already discussed this for several nights.

They agreed that the jewels should be turned to cash as soon as possible. Storing it indefinitely would be like leaving it buried underwater. Some things cannot just wait. To carry this out, funds were needed, and the best markets for old jewellery lay outside the country.

Mando realized that, like a diamond, he needed more expert cutting. Indeed, his college education gave him a solid foundation. He also read widely and well; the experiences of the war further deepened his knowledge about life. But still, he felt inadequate. Much more was needed, just as wood for a pillar should be cut only at the right time. He felt he could still learn more by travelling and observing people, by visiting other countries, and attending different events. If all of these could only be distilled in one vessel, they would give Mando the experience, ability and wisdom that could count for more than all of Simoun's glittering wealth.

Like ice, any amount of wealth could melt in the hands of one who does not know how to use it. The best plan could come to nought despite the noble aim of its proponents, unless they had the knowledge, vision, and good judgement to turn ideas and ideals into action.

'What you wish for is necessary,' said Tata Matias. 'Of course, the problems are here, and we know both the illness and the cure. But, as I've said, it's best to consult doctors with more experience and to search for more effective medicine. Is this how you feel?'

'Yes, Tata Matias,' Mando said. 'We both realize that the wealth entrusted in our hands is not a privilege, but a great responsibility. That it's not for our personal welfare, but for that of the majority. How should we use this weapon? What should we do? How? These questions demand honest and intelligent answers. The right answers shall then guide us; they'll be our lodestars. Is that right, Tatang?'

'I'm pleased with your analysis,' the old man said with a smile. 'Yesterday is the foundation of today, and today is the pillar of tomorrow. The spirit of our heroes who fell in the night should light the way for those who love their country in these fraught times. The fruit of your efforts will strengthen those who will follow you.'

Mando also consulted Dr Sabio on their common plans like Freedom University, the Montero Village, and others. Mando had great respect for his former teacher Dr Sabio, for not only was he a lawyer, professor, sociologist, and an advocate of Philippine Studies, but he had also continued to study and research ancient history and current events in the Philippines and overseas. Still, the professor did not know the source of Mando's wealth. He thought Mando was the heir of Tata Matias.

Dr Sabio had already travelled to many lands. He had a wide knowledge of solutions to the land problems in the new republics of Eastern Europe and the successful management of cooperatives in Scandinavia. While they were at the evacuation place, Dr Sabio convinced Mando of the importance of knowledge. Then they discussed the creation of Freedom University.

Mando still remembered this conversation, the words dipping and rising in his memory.

'What was the aim of Rizal and the other heroes?' Dr Sabio had asked. 'To free our country from darkness. Our ancestors were enslaved by foreigners, not so much by physical force but by blinding. Do you remember Rizal's letter to the women of Malolos, which he wrote at the request of Marcelo H. del Pilar? At the same time, Bonifacio and Jacinto were trying to spread the Katipunan's vision. They also had a newspaper, which would spread their message to the citizens. Ignorance is the mother of slavery. Rizal wanted nothing else than to open the Filipinos' eyes so they could see the truth, so that they would want to be free. As he said, "There are no masters where there are no slaves".'

'We can see that in this war,' answered Mando. 'Some kowtowed to the Japs, but the country remained free.'

'Still, ignorance is our country's most serious illness,' said Dr Sabio. 'The Filipino believed that the foreigners who came here liberated him, although they robbed him; believed that life in this world is not real life, for there is a heaven without end. He believed that he would enjoy life's glory if he died suffering, which he equated with holiness. Indeed, the Filipino endured more suffering than Job did. He bought everything sold by the liars, who chained his neck and blindfolded his eyes and mind.'

Mando said, 'These are indeed the painful truths that Rizal showed in his books.'

'You sound like a Rizalist, Mando,' Dr Sabio said.

'Like you and the other nationalists, I also love our country.'

'Very well, then. You're also aware of the bitter truth described by our martyrs.' As if reading passages from the *Fili* on Mando's face, he said, 'Throughout centuries of slavery, the Filipino who before held his head high and enjoyed freedom, was now shorn of his identity and culture. The Filipino forgot his old legends, alphabet, songs, poems, laws and customs. He memorized doctrines, prayers and beliefs from foreign places, which he didn't even understand. He blindly imitated alien manners, ways and wants, which didn't even fit his situation. He humbled himself until he became ashamed of anything native, while he adopted everything that was foreign.'

Dr Sabio stopped and looked into the distance. Mando remained silent, reflecting on the words that he had just heard.

'We can't hope to prosper,' Dr Sabio said, 'while these illnesses are not attacked at their roots. Expose the sick on the steps of the temple. Rizal exposed the evil of the powerful, the rottenness of the Filipinos whom they had brainwashed, and the ignorance of the country. He didn't stop at writing books and pamphlets. He took practical steps. He organized the Filipinos in Europe, set up the *La Liga Filipina* in Manila to knit the patriotic intellectuals together. When he was captured and exiled to Dapitan, the *Liga* became the flame that lit Bonifacio's Katipunan. But even when he was already in exile, Rizal did not stop. He opened a school, taught the young, and set a good example. Neither place nor situation prevented him from working for the country's welfare. He was a noble example at every turn.'

Mando admitted his great admiration for Rizal, but he felt that every hero belonged to his own time.

'It's true, Dr Sabio,' said Mando, 'Rizal's wisdom can guide the nation. But some conditions demand certain decisions. This is true in war, as in a new life. The intellectual's passive attitude sometimes stalls a programme. This is where Bonifacio differed from them. He was decisive. Therefore, Doctor, what our country needs after the war is a leadership that not only thinks, but also acts.'

'A brilliant combination of wisdom and action then,' agreed Dr Sabio. 'In short, a Rizal and a Bonifacio combined into one.'

'Yes, sir, that's it,' said Mando. 'Of the millions of Filipinos, there has to be someone with the same qualities. Although, sad to say, in our so-called democracy—for I was only a student and a houseboy then— it's not always the best person who wins the elections.'

'Indeed, for in an election, the ones who vote are the majority,' answered Dr Sabio. 'And among the many, only a few people have principles. Many are guided by personal interests, twisted by emotions, or distorted by greed.'

The two continued to discuss the country's various illnesses. They agreed on Mando's need to travel. The wise old professor gave his stamp of approval on Mando's itinerary.

'May you return whole in body and mind,' Dr Sabio said, in parting.

'I solemnly promise,' Mando answered, smiling.

'Very good,' Dr Sabio said and gave Mando some additional instructions. He also prepared letters of introduction to his friends at different universities and cultural organizations.

He then explained the programme of Freedom University.

'We don't need a university if it will just become a diploma mill,' he said, 'or if it will just make the capitalists richer. We'll make it a forge to mould the nationalistic youth who'll help the country in various ways. From them will come our future leaders in government, in society, in economics, in natural sciences, and in political science.'

'In other words, you won't turn education into a business.'

'Certainly not,' was the professor's answer. 'For half a century, we've invested money, time and the lives of the youth in the old educational system from America. And what did we see? Unemployed professionals. Do you know that many teachers are selling on the sidewalks because they don't have jobs for them? How many lawyers are willing to be ordinary policemen and dentists, or work as messengers? How many took the civil service exams a year after the war and ended up as clerks? 40,000! Is this the future of the youth? Oh, Mando, it would be a thousand times better to have a nation of farmers and fishermen than a nation of clerks.'

Mando relayed to his adopted father his conversation with Dr Sabio.

'It's only right to consult him before you leave,' said Tata Matias. 'It would even be better if he could come with you.'

'I've reasons for going alone,' said Mando. 'Just think, Tatang. There are secrets known only to the two of us.'

'That's true,' said the old man. He added, 'You'll travel to other lands for the sake of your work here. When you return, remember how Ibarra, the hero of the *Noli*, returned after finishing his studies. He was filled with hope. But later, he had to leave as a fugitive and travel alone as one persecuted. When he came home again, he was already a Simoun, who had no aim but seeking revenge against those who had snuffed out his hopes.'

Tata Matias picked up a copy of the *Fili* from his side. He gave it to Mando and asked him to read aloud Simoun's confession to Father Florentino before his death.

Mando read up to the part where Simoun expressed doubts about a God of Justice who had denied him any help. But Father Florentino answered, 'Never will one who helped oppress a country be honoured for its salvation. Hate will bear nothing but horror. Sin is a crime. Salvation means courage and sacrifice. And sacrifice is love . . .'

Mando closed the book and handed it to Tata Matias.

'I expect you to return from your trip neither a Crisostomo Ibarra nor a Simoun,' said the old man.

'I'm sure I shall return with the money from the jewellery.' And in a low voice, he said, 'And also with knowledge that money can't buy.'

'You'll return as the fulfilment of Rizal's hope in the youth. You won't be like the poet Isagani, who was content with hope; nor the pitiful Basilio, who aspired only for an easy life as a doctor and closed his eyes to the evils around him. Especially not an Attorney Pasta, a tool of our country's enemies, who became rich from his various schemes. Now, our so-called upper crust is full of Attorney Pastas.' The old man sadly shook his head. 'Oh, you will not return a foreigner in his own land.'

'I'll return as a brown American,' Mando said, laughing. Then he added seriously, 'The Mando Plaridels and Matias Dipasupils become foreigners in their own land only when foreign masters and their Attorney Pastas and other hired tools are allowed to prevail. But the country will not be fooled all the time. We won't allow this, Tata Matias. And it won't be long—I'll be gone for only two or three years. On my return, we'll do things that would justify to Father Florentino our taking of the jewellery from the bottom of the sea. And even Rizal would be mighty proud of us.'

When again he glanced at Tata Matias, Mando noticed that the old man could hardly keep his eyes open.

XX

After breakfast, Mando and Magat left in a Jeep for the Montero Plantation in Central Luzon.

The two had agreed to look into the situation at the plantation. They heard that after the war, the gulf had widened even further between the owners and the tenants on the vast agricultural lands. The landlord insisted on going back to the pre-war policy on farming and leasing and, for their part, the tenants cried for reforms.

Dr Sabio had planned to join them, but he had to attend to some business in Cabanatuan. Montero was a forty-five-minute ride away from Cabanatuan, so he could join them later, perhaps after lunch. The professor knew about the agrarian history in Luzon and had made an intensive study of agrarian relations. Nonetheless, he wanted to have a clearer picture of the current conditions at Montero Plantation. Freedom University planned to buy the said lands in Central Luzon.

The two friends discussed various aspects of agrarian reform. They knew about the claims of both sides.

'Everything has changed except the way the plantation owner treated us,' the farmers said.

'The law is in force again,' the landlords claimed. 'We should obey the law.'

They also discussed the role of the *Kampilan* in the face of these complications. Mando noted that newspapers should publish both sides of an issue. But he believed its greater duty was to reveal the truth. This is the stand of journalists who do not compromise.

'In the wake of the war came a period of excessive propaganda,' Mando said. 'Let's not depend on the press release alone, or be carried away by chatter. Let's sift the truth from the lies all around.'

For example, he cited a government office whose main job was to spread fake news. He also mentioned a loud-mouthed official who based his decisions on newspaper and radio announcements. He spent most of his time in places of leisure.

Mando told Magat of his wish to see the different parts of the Philippines, if only he did not have to take this trip overseas. 'This bad practice should be changed,' he said. 'We should first know our country and people before we travel to other lands.'

'But this inclination came from our training,' said Magat. 'As a conquered country, the first thing we learnt was to look up to our colonizer. We were made to believe that they came here to help us. We were also made to believe that they sell what's good for us. These include their language, commerce, way of life, and surely, even their vices. The Filipino became a great imitator. But the trouble was, we imitated even the bad. Our women don't wear our native attire any more and prefer sheer textiles that hug the body. Young people are drawn to leisure instead of work. The children now prefer bread over rice, candy over native sweets, apples over bananas. That's what the teacher taught: "An apple" . . . But the teacher did not clarify to the students that the Americans eat apples because they don't have bananas.'

Mando chuckled at Magat's colourful description.

'This slave mentality is rooted in our countrymen,' said Magat. 'Our leaders have been overseas many times, but have not seen Batanes or the beautiful southern islands. Everyone taking medicine or law who has the funds, flies away to the United States to "specialize". That would have been fine if their real aim was to gain knowledge. But what hurts is the implication that what they learnt here isn't enough.'

'That is one of the things I discussed with Dr Sabio,' Mando said. 'He wants Freedom University's first aim to be an awareness of life's realities. According to him, most universities aim to prepare a student for a definite work, and that is all. So they fall into the trap of what George Santayana calls "the barbarians of specialization". On the other hand, Dr Sabio's programme has three bases: scientific—that is, to discard superstitions; nationalistic—to place the welfare of the country and people above all. For example, while teaching Philippine history, we shall not say that Ferdinand Magellan discovered the country, but rather, that he was the first white person to come here. And finally, a good education will be for all, not just for the rich few. Scholarships will be offered to the talented but poor, but its doors will be closed to the rich and the braindead.'

'That will be a hard blow to the diploma mills.'

'Indeed, it will be. But just imagine, these diploma mills make more profit than factories. It will also expose some exclusive colleges for the elite's children for what they really are.'

Mando also spoke of Dr Sabio's plans to teach practical things to high-school students. 'Rice and sugar are the two major food items of the Filipinos. Yet how many city folks know how rice is produced—the tilling of fields, sowing of seeds, transplanting of seedlings, harvesting, threshing and milling? It's the same with sugar. Our young people should know how sugarcane is planted, tended, cut in the fields, crushed by machines, boiled in vats, filtered, and refined, before it is mixed with coffee or ginger tea and with various food.'

The Jeep stopped at the foot of a temporary wooden bridge, which was the only way across the river. The old stone bridge that had been blown by dynamite during the war had not yet been repaired. Rows of trucks, Jeeps and some cars waited on both sides.

'Just like those vehicles,' Magat said. 'They seem to be signs of progress; maybe so. But we don't have car factories, no local source of petroleum, so these are a burden on the economy. Even before the war, we were the foremost Asian country importing cars and petrol from America.'

'That's a necessary evil,' answered Mando.

'We need more railroads for electric trains. Our hydroelectric plants can supply our electricity needs, if only we could harness the power of our rivers and waterfalls. It's cheaper to run a railroad system and the parts of trains don't need to be replaced often. Motor vehicles, especially heavy trucks, are like demons destroying our roads and wasting our money. The streetcar should be restored in Manila and the suburbs.'

'The streetcar is a good idea,' said Mando. 'We can publish an article on that in the *Kampilan*. It's time we wake up our leaders to industry and the use of our natural resources. We don't lack capital; we're just timid. We prefer pawnshops with a sure income, rather than investing in fishing. We would rather build a cinema than a factory.'

'If the Japanese had stayed long,' Magat added, 'many of our natural resources would surely have been dug up.'

'The Americans will do the same, too. That's why they insist on equal rights in mining and agriculture.'

'The problem is,' Magat said, 'if foreigners dig up our mines, our wealth falls into their hands. In time, we'll be like Hawaii, Panama, and the other banana republics. They've got progressive industries, but the natives remain poor.'

As their Jeep covered the length of the bumpy road between Bulacan and Nueva Ecija, Mando said it was no longer dangerous to travel here the way it had been during the Japanese times. Then, there was horrifying news of robbery, kidnapping and killing along the provincial roads.

'They have gone down from the towns. Now it's hard to tell the wolves from the sheep,' Mando said in a teasing tone.

Magat doubted there was no more danger. 'There will always be danger until the simmering discontent is gone,' Magat said. 'Are we not on our way to the plantation where there is unrest?'

'Oh, banditry is different,' said Mando. But Magat could not be appeased.

'Why is it different?' repeated Magat, stepping lightly on the gas. 'You might say they're probably the children of one mother. Cabesang Tales was an honourable and hardworking citizen named Telesforo Juan de Dios before he was robbed of his land. In the end, he became the fearsome bandit, Matanglawin.'

Mando understood his friend, but he kept his peace. Magat's mention of Cabesang Tales reminded him of Simoun. Did he not have

Maria Clara's medallion, the storied jewel she gave as alms to a leper, who in turn gave it to Basilio for treating him and which Basilio gave later to Huli, Cabesang Tales' daughter, as a token of his love? In the end, when Cabesang Tales stole Simoun's gun, the old man left the medallion as payment, although only the night before, he had refused an offer of 500 pesos, or trade for any important item from the treasure chest of jewellery.

They were already entering the plantation when Mando was startled from his thoughts.

'This looks like it,' he told Magat.

'This is it, then,' he said, pointing to a wooden sign, which said 'Montero Plantation'.

Mando remembered that during the war, sometime in 1943, he went to some areas near Montero Plantation while on a mission. The places were not new to him, for he was born there. Even while serving the Monteros, he sometimes came along. He was unhappy to see the plantation's miserable condition and the sorry clump of farmers' dwellings.

He asked about his uncle and cousin. After learning that they were alive and well, he stifled his intense desire to see them. This was against the order given to him. The mission was secret. He needed to assess the enemy's situation at the plantation and that of the townspeople, and make a report right away. So Mando left the next day.

If he had given in to his desire to see his uncle, he would have met his only cousin, who was then growing into a lovely woman.

The plantation covered almost two adjacent villages in Central Luzon. The first town consisted of a clump of nipa huts clustered around a yard with an average-sized house and a warehouse where Pastor and Puri lived.

Mando and Magat noticed that only a small portion of the land was cultivated. The rest was idle and full of cogon grasses.

The silence was odd. Magat thought it was like the silence that reigned during the war, before both sides started firing.

Mando wondered if he should tell his friend the other reason for this visit, which was more important for him. He wanted to see his uncle, Tata Pastor. He knew his uncle was a tenant. Mando had left Manila when Pastor was made an overseer, after the former overseer had been kidnapped by the outlaws.

Mando recalled the last time he saw his uncle was during his mother's funeral wake. He was then a young man called Andoy. With Tata Pastor were his wife and daughter. His uncle wanted to bring him back to the province, but Don Segundo would not let him go. He said that in honour of Andoy's parents' long service, he would send Andoy to school. In truth, Andoy was useful to the Monteros.

Pastor was persuaded to let Andoy stay, thinking that his nephew would have a brighter future in the house where his parents had worked. In the fields, he would just remain a farmer all his life.

Mando could not remember seeing his uncle again. Even when Tata Pastor's wife, Nana Hilda died, he did not go, for Don Segundo did not tell him that she had died. By the time Pastor became the overseer and started bringing rice and other provisions to Manila, Mando had already become a guerrilla in the Sierra Madre mountains.

So when Pastor asked about his nephew, Don Segundo answered that he had left suddenly and that he had been taken by the Japanese military police. He was supposed to have been involved in some 'deviltry'—of course, the Don did not say that he had reported Andoy to the Japanese, and that Andoy had escaped.

In the end, Mando decided not to tell Magat about his uncle, since Magat also did not know his other secrets.

Magat stopped the Jeep at the gate. They got off, walked to the house, and called out a greeting. At the second call, a young girl looked out of the window. Her thick hair hung loose down her shoulders, as if she had just taken a bath. Magat nudged Mando.

'Good morning,' said the two men.

'Good morning to you,' she said.

'We'd like to ask where we can find the overseer,' asked Mando in a courteous manner.

'Yes, he lives here,' said the girl. 'Please wait.' She came down and asked them to come in.

'Is he home?' Mando asked.

'If it's Tatang whom you want, he left for a while, but he'll be coming back soon. Please sit down.'

The two men sat on a long wooden bench. The living room had no expensive furniture. There was just a table in the centre and two long benches near the opposite walls and three old chairs.

Mando and Magat barely noticed the surroundings. Like the eyes of a wild bird attracted by light, their eyes hardly left the girl. She was just wearing a plain house dress, but it only seemed to deepen her beauty.

To Magat, she was a rare orchid hidden under the leaves of a vine in a forest. Mando thought of the immaculate pearls in the treasure chest of Simoun.

'Such beauty, like that of a country flower,' thought Magat as he looked at the dreamy eyes and the deep dimples on her light olive cheeks.

Mando remembered Dolly Montero. Even though he never liked her, Mando could not deny that she was attractive, like a gaudy colour or a heady perfume. Dolly was like the sparkling champagne in a crystal goblet that one is tempted to drink in one gulp. But this young girl was different. Her purity and modesty were alluring, not intoxicating but enchanting. She was like a brilliant star peeping through the bank of clouds.

Mando stood up and introduced himself and Magat. 'I'm Mando Plaridel, and this is my friend, Magat. We're journalists from Manila.'

'Magat Dalisay, ma'am,' added the guerrilla.

'I'm the daughter of Pastor, the overseer. I'm called Puri.' Mando started in surprise when he heard the names.

'If this is Pastor's daughter, she must be my cousin,' he told himself.

Once more, he marvelled at his cousin's beauty.

XXI

Magat was not at all impatient while waiting for the overseer. *So what if he is delayed?* he told himself. He was immensely enjoying talking to Puri.

On the other hand, Mando would have dragged the minutes along, so Mang Pastor would come home at once. He was eager to know if this Pastor and this Puri were his uncle and cousin. They had not met for a long time, and he wanted to be sure.

Mando hesitated about what he should do, now that his original plan had changed after seeing Puri. On his way to the plantation, he thought only of Tata Pastor. Now he felt that his first concern had shifted to Puri. Should he make himself known, or should he keep his identity secret? Immediate recognition would bring the usual joy of a reunion among relatives long separated by the war. On the other hand, his secret might be exposed to the Monteros and the others, who considered him an enemy. Mando was still wracked with doubts when Pastor arrived.

The two guests stood up respectfully, and Puri told her father who they were. Mando tried to see in Pastor's face some resemblance to his mother.

'Sit down,' Pastor welcomed them after learning their purpose. 'Take these chairs.' And he brought the old chairs nearer.

'This is fine,' Magat declined and sat again on the bench. Mando did the same.

Pastor whispered to his daughter, who then went to the kitchen. The father took one of the chairs.

Magat continued the short explanation by Puri. He said they wanted to learn what was happening at the plantation and to expose the farmers' oppression.

'The problem of the workers is the problem of the nation,' said Magat, 'whether in the factory in the city or on the farm in the province. The worker sacrificed the most during the war. But what's his reward during times of peace?'

Pastor nodded several times. Mando looked at Pastor. Now he could see signs that this man and his late mother were indeed related.

'Good,' said Pastor, 'the tenants will be glad their case has caught the attention of those who live in the city. The plantation owner lives in the city. Perhaps you know him?'

'He is well-known, sir,' agreed Mando. 'Is he not Segundo Montero?'

'Yes,' Pastor added a slight correction, 'Don Segundo Montero.'

'As I've said,' Magat continued, 'the case of the worker is important. Social justice is concerned with the workers and the well-being of the nation.'

'I agree with you,' Pastor said.

'That is the mission of good newspapers, sir,' added Magat. 'Other Manila newspapers reported that troublemakers started the disorder in the plantation. That is also Montero's accusation. We want to know the truth, that's why we came. For our paper, truth comes first.'

'Perhaps I should not say this because I'm the overseer,' Pastor said gently. 'You should hear the leaders of the farm. But as you've said, truth comes first. We can't deny the farmers' oppression, sir.'

'That's your opinion,' said Magat. 'Haven't you said this to the owner?'

'Ay, it's just like talking to the deaf,' Pastor sighed. 'How many times have I told this to him? Every time I go to Manila. And what do I get? Scolding and blame. The last time he threatened that if his orders were not carried out, he would get another overseer. It's up to him.'

Pastor narrated that during the first months of the Japanese occupation, the overseer had insisted on a one-sided arrangement.

He stated bluntly that the harvest had to be increased because the Japanese needed it. 'But one night, the outlaws came, and the overseer simply vanished. I don't want that to happen to me. I've a daughter . . .'

Mando and Magat glanced at Puri, who was standing in the doorway.

The girl smiled.

Pastor went on.

'Might should end; right should prevail.'

'Have the people sought the government's help?' asked Mando.

'They're already fed up,' Pastor said. 'First, they went to the governor, who told them to be patient. Seeing that they were stubborn, he promised to talk to Don Segundo. But until now, there are still no results.'

'That's unfair,' said Magat.

'Because the governor and Don Segundo are like that,' Pastor entwined his two forefingers to show what he meant. 'So . . .'

'So, the tenants have lost their patience,' Magat said. Pastor nodded.

Puri came in and whispered to her father.

'Well, friends,' Pastor stood up. 'Let's have lunch first.'

Mando and Magat exchanged glances. They didn't realize it was already noontime.

'Oh no, thank you. We have to go,' Mando said.

'Thank you, sir, but we should not put you to any trouble,' said Magat.

'No trouble at all.' Pastor held Mando by the arm and moved towards the dining room. 'But do you eat milkfish in tamarind soup?'

'You don't have to ask,' Magat said. 'We were both in the mountains during the war.'

'Oh, guerrillas?'

'If that is still honourable, sir,' Magat answered.

'Then consider this house yours as well,' said Pastor.

The old man sat at the end of the table with the two on opposite sides. Puri stood by, ready to wait on them.

'Join us, daughter,' Pastor said.

'Yes, please,' urged Magat.

The girl first served them steaming rice, a cup each of the tamarind soup with a slice of milkfish and fish sauce in saucers. In the centre was a plate of beef jerky. Puri also set down glasses of water.

'I'm sorry we have no ice here,' she said, smiling. Then she sat at the other end.

'We also came from small villages,' Magat said.

'If you are guerrillas,' Pastor said, 'then perhaps, you've met my nephew, Andoy.' He looked at his two visitors.

'Andoy?' Magat repeated. Trying to remember, he puckered his lips and stared at the tiny holes in the thatched roof.

Mando drank water. He felt very hot indeed.

'He's about your age,' Pastor continued. 'When I last saw that boy, he was in his teens. The only child of my elder sister, who took care of me. He was living in Manila with the plantation owner. But he disappeared. There was news that he was taken by the Japanese military. Some said that he went to the mountains. We never saw each other again.' Pastor sighed. 'Poor boy.'

He stopped. His sorrow over his nephew's fate was obvious.

'No, I haven't met anyone named Andoy,' Magat said. 'How about you, Mando?' He turned to his friend.

Mando pretended to reflect, felt his scar, then exclaimed, 'Andoy! How could I forget Andoy? But we used to call him Andy. Tall and thin, but strong. Before the war, he was studying at university and lived with the family of Monte . . . Montero, that's it. That must be the same Don Segundo Montero.'

'Is he alive?' asked Pastor with eagerness in his voice.

'He was alive and well when we last met,' Mando said. 'He left for Infanta before the Japanese attacked Sampitan in 1944. When we parted our separate ways, he left a box with me and told me if I should go near the plains—for I was then assigned on secret missions here—I should ask around for his uncle named . . . Castor. Oh, yes, Pastor. He had a daughter who should be a young woman by now . . . He asked me to give him that box.'

'That's him,' Pastor said. 'Do you recall your Andoy, Puri?' he asked.

She nodded, her lips slightly parted.

'I've the box with me,' Mando said.

'What could it contain?' Pastor wondered aloud.

'He didn't say, sir, and I haven't opened it. I'll bring it soon,' he promised.

'Maybe I should go to your place, then,' Pastor offered. 'It's too much trouble . . .'

'Don't worry,' Mando said. 'The truth is, I've been remiss. I should have looked for you right away . . .' He looked at Puri's pretty face. She looked away.

Magat stared at Mando, puzzled. What is this story about Andoy and a box? But he knew that Mando had secrets, which he knew only because Mando had told him, such as the scar that was not there when they had first met.

XXII

After lunch, Mang Tomas and Danoy came, the eldest and youngest leaders of the farmers.

'We were passing by when we saw the Jeep,' Mang Tomas said. 'We thought there might be news about our petition.'

'It's lucky you passed by,' Pastor welcomed them. He introduced the two leaders to the guests from Manila.

'They want to get information about what is happening here,' he added.

'Really, we came to see you,' said the *Kampilan* editor.

Mang Tomas and Danoy were delighted to learn that Mando and Magat were the publisher and editor of the paper which was read by many people in the agricultural regions. When they were already seated around the table, Mang Tomas related the story of the present conflict at the plantation. Danoy added to the explanation.

'We inherited this problem from our parents and Mr Montero, from the former owners,' said Mang Tomas.

'An old issue which was left hanging for many years, but with an easy solution if we want it. Just one word: justice.'

Magat pointed out that justice is often seen according to the colour of the viewer's glasses.

'Real justice is not changed by the colour of one's glasses,' said Mang Tomas. 'What is the basis of our petition?'

From his pocket, he got an old wallet and took out an envelope that had turned yellow with age. He brought out a newspaper clipping with letters that were already hardly readable. It was a news item with a photograph of Manuel Quezon, the first president of the Commonwealth.

'This is the basis of our petition.' He handed the clipping to Mando. 'The late President Quezon was also a landowner; he had lands in Arayat,' related Mang Tomas. 'A few years before the war, he gathered his tenants and voluntarily gave this charter. A bible of harmonious relationships on the farms. So I always carry it.'

Mando handed the item to Magat, who calmly read it.

'Please read it out aloud,' asked Mang Tomas. Magat read the following paragraphs:

Friends: The term *Kasama* (tenant), which is the Tagalog word for the tiller of the land, means sharer, and this title which we inherited from our ancestors gives the true spirit and meaning of the relationship between landowner and farmer.

For, in fact and in law, they are sharers. The landowner puts in his capital, which is the land; the tenant tills this and they then share the harvest.

At first, the tenant was not just a sharer, but he and his family were regarded as relatives.

This is a human and profitable relation. However, as time passed, because of avarice and greed, the landlords took advantage of the tenant. The tenant was cheated of the fruits of his labour through various means, the most common being the high interest for his debts.

Pastor said, 'Quezon had a deep understanding of history.'

'He knew how to look back on the past,' said Mang Tomas. Magat continued his reading:

For many years, we owned this land, but we did nothing. One reason why my wife and I wanted to own land was because we wanted to show by deed what we preached regarding the relation of the landlord to his tenant. Example is always better than words.

We will be real sharers; we shall give you work animals. You will pay
for them on a yearly instalment, but those who are industrious in tilling
the soul and caring for the water buffaloes will get back the amount
they paid.

First, we shall erase your old debts. Those who have debts to the
former owners have no more accounts with us, although in the sale,
these debts are included and transferred to us.

Any debts you might have with us in the future, like advance
payment for your food, clothes, rice, and money, if repaid in rice, will
be according to current market prices. However, we shall not lend you
money for gambling.

Mando's laughter was contagious. 'That's the weakness of the
poor—gambling,' he said.

'The government should be blamed for the spread of gambling,'
said Magat. 'All big-time gambling is licensed: sweepstakes, horse
racing, jai alai, cockfighting.'

'And small-town lottery,' said Pastor.

'It's tolerated by officials who accept bribes,' answered Magat.
After a brief exchange of words, he continued reading:

We will give every family half a hectare of land that you can plant with
vegetables or bananas or use for poultry and pig-raising. We will make
improvements to increase the harvest, but you will not spend a centavo.

If you have any complaints, you can bring them to either Mrs
Quezon or to me. And if we don't give you justice, you can then go to
court. For, like all citizens, we are under the power of the court if we
break the law.

Be industrious and work hard. Consider the fields you till your
own, for you can depend on this land as long as you wish and while you
fulfil your responsibilities according to our agreement.

Here you are free to become Communists, Socialists, Popular
Front, or anything. Even though I'm a Nationalist, you don't have to
join my party or vote for its candidate.

I will do the best for you. Besides giving you what is according to
law, I will reward you if you work hard.

But remember that no one who does not strive will get anything
from me. No one has a right to live on another's sweat.

'Hear that,' Mang Tomas repeated, stressing each word, '"No one
has a right to live on another's sweat." Is that not lacking among the
Segundo Monteros?'

'But he's a capitalist,' Mando mocked.

'So, the product of our toil belongs to the capitalist?' asked
Mang Tomas.

'According to law, the landowner has a right—'

'To live on another's toil?' Mang Tomas sneered. 'To make a
profit, too.'

'Let's finish this.' Magat read the last part:

We shall be real partners and sharers. What is good for you is good
for me, and what is good for me is good for you. By means of this
understanding, we shall be not merely partners, but we will be friends.

'Truly, Quezon had no peer in his time,' said Pastor.

'If Quezon, the landlord, could do that before the war,' Mang
Tomas declared. 'Why can't other landlords do it now? It needs only a
little consideration.'

'Therein lies the difficulty—consideration,' said Magat.

'Or fear,' warned Danoy.

'What I like best is freedom in politics, that anyone is free to be a
nationalist or a Communist,' said Danoy.

At this point, they heard someone call out. Puri went to see who it
was and returned at once.

'It's Dr Sabio,' she said. 'He's looking for you, Mr Plaridel.' The
professor followed Puri. Pastor and Mando stood up.

'Come in, Doctor,' Pastor welcomed him.

'Doctor, I knew you'd come,' Mando greeted him happily. He
introduced him to the group as the president of Freedom University,
a learned sympathizer of tenants, who planned to buy the Montero
Plantation, among others.

'What for?' asked Mang Tomas regarding the plan to buy the plantation.

'For the sake of farmers and the country,' Mando answered promptly.

'We shall discuss that,' added Dr Sabio.

When everyone was seated, Magat told Dr Sabio about their talk on the late President Quezon's agreement with his tenants in Arayat. Mando took the clipping from Magat and gave it to Dr Sabio.

'I'm familiar with this,' said the professor, glancing at the old clipping. 'He's an example of a good plantation owner,' he added. 'During his time and in the face of the anomalous practices of most landowners, Quezon's terms were just.'

'They're really good,' cut in Mang Tomas, who was so used to unfair treatment.

'But during these times, they are no longer ideal,' said Dr Sabio. 'Quezon's justice was based on paternalism. In spite of all his kindness as the father of a family, he was still the landowner and the tenant only shared in the plantation. His capital was the land, which he bought for a fixed amount, while the investment of the tenants was their strength, their very lives. But in the end, he got an equal share with each tenant. If he had a hundred tenants, he would receive a hundred shares, while the tenant got nothing but a part of his labour.'

'Nevertheless,' Dr Sabio added, 'President Quezon himself said that in the struggle between the right to life and the right to property, the right to life should prevail. That was the basis of his programme of social justice, although even now, in our courts, the right of property always wins.'

The farmers were amazed at the logic of the president of Freedom University. He was very bright, indeed; they were convinced and ready to listen to him.

'The ideal land system at this time,' continued Dr Sabio, 'is for the tiller of the land to be the owner, or he should have a greater share of the harvest. Not based on one or separate parcels, as is the practice in our provinces, but by means of cooperatives. A cooperative is a kind of association owned by everyone who lives and works on farms. The organization spends, but the harvest is for all the members, with equal shares and no landowner to monopolize it. The storehouse is the property of the association, which is made up of all the former tenants, not just one plantation owner or his family.'

'That has long been our dream,' said Mang Tomas, 'but we don't know how to carry it out. First, we don't have any right over the land; second, where would we get the capital?'

'That will be the role of Freedom University,' replied Dr Sabio. 'The university will put up the capital. It will collect its capital, but little by little, and the tenants will hardly feel it. The cooperative will manage the plantation.'

The farmer leaders were for Dr Sabio's plan and were ready to help carry it out.

'That's the only proper solution,' said Dr Sabio, 'not only in agriculture but also in large industries. Change the old system. Reap and produce to take care of everyone's needs, instead of just to enrich a few.'

'I think that's socialism,' said Danoy.

'Yes, more or less,' agreed the professor. 'Socialism means ownership by the state of all means of production and of production itself, to be used for the good of the country. At present, society is divided into two classes with conflicting interests. The first class lives and becomes rich from owning the means of production, like land, mines, factories, electricity, transportation and raw materials. This is the capitalist class. The second is the labouring class, which is used by the capitalists to serve them. In other words, the capitalist class buys labour at a low price; that is, the first buys the second, not for the whole of production, but only for the time he works. The capitalist then pockets the profit.'

He added, 'On the other hand, the labourer lives by the sweat on his brow. There are different types of labourers, but most use their arms or their brains. The condition of the intellectual labourer is a little better, but they are also workers. They produce garments, houses, medicine, cars, radio, television, refrigerators, office papers and more. But because their pay is not enough, they're always in need. Often, they can't buy or enjoy their products. For under capitalism, it's not the ones who work themselves to the bone who earn much and profit, but those who own more and don't sweat, and live in luxury and ease.'

'Just look at the Montero family,' Pastor said.

'All the Segundo Monteros,' corrected Dr Sabio.

The brilliant educator cited some examples of the sudden wealth of the Segundo Monteros. He described the outright exploitation in factories and business firms, where labourers and employees work from ten to twelve hours, which is illegal, and are paid beggars' wages. The capitalists know that four to five hours of work from each labourer is enough to finish work equal to his pay. Thus, his production during the extra five to six hours is free and is the sole profit of the capitalist. If he has a hundred labourers, the capitalist gains 500 hours a day. Thus, he receives for free the produce of a hundred labourers for 500 hours.

Dr Sabio added that the small salary becomes even less, for the money is just enough to meet only his basic needs.

'Money in itself has no value,' said Dr Sabio. 'But it's important because it buys the family's needs. While prices of goods are high, as they are now, the value of money becomes less. Under socialism . . .'

Mang Tomas cut in, 'But it is often said that socialism is a dream which cannot be realized, a . . .' Mang Tomas groped for the right word.

'Utopia,' said Mando.

'Utopia?' asked Dr Sabio. 'Because they don't want change; they fear change. The leeches and fleas who live by sucking others' blood die when there is no more blood. It's the same with those who have become rich and fat by exploiting their fellow men.'

The professor went on. 'Of course, we should not hope that socialism will cure all problems. But without a doubt, it will lessen the suffering of many—unemployment, hunger, sickness, ignorance, superstition and crime. Excessive opportunism will be stopped. Food, clothes, medicine and other prime commodities will be for the people's use, not to make millions for the greedy few.

'A five- to ten-year economic programme will regulate the production of many prime commodities. Thus, it will stop anarchy and monopoly in the industry in this system called free enterprise, where production is based on what will net more profit and not on what is more needed by the public. For example, why do we have a shortage of rice, fish and meat, which are the Filipinos' food? In a socialist system, the citizens' needs will be given priority, instead of the interests of the small band of industrialists and businessmen. The real profit will not be the money hoarded in the bags of the rich or as additional tools of production, but the consumer's comfort.'

'Therefore, socialism is good,' said the three farmer leaders, seemingly in unison.

Dr Sabio had hardly caught his breath when Mang Tomas asked for another favour.

'Please explain communism to us. We are often called communists, and we don't know why. Is it communism to join a fraternity? To protect ourselves against a bad landowner? Is it communism to protest against the cruelty of the soldiers and the civilian guards? To vote contrary to the order of the landowner and against their candidates? Dr Sabio, we are often caught, jailed, or beaten up for these things, for they claim that these are what the communists do.'

Dr Sabio frowned, shook his head, and answered slowly. 'Unfortunately, communism is misunderstood not only by you, but also by the soldiers and civilian guards hired by those in power. Ignorance is widespread and it's dangerous.' The professor stressed the last. 'What you are doing is not communism, and you aren't communists. These are all rights guaranteed by our constitution and the laws of the land. These are the inherent freedoms of people in a democracy, in a government set up for the good of the country. But you're threatened, and force is used so you won't fight for your rights. They just want labour to remain docile and ignorant.'

'Then, what is communism?' asked Mang Tomas.

Dr Sabio looked around before speaking. 'Well, the answer is probably known to our friends, Mando and Magat. It should also be made known to all labour leaders and labourers. The word communism is older than Christ, for in ancient Greece, there was already a class of communists who didn't allow private property. Just think, private property was illegal. But the modern Marxist communist is different. The philosopher Karl Marx talked about this in his book, *Das Kapital*. Marx was a German who spent most of his life in England. His close collaborator, Frederick Engels, grew up in Manchester, England, so *Das Kapital* and their combined work, the *Communist Manifesto*, was based on the social conditions in England before the Industrial Revolution. Thus, communism is not a Russian ideology; rather, the Union of Soviet Socialist Republics was a result of this ideology. Marx traced the roots of capitalism to the profit accumulated from the exploitation of labour. Marx complained that many learned men gave too much importance to the world; for him, it's the world that should be changed. What resulted was a new kind of communism, which is called scientific Marxism, or revolutionary communism.'

Dr Sabio paused and asked, 'Do you follow me?'

'It's very clear, Doctor,' said Mang Tomas. Pastor and Danoy nodded.

'As I have said,' continued the professor, 'communism is revolutionary, while socialism is somewhat evolutionary. The aim of the first is to grab power from society or the state by means of class struggle or by revolution. When it gains power, it will establish the dictatorship of the labouring class, based on the principle that being the majority, they produce all the goods. The rich and poor classes will be abolished, as well as capitalists and measly wages. The goal is to establish what you often hear—a classless society, which aims for equality.'

The professor cleared his throat and looked at Mang Tomas.

'Before, this state was called a utopia or a dream, as you noted a while ago. But now, it's a reality. There is the Soviet Union, and we have heard of the People's Republic of China. Like twin world powers, they compare with the US, but it is misleading to compare the present strength of these two camps. For America, the most prosperous of the capitalist states, is at its peak, while the Soviet Union is just starting, crippled by two world wars. Hardly half a century has passed since the revolution against the Tsar's empire in 1917.'

'What then is the difference between socialism and capitalism?' asked Pastor.

'Socialism has many forms. With the loss of the people's belief in kings, and when science proved that these kings were not sons of heaven, the republic was born and people raised the banner of socialism. There are still kings in Scandinavia, but their framework of government is now socialist. Quite a few are called Christian Socialists. Socialism has also risen in Britain and is now found in Indonesia, India and some new

African states after they got rid of colonialism. Britain and India have not gone far from utopian socialism. Their steps are careful because the conservatives are still powerful. Some means of production have been bought and are now run by the government, but most are losing enterprises. The transfer of power is through democratic process, by election or expropriation. There is no plan to have a dictatorship of the proletariat.'

'Sir, why are the Soviet Union and China also called socialist countries?' Danoy asked.

'Because both follow Marxist socialism or scientific socialism. Both are moving towards communism, which depends on revolution, the downfall of capitalism not just in one country, but everywhere. That is why even if there are similarities in their policies on ownership of means of production, socialism and communism differ in methods and goals. Thus, they are often close rivals, like India and China. At any rate, they have similar aims—to expect the citizen to give his best to the state and to receive from the state according to his need.'

'Doctor, you mentioned revolution. Is that what we often hear—a peaceful or bloodless revolution?' Danoy asked in a puzzled tone.

'The term peaceful or bloodless revolution comes from reformers, who are also for the status quo. They think that illness can be cured by band-aid treatments. Give a dog more food, and it won't bark any more. Loosen the prisoner's chains, and he won't grab a knife. But how can bloodshed be avoided in a revolution, when the very defenders of the status quo—the heads of the establishments, capitalists, landlords, the financiers and monopolists, aristocrats and their tools—the army, the police and other armed forces—are the first to use force? Just look at the strikes, demonstrations, and picket lines; those in power show violence. Would they be calm during a real revolution? A revolution has to be bloody, not because of those who seek justice but because of the cruelty of the enemies of change.'

'So, is peaceful revolution just an empty phrase?'

'A phrase of the turncoat politicians who are for both sides; of priests who don't fear God; of the greedy who want to halt progress.'

Mang Tomas, Danoy and Pastor looked at each other and thought about Dr Sabio's words. Each one wondered whether the professor wanted a revolution or was merely stating an observation. Danoy broke the silence with a question.

'Then, Professor, do you feel that because of the unfortunate events after the war, one of which is the land problem, we cannot avoid this bloody revolution?'

Dr Sabio hesitated, but after a while, he answered quietly. 'There are two inevitable laws, my friends,' he said. 'These are evolution and revolution. Both of them mean change. Evolution is slow, while revolution is like a big and sudden leap. A socialist revolution, which is surely what you have in mind, is the revolt of a class against the opposing class. The aim is to change the old framework and set up a progressive one. But to succeed, first it needs the disenchantment of the majority with the existing conditions; and second, the weakness of the power to be replaced. This is called a "revolutionary situation". When this situation comes, then the powder keg of the struggle happens. This was the scenario in the Philippines when Bonifacio started the Revolution of 1896.'

When Dr Sabio paused, Pastor spoke. 'In your opinion, what is a good system of government for the Filipinos? Would socialism be right for us?'

Everyone's attention was focused on the president of Freedom University.

'That's a good question, and a timely one as well. But you, Pastor, Mang Tomas and Danoy, should answer it. For a long time, you have worked on the land under a landlord, and you have experienced oppression. It is the same with workers in factories, shops, mines, sugar mills, and business firms. They work long hours and have meagre wages. All profits go to the capitalists. In socialism, all means of production are state-owned; the state is the whole nation and its government. In installing leaders, there is also a big difference when compared to personality politics, which is the termite in a democracy. In our democracy, all important government positions are monopolized by the powerful—Malacañang Palace, Congress, the judiciary and the army. Because money is powerful, as are mass media, which act as messengers for all sorts of propaganda.'

He sighed and glanced at the others, who all seemed to agree.

'On the one hand,' Dr Sabio said, 'any system of government is not a cure-all. Every country has its specific set of problems. We should always consider the conditions, customs, habits, education, culture, religion and, especially, the economy of the country and its people. We can be sure that the kind of socialism that meets the conditions of our country will be a greater blessing than the promises of democratic capitalism, which is only for a small group. We can't deny that the unity of the Filipinos during the revolution against Spain and the war against the United States has been torn apart by two opposing classes.'

They were so engrossed in the lecture that they didn't notice that it was almost dusk, until Puri came with refreshments.

'I'm sure this can't compare with your discussion,' she remarked as she served the guests.

'We shall have another talk, then,' Mando said, ending the meeting.

'Thank you. We learnt a lot,' Mang Tomas said.

After some more exchange of views, the three guests from Manila started to leave.

'We shall publish your side in the *Kampilan*,' said Magat.

'Our side,' corrected Pastor.

'Yes, our side,' repeated Magat.

Mando went to Puri and thanked her. He held her hand for a long time as he said goodbye.

'I will return soon,' he said, 'and bring your cousin's gift.'

'It's up to you.' Her lips were like twin rose petals as she smiled. Her gentle eyes revealed that she would be waiting for his return.

XXIII

After a few days, Mando returned to the plantation alone. He drove the Jeep straight into the yard.

Before he got off, Pastor graciously met him.

'Good morning,' greeted the overseer. 'What has brought you here?'

'I brought your nephew's package.'

'Oh.' Pastor asked him to come in. He looked up the stairway and called his daughter.

'Puri,' he said, 'we have a guest.' He turned to Mando. 'I told you not to trouble yourself.'

'It's no bother. Anyway, I have the Jeep.'

Upstairs, Puri knew who the guest was. She heard the sound of the Jeep and looked out the window. She hurriedly fixed herself, changed her dress and powdered her face a little.

'Puri,' her father called again.

'I'm coming, Tatang.' And she went down. She shook hands with Mando.

'You are alone,' she said.

'I didn't come for news; my trip is personal,' said Mando with a smile.

'He brought Andoy's package,' Pastor told her.

On the table was a small box wrapped in newspapers. Mando got it and handed it to Pastor, who turned it over to Puri. She held it, looked at it, and then returned it to her father.

152

'Why don't you open it?' Mando said. 'I've had it for years.'

Carefully, Pastor removed the wrapping, as if he was afraid it would be torn. It was an ordinary cardboard box. Pastor removed the cover. Inside was a small package wrapped in silver foil, the kind used for cigarettes. A folded note was attached to it by a rubber band. Pastor opened the note and read.

August 1944
Dear Tata Pastor,

Nanang told me before she died to regard you as my parent. However, events have kept me from seeing you for a long time.

Now I am with the guerrillas in the Sierra Madre. Only God knows the fate of one who defends his country.

In my sleep, I see Nanang, and she says your name.

I leave with my comrade, Mando, this small token for you and my cousin, who must be grown up by now. He often goes to the plains, so I asked him to look for you. May this at least show that I think of you as Nanang had wished.

Your nephew kisses your hand,
Andoy

After Pastor read the letter aloud, tears welled in his eyes. Puri was crying.

'Where could he be? Is he still alive?' he asked, his voice filled with anxiety. Mando was just silent.

Then Pastor opened the package. He and Puri were amazed. The package contained money—plenty of money. Twenty- and ten-peso bills with 'Victory' stamped on them. While Pastor was counting, a small object fell on the floor. It was a ring. He picked it up.

He held it with his thumb and forefinger, then he showed it to Mando and Puri.

'A diamond ring!' exclaimed Pastor.

He handed it to his daughter. Puri's eyes widened.

'Please wear it,' said Mando.

Puri appeared shy, so Mando took the ring and put it on her left middle finger. Puri wanted to draw back her hand, but Mando held it firmly.

'There!' he exclaimed, 'it fits perfectly.'

Puri felt uneasy and immediately removed the ring. She was blushing and then spoke in a tone of protest, 'I don't want to wear it. People might think that I already have a sweetheart.' She pouted.

'Don't you?' asked Mando.

'No.' The girl blushed deeper.

Puri seemed embarrassed, but Mando was obviously pleased. After removing the ring, she handed it back to her father.

'Use it or keep it,' said Pastor. 'It is for you.'

'It fits,' added Mando.

Pastor finished counting the bills. 1,000. He glanced at the ring glinting in Puri's hand.

'Where did Andoy get this money and that ring?' The joy in his eyes dimmed. 'Weren't the guerrillas poor, with hardly any food?' he asked.

'Not after the submarines came,' Mando said. 'The paper bills marked "Victory" were brought by the Americans and given as advance payment to the guerrillas. The ring was given by a family whom Andoy had saved from the Japanese soldiers.'

'I see.' And Pastor's eyes brightened again. A slight smile appeared on Puri's lips.

'I wonder how much this ring would cost?' said Pastor.

'I heard Andoy say it cost 3,000 pesos.'

'Good Lord! That's a fortune,' exclaimed Pastor.

'Then I really can't wear it, if it's that expensive,' said Puri.

'Why not?' asked Mando.

'People in the village might think I'm showing off. You know how people talk.'

'As long as it's not stolen, there's nothing to fear,' Pastor said.

'In Manila, the newly rich wear very large diamonds. Good if they became rich through hard work.' Mando was thinking of some people who had bought Simoun's jewels.

'Even then,' Puri still refused. 'A simple girl's hand should not be covered in jewels, but should be used for work.'

'The hands of one who works have more right to wear jewels,' Mando said.

'And to hold money,' Pastor added.

Finally, Puri agreed to keep the ring, because it was her cousin's gift, her cousin whose fate they worried about.

'What could have happened to that boy?' Pastor asked. 'Have you had any news since you separated?' Pastor asked Mando.

'None. I have a hunch, though, that he is still alive,' Mando answered. 'He could have joined the US Army during liberation. I would not be surprised if Andoy were among the guerrillas sent to America.'

'May God bless that boy.'

Mando told them of his plan to travel, perhaps the following week. 'It's for the newspaper,' he explained to Pastor.

'That is a long time,' said Pastor when he learnt Mando would be gone for two or three years.

'Travel is easy these days,' said Mando. 'One can reach any place in thirty-six hours. Wherever I am, I can come home at once, if necessary. About the farmers' petition on the plantation, even if I'm far away . . .'

'Many people are now feeling bad,' Pastor said. 'I'm not sure I'll stay as overseer. I've been offered a parcel of land at the edge of the village. I might buy it with Andoy's money. Puri and I can stay there.'

'That's a good plan. Besides the move of the farmer's federation, a Filipino corporation wants to buy the plantation, the same corporation that owns Freedom University in Manila. Oh, yes, you have met Dr Sabio. They plan to set up a big laboratory at the plantation, to improve the harvest and the farmers' condition.'

'Yes, I remember his plans,' said Pastor.

'So, if the plantation can be bought from Montero, they will then put in place a modern programme. The former tenants will remain under good terms. Meanwhile, they will assign land, students and agricultural experts to help the farmers. In short, as the students learn agriculture and sociology, they also help boost the farmers' living conditions.

In the final analysis, more than agricultural land, the farmers need a just share of the fruits of their toil. Is that not so, sir?'

'Only the blind won't see that truth. Because the tenants of Don Segundo are fed up, many want to go to Mindanao if they can get homesteads there. Or to try their fortune on the plantations in Hawaii or California. They go wherever they can live in comfort.'

'Even Mindanao is now owned by big landowners, mostly high government officials,' said Mando. 'During the past fifty years, many homesteaders went there, sweated blood clearing the forest and the mountains, until they died from hardship and sickness. Later, their children learnt that the land they and their parents cultivated for years was titled in the name of persons with high positions. In the end, many were jailed or even killed, for they refused to leave the land.'

'Why does God allow such evil?' Pastor said.

'About the plan to go to Hawaii or California,' Mando explained, 'they should know that there is no shortage of labour there. The US is near Mexico, where they could get workers besides their fifteen million black people, aside from the Chinese, Japanese, Cubans, Porto Ricans and other races.

But the Filipino receives the lowest pay among all the foreigners, which is still better than the conditions in the Philippines. I think the Filipino farmer should not go to other lands, for wherever he goes, he will be enslaved by exploiters. He should stay here where he has invested much and fight for his rights.'

'By nature, the Filipino farmer is peaceful,' Pastor said. 'He wants to avoid quarrels. But he is not a coward. There is no farmer's house without a machete for chopping wood. At times, this can be used to split the skull of the wicked.'

When a shareholder came to see Pastor, Puri came in from the kitchen to be with Mando while her father was busy.

'Please stay for lunch, sir,' Puri asked Mando. 'Thank you for your trouble coming here, although you are a busy man.'

'It's a pleasure. Here, I can enjoy the fresh air.'

Puri glanced at her father and his guest in the doorway. She and Mando were seated at the table facing each other.

'During my travels, I shall write to you whenever I can, if it won't bother you.'

'It might be a bother to you,' said Puri, 'to be wasting time on a nobody from the village. When you're there, it won't be likely that you will remember us.'

'I won't say you think low of me,' Mando reproached her, 'for you have a noble heart. But if I did not forget your cousin's request after three years, although I had not met you, how can I forget you when I'm gone, now that I have promised it?'

'Because there are so many pleasures there,' Puri said, 'beautiful views, various forms of entertainment, such lovely women.'

'I will travel not for pleasure or amusement,' Mando said. 'And regarding beautiful women, no one can hold a candle to you.'

Puri stood up and was about to leave, but Mando held her hand. Pastor and his guest had their backs turned.

'Promise me,' asked Mando, 'that when I return, you will be the same Puri.'

'Why should I promise?' she pretended not to understand.

'Because . . .'

Just then, Mando heard Pastor call his name. The guest had already gone.

So Mando said goodbye as well and could not be prevailed upon to stay for lunch.

'I shall write often,' he addressed the two, but his eyes were only on Puri.

'God be with you in your travels,' Pastor said. 'Let us know in case you meet my nephew.'

'You can count on it . . .' He bade them farewell and waved as his Jeep left the yard.

XXIV

Mando Plaridel was travelling outside the Philippines for the first time. He climbed the steps to the aeroplane without looking back. There was no announcement about his leaving, so no one except Magat and Andres saw him off at the airport. He would travel alone. He brought some letters from Dr Sabio. The professor had stayed long in Europe and America before the Second World War. Before the plane took off, Mando fastened the seatbelt. Just once, he peeped through the small, thick glass window and saw a group of people waving to the passengers. Magat and Andres stood apart from the crowd.

In two days, Mando would arrive on the other side of the world. The plane would make several stopovers in Eastern Europe. He would get off in Madrid.

Mando brought most of Simoun's jewels. He left the rest with Tata Matias.

Mando had secret partitions made at the bottom of two large portable suitcases where he hid the jewels.

Even if the suitcases were examined, these would not be noticed, unless they were slashed. But this was not done unless the traveller was under a cloud of suspicion.

Mando travelled for two reasons: first, to sell the jewellery at the best price; second, to study and observe. Mando wanted to deepen his storehouse of knowledge and experience.

He realized he was young and still had many things to learn. He had a vast and ambitious programme. It was his duty to prepare for it; but first, he had to prepare himself. He had vast sums of money, but money was only one of his tools. If he lacked preparation, strength and vision, the money might even lead to ruin.

Among other things, he wanted to learn more about organizing a modern newspaper: low-cost printing, efficient and fast distribution and marketing. He also wanted to learn how to print cheaper books, which Mando planned to do when he returned.

He also wanted to observe new methods of raising animals, how to shorten the time so there could be earlier gains.

He would learn about cooperatives, how the farmers could enjoy the fruits of their toil without being exploited. What he wanted was practical learning and best practices, not untried theories. He believed theory should be based on specific experiences, not on opinions. Otherwise, a theory would remain floating only in the mind.

Some months before he left, Mando had quietly sold some of the jewellery. From these, he had gathered funds for his trip and the press.

He made some discreet enquiries about those who had amassed wealth during the Japanese times and liberation. The bloated ones had hurriedly bought lands, houses, and jewellery.

One of those approached by Mando's agent was Doña Julia. Her mouth watered each time she touched the veritable garden of jewellery laid before her eyes. But her throat went dry when she heard the prices. Her 10,000 pesos was only able to buy one ring with a gem as big as a cat's eye shimmering in the dark.

A well-known woman who belonged to the upper crust, one of those whom Doña Julia had mentioned to Dolly, wanted the three perfectly cut diamonds, but did not want large ones. She could not let them go, just as she could not let go of a sugar baron, her lover. More so when she learnt that the Maharajah of India had offered 12,000 pounds sterling for the item. At the equivalent of even four dollars to a pound, the rate of exchange after the Second World War, the piece of jewellery would be worth 90,000 Philippine pesos.

The woman was apparently fascinated by the first customer's identity. She asked for a few days, for her sugar daddy was not yet in Manila. The next week, she heard that a famous foreign actress, a friend of a shipping magnate, was looking at the gems. The sugar daddy's mistress was vexed and told the agent to get them at once. She immediately bought them for 50,000 pesos.

Mando agreed to the price because he needed the money immediately. A Cabinet member bought a ring for 7,000 pesos.

'For his wife?' Mando asked his agent.

'For his secretary.'

'So the Cabinet member is rich, hmm?'

'It's his wife who is rich, but she looks like a Japanese tank. Naturally, she doesn't know that the 7,000 pesos was used to buy a solitaire for his private secretary.'

There was also a matron noted for her long experience as a connoisseur of art, and her short experience as an actress. Her husband was a millionaire who collected relics. She bought a ring of a former general of Alexander the Great. She paid 1,000 pesos for the ring, which she later gave to a young and handsome army officer, who was her secret lover.

The matron and the gallant officer became close during several relief operations in the rural areas after the devastating floods and tropical cyclones, according to gossip. The operations for charity became romantic operations. Both risked their names and positions, and met in various places in Baguio, Tagaytay, Hong Kong. Their affair certainly created a stir.

'The matron said that her husband is gay and not circumcised,' said a rumour monger.

'Then how come they have three children? Or is it four?'

'Well, even gay men have penises. But how do we know who the real fathers are?'

'But the officer is also married.'

'You mean, he has a collection; a complete collection.'

'Oh, these women. The moment the itch starts . . .'

'They'll die for their desires. But a woman goes wrong because of the man. If he knows how to hold the reins, the horse won't buck.'

'Then, it's up to the jockey on the horse, ha?'

'On the rider and on the horse. They should be an equal match.'

The two gossips laughed, noting where the talk about the ring had led.

Two other buyers were also mentioned. The first was a senator who chose a bracelet with stunning rubies and emeralds. He gave it to a popular matron who belonged to the upper crust. This woman, noted for her beauty in her prime, was the daughter of a low-ranking employee. She married a wealthy businessman, a semi-invalid, so that, like D.H. Lawrence's Lady Chatterley, she was thirsty even if she were surrounded by water. And she fell for the senator, who was supposed to be a stud. But the bracelet bought by the senator was only a token. The matron reciprocated with gifts double the price, which were also bought from Mando.

But the most unusual sale was that of a circle of five society matrons who bought wholesale a set consisting of a gold ring with five small diamonds, a man's bracelet, cuff links, and a tie pin with five rubies. This did not seem extraordinary, unless one knew the reason and the recipient.

The five matrons, in a reversal of the usual situation, took care of a gigolo. A young *mestizo*, tall and robust, with hard muscles and sturdy arms and knees. He did not finish his studies, but he could speak fluent Spanish and English. He did nothing but keep his body in good condition, his chest like a hard shield. He was supported by the five matrons, whose ages ranged from forty to fifty. They paid for his apartment, bought him a second-hand car and in addition to household expenses, he received a monthly allowance of 500 pesos.

His role was to sleep with each of them once a week in his apartment. One was scheduled for a day from Monday to Friday with a special benefit on Saturdays, when each took turns. His Sundays were free; Sunday was for his real girlfriend, a sexy mestiza, who was none other than Lilibeth.

Like a jockey, he rode six different horses, seven days and nights, so he knew the various ways of horse riding. Some were hot and eager, ready to gallop two miles, non-stop; some wanted to have sex only for a short time, but flamed like a dynamo. While he gave pleasure to the five in a replica of the Marquis de Sade's harem, he was made happy by his own client, Lilibeth, the whole day and night every Sunday in his apartment.

The husbands of the five were all rich and well-known, but just as man does not live by bread alone, a woman is not made happy by money alone. Sex is needed now and then by a healthy woman, just as a plant needs the nourishment of water and sunlight.

Of the five, one or two had insatiable sexual appetites and would look for other partners in bed. If the mestizo were to be interviewed, he would likely tattle about the likes, ways, and hunger of the daughters of Eve, just like Dr Kinsey's famous survey on sex.

This seemed natural to them, unnoticed by their husbands and social circles. In fact, they were always present at social gatherings like the frequent parties for those who were leaving or just arriving. They always looked happy in the group pictures that appeared on the society pages of the newspapers. 'If the jewellery on the lovely women and handsome men could tell their stories,' said Mando, 'there would be a reenactment of Jehovah's anger against Sodom and Gomorrah.'

'The stories from *One Thousand and One Nights* are nothing compared to this,' answered the agent with a laugh.

Mando sold the other pieces to a number of wealthy people for about half a million pesos.

XXV

Dolly's ordeal was finally over. The seed in her womb had been secretly put away in the hospital in Hong Kong. As her mother had said, this also happened to many other women of the upper crust in Manila and some Visayan cities. They were maidens only in name.

'You can count the virgins on your fingers,' said Doña Julia, whose ears were keen on such gossip.

Dolly was back to her old self. She was whole again. After her 'vacation', she wanted to return to Manila. Her health did not suffer and she felt good. She did not even have a scratch on any part of her body.

But Doña Julia would not allow it and asked Dolly to go to Europe instead and tour its famous cities. She also advised her daughter to stay in Paris and study fashion or interior decoration. Then she could come home when their mansion was already finished.

Dolly agreed; Doña Julia supposed that her heart had not yet healed as quickly as her figure, which had regained its freshness. Besides, her studying in Europe would erase any suspicion from their friends because of their sudden trip to Hong Kong.

So Dolly went to Europe and Doña Julia returned alone to Manila. On her return, she told Don Segundo that Dolly would study in Paris. Dolly had written of the same to her father.

'Why didn't you go with your daughter to Paris?' asked Don Segundo, who had no idea what had happened in Hong Kong.

Doña Julia answered, kissing Don Segundo's cheek, that she was also thinking of him, who was all alone in Manila.

Those days, Montero was busy renovating his mansion in Singalong. He had signed a contract with a young architect, the Chinese mestizo Pong Tua-son. He was the son of the businessman Son Tua, who was well-known in the Chinese community and to the authorities in Metro Manila.

Rumours had it that Son Tua arrived at a southern port wearing a pigtail. He came from Sungsong, stowed inside a large crate of goods. He left China with the help of a port guard who had taken a bribe from an old Chinese man in the Philippines. Son Tua served this Chinese until he grew up. When the old man died, Son Tua left for Manila to try his luck.

Son Tua had his start buying old furniture and was known as a junkman. After some years of hard work, he opened his own textile store.

He married a young, childless widow who had inherited some property from her first husband.

Son Tua bolstered the widow's assets, sold the textile store, and started a den for opium and gambling. In this business, he became close to the high government officials in Manila and the nearby provinces.

The role he played during the war was not very clear, but it was rumoured that he had associated with both the Americans and the Japanese. After the war, he was already a millionaire, just like Don Segundo Montero.

Pong Tua-son was one of the many children of Son Tua and the widow. He easily made a name for himself, for his fees were lower than the others, and he had quick access to construction materials. The children had reversed their father's name to Tua-son. Their rise in society was as fast as that of an elevator in a new building.

One of the Tua-son girls married a rising army officer, Major Bayoneta. He became a collaborator after coming from the Capas detention camp and even became a general, two years after liberation. Another daughter married a prosecutor. As for Pong, it was said that he only had moist eyes for Dolly.

Don Segundo asked Pong to give his best at building his mansion on his old lot in Singalong. 'The most beautiful house in the Philippines.

That is what I want,' Montero told Pong as he looked over the old house, which was still in good condition.

'I'll do as you wish, Don Segundo,' said Pong. 'It will be even more beautiful than the Malacañang Palace of the president.'

Monty clucked with pleasure, and he declared that he would invite the papal representative to officiate at the house blessing unless the Philippines already has its own cardinal by that time. He would ask the president to be a sponsor so that they would have a closer relationship.

'And your room, we'll make it grander than the President's. And air-conditioned.'

'Of course.'

'A bed worth 10,000 pesos?' asked the architect.

'Agree,' said Monty, 'but regarding the bed, better ask Señora Montero. Ever since our wedding, she has always chosen the bed.'

Pong nodded. 'Well, the room of Doña Julia will be more elegant than the First Lady's.'

'Excellent, Pong, excellent.'

'And as for Señorita Dolly's room, I'll use everything I know in architecture,' promised Pong Tua-son.

Son Tua, Pong's father, had noticed his son's interest in Dolly.

When apprised about this, Monty answered, 'The wooer brings sweets.'

'Now, what will you do with Señorita Dolly's room?' asked Don Segundo.

'I was thinking of a room similar to Princess Margaret's in Buckingham Palace. But Dolly is more beautiful than Princess Margaret.'

'Of course,' the father said, basking in the compliment. 'Have you seen the princess's room?' he asked.

'I have seen pictures, including of the dresser, bed and bathroom. We'll copy it, but it will be more special.'

Don Segundo had no doubt in his mind that he had found the best architect.

In two weeks, Pong finished the plans. It would be a three-storey house with a sprawling garden, a big garage, and a wide swimming pool. The servants' quarters would be behind the garage.

The ground floor would have a large hall, a private office for Don Segundo, a bathroom, and a dressing room.

On the second floor would be the rooms of the family with a bathroom in every room. There would also be guest rooms.

The third floor, which would be high and airy, would be for entertainment. It would have a small bar and dining room, a poker and mah-jongg den, a radio and TV set, and a library. Here, Don Segundo would talk about business and politics with his friends. An elevator would connect the various floors.

Not satisfied with the old one-hectare lot, Don Segundo did not rest until he was able to get the nearby lots. He found out that being owned by foreigners, these lots were taken by the Japanese during the occupation. After the war, they were transferred to the government office that handled the properties owned by the enemy. Using influence and bribes, Montero had these nearby lots transferred to him. The widened grounds were just right for a three-storey building.

In those days, there were no obstacles to the wishes of a Montero and to the vision of an architect as long as, in Pong Tua-son's words, 'There are enough funds.'

Meanwhile, within shouting distance from the Montero garden, a thousand families who had lost their roofs because of the Japanese occupation and the liberation became squatters in schoolhouses and private buildings that had escaped the bullets and fire.

Many gathered the burnt roofs and blackened wood. They built small hovels on the vacant lots, in a race against the monsoon rain and the sweltering heat of the sun.

Groups of dirty children roamed the streets by day, like stray dogs. But at night, after their hunger had been quelled by whatever they could pick up or steal, they would curl up together under a ruined building or a demolished bridge. They would try to snatch a few hours of sleep until they would be awakened by the wheels of a passing truck or be driven away by a policeman.

More fortunate than these children were their parents, who had already died during the war, for they were now sleeping soundly in graves with no names.

XXVI

Governor Oscar Doblado rose early, even if it was a Saturday. It was only nine o'clock in the morning, and he was having breakfast. He had just attended the High Mass at the San Agustin Church an hour earlier, where he received communion.

He was alone. In his left hand was the morning paper, a cup of coffee in his right hand.

His wife, Doña Ninay, was in her room on the second floor of their house in Quezon City. Food was brought up to her. Doña Ninay went down only occasionally, and her personal maid ministered to her. Since she had become bedridden and half-paralysed, she preferred to stay alone in her room, read Spanish novels, and amuse herself by watching TV. Once a day, Oscar would come up to check on her.

The governor rose early, even though he had stayed up late the night before. He had invited some friends to play poker at his house. But before he played poker, he also went to Mass, for luck.

'Come before noon,' he called up his friends. 'We shall have roaster fish and newly caught fish with white sauce.'

After breakfast, Oscar told his cook that he had ordered food from a restaurant. He also checked to see if there were enough bottles of wine at the bar.

He was governor of the province where the Montero Plantation was located. He travelled between his mansion in Quezon City and his office in the capital. His car could make it in one and a half hours.

He would start working after breakfast, and at ten o'clock, he would begin receiving guests at his office.

Receiving visitors and signing papers would take up all his time in the morning. Once a week, he would meet the provincial board.

When Governor Doblado left his office at noon, he would not return that day. Anyone who asked was told, 'The governor is out on inspection.' In a house of durable materials on an average-sized lot surrounded by a concrete fence in a town near the capital, the governor would relax. There, he would have lunch and rest until it was time to go home to Quezon City.

This house was owned by Tindeng, a young and good-looking woman, who was said to be a relative of the governor's wife's. Being an orphan, she was sent to school by Doña Ninay. Tindeng only had two children as companions in her house. One was a seven-year-old girl and the other, a four-year-old boy. They were supposed to be her niece and nephew. Nevertheless, some rumour-mongers gathered around the store across from her house said that she was the governor's mistress and that the two children were the children of their affair.

If the governor's wife in Quezon City was aware of this, she showed no signs. Perhaps, she had left everything in God's hands, especially now that she could hardly leave her room after a near-fatal stroke.

Born to wealthy parents, Oscar Doblado had been a loser even as a student. He learnt vice before he gained knowledge. He graduated without any distinction; rather, he was among the 'fortunate' ones. His diploma was framed and used as a decoration on the wall of his parents' home. His first appearance in court was not as a lawyer, but because of a brawl at a gambling place, and another lawyer had defended him.

Before his father died, Oscar married the wealthy Ninay. He knew he married well, and the next step was to enter politics. His must have been a life, a truly charmed and favoured life, for he ran and won as a governor in the first postwar elections.

However, his sickly wife bore him no child in their marriage of twenty years. She used to say in a teasing manner that she actually had a child, for Osky, her husband, was equal to six teenagers.

Governor Doblado didn't invite many to his games of poker. Four to six was a good number, but each one brought capital no less than 20,000 pesos. They would play continuously after lunch until midnight. And the earnings were more than enough for all of Osky's expenses. He would make from 6,000 to 10,000 pesos per game.

From lunch to snacks to supper, they had the excellent services of a well-known restaurant. Like condemned men before being hanged, the poker players could ask for any food or wine from the catering service, or smoke the most expensive cigar.

Even before any guest came, a roasted pig was already steaming on a large platter, along with other food, on a grand table on one side of the room. There were bottles of scotch, brandy, port, sherry, burgundy and ice cubes in a deep crystal container, olives, pickles, peanuts and empty glasses and cups. A houseboy stood beside the table, waiting for their orders.

The first to arrive were Bishop Dumas and Judge Pilato. The bishop was older than the judge and wore a black habit; the judge wore white formal clothes made from the spun fibres of pineapple. 'We're early, Governor, aren't we?' the bishop answered cheerfully when Oscar greeted them.

'Just right, Monsignor. Monty called and said he would fetch Senator Botin.'

They had hardly sat down when Oscar began to offer them drinks. 'Have a drink first. Judge, what will you have?'

'Scotch and soda.'

'Monsignor?'

'Don't bother. I'll pour my own.' Taking a bottle of brandy, he poured some into a goblet and drank it straight.

'This is excellent,' he said, savouring the liquor on his tongue. 'Nothing can compare to truly aged brandy.'

Then they began to nibble the crispy skin of the roasted pig.

Before they could finish their drinks, they heard the loud words of Montero and saw the large face of Senator Botin. There was no need for introductions, for they often met at such gatherings. They all stood up and shook hands.

'I better have lunch served,' said Governor Doblado. 'You all must be hungry by now.'

'Who cares for food?' said Monty looking at the roasted pig and the vast amounts of alcohol. 'These will be enough.'

'But those are only the snacks. Wait till you see the real meal,' said Osky. 'I won't invite you unless it's special. What drink can I serve you, Senator?'

'Martini, if there's any.'

Osky asked the servant for a martini and poured some into a glass for Senator Botin.

Monty poured his own drink into a glass.

'Sherry for me, upon my doctor's advice,' he said. 'Sherry comes from fruit juice while whisky is 50 per cent alcohol. I prefer whisky and didn't learn to drink any other, but *señores*, whoever wishes to live long should obey his doctor.'

'Do you have high blood pressure?' asked the judge.

'My heart is overworked,' said the landlord.

'That fatigue is not due to whisky,' said Oscar with a meaningful look.

'I'm tired of muscatel,' said Bishop Dumas. 'That's what the altar boy hands me every Mass. So, outside the church, my stomach craves another—straight brandy, which is not as strong as scotch.'

'So that is why you can take more brandy than muscatel,' teased Senator Botin.

'Hey, Monty,' said Judge Pilato, 'is that your palace being built in Singalong?'

'At your service, Judge,' said Monty.

'I thought it was another temple of the Church of Christ,' said Pilato in a teasing tone. He glanced at the bishop, who pointedly ignored him.

'It's getting to be a problem,' said Monty, 'the cost of materials is already too high.'

'For one as rich as you,' said Pilato, 'the sky's the limit. And you're in luck. If you were in Australia, you couldn't build a mansion. How many are you in your family?'

'Three,' said Monty.

'Only three—ah, you can't have a mansion. There is a definite size allowed according to the family. After the war, the Australian government set up a housing programme—homes for the homeless.

No one can hoard more materials than he needs. You can get materials for a house for just three people, because if the rich can buy all the materials they want, the others won't have houses.'

'That's why I live here rather than Australia or elsewhere,' said Montero. 'Here, people are free. As long as you have the money, you can do what you want.'

'When is the inauguration?' asked Oscar.

'It's not even finished yet, and it still lacks many things. But maybe we will have it when Dolores comes back,' said Montero. 'Julia won't allow it while her princess is away.'

'Is your daughter still in Paris, Monty?' asked the bishop.

'Yes, Monsignor, she is studying at the Sorbonne.' The father was not sure what the school was, but he just said 'the Sorbonne' because the syllables rolled smoothly off his tongue.

'The Sorbonne?' The bishop thought awhile. 'Ah, the Sorbonne is very good. It is a Catholic institution. Cardinal Richelieu founded one of the first colleges in the Sorbonne, and it's now one of the best schools of theology in Europe. Paris is a city of temptations, but those studying at the Sorbonne are safe from worldly pleasures.' After saying this, Bishop Dumas gulped down the remaining alcohol in his goblet.

'Lunch is ready. Let's go to the dining room,' said Osky. He led the bishop ahead of the other guests.

When he came to the head of the table, Bishop Dumas looked back at Senator Botin and offered his seat.

'You may stay here,' he said.

'Bishop, you should,' declined the lawmaker.

'If we follow protocol . . .' said the bishop.

'Then the more you have the right,' finished the senator and added, smiling, 'I am only a lawmaker, while you are a prince of Rome.'

'If all lawmakers were like you, Senator,' the bishop teased in return, 'then there would be no conflict between the state and the church.'

'This is my position: give to Caesar what is Caesar's, and to God what is God's.'

Osky settled the discussion by asking the bishop to sit at the head of the table. Senator Botin then sat at his right, Judge Pilato at his left, and Montero and Osky sat across from each other.

'Are there no others, Governor?' Bishop Dumas looked at Doblado before scooping his spoon into the soup bowl.

'General Bayoneta promised to come, but he was delayed,' said Osky.

'The general will raid us?' Montero asked in mock protest.

'Have you heard of any gambling of the elite being raided?' said the governor. 'Anyway, you know, Senator Botin, Monty, that his wife is the daughter of the Chinese millionaire Son Tua, I mean, Tua-son.'

'That's why I cannot imagine how he can be an enemy of vice. Would you believe his father-in-law worked to place him in his present position?'

'He is the enemy of small-town lottery,' said Osky. 'I should know . . .'

'Because his father-in-law does not deal in small-town lottery,' said the senator. 'But he is not the enemy of gentlemen's games like monte, poker, *chemin de fer*. These are safe from him. And he plays for high stakes.'

'Of course, because he does not have to say Mass at the crack of dawn just to earn money,' Bishop Dumas said with a smile.

'What would you do if you could carry the campaign against vice,' said Osky, 'and be the son-in-law of the financial broker of the majority party? It's going to be sheer profit, coming and going, like a saw.'

'I believe what an authority says about such things,' Senator Botin said, and everyone laughed.

Then a servant approached Oscar and whispered that there was another guest. Oscar went to the door and returned with General Bayoneta. Oscar introduced the new arrival, who bowed and told them to continue eating. The servant handed his master a bottle of scotch and a glass with ice.

'General,' greeted Judge Pilato, 'we thought you would raid our poker game, but we have not even started yet.'

'I'll wipe you out in a legal way,' said the general. 'The governor knows me very well,' he added.

'What kept you?' asked Oscar.

'There was a conference on exterminating rats in Mindanao. Reports say they destroy not only plants but also property.' Bayoneta quickly drank his whisky. He was seated by the host at the other end of the table, opposite the bishop.

'Why exterminate only the rats in Mindanao?' asked Monty. 'Are there not many big rats in all corners of the government?'

'When you began taking the sherry, Monty,' the senator said, 'the more easily you became drunk. Remember the saying "he who spits at the sky . . ."'

'I didn't mention any names, Senator,' Monty said. 'So I think not of "spitting at the sky" but of the children's game of "he who has the gold should run".'

'Oh, the general is not eating?' asked the bishop.

'I have already finished, Monsignor. Lunch was part of the conference.'

'Then let's go.' The bishop stood up. 'Thank you, Governor, for a grand feast.'

And with that, the others also stood up to begin their long and expensive game of poker.

XXVII

From the dining room, Governor Doblado led the guests to another airconditioned room on the same floor. It was his den.

The floor was softly carpeted. There were sofas, some lounging chairs, and a small, low table made of native hardwood. At the centre was a round table made from one piece of thick wood covered with green velvet. It could easily accommodate ten people.

A copy of the famous painting, *September Morn*, hung on the wall. On top of a wide hardwood cabinet was an ivory bust of Psyche. There was also an electric clock on top of the cabinet.

In the afternoon, the room was bright because of the crystal panelling. At night, it was lit by fluorescent lamps in the four corners of the room, or by the elegant lamps standing on pedestals.

Oscar had bottles of wine, glasses and cups brought with ice cubes.

He opened a box of Coronas.

'Let me pour you some brandy, Monsignor,' Oscar offered.

'Thanks,' said the bishop, 'but I don't drink during a game. I prefer Coronas.'

'As for me,' said Monty, 'the more I drink, the more I enjoy the game. Unfortunately, *señores*, now I can only drink sherry and in limited amounts, at that.'

'There are reasons both for drinking and not drinking while playing,' Judge Pilato said. 'Those who don't drink want to have greater concentration. Those who drink need the alcohol to give them courage.'

'I drink because I want to, not to have courage,' Monty said. 'I bet not on the strength of the wine, but on my cards. If I hold five aces, wild, you can have all the saints of the Roman Church.'

'Let us not drag sacred things into gambling,' said the bishop sharply.

'With me, it's different,' said General Bayoneta, 'I'll tell you my secret in poker.' He looked around as if he would reveal a planned *coup d'état*. 'When the cards are weak, that's when I push the chips and "top me".'

'Therefore, General,' Senator Botin said, 'your method is like the old military tactic. Whenever you are losing, that's when your noisy propaganda says you're winning.'

The group laughed at the comparison, but General Bayoneta said, 'If my tactics are poor, you know what to do when I say, "Top me."'

'I'll remember that,' laughed the senator.

Oscar then took a new set of cards from the cabinet. He broke the blue seal and gave the bishop the cards still wrapped in cellophane. Oscar also took out the box of chips attached to a pen and a list.

Bishop Dumas removed all the cellophane, riffled through the pack, then separated the twos, threes, fours and fives. He also did the same for the jokers. He shuffled the remaining cards.

'The old rules,' Oscar informed everyone, as he piled the chips of four colours.

'Strictly cash, isn't it?' said Monty.

'If you wish,' Oscar answered like a diplomat.

'Among friends, that is the proper thing,' Monty agreed. 'We're different, of course, but at a poker table, *señores*, the unexpected often takes place. Maybe you haven't heard of the president who gave the invitations but played without capital? Now, who can refuse a president? You also heard of the bank director who left a debt before the war. The war is over, but he has not yet redeemed his IOU, although the house has paid for it. A banker, just think of that.'

'It is said,' Oscar confirmed Monty's story, 'that the place to know a real gentleman is at the gambling table.'

'Very well then, how much are the stakes?' asked Senator Botin, looking bored.

'Small stakes only, Senator,' said the host-cashier, '1,000 pesos each, but you can get as many as you like.'

'*Hombre*, is 1,000 pesos small?' objected Botin. 'The salary of a member of Congress is only 600 pesos a month.'

'What is salary compared to allowance and sideline?' Monty said.

The senator threw Monty a sharp look, but he said nothing.

'Give me three for a start,' he told the governor and took out six 500-peso bills for his chips.

'Fresh from the Central Bank,' Oscar said and waved the neat and crisp bills for everyone to see.

'Hey, I'm no 10 per center,' said Botin in protest.

The host-cashier counted out twenty white chips worth ten pesos each, eight red chips at 100 pesos each, two blue at 500 each, and one yellow worth 1,000.

'Is that enough, Senator?' asked Oscar. 'It seems slight.'

'Simple living,' the senator winked. 'If only we had something from reparations, or got a share in the booming barter trade.'

Oscar took the 3,000, placed it in the box and entered in his list: 'Senator B, 3'.

Senator Botin got his chips, counted them and arranged them in three piles before him.

'Judge?' The cashier turned to Judge Pilato.

'Three also.'

The cash and chips swiftly changed hands. The cashier entered: 'Judge, 3'.

Bishop Dumas asked for five; Montero and Bayoneta, six each. Oscar added to the list: 'Bishop, 5; Monty, 6; General, 6; total 23'.

They sat around the table. From Bishop Dumas, going left, there were Judge Pilato, Senator Botin, Montero and General Bayoneta.

'Won't you play, Osky?' the bishop asked the governor.

'The five of you may start.'

'Six can play.'

'I'll attend to our snacks first,' he said, then he excused himself.

'And the tong,' added Monty. 'We should not forget Osky's share of the pot for hosting the game.

'Very well, then, let's start,' said Bishop Dumas. He appeared to bless the pack of cards with his right hand.

'Amen,' whispered Senator Botin.

The bishop gave each a card. Judge Pilato showed an ace, so he was the first dealer.

The judge shuffled the cards again and threw a white chip to the centre, then he said, 'Stud, simple.'

The four followed the dealer, and each placed a white chip.

Judge Pilato dealt each player one card face down from Senator Botin to himself. He followed with one card each, face up. The card of Senator Botin was a seven, Monty a queen, General Bayoneta a ten, Bishop Dumas, a knight and Judge Pilato, the dealer, an eight.

'Queen,' called the dealer.

'Size of the pot.' Monty placed five white chips in the middle, together with the rest.

'Call,' answered Bayoneta, which meant he would pit his cards with a ten on top against Monty's cards with his queen. The general put a red chip and got his change of five white.

'That's good enough for me,' Judge Pilato said, on retreat. He turned his eight on top of his other cards and did not add to the pot any more. Thus he showed he would not pit his cards against those who said 'call'.

'Deal,' warned Pilato and gave Montero a third open card. 'King,' said the dealer.

He threw a third before the general and said, 'Knight.'

The bishop got an ace.

'Bet the ace,' said the dealer.

'Let's sweeten the pot with 200 pesos.' Bishop Dumas smiled and threw two red chips on the pile at the centre.

'And whom will the king fear?' said Montero, who also placed two red chips.

'And who will overcome the general who's riding a high horse?' said Bayoneta.

His red chips were added to the pile.

'Deal,' said Pilato and gave each of the three an open card.

Montero got an ace, the general a king, the bishop a knight. Each had four cards: three open, and one face down. Before Montero could be seen a queen, a king, an ace, and one more card. The general had a ten, a knight, a king and one hidden. The bishop had a knave, an ace, a knave, and one more.

It appeared that based on the open cards, Bishop Dumas was ahead of them all, for he had a pair and an ace. Montero and Bayoneta had no open pair, besides being crippled by the king and the ace.

Without raising his eyes or showing any change in his facial expression, the bishop threw a yellow chip at the centre. He looked like a priest who remained unruffled, while listening to the confession of a married woman having an affair.

Montero said nothing. He turned down all his cards, as a gesture of surrender.

General Bayoneta held a yellow chip, but he did not let it go. He just stared at the bishop as one would stare at a captive to make him admit to the charges hurled at him. He remained like this for more than a minute, while the bishop looked at the yellow chip, which stood out at the centre of whites, reds and blues.

'Very well, then,' said the general. 'Call.' And he put the yellow chip on top of the one placed by the bishop.

From behind, Governor Doblado picked up with two fingers a blue chip for the tong. He wanted to make sure he got his share in the heated game.

'Deal,' said the dealer and gave a last card each to the bishop and the general.

The bishop looked at the playing card and caught the last card meant for him.

Also face down, Judge Pilato dealt General Bayoneta a card. The two poker players peeped at their last cards, but one could not tell whether they were good or bad. Not from the movements of their eyelashes, nor the curl of their lips, nor from their breathing. Both wore faces that nobody could read.

Without a word, the bishop showed a ten and the general, a horse. Therefore, of the two sets of four open cards, there was a pair of horses, a king, and a ten for the general, while the bishop had a pair of knights, an ace, and a ten.

'I told you, a horse ridden by a general is very rare, indeed,' said Bayoneta in a jeering manner. 'See now, there are two.'

'I was put to shame by the knight,' Bishop Dumas said, shaking his head.

'In honour of the two horses, then, top me,' said the general, and he pushed all his chips forward.

The bishop looked at him. All stared but did not make any noise. Senator Botin, Montero, and the dealer Judge Pilato were all silenced by the first deal.

Then the bishop looked at his cards, at the cards of Bayoneta, then at the general's face. He counted with his eyes the pile of chips pushed by the general and the chips that lay before him.

'I can't top you, General, for you have more chips,' the bishop said in a cold manner.

'Then,' answered Bayoneta, 'I'll top you.'

'You were right, Governor,' said the bishop. He meant that Bayoneta was really a heavy gambler.

'I revealed my secret earlier, didn't I, Senator?' the general said.

'I won't be carried by propaganda,' Bishop Dumas said with a sneer. 'Even with the radio, I don't listen to the commercials.'

'Well, you have the last word, Monsignor.'

'How much is this?' the bishop asked himself and slowly counted his chips with two fingers. '3,290,' he said. 'Oh, the general wants to get such a big amount. This is not easily earned by an old priest. How many Masses, weddings, baptisms, confirmations, burials would these take?'

'You still have time to retreat,' said Bayoneta. Then as if against his will, he removed some of his chips, to leave only the equivalent of the bishop's. 'How much did you say, Monsignor? 3,290?'

'Right,' answered the bishop quickly, at the same time pushing his chips toward the centre. 'Call.'

Absolute silence reigned around the table. The general was the first to speak.

'Two pairs,' he announced in a triumphant tone, as if accepting the surrender of the Muslim fighter, Datu Kamlon. Quickly, he showed the hidden card, which was a ten. So he had a pair of knights and a pair of tens back to back.

Bayoneta thought he had already won, so when the bishop was silent, he was about to draw the chips. But he stopped dead cold when he heard the voice of the Monsignor.

'No good,' he objected. He showed his hidden card, which was also a knave. So he had three knaves—a trio. A trio is higher than two pairs.

The general was shocked, but the bishop paid no more attention to his reaction, for both of his hands had begun gathering the chips. One more blue was fished out by Doblado's two fingers.

'What was found in water, to water will return,' Senator Botin whispered to Judge Pilato. But he was careful not to be overheard by the general, who was sweating profusely by that time.

In that single encounter, Bishop Dumas won 5,000 and the general lost 4,600. Oscar got his share of 150.

'Between a good poker player and a good bishop, I'll choose the poker player,' said Senator Botin.

'But of course,' agreed Judge Pilato, 'more than a senator.'

'Even in poker,' Bishop Dumas said in a solemn tone, 'a sincere prayer is heeded by God.'

'Or by Satan,' said General Bayoneta, slashing the air with his words.

XXVIII

'Señores, the game is fun, but the snacks waiting for us are more delicious,' the host, Governor Doblado, said. He asked the poker players to take a break. A senator, a bishop, a general, a judge, and a landlord-businessman—this gathering of the powerful elite could bet on a fortune that could save thousands of poor people from hunger in just one round of poker.

The five guests had spent three hours in the four kingdoms of the air-conditioned room. Bishop Dumas continued raking it in while General Bayoneta was losing. All in all, the military chief had lost 20,000, and the same amount of chips had gone to the monsignor. Senator Botin and Monty had each lost 3,000; Judge Pilato had recovered his capital.

In one round, General Bayoneta asked for a new deck of cards. This was their third change. The scotch bottle on his left was less than half full.

Actually, the five poker players were about the same in skill and not one of them would hesitate to face Professor Hoyle, the famous author of the poker bible, if the said expert would only dare to show enough capital. More than a cheat, the one person most avoided in this game was the one who played without money. The cheat could be beaten, but what could you win from the penniless one?

Just like any other game of luck, in poker, one's skill was only half the game. If the player did not get a good hand, he would just keep placing ante in the pot and not be able to 'call'. And if he should stick to the game without a fighting chance, it would be like throwing a live cat to a hungry crocodile. So, as in a horse race, he would be included only at the start.

Bluffing can be profitable occasionally, but only if the opponent is uncertain. But if his cards are good, the bluff is nothing but a blow against a strong wall.

More or less, this was what happened to General Bayoneta that afternoon. No player escapes superstition during a game. He often counted on this; he hoped that his bad luck would be replaced by a lucky streak and the tide would turn against the opposition. Thus, the general would change his seat, ask for a new glass of whisky, press his heel on the face of an animal in the carpet's design. Once, he asked for a new deck when it was his turn to deal.

But it seemed that bad luck dogged him. No matter what he did, two-thirds of his 30,000 still took flight.

'General, it seems that the peace and order situation is getting serious in many places,' said Montero. 'What's going on?

General Bayoneta straightened his shoulders, thinking that this was one topic he could answer without losing any of his chips. Nevertheless, he was careful in expressing his views.

'In this group,' Bayoneta told Montero, 'I should not answer this alone. Here are Senator Botin and the governor. Maybe they know more than I do about the lack of peace and order. Judge Pilato and the monsignor surely have their views on the issue. I'm only a soldier, and my primary duty is to enforce the law; in a word, to prosecute the enemy of the law.'

'Perhaps, we can all agree that the root cause of what's happening now is the last war,' Governor Doblado said. 'The war destroyed our economy, and this can't be easily restored. Trailing it are unemployment, poverty, hunger. An empty stomach is a bad counsellor. There are many robberies not because of the inborn evil among the thieves, but often, because they just want to live. I know. In my province alone, many are jailed for this. It's worse in the city. They look for jobs, but they can't find work. They beg, but no one gives them alms. What will they do then?'

'During the war and even afterwards, man has forgotten God,' Bishop Dumas said slowly, then shook his head. 'That is the first sign. Both the wealthy and the poor. The wealthy became more greedy and decided to keep for himself all the bounty entrusted to him. The latter believed that society is to blame for his poverty, and because of this, he has the right to get others' property. When a man forgets God, he becomes a follower of Satan.'

'Oh, I don't neglect my duties,' said Montero in a defensive manner. 'Magno, you know about my donation to the church. My wife heads the Catholic women, and my daughter always raises funds for the Red Cross. So what more is expected of me?'

'I wasn't referring to you,' Dumas said. 'You're not the only rich man in the country.'

Governor Doblado tried to get Montero's goat.

'Hey, Señor Millionaire,' said Oscar, 'don't boast like the Pharisee that gives alms one day and then exploits other people for one whole year.'

'Osky, you're dragging your own tail,' Montero said.

Judge Pilato dropped the ashes of his cigar before speaking. 'Even the courts are often blamed for the situation,' he said. 'If the sentence is light, we are condoning crime. If it's heavy, then we're cruel. If an important person wins, the judge was bribed. If nobody is sentenced, the poor have no chance. But we judge the case, not the person. We did not make the laws. The judge does not sentence according to his wishes, but according to the law.'

Judge Pilato puffed on his cigar before continuing. 'Look, a father steals money to buy rice. If caught, he has to be jailed. But a powerful person steals a hundred thousand, but he cannot be charged because there is no evidence nor witness. Now . . .'

'That's what I mean,' the general said. 'In performing our duty, we set aside our personal feelings. If in bringing about peace and order, the soldier must use force, don't blame him for doing his duty.'

'Who was the wise man who said that when a person is ashamed of his actions, he uses duty as a pretext?' Senator Botin said in a pointed way. The general threw him a sharp look.

'If a soldier is afraid to do his duty, then he should look for another profession. He should be a politician,' Bayoneta answered.

'Why?' the senator asked in an angry voice. 'Doesn't a politician know how to do his duty?'

'I mean to say, Senator, that when he pleases the public or his district, the politician thinks everything is all right. On the other hand, fulfilling his mission is the sole aim of the soldier, no matter who gets hurt. The politician is swayed by public opinion, but the soldier is not . . .'

'Do you mean that the army does not believe in democracy?' asked Senator Botin.

'I mean, the army is not politics.'

'I think there's a big gap between government policy and your methods. In a republic, all government agencies, the army included, should follow the democratic system. Isn't your policy too harsh? That remedy is worse than the disease. Are you aware that people in rural areas complain about the army's ferocity? They say that every time we start a peace and order campaign, the peaceful folk suffer more than the outlaws. You want to stop the fire, but you are pouring oil.'

A sour smile played on the general's lips. His jaw was hard-set as he fenced off the lawmaker's thrust.

'Some diseases like cancer require an operation. The army is often caught between the sword and the wall. Should he allow the enemies of the law to prevail, or should he restore the prestige of the government? Deny it if you will, but at this stage, the army is the pillar of democracy. Those who don't heed the church and don't fear the courts are forced to listen to the gun.'

'But a social problem can never be solved by the sword,' said the senator.

A guest arrived just in time to catch the general's last remarks and the senator's firm answer. Governor Doblado introduced Dr Sabio, who was already known to some as the head of Freedom University and a respected expert on political science.

'You will enjoy this discussion, Doctor,' said Osky, 'but you should have snacks first.'

'Coffee would be fine,' said the new arrival.

'We were just discussing the alarming peace and order situation,' the governor told Dr Sabio. 'Thefts, burglaries, killings, disorder everywhere. These are obviously the result of poverty and crimes caused by the war.'

Dr Sabio first sipped his coffee.

'I heard the last remarks of General Bayoneta and Senator Botin. Don't blame the war. These problems could have been worsened by the war, but they were not caused by it. How can the creature precede the creator? The social problem is similar to the question: which came first—the chicken or the egg? We have to admit that ten to twenty years before the war, a governor was killed by his political opponent, a landlord was slain by a farmer, a doctor was killed by the husband of a patient. There were already big strikes long before the war. The colorum uprising in Pangasinan, the *tanggulan* troubles in Bulacan and Manila, the *sakdalistas'* revolt in southern Luzon, the fighting between the constabulary and the Moros in Mindanao. Therefore, these are not recent. The root causes were there even before the war.'

Dr Sabio finished his coffee. No one objected to him; he was like a professor lecturing a class.

'What are these root causes? A man's taking advantage of another through position, money, or brains. Taking economic advantage in many forms and schemes. This is the source of a man's discontent. And it spreads. We know that a spark easily causes fire.'

'I said earlier that both the wealthy and the poor are to blame,' the bishop said.

'That's true, Monsignor, if you refer to the worsening of the situation,' agreed Dr Sabio. 'But at the start, only one could be blamed: the opportunist. You will agree with me, Monsignor, that God knew and He, Himself, sowed in Paradise the seeds of sin.'

'God gave man the intelligence to know good from evil, and the freedom to choose,' answered the bishop.

The rest were silent. Dr Sabio continued.

'Now what do we see? Each man for himself. Those on the top of the hierarchy step on those below. The favoured ones, even those with duties to the country, focus only on their own welfare. They have hardly warmed their seats in their positions when they begin to build palaces, buy two cars, and amass money for their vices. I'm not against fair profit and just rewards, but I think those in the government have no right to live differently from the ordinary citizens whom they lead.'

'Even if he spends his own money?' asked Senator Botin.

'Even then, Senator. A leader should set a good example for the public. If the nation is in dire straits, it is immoral for a leader and his family to wallow in luxury. If a citizen walks on muddy streets, it is indecent for a leader to recline in his Cadillac. Don't you think so?'

'As long as my conscience is clear,' answered the senator, 'I have nothing to fear. Why, does one have no right to live the way he wants?'

'You see,' the general reproached him, 'now you say "while your conscience is clear". Earlier, you objected when I said, "As long as I do my duty, never mind who gets hurt."'

'What do you suggest, Doctor?' asked Judge Pilato.

'Better education, especially for those below, not just learning their professions,' said the professor, 'but a deep understanding of morality, one's obligation to his fellow men and women, and to society. In short, training to be responsible citizens.'

'Religion!' Bishop Dumas boomed. 'More religion is what the nation needs. Those who grow up in these times are steeped in materialism. What do you think, Doctor? Isn't religion needed in school?' The bishop had an idea that this was not the policy at Freedom University, but he asked the question anyway.

Dr Sabio gave the bishop a respectful look and answered in a calm manner. 'The knowledge and fear of God are the first things that man learns. Because of a lack of faith in himself and in the face of nature's wonders, man worshipped the power that created these mysteries and everything his limited mind couldn't understand. But science has conquered nature. Man learnt that he is like any other being on earth and that even the earth is not the centre of the universe, but only one of the planets revolving around the sun. Hardly anything is now left unchallenged by the mind of man. Thus, what happened was to be expected. Man developed a greater concern for everyday life than for his dream of the next life. So, the power of religion diminished. But the ethics and morality taught by religion, the humanitarian basis of all creeds and all prophets from Moses to Buddha and from Christ to

Muhammad, are still the golden rule of all churches, philosophies and secular institutions. I refer to the commandments, "Love others as you love yourself" and "Don't do unto others what you would not have others do unto you."'

'The moment mankind forgets to behave thus, what difference is there between a man and a beast? Voltaire, an agnostic, said, "If there is no God, man should create one." Monsignor, it may be that compulsory religious instruction is against the separation of church and state, but we agree, I think, that morality is what the country needs at this time.'

'Although I don't fully subscribe to your theory,' said the bishop, 'I don't completely object. Even science is limited, just as man's knowledge is limited. Only God is omniscient. What science lacks should be supplemented by faith. Or we could follow St. Thomas Aquinas who said, "There is only one Truth," so that truth of science and truth of faith should coincide.'

Then the bishop turned to the professor and asked suddenly, 'Doctor, may I know your religion?'

All eyes turned to Dr Sabio at the thrust of Bishop Dumas. But the professor was not rattled and parried quickly.

'Religion is the secret of every man's conscience,' he said. 'But if you wish to know, my religion is truth.'

'God is truth. He is the Way; He is Life.'

'With apologies to St. Thomas Aquinas, that is where science differs from religion,' Dr Sabio said.

'Therefore, you are an agnostic?'

'I look for proof in everything.'

'And without proof, you don't believe?'

'That, sir, is the law of truth.'

'And who made such a law?'

'Nature.'

'And who made nature?'

'Nature itself.'

The Bishop gave a soft, sceptical laugh. He told himself he had found an enjoyable opponent, although one who is hard to convince.

He said in a pleasant manner, 'I would be delighted, Dr Sabio, if we could have a long discussion sometime.'

'Thank you, Monsignor. When I find time, I shall pay you a visit.' He added, 'I hope that someday, those who rely on faith and those who rely on truth can have worthwhile discussions. They could agree to disagree.'

The host, Governor Doblado, looked at his wristwatch, hinting that it was time to go back to the round table.

'Maybe we should settle things at the poker table?' said General Bayoneta, who was getting bored. He was losing a lot. 'You play, don't you, Doctor?'

'Rarely, and for small stakes,' said Dr Sabio.

'The Doctor came for another purpose,' said Governor Doblado. 'He wanted to discuss his university's plans about a plantation in my province.'

At the word 'plantation', Montero looked at Oscar. 'What plantation?' he asked.

'He owns the Montero Plantation,' said Oscar by way of introduction.

'Then he is the one I should see,' said Dr Sabio, 'but some other time.'

'We shall see,' was Montero's only reply.

Dr Sabio said goodbye. After he left, the poker players went back to the air-conditioned room and continued to play.

XXIX

The phone was ringing at the desk of the *Kampilan* news editor. Andres picked up the receiver.

'Hello, yes, Santi? Two children killed by their mother. She stabbed herself . . . Now in serious condition . . . Why did it happen? How's that? . . . From extreme poverty . . . No food available . . . No one to help . . . Husband in jail . . . What? Social services refused help . . . Yes, I've got the names and ages . . . Good . . . Get other details . . . Living in the slums . . . The children's bodies at the morgue . . . Mother is in the hospital. Okay, call back . . .'

Andres was looking at the line-up of the news for the front page when Magat came in from the editorial room. He had a copy of the afternoon paper.

'Andy, is there anything new on the Blue Ribbon exposé?' asked Magat. 'That's a big scandal.'

'I asked Iman to interview those who are involved. He will get statements from the two department secretaries and the matron. I also sent a reporter to the chief investigator to find out if there is evidence.'

The two cabinet members exposed by the Blue Ribbon Committee were charged with receiving bribes in big deals. One allegedly got a fishpond, and the other was rewarded with a house and lot in Baguio. The matron, the wife of a government official, was said to finance some members of the Cabinet who make frequent visits to Hong Kong,

Tokyo, Bangkok and Singapore. They bring out more than the allowed 1,000 dollars, and they smuggle contraband goods, which give them huge profits.

Andy told Magat Santi's news about the desperate mother.

'Is there any good news about the strike at the pier?'

'What do you mean by good?' Andy looked up at Magat, who remained standing. 'Bloodshed? Yes. The police attacked the picketers, wounding two workers. The cops will be charged with physical injuries and the workers with resisting the law enforcers.'

'Good,' said Magat. Andres was puzzled. He was not used to what went on in the copy room of a newspaper.

'Why do we say "good" when something bad happens? Like the mauling of the workers by the police?'

'The event is bad, but the news is good,' Magat answered. 'The reader likes to read about the unusual and the sensational. So, it's not news when a dog bites a man; it's news when a man bites a dog. What's been done about the school crisis?'

'What else but the old solutions? Pour more funds, look for more buildings to be rented, hire new teachers,' Andres said.

'Where will they get the funds?'

'There's a plan to double the students' tuition fees and to hold twenty lotteries every year. The money earned will be added to the educational funds.'

'Therefore, our twenty-four sweepstakes and lotteries will now become forty-four,' Magat said.

'Twenty-four for charity, twenty for education,' explained Andres. 'Is there no way other than gambling to pay for good proposals?'

'Any proposal of the present officials will have the same result; the country will just be fried in its own lard.'

'What about the tenants' petition for the government to buy the plantation?'

'They have presented this to the office, but they have not yet received any answer except the words "wait . . . it will be studied . . . that is the policy of the government, but the problem is money . . ."'

'The problem, Andy, is not lack of money but lack of action,' Magat said. 'There are many bright people in the government who have many good ideas. But they end there. When it comes to implementation, they hesitate, their tails between their legs. The proposal is left hanging, forgotten, until they are jolted awake by the grave consequences of their negligence.'

'The government is like a spider that spins a web and sleeps at the centre, just waiting for the fly or moth that would make the mistake of entering the trap,' Andres said, and then he laughed.

'That's a good comparison,' Magat said. 'So it is just caught in its own web. We shall fight then against this indolence,' said the editor. 'We shall unmask the hypocrites, wake up the people who are asleep. On the other hand, we shall praise the deserving. As Jefferson said, a good newspaper is preferable to a bad government. In critical times, the newspaper should be a fort of truth.'

'Napoleon admitted that he was more afraid to fight a newspaper than a thousand bayonets. Sometimes, a powerful editorial can shock more than a bomb.'

'That's true,' said Magat, 'but don't forget, Andy, that our goal is not just to expose and destroy. We also want to help in building, in creating. That is the difference between guns and ideas. A weapon only destroys and kills, while an idea destroys and builds; it also kills and gives life.'

The phone rang. Andres answered it.

'Yes, Santi? Oh, the mother of the two children died. Is that all? . . . Okay.'

Then a messenger came and gave Andres a picture attached to a typed news item.

'Oh, a pre-war Miss Philippines,' he said after glancing at the press release. 'Now she's married to Gordo, the banker. She will hold a dance at the Manila Hotel and has invited a thousand guests on her birthday.' Andres looked at the postscript. 'Don't fail to include this latest picture and send a photographer to the affair.'

The two editors burst into laughter.

'Maybe I should use this picture on the front page,' he said in a mock-serious tone. 'Let's use the headline "Feast for 1,000" and beside it, the picture of the mother who killed her two children, then killed herself afterwards. Then we'll put headline: "Three Killed by Hunger". What do you think?'

'You're the news editor, my friend,' Magat said, laughing.

Iman strode into the copy room and went to Andres's desk.

'What have you got?' Andres asked.

'The two secretaries will sue the Blue Ribbon chairman for libel,' answered the reporter. 'According to them, their respective wives bought the property, which was alleged as the bribe. They have photocopies of the deeds of the sale. Secretary A has the title to the fishpond and Secretary B, the lot and bungalow in Baguio.'

'Naturally,' said Andres.

'And Madame XX?'

'She refused to talk, as counselled by her lawyer.'

'Naturally,' said Andres again.

They were commenting on Iman's report when the phone rang again. It was the lawyer of Madame XX.

'You'll answer for libel if you mention my client's name,' he said in a threatening tone.

'Then,' answered Andres, 'we shall report your phone call and your threat of libel if . . .'

'Don't even mention it . . .'

'Mister,' Andres's voice had a hard edge, 'the *Kampilan* is a free newspaper, and it has no master. No one tells us what we should print or not print . . .'

'It's up to you.' And the lawyer cut off the conversation.

Magat invited Andres to the editor's office.

'Come in,' said Magat, 'let's discuss my editorial.'

When they were already seated and Magat had lit a cigarette, he handed Andres three typewritten sheets.

'There, see if it's not too much or too little.'

After reading the title and the first paragraph, he looked intently at Magat.

'Fifty years ago, or on 30 October 1908,' Magat said, 'the newspaper *El Renacimiento* published an editorial titled '*Aves de Rapiña*', or 'The Preying Birds'. The courageous Filipino newspaper was sued by an American high official because the editorial created a big scandal involving the American. The newspaper's owner and editor lost the case, his property was confiscated. In the end, the *Renacimiento* had no choice but to fold up. But its editorial was a shout of protest that was not stilled down over the years, and every time there is oppression, exploitation and injustice, that editorial resounds again.'

'I have heard of that editorial,' answered Andres. 'But this is the first time I've read it.'

'It's half a century old, but the situation during the time of its writing is not any different from what we see today. Perhaps, we now have a thicker swarm of preying birds.'

'Without a doubt,' said Andres, and he went on reading.

The Preying Birds

On this earth, some are born to eat and devour, others to be eaten and swallowed . . . Their relationship depends on the greed and strength of the first until he has been satisfied at the other's expense.

There are some people not only want to be like the merciless eagle, but also have some of the qualities of a vulture, an owl, and a big vampire, which sucks human blood.

To climb the mountains of Benguet to classify and measure the skulls of the Igorots in order to study and enlighten this race while having the sight of the preying birds, at the same time spying on the location of large gold deposits kept by the Igorots in the vastness of the lonely hills, to claim these afterwards, thanks to legal procedures that are changed on a regular basis, but always for his own benefit.

To allow, against law and health, the forbidden slaughter of diseased cows to profit from the decayed meat that he himself forbids by virtue of his position.

To introduce himself at every opportunity as a scientist with lines on his forehead and devote his life to the wonders of the science laboratory, although his only scientific works are classifying insects and importing fish eggs, as if the fish in this country lacked nutrients and flavour, so that they have to be replaced with fish from other countries.

To scheme, with the help of secret agents and partners, to sell to the city at fantastic prices worthless lands that the councillors cannot refuse because they are afraid of the man behind the scheme; and they cannot refuse, because it is also for their own gain.

To patronize concessions of hotels on unclaimed land, hoping to make large profits from the blood of the people.

These are the qualities of this person, who is also an eagle that spies and devours, a vulture that fattens on the dead and on decayed flesh, an owl that pretends to possess all knowledge, and a vampire that sucks the blood of its victim until everything has dried up.

These preying birds always triumph. Their flight and their schemes cannot be stopped.

Who will stand in their way?

Some share in the loot. Others cannot protest because of their weak voices. And still others die from the frightening erasure of their own strength and welfare.

And suddenly, the deathless phrase appears: '*Mane, Thecel, Phares*'.

* * *

Gone is the loathsome creature who used the disguise of the eagle, the vulture, the owl and the vampire, but he left his descendants and the descendants of his agents and partners. They can be found not only in the mountains but also on the plains, fields, lakes, seas, towns, and cities; in tall buildings, in high positions, in important causes. Their sharp beaks, teeth, and claws still devour and suck the blood of their victims.

But one day, and that day must come, no longer will it be the mysterious hand of fate that would write on the wall the warning of disaster, like the words read by Belshazzar. The hand of the oppressed will put things right.

This is not a prophecy but a certainty that cannot be delayed, for it is inevitable.

* * *

'This is the editorial,' Andres said with admiration when he finished it.

'A thrust of the *Kampilan*,' said Magat, as he lit another cigarette.

XXX

In the past few days, the newspapers reported that Congress was about to pass a bill that would make retail trade, including that of the variety stores on the streets, owned by the Filipinos. Crowds flocked to Congress during the last days of the discussion of the bill.

The session was scheduled for nine in the morning. It was already eleven and many seats in the Senate were still empty.

Meanwhile, on both sides of the hall, the gallery was filled with people. In the front row sat the small businessmen, who wanted to see what would happen to the proposal. Although the newspapers had predicted the passage of the bill, they were worried because of persistent rumours that foreigners had offered millions of pesos in bribes so that the lawmakers would kill the bill. The campaign for and against this controversial bill had started even before the war.

There was already a big crowd of curious onlookers inside the hall and outside. They were all there: the jobless who hoped to see their representative or senator, the law students, the idle who enjoyed watching the sideshow in Congress.

'Some senators are better comedians than our bald Pugo and Tugo,' said one.

'But imagine how much the country spends on them,' said another.

Some young women in the front rows fanned themselves, or fixed their lipsticks. Sometimes, they would wave their fans at a senator who happened to glance back at them. One onlooker whispered to another that these women were like the lobbyists' bait. The other couldn't get the drift of his words.

To the left, facing the chairman's table on a platform, was the press section. It looked like a deserted fort.

In contrast, the Congress's employees and clerks, the secretaries, the stenographer, and the messenger had been in their places for some time. From their expression and glances at the gallery, and their words, one could see how self-important they felt.

'The way those monkeys behave, you'd think they were the senators themselves,' said an annoyed student. 'Someday, when we occupy those seats, the first thing I'd do is to kick out that one, if he's still around.' And he pointed out a security guard who had vexed him earlier.

The platform with a large table and throne-like chairs was still waiting for the Senate president. The guards flitted all around the entrances on both sides of the hall. They bowed before the high officials but threw dagger looks at the common people, as if they were suspected of carrying bombs.

The onlookers had already dissected the personalities of each of the few who had arrived. Two oppositionists were speaking noisily and making expansive gestures with their hands. Another explained that the division between the majority and the minority was vague. The two often exchanged members.

'The practice is to join the party where there are more benefits. This is the politics of the stomach.'

'Like Senator Batalla.' And he pointed with his lips towards one of the two men noisily talking on one side of the hall.

'That one does nothing but contradict any popular bill, whether it's good or bad. But once, he gave himself away. He kept attacking a bill; it turned out that he was the author.'

Each time the front door opened and disgorged a gentleman with an unusual attire or bearing, the whispering would grow louder and the gossip would float with the smoke of cigars and cigarettes in the cramped air. They would whisper loudly about the newly arrived and discuss his public and private affairs, both as a legislator and as an individual.

'There's Senator Discurso,' said the first onlooker to his seatmate, who hardly spoke and pointed to someone rushing in—a short, stout man with a wide mouth and large eyes.

'That one is fond of making speeches, even if he is already out of order,' said the onlooker. 'It's hard to stop him unless his false teeth fall out.'

A man then entered with faltering steps. He seemed to be deep in thought. He carried a cane with one hand, and on the left lapel of his woollen coat was pinned a gaudy rose. Eyes followed him, until he put down his cane on his table and sat back on his swivel chair. Then he raised an arm to return the greeting of the newspapermen.

'That's Senator Estrellado,' whispered the onlooker. 'He is always well-dressed and elegant. You'd think he would do something worthwhile, but he does nothing but wear out his seat. He never joins a discussion or say "yes" or "no". Nevertheless, he always wins in the elections.'

'Really? How does he do that?'

'By overspending,' said the gossip. 'Some newsmen and photographers are on his payroll, so his statements and pictures always appear in the papers. Every time the reporters choose outstanding legislators, he is always on the list. Even if he did nothing during the whole session. Naturally, he always gives them envelopes.'

'So, that's it, huh?'

'Yes, money talks—and how! Many are carried away by propaganda on the radio and in the papers. With money, it's easy to make a crow turn white and a heron black.' And then he snapped his fingers softly.

'You can't believe there are many clean ones among those legislators.'

'So it seems.'

Two more senators came together. Senator Botin, whom we had met before, was in wearing a sharkskin suit; the other was in native formal wear made of spun pineapple fibres. The latter looked young and energetic despite his white hair.

'Those two are very good,' said the gossipy onlooker. 'The one in the coat, Senator Botin, is good at gambling. The other in formal native wear is Senator Maliwanag. He has the most brilliant mind in Congress.'

The other laughed at the amusing comparison.

'Maliwanag is good,' continued the gossip. 'Because of this, he is often alone. He seems to be just like a prophet in the middle of the wilderness. In gatherings like this, one should not be intelligent or patriotic. An acrobat or a poker player is better. Senator Botin could bring home more money than Maliwanag, for he is a wily gambler and an expert bluffer.'

After eleven-thirty by the big Senate clock, the Senate president walked over to the platform, took the mallet and pounded it.

'The session is open,' he declared briskly. Then he sat on his large chair, rested his head on the back, and began to puff his cigar.

The floor leader rose and asked that they omit the roll call and the minutes of the preceding session. There was no objection. He then presented the first item on the agenda. The opposition leader quickly stood up and questioned the quorum.

'Ask for a quorum when voting on a bill,' reminded the floor leader with some heat in his voice.

'But if you always take note of the quorum, no session will take place.'

'In *dat keys*,' shouted the oppositionist, '*dis siyempul* anomaly is *di responsibility ob di madyuriti*. According to *di* rules *ob di* house . . .'

'Let's set aside the rules first,' the floor leader screamed back. 'We need to finish as soon as possible, so don't waste time on the rules.'

The veins on the neck of the opposition leader bulged as he screamed in his own brand of English.

'Mr Senate President, Your Honour,' he said, stuttering, '*Di* members *ob di madjuriti* are *olwis* absent in *awir* sessions. We were sent *hiyer* by Uncle Sam, no, I mean, by Juan de la Cruz, to work, *en* work religiously. But many *ob* you abandoned your duties. You simply *istil di* money *ob di pipol*. What do members *ob di madjurity* do? Waste time on money in junkets *en* junkets. It's *imposibol to heb* a quorum because one *hap ob di Senit* is elsewhere, outside *ob di Pilipins*. At least five senators are in the United *Estets*, one is in *Espin*, one in England, one in France, one in Argentina, and three in Japan, cutting deals on the *reperesyons*. *Wid dem* are *dyr waibs, tsildren en* company,

at *di* expense *ob awir guberment en pipol.* Your Honor, *dis abuses* are a
national *iskandal en* calamity. *Di iliktorit* will *siyurli panis* your party in
di coming *iliktions.*'

The gallery burst into loud applause after hearing the fusillade
of attacks from the opposition. The majority floor leader objected,
claiming that the opposition was out of order.

'We have an agenda, Mr President,' he pointed out.

'Please go ahead,' the chairman said.

'The bill Filipinizing retail trade is up for decision today,' said the
floor leader. 'The committee has recommended its approval.'

'The intention of the bill on Filipinization is to exclude the
foreigners from running small variety stores, am I correct?' Senator
Discurso asked, speaking in Spanish.

'*Mas y menos,*' the floor leader agreed.

'Therefore, this bill is unjust, for it will just use the law as an
instrument,' Discurso said with vehemence, in a mixture of Spanish
and Tagalog.

'It's a nation's duty to itself to pass laws to protect its interests,' the
floor leader informed him.

'Mr President,' Discurso shouted in English, and then he spoke in
Spanish, indicating his opposition to the bill. '*Quiero hablar en contra
de la proyecto.*'

'Senator Discurso,' the chairman of the committee said, 'please
wait for your turn. Senator Maliwanag still has the floor.'

Calmly, the floor leader asked Senator Discurso not to oppose the
administration, for he was a member of the majority. The senator's face
turned red at this reminder, so he screamed back in a merry mixture of
three languages. 'Mr President, I believe that our nation is a democracy.
Everyone has the right to exercise the freedom of judgement and
opinion. I'm against the Filipinization of retail trade because I'm for
equal rights and opportunity before the law. Many Chinese-owned
shops prosper not because the owners are Chinese but because they
are good managers, more hardworking and diligent and more frugal in
their business. They are not to blame. On the contrary, we should be
grateful to the Chinese for giving Filipinos a valuable lesson on hard

work. I'm afraid that the moment the businesses are transferred to the hands of our compatriots, they will exploit our countrymen. We have enough proof of this. What is also happening is that the fish that are abundant in our rivers and seas are more expensive than the meats imported from Australia and Argentina. Likewise, the prices of bananas from our land are higher than apples and oranges from the United States. *Que barbaridad*!'

'Que barbaridad' was not a part of his speech, but it was an outburst when his dentures leapt from his mouth. Luckily, he caught them with his hand. He stared open-mouthed as loud laughter echoed from the crowded gallery. The chairman pounded his mallet, and the crowd was quickly silenced. The chairman told the house security to warn those who made noise. But even the senators were laughing hard.

'That serves him right,' said one onlooker who favoured the bill. 'The Chinese must have paid him a large sum.'

When order was finally restored, Senator Maliwanag stood up. He was recognized by the chairman.

'I shall explain why we should approve the bill giving retail trade to our countrymen,' said the handsome senator. He spoke in flawless and eloquent Tagalog.

'You should speak in English,' said Senator Batalla.

'*En Castellano*,' said Senator Discurso.

'Gentlemen of the Legislature,' continued Senator Maliwanag, calmly dismissing the requests. 'I thought that every member of this body knows what is known to every ordinary citizen—that the Philippines is free and independent. But because we have not yet been independent for a long time, colonial mentality is still found in our midst.'

The buzz in the gallery expressed approval.

'I saw one of these signs when I began to speak. In the legislature of a free and independent country, when a member uses his native language, members don't ask him to speak a foreign language. In the legislature of a free country, the wretch who behaves in this manner will be brought out of the assembly hall by security. He will either be charged with disturbance of the peace, or have his head examined. Here, this merely arouses laughter instead of shame.'

Sudden applause burst from the gallery.

'But I prefer English,' insisted Batalla.

'*Hangal!*' said Senator Maliwanag.

'Who is the fool?' The one who did not approve of Tagalog stood up.

'If you understand Hangal, then you understand Tagalog,' said Maliwanag. 'But if you don't, then I'm sorry.'

Laughter resounded from the gallery. The senator continued.

'The Philippines is the land God gave to the Filipinos. But look at the unhappy turn of events. Here, the Filipinos are poor and the foreigners are rich. Who owns the mines? The foreigners. Who owns the banks? The foreigners. Who owns the major industries and business firms? The foreigners. Who owns the utility companies? The foreigners. Who owns the communications services? The foreigners. To whom belong almost all the big factories and businesses? The foreigners. Go to Santa Cruz, Binondo, Quiapo, and you can see the painful irony. The big stores all belong to foreigners, while our countrymen sell wares in a box or a basket or a table on the sidewalk. And they are chased by the police and dragged like animals to the police vans.'

'One question.' Senator Botin rose. Maliwanag nodded.

'Will the Filipinization of retail trade correct this?' asked Batalla. 'Is that not just a balm on a wound?'

'That's a good question,' said Maliwanag. 'The retail trade in the hands of foreigners is a symptom of a serious illness. Just like unemployment, poverty is the offspring of the same mother. They're different wounds from one source. You're right: applying a poultice to a painful wound brings only temporary relief to the patient. But this doesn't mean that the treatment will stop there. If an operation is needed, then, by all means, that operation should be done.'

'Could you specify the illness that caused our people to suffer?' Senator Botin asked again.

'Perhaps it's no longer a secret,' Maliwanag answered. 'It's caused by colonialism. During the four centuries of Spanish rule, the Philippines was used to chopping wood and drawing water from the well and was asked to attend solely to the needs of the master. The Philippines only produced raw materials and imported finished products. She sold cheap and bought dear. It was inevitable that this situation would lead to poverty, unemployment and discontent. Nationalism is the cure, and that's why I am asking for the unanimous approval of this bill.'

'Approve! Approve!' shouted the gallery seemingly as one.

But the senator had hardly returned to his seat to drink water when he heard Senator Batalla calling attention again to the lack of quorum.

'To pass an important bill without a quorum is equivalent to falsification,' he shouted.

Indeed, there was no quorum, but because their stomachs were growling, the Senate adjourned without acting on the Filipinization bill.

'The foreigners will rejoice again,' groaned the Filipino owner of a small store on the street corner.

XXXI

A man five feet, ten inches tall, with an elegant bearing, took twin rooms *en suite* at the Hotel Ritz in Paris. He strode into the plush hotel in a grey suit made of English wool. He wore black leather shoes, a white long-sleeved shirt, and a purple tie with small silver dots. Under his right arm was a portfolio; his left held a Homburg hat from Rome. Even the very atoms in the air seemed to give way to this man of destiny.

When he approached the reception desk, he spoke in fluent English. The first thing that the employee noticed was his white teeth and the large scar on his cheek. The employee wondered what kind of sharp weapon could have caused such a scar. The wealthy gentleman also wore light-green sunglasses.

He quickly signed his name beside the suite's number in the guest book.

MANDO PLARIDEL

'Mando Plaridel,' read the clerk. 'Are you Mexican?' he asked, handing the guest the key to the suite.

'No,' he said, 'I'm a Filipino.'

The clerk did not catch the answer, but he just said nothing. He thought that this rich man came from Spain, or the Near East. He just followed a long-standing policy of the owner of the Ritz, who began as a waiter and ended up a millionaire. The owner had told all his employees to see everything without looking, to hear everything without listening, and to learn everything without asking.

The clerk knew the physical characteristics shared by the Chinese and the Japanese: pale, yellowish faces and almond-shaped eyes. But this man had reddish-brown skin, and his round eyes were black as coal.

Mando took the elevator to his room on the third floor, followed by a bellboy carrying his suitcases.

Mando had just arrived that afternoon from London. He had taken a BOAC plane from the Croydon Airport in England. He reclined in his comfortable seat, read the English paper and drank a martini. The plane smoothly crossed the Canal de la Mancha and gently landed at the Le Bourget Airport in Paris in an hour.

The queries at the immigration counter were respectful and brief. In less than half an hour, he had breezed through immigration and customs. There were no annoying questions, and his luggage was not searched. The employees accepted the customs declarations of the guests. Indeed, the French showed their visitors their delight in having tourists. Their greeting 'Welcome to Paris!' tinkled like bells.

After exchanging dollars for francs at a counter at the airport, Mando took a Citroën taxi to the Ritz Hotel.

Now in the hotel, he arranged his suitcases, looked around his elegant room, and then went to the bathroom.

After a bath and a change of clothes, he lifted the phone's receiver and asked for a waiter. It was about seven in the evening. He ordered drinks and dinner. In Paris and other cities on the continent, the drink is not cold water but wine. Two or three kinds of wine were served with the food.

While waiting for his order, Mando took out his diary and sat on the sofa. He wrote down the date and time of his arrival in Paris. He turned the pages of the diary.

After dinner, Mando wondered if he should go out and begin his adventures in the enchanting city. Paris was indeed beautiful by day, but it was enchanting by night.

Mando could breathe the delicate breeze from the window of his room. He looked at the sky, which hung like a huge canopy over the lovely city. The darkness vanished with the bright lights, which were like long necklaces that glittered along the twelve boulevards, that were, in turn, linked at the sparkling Place de l'Étoile. Mando saw at once that the brightest boulevard was the Champs-Élysées, where his taxi had driven that afternoon from the airport. The driver had stopped for a while beside the Arc de Triomphe. In halting English, he said that Napoleon had built this to commemorate the victory of France during the war. Only after Mando showed he understood did the taxi driver continue on its trip to the Ritz Hotel.

In the view from his window, the famous Eiffel Tower, with its height of 934 feet, looked like a giant standing at the Champ de Mars. A red light glowed on the tip, like the eye of a giant bird.

Mando's attention was also riveted by the waters of River Seine, which were like the silver scales of a long serpent reflecting the lights. Not far was the silhouette of the Trocadéro Palace. He looked beyond the shady trees of Champs Élysées. On the west of the Tuileries, stood the Place de la Concorde, formerly called Place de la Guillotine. The square had a new look and décor . . .

There was no more trace of the disorder, panic and horror of the day when King Louis XVI and his queen, Marie Antoinette, had died at the hands of the revolutionists. After a few years, the leaders of the revolution themselves were trapped by the cycle of intrigue and revenge. The wheel of politics turned. Mando felt the breeze, but it was not the lament of Madame Roland that he heard, the beautiful woman who helped the revolution but was later killed by the same revolution she had aided—she, who before the guillotine cut her head, exclaimed in defiance, 'Oh liberty, how many crimes are committed in thy name?'

After having his fill of the City of Lights, Mando returned to his seat and drank his martini. Silently, he ate the hot and lovely dinner brought by the waiter, then drank strong coffee. He lit a cigarette and poured himself another glass of martini.

Then he looked up some names in the telephone directory and listed these on a sheet of paper.

Mando decided not to go out that night. Instead, he changed into pyjamas, reclined on the bed, and held his diary.

He recalled the events from the time he had quietly left Manila, almost a year before.

XXXII

Mando had gone to the most important cities in Europe. He saw and learnt many things there. Now he had a wider vision, which would be hard to measure and describe. There was a change in the way he looked, dressed and moved. He now seemed self-possessed and cultured.

According to his diary, he first stayed in Saigon, then he flew to Bangkok, Rangoon, Karachi, and finally Cairo, in the first leg of his trip. Then, he crossed the Mediterranean to go to Ankara, Milan and Madrid.

In some of the Asian cities, he was tempted to stay and see the ancient places he had only read about in the books. But Mando stifled such a desire and told himself that he would visit later, because his aim was to reach the famous cities in Europe.

Although he only stayed briefly in Asia, Mando got important information about their conditions, people, cities, government, progress or lack thereof, strengths and weaknesses.

He thought it best to stay longer in Madrid and there, learn about Mother Spain at close range. He often travelled from Madrid to Barcelona. These two cities were the intellectual, commercial and social centres of the former conqueror that had given the Philippines the name of its king. Some ancient parts of these cities reminded him of Intramuros and San Nicolas in Manila.

He met some Filipinos who enjoyed living there and had no plans of going home to the Philippines. Likewise, there were Spaniards in

Manila, Iloilo, Zamboanga, and other places in the archipelago, who did not want to return to Spain any more. Mando thought that people were like plants that live in places where they take root and find the climate agreeable.

Mando often visited the former palace at the Congress of Representatives and the famous Central University of Madrid. The visitors' credentials were closely examined before anyone could enter the palace. This was done upon the order of Generalissimo Francisco Franco, who had survived several assassination attempts, allegedly perpetrated by the nationalist foes of his dictatorship.

Mando looked for the former printing press of the newspaper *La Solidaridad* that was published by del Pilar, Lopez Jaena, and Rizal as the voice of the expatriate Filipinos in Europe. The house had been replaced by a modern building, and not even a humble marker was put on the historical site.

He spent many days at the National Library. In its foremost museum, he examined books and looked at relics of the Spanish colonization of the Philippines. He copied some important information that he could use later to correct some wrong accounts of the history of the archipelago.

To his delight, Mando discovered that the Spaniards were very friendly towards Filipino tourists. Their women had sweet smiles, their grass wine and dry sherry gave heat, and their sardines and tomato-pepper sauce were spicy. At first, he could not understand why they had this special fondness for Filipinos. The Filipinos were treated like relatives who had long been separated and missed.

Mando thought that all advanced countries were almost the same: peaceful and generous, quiet and kind-hearted. But often, the representatives they had sent to the colonies were rascals who just committed abuses. He felt that if the Spanish officials and friars had been just like these ordinary citizens in Madrid and Barcelona in the way they treated the Filipinos, perhaps the ties that bound the Philippines and Mother Spain would not have ended in blood. Nevertheless, Mando felt it was best that way, for a steel chain and a gold necklace have the same effect if used by the master to choke a slave. Once, Mando asked a Filipino who had been living in Spain for a long time, about his thoughts on colonialism. The man said, 'Spain was a good and honourable country, but its ministers were to blame. Colonizers often send undesirable people to the colonies. Secondly, the Spaniards changed their impression of the Filipinos when they rose up in 1896. That was when they realized that the Filipinos were not a tribe of slaves.'

In Madrid, Mando visited some old churches, which had the same style and size as the churches built by the Spaniards in the Philippines. He watched the popular bullfights. He noticed the contradiction between the state religion and the state amusement of Spain. The first preached holiness, but the second displayed cold-blooded cruelty. He guessed that it was the same reason education was in the gentle hands of the religious orders, and the government was controlled by the iron hand of autocracy. But occasionally, they were reversed or fused.

After a few months in Spain, he moved to Italy. He stayed in Rome.

Rome was one of the oldest cities in the world. According to legend, it was built by the twins Romulus and Remus, who had been found and reared by a wolf. One of the fast-selling souvenirs in Rome is that of two infants being nursed by a large wolf, their foster mother.

The centre of the religious and political power of the Roman Catholic Church was the Vatican. It was an independent state, separate from Italy, a sovereign power with an area of less than fifty hectares. Here lived the pope and 1,000 residents, many of whom were employees, guards and servants of the Roman Catholic Church. The Vatican was surrounded by high walls.

On the other hand, Rome had a population of two million people. Mando was surprised that the holy city of the Vatican also had the greatest number of communists outside the Soviet Union.

The first thing that Mando noticed at the airport was the abundance of crucifixes and small statues of Venus de Milo. Both were naked. Christ was bare of all vanity and worldliness at the moment of his sacrifice at Mount Calvary, while Venus de Milo showed the unadorned and natural beauty of a woman.

Rome was a city of contrasts. The ruins of a coliseum built before Christ sat near the modern building of the United Nations.

Just like in Manila, government offices, banks and other establishments in Rome were closed on Saturdays and Sundays. However, the theatres, stores, restaurants, and bars were open. But on Sunday, the whole city stood still. There was complete abstinence—no business for the stores, for everything was closed. On the other hand, the 300 Catholic churches were open, and there was a brisk sale of religious objects like crucifixes, rosaries, veils, medals, sacred pictures, prayer books, images, candles, and all kinds of stamps showing the activities of the pope and the Holy Church, countless relics and souvenirs prized by pilgrims and Catholic tourists.

Tourism was the chief industry of Rome and other famous Italian cities. Besides Italy's noble ruins of more than 2,000 years, its art, opera, architecture, sculpture and other cultural forms were some of the most impressive in Europe.

Mando joined a tour of Rome and its suburbs. The usual tour, which took the passenger to historical places, lasted three hours. But tours that included Naples, Capri, Pompeii, Sorrento, Amalfi and other places, lasted for several days. So the traveller's budget should include food, hotel and other necessities.

Mando stayed at a hotel near the Basilica of Saint Mary Major, one of the four patriarchal temples of Rome. The other three were Saint Peter's Basilica, the world's largest and most famous; the Basilica of Saint John Lateran; and the Basilica of Saint Paul. According to legend, in August 352 AD, the image of the Blessed Virgin Mary appeared to Pope Liberius, and told him to build a church where snow fell that night.

During one outing, Mando went around the large Basilica of St. John Lateran, where he saw the huge statues of the twelve apostles and the mausoleum of the painter Raphael. He also signed the old book of guests who came from all parts of the world.

He also visited the Basilica of Saint Paul. In front was a statue of Saint Paul holding a sword, showing that he was not only a ferocious Roman guard against the first Christians but also a martyr beheaded for being a devout follower of Jesus.

But of them all, the grandest, most powerful and impressive was the Basilica of Saint Peter in the heart of the Vatican. Every day, thousands of people visit this holy centre of Christianity to fulfil a vow, to hear Mass, to see the pope, or to stand in rapt attention while looking at the peerless works of civilization and art. Almost all religions, Christian and non-Christian alike, Muslim, freethinkers and atheists, were fascinated by the ceremonies of the most widespread religion and the monuments of its history and culture.

Upon alighting at Saint Peter's Square, one would come face to face with the tall obelisk that Caligula brought home from Heliopolis during his Egyptian campaign. The cathedral and the pope's palace stood grandly on one side. By the wide door of the cathedral was a tall Swiss guard as rigid as a statue, wearing a colourful uniform and holding a spear. On each side of the stairway stood the monuments of Saint Peter and Saint Paul. There were also five doors to the portico. On the left was the statue of Charlemagne, and on the right was the statue of Constantine, who built the first basilica. It was said to have been built on the exact burial place of Saint Peter. Mando noticed the bronze statue of Saint Peter, who was seated. Its feet had been worn out from the pilgrims' countless kisses.

After the rites celebrated by cardinals and bishops at the main altar, the pilgrims and other onlookers flowed out of the cathedral into the middle of the square. All eyes were fixed on the window on the third floor of the palace. Then a white banner was unfurled from the second window. In a few seconds, the pope would appear, with his hand raised to bless the crowd below. It was high noon, but the sun was mild.

On other excursions, Mando saw the remaining ivory columns of the Roman Forum, the old meeting place of the citizens, and the Curia, the former conference hall of the senators. At the Curia was enacted the tragedy of Julius Caesar, who was killed by Brutus, his adopted son, along with other conspirators. They were afraid that Caesar would be crowned and said they also wanted to save democracy. But in a stroke of irony, this paved the way for the rise of a series of Roman emperors called Caesar. This was followed by the autocrats of the other kingdoms. Later on, the horizon would appear the *kaiser* of Germany and the *tsar* of Russia.

Mando also went to see the arches and monuments made by famous sculptors, like the arches of Constantine and Titus, the monuments of Marcus Aurelius in older times and of King Emmanuel of a new Italy. He also looked at the works of Galileo, Garibaldi and Cavour. Surprisingly, on one side of the shore of River Tiber, still stood a tall column. According to the guide, it was built by Benito Mussolini in honour of his closest friend—himself. In fact, the concierge at the hotel where Mando was staying loudly proclaimed that Mussolini was the greatest Italian after Julius Caesar. This reminded Mando that there were still many fascists in the country, despite the numerous socialists in Rome.

One of the most interesting excursions brought him to the rows of catacombs, or underground graves, which he saw after the bus had travelled several kilometres in the Appian Way. There were nine different catacombs, and they visited the one belonging to Domatillus. They went down the long and winding passages lined with tall niches. They further climbed down the stone steps around a platform, went down many stops again, until they finally reached a chapel. There, they were received by an old priest whose deep-set eyes and pointed nose made him look like a mummy that had come from one of the niches. The priest related the history of the catacombs. There used to be four floors, he said, but these were buried under the ruins and had been dug up only eighty years ago. During the early days of Christianity, the Roman pagans had killed thousands of people. He then mentioned the names of the saints and martyrs that had been buried there. Then they visited the other sacred rooms of an old cemetery. The paths were made of hard earth, and the dim light only served to emphasize the darkness.

As Mando stood in a corner looking at the niches, which were empty except for the dust of those who had been buried for twenty centuries, he thought how easy it was to kill and dissolve a person's body, but not his spirit. It has been proven every time. The first Christians were persecuted, imprisoned, nailed to the cross and killed. But they did not surrender, and they did not fear death. When they were gone, the truths for which they died, flourished. And in a grand stroke of irony, the heartless group of executioners were the first to bow and wave the flag of the new faith.

On their way back from the catacombs, they stopped by the Quo Vadis Chapel along the Appian Way. Saint Peter and Jesus Christ were supposed to have met here. At that time, the persecution of the Christians was at its peak, and Christ had died on the cross outside Jerusalem. Saint Peter was fleeing from Rome when he met Jesus of Nazareth.

St. Peter was startled and asked his teacher in wonder, '*Domine, quo vadis?* (Lord, where are you going?)' Christ quickly answered, 'To Rome, to be crucified once more.' Saint Peter felt ashamed as he did when he denied his master in the garden of Gethsemane, and the rooster crowed at dawn. So the foremost apostle turned his footsteps and then hurried back to Rome, to face his death.

Mando then realized that the real greatness of Rome or Greece and Athens was not because of their feared legions, which were finally vanquished at that time. Their real wealth lay in their rich civilization and culture found in Greek literature and Latin laws, which were handed down the ages.

Mando was also fascinated by the Vatican's mystery and truth. It was the official residence of the Holy Father and the seat of power of the Roman Catholic Church. Just one square mile and with less than a thousand residents, its voice is heard and heeded by five million followers all over the earth.

Mando sat many times on a pew in the large Saint Peter's Cathedral and meditated. He visited the honoured Basilica of the Vatican, which was even grander than King Solomon's Palace. He also visited the tombs of Saint Peter and his successors, from Linus to Pius XI. He saw not one of the thirty-eight anti-popes, who claimed to be the true pontiffs from the second century until 1440.

More than the statues of those who established the different religious orders of the church, Mando admired the murals and paintings of Raphael. He also did research at the Vatican Library. There, he saw manuscripts older than the Christian religion. These were the first copies of the Bible made of papyrus and written by hand in Hebrew, Greek and Latin.

Mando was startled to see the so-called Index and *Propaganda Fide*, a blacklist of forbidden books and reading materials. Mando did not read the whole list, which ran into thousands of authors and works, covering all topics.

He had sinned many times, he found out, by reading the works of Voltaire, Victor Hugo, the Dumas father and son, Zola, Rabelais, Stendhal, Flaubert, Anatole France, George Sand, D.H. Lawrence, and other famous authors. Several times, he had also read the plays of Maeterlinck and Bernard Shaw, which he enjoyed thoroughly. He had no idea that he was endangering the salvation of his soul in the next world. Looking at the Index, he recalled *Paradise Lost* by Milton and *Faust* by Goethe, which were hailed as world masterpieces. In the English epic, Satan was the protagonist when the king of the devils rebelled against God. In the German poem, the chief character was Dr Faustus, who sold his soul to Mephistopheles in return for a woman, pomp and power.

Mando also recalled his student days. Every Lent, he would read the *Life of Jesus* by Ernest Renan. This book was also banned, he learnt. He could not imagine how this came to be, for Renan had studied to be a priest before he became interested in writing history and biography. The Index on Prohibited Books also included the works on astronomy by Copernicus, Kepler and Galileo, from which he drank in his intense thirst for knowledge. Did not these books change the outmoded beliefs about the place, shape, size, elements, purpose and meaning of the planets, sun, moon and stars?

Mando doubted if he could still gain pardon for long-past pleasures he had derived from the philosophers of the ages: Spinoza, Bacon, Hobbes, Bergson, Swedenborg and Kant; Darwin, Adam Smith, Proudhon and Hegel; Marx, Engels,and Lenin. Why should he wonder that the novels and other works of Rizal should be opposed by faithful followers of the church, although they honoured the martyr of the race?

Mando closed his eyes for a while. Then he approached an old employee of the library and asked with courtesy about the question bothering him.

'Bad reading material is more dangerous than swords,' the employee said bluntly. 'Saint Paul showed what should be done with bad books. He burnt them. The popes succeeding Saint Peter did likewise. For the Holy Church cannot err, and in guiding all Catholics, it is her duty to keep all their reading material clean.'

Then he took another list and handed it to Mando.

'This is the blue list,' he said. 'There is no lack of good things to read. You can see that on this list.' Then he turned on his heels and left.

Mando looked at the blue list with its recommended books. It contained the *nihil obstat* of the church censor and the imprimatur of the bishop of the diocese where it was published.

It mentioned the Catholic Bible, especially the New Testament; the prayer book of Father Alsace; the *Imitation of Christ* by Saint Thomas A. Kempis; the writings of Saint Thomas Aquinas, Saint Ignatius de Loyola, and Saint Alphonse de Liguori; some works of G.K. Chesterton and Graham Greene; all the books of Cardinal Spellman and Monsignor Sheen; *Lives of the Saints* by Butler; and the encyclicals of different popes, especially *Rerum Novarum* and *Matrimonio Cristiano* by Pope Leo XIII and *Cuadragesimo Anno* by Pope Pius XI.

Mando left the Vatican Library and crossed the square to the cathedral. He entered the door and dropped a hundred liras into the box for alms near the front.

When he left the cathedral, Mando was still thinking of what the old library employee had said about burning bad books. He recalled that Hitler and Mussolini became known for book burning, and that the Japanese in the Philippines often made bonfires of mountains of books, which they said were not worth reading.

Mando reassured himself by thinking that it was better to burn books than roast in the fires of hell. He continued comparing the pictures deeply etched in his memory with the entries in his diary.

He recalled his trip to Switzerland, a small country nestled amid the beautiful Alps. As a boy, Mando had read the story of William Tell, the archer who was a Swiss hero. Mando discovered that this country still had the same heroism and courage, undiminished by time.

Mando was impressed by the small republic, which was less than one-seventh of the Philippines and with only five million people. It remained free and was economically and politically stable. It remained neutral, peaceful and safe during the Second World War. It didn't have to pour money for armaments, although it was surrounded by warlike countries such as Germany, France, and Italy.

Mando's tourist guide explained that the Swiss were not concerned with politics but with industry, agriculture and other productive activities.

'The president serves for only a year, without reelection,' said the guide. 'He is elected by the legislature from among the members of the council, whose two houses are both elected by the people.'

While Mando and his guide were talking at a street corner in the city of Berne, a middle-aged man passed by on a bicycle.

'Look at that man,' the guide told Mando. 'He was a watchmaker who later became our vice president. After his term, he went back to making watches.'

The guide explained with pride that making watches is an important profession in Switzerland and that Swiss watches were the best in the world.

Oh, such an important person goes around on a bicycle, Mando wondered to himself.

'Here, one does not enrich himself in a government position.'

Mando raised his eyebrows but made no comment. He observed that the Swiss were also as industrious as ants. The tourists were the only ones who wandered about, seeking pleasures. The Swiss made much money from tourism. At the stations, the trains brought products from different parts of the country, from giant locomotives to small rings and watches and especially cheese, butter and canned milk. Their quality was the best in the world.

Mando passed by Geneva, the city by a lake, where international conferences had been held since it became the seat of the League of Nations after the First World War. At present, there were many standing committees and commissions of the United Nations in Geneva. The representatives from different nations gathered and worked here, trying to cobble peace in an uncertain world.

Before he left for other countries, Mando deposited several million francs and some of Simoun's jewels in a reputable bank in Switzerland.

After coming back from Geneva, Mando spent some weeks in the countries of Benelux (Belgium, Netherlands, and Luxembourg). These three countries set good examples of how to remain independent and prosperous. Even if the first two were ruled by kings and the last by a duke, their constitutions guaranteed religious and political freedoms to every citizen. Neither the king nor the government could impose state beliefs on the individual.

Mando was in London when England turned socialist. He could not imagine why the party of Winston Churchill fell, when this premier during the war, along with Franklin Roosevelt of the United States, counted as the foremost leader of democracy.

An English writer whom Mando had met on his trip greeted him upon his arrival in London.

'Not all war heroes make for good leaders during the period of reconstruction,' said the Englishman. He mentioned the great generals, from Alexander the Great to George Washington, who did not turn out to be good administrators. He added that every leader has his own time, and every period has its leader.

The English writer boasted that England not only developed its culture but also brought civilization to the jungles of America, Africa and Australia.

'But you are a colonizer,' said Mando. 'You bring civilization and take out gold. Spain did the same earlier, but it brought religion, which was also paid for in gold.'

His English friend respected Mando's opinion, but insisted on what he said about civilization. Although Mando knew its history, he listened patiently to the story of the birth of the English Constitution when King John signed the Magna Carta in 1215 on the fields of Runnymede. This document recognized the rights of the nobles. Mando agreed that the Magna Carta became the model for the Bill of Rights of the United States, which was, in turn, the model for the citizens' rights in the Philippine Constitution. He also mentioned the Industrial Revolution, which began in England in the middle of the eighteenth century. Since then, the belief that work is heaven's curse was supposed to have vanished, for with the miracle of the machine, man had been freed from the yoke of hardship until he reached a new dignity and living standard.

On the other hand, Mando reminded him that the Industrial Revolution nourished capitalism and was the foundation of the Machine Age, where the means of production were more important than people. 'Man became a slave of the machine,' said Mando.

Mando was taken by his friend to different places. They entered the gardens of Buckingham Palace. His friend explained that the queen in the palace is only a symbol. The real power is at Whitehall, the centre of the government that had been elected by the people, which then happened to be socialist.

They also visited the large printing presses on Fleet Street. Mando observed the different parts and activities of a modern newspaper, and how they were managed. He learnt that thousands of people read the English newspapers such as the *London Times*, *Daily Mail* and *News of the World*.

'Here, democracy is not just a flower blooming on the tongue,' Mando's friend said with pride.

And they went to Hyde Park, the famous park in London, and listened to the speeches of different groups on the wide square. One criticized the queen, while another bashed the prime minister. One gathering was about communism.

'They are free to float all kinds of ideas,' said Mando's friend. 'They don't even need to ask for a permit from anyone. No policeman will bother them.'

Meanwhile, Mando saw that the leaders had also learnt to practise self-discipline. They were not used to putting themselves above the law. One afternoon, Mando was brought by his writer friend to the house of a member of parliament. It was a small flat compared to the mansion of the typical Filipino legislator. After receiving them in his library, the MP lit the fireplace. He was going to boil water for tea.

'Is there no electricity?' asked the writer.

'Because of austerity,' answered the host, 'we're not allowed to use electricity before six in the evening.'

Mando looked at the clock on top of the table. It was already five-thirty. Half an hour more. Mando's eyes glistened with admiration for the English legislator. Then a sigh escaped him when he thought of what a Filipino lawmaker would do if he needed to make coffee in the face of such a ban in Manila. Would he still light a fire, or just switch on the light? Mando knew what the answer would be.

As they drank tea, they discussed various things. Mando asked, 'The war has long ended, yet why do you still use coupons for buying and selling?'

'To avoid the black market, to prevent hoarding by the rich, so that goods will be available to the ordinary consumer. We can do this because production is adequate. Supply and demand are balanced.'

'Why are American cigarettes so expensive at two dollars a pack?'

'Sometimes even more,' said the official, 'because we want to protect our own production. Our cigarettes aren't inferior to the imported ones. If we don't charge high taxes on those made in the USA, we'd be killing our industry. We have our own; therefore, those from the other countries are just mere luxuries and should be made expensive.'

Mando saw clearly why Filipino producers did not prosper and why imported products sold quickly in Manila.

Like any tourist, Mando did not tire of visiting the historical places and buildings in the two parts of London divided by River Thames. He climbed the London Tower, strolled at Mayfair Park, visited Westminster Abbey, and watched a meeting of the parliament. He bought a few souvenirs at Piccadilly Circus and at Trafalgar Square. He also bought some books at Haymarket on Chancery Lane.

Whenever he had time, Mando always went to the incomparable British Museum, which housed a big library. Every time he went, Mando felt like he was entering a holy temple.

The first time he went there, he was with his friend, who informed Mando that it contained more than five million books and two million manuscripts. If the bookshelves were placed side by side, they would reach sixty miles, which was the distance from Manila to San Miguel de Mayumo.

The complete collection of English poems from Chaucer's *The Canterbury Tales* to the last collection of Dylan Thomas were all deposited there. Attracting the most attention were the plays and poems of William Shakespeare, with copies of the translations in many languages.

As Mando read a yellowing book on the history of socialism on an old table in the reading room, he seemed to see the shadows of Garibaldi, Marx, Lenin, Rizal, Sun Yat-sen, Gandhi and other revolutionaries, hovering around him. They had also spent many long and fruitful hours in this reading room.

Mando was mesmerized by the English genius in industry and commerce. An island only slightly bigger than the Philippines, England produced almost all of man's needs, from pins to giant ships, from candy to giant hydraulic plants, and everywhere it sent its ships and aeroplanes. While the Philippines could not even produce mediocre toilet paper.

After reading the last pages with the entries on his travels, Mando took out from his portfolio a small notebook and studied it closely. It was an important list of Simoun's jewellery that had been sold, to whom and from where, and the price. When Mando summed up, the sales had reached a few million dollars. Less than half the jewellery had been sold. He had made no transaction in Paris, and his contact in the United States was getting impatient.

He deposited the money in the banks, bought bonds and invested in stable industries. In all his financial transactions, he hired an internationally known Swiss corporation as his consultant. In Madrid, he deposited several hundred thousand dollars at the national bank, almost a million at the international bank in Geneva, and more than two million at the London bank. Half a million was used to buy stocks in the railroad industry in Switzerland, and he also bought bonds in Berlin. He had enough traveller's checks in Swiss francs and American dollars, two of the most stable currencies in the world.

He had 5 million dollars to his credit at that time.

That's more than fifteen million Philippine pesos, he told himself. He reassured himself that this was not a dream but a fact.

Mando noticed that it was almost midnight. He became immersed in his diary and in the deep well of his thoughts. He got up and lit a cigar.

When he stood again by the window, the red light atop the Eiffel Tower seemed to wink at him. It was already very late, but just like a beautiful and enchanting princess, Paris was just starting its nightlife.

XXXIII

Mando remained an early riser. Ever since he had worked at the Monteros' before the war, he would rise at dawn. And more so as a guerrilla hiding in the Sierra Madre mountains.

But the next morning at the Ritz Hotel, he had not yet even brushed his teeth when the telephone rang. It was Helen, a Spanish-Irish mestiza, who was born in Intramuros, Manila but had lived in Europe during the war. Helen had lost both parents and lived a cosmopolitan life, travelling all over the continent. She lived on her earnings as an agent for anything she could sell, from a fort in Gibraltar to the crown of King Farouk. When she was younger, it was said that she received offers for her smooth and alluring body for a night at the Grand Hotel, or a week at the Riviera, instead of her wares.

Mando had met Helen in Geneva on business. The Spanish-Irish Filipina had helped Mando sell his jewellery at a good price. He gave Helen 5 per cent of any cash sale, and her commission was not small. To a young king in the Near East, she sold a set of jewellery worth a million dollars. This was a gift to a Hollywood star with whom he was infatuated. The king and the star met on vacation while in Switzerland, and Helen rightly guessed what spell could attract both the king's gold, which came from his petroleum wells, and the heart of the actress. In that transaction, Helen earned a clean 50,000 dollars.

This was one of the biggest sales listed in his notebook. In Madrid, he sold some jewellery to a famous Spanish millionaire from Manila who was then on vacation in Spain. He was delighted to see the items, and he bought them without haggling over the original quoted price of half a million dollars. Mando heard that the jewellery was given as a gift at the wedding of Generalissimo Franco's daughter. In exchange, he received a gold medal and a citation for his deeds in honour of Spain in the former colony.

Cleopatra's collar was bought by a bank of the Rothschilds in England at 600,000 pounds sterling—or about 2 million dollars. The bank official expected to profit by no less than 50 per cent for its investment in the famous collar, which it later sold to a multimillionaire collector in Chicago.

Before the bank of the Rothschilds had bought the famous collar, Mando's agent had offered it to the English government.

'Such a collar and similar jewellery are only for aristocrats,' said the spokesman of the socialist government. 'We won't waste a single penny on anything not needed by the country. Our funds are reserved only for food, housing and coal.' If it were not for his moral responsibility, Mando would have given the collar as a gift to the socialist government in London. He felt then that the gap between the new government and the old conservative regime was like that between heaven and earth. After a time, he was startled to learn that the opposing parties were both made up of politicians. They were then just two faces of the same coin.

Mando invited Helen to breakfast. When she arrived, they went down to the restaurant of the hotel. According to Helen, she had just arrived in Paris and immediately sought out Mando. She was staying at the Normandy Hotel.

'A New York playboy is here,' said Helen as they were having coffee. She mentioned an American heir who had been married and divorced several times. Each of his romantic adventures was international news.

'Does he have a prospect?' Mando asked.

'I heard that he keeps on following a ballet dancer, a Viennese, who is now the toast of Paris,' said Helen. 'He is said to be throwing away a fortune in flowers and perfume alone.'

'Very well then, you'll see what the playboy will like.'

'What the *ballet dancer* will like,' Helen quickly corrected him.

After breakfast, they returned to Mando's suite, and he showed her a list of the jewellery. Then he brought out a case of different gems, which Helen had not seen before. Rings and earrings, necklaces, bracelets, pendants, pins, combs and other pieces of all shapes, colours, and styles. Some were shaped like butterflies, dragonflies, bees, centipedes, fish, elephants, tigers, serpents, flowers, stars, statues and even human heads. Some were made of gold—yellow or white—and sprinkled with diamonds, pearls, emeralds, rubies, turquoise, garnets, sapphires, opals and stones with all the colours of the rainbow. Helen picked a few and asked for their prices.

'I'll go to the ballerina's hotel,' said Helen. 'It's said that she does not wake up before eleven.' She looked at her watch. It was already past ten o'clock. 'Very well then,' she said, 'I'll see you.'

'Come back this afternoon,' Mando said. 'I'd like to see Paris. Please be my guide.'

'Okay, *monsieur.*' Helen waved her hand and then left.

Helen returned in time for dinner. She happily informed Mando that she had firmed up a deal amounting to 300,000 dollars.

'It's in the bag,' she said proudly. The ballet dancer could not let go of the jewels. Helen had asked for an appointment with the playboy heir. 'If you have the head, the business is easy.'

'First, you need something to sell,' answered Mando.

'Of course,' Helen said. 'Only a racketeer sells nothing.'

'In Manila, influence peddling is different. Nothing to sell and no capital, except their saliva.'

'The influence peddler, wherever he may be—Manila, Paris, or Washington—is a racketeer,' said Helen. 'Most of them are politicians in power.'

'You're really a wise woman, Helen,' said Mando in admiration.

'I've been around.' Helen winked her blue eyes.

'Hats off to you, then.'

Mando asked the telephone operator to send up some drinks. 'I'll just change,' Mando told Helen. Their car was already waiting for them when they went down. They went to a small restaurant on the bank of the River Seine. Despite Sun Yat-sen's claim that the Chinese were the best cooks in the world, the French were considered the experts, especially by gourmets. They said that the Chinese discovered more dishes, but the French were more choosy; they have rare sauces and their food does not cloy with too much lard or seasoning.

Helen asked for stewed rabbit, and Mando ordered a pigeon breast sautéed in champagne.

After dinner, Mando asked what Helen wanted to see—the Opera or the Folies Bergère.

'For you, let's go to the Folies Bergère,' said Helen. 'There are operas in all the big cities, but there is only one Folies Bergère of Paris. It was imitated by the Ziegfeld Follies in New York, but an imitation is just a mere imitation.'

They had to pay extra for tickets, for the ticket booth was already closed. Tourists from all over the world filled the famed burlesque theatre every night.

That night, impresario Paul Derval was presenting *C'est de la Folie*, which would last about two hours.

According to the programme, which was sold at 300 francs, the women's costumes were exclusive creations of a famous couturier, and it warned that they could not be copied without his permission.

The well-applauded scene where the audience hardly blinked was the one titled '*L'Enfer des Femmes*' that showed hell in flames. At the side stood a well-built Lucifer who looked more like a Mr Universe. Then, like a swarm of moths, appeared the beautiful women, young, fair and shapely, with nothing to distract the eyes except the flowers in their hair and the rings on their fingers.

Such was the delight of the audience that two American sailors seated behind Mando and Helen decided there and then to look for hell.

'Buddy, surely there's heaven in that place,' the sailor said to his companion. The two agreed to search for the place immediately.

Mando whispered to Helen that this kind of show was not allowed by the authorities in Manila and would be opposed by the good matrons who were the guardians of morality.

'But this is art,' protested Helen.

'In Manila, it would be called indecent, obscene.'

'Indecency and obscenity are in the eyes of the beholder. When did a beautiful body become indecent? Then we should destroy statues and paintings from Venus de Milo, *Adam* by Michelangelo, and *The Naked Maja* by Goya.'

'But Manila is a Catholic city.'

'So is Paris,' answered Helen. 'But she sees art in a nude, not ugliness and indecency. Otherwise, she wouldn't be Paris.'

From the Folies Bergère, Mando and Helen went to Bal Tabarin, a popular nightclub in Pigalle. The place was already full, but they were assured of a good table when Mando gave the floor manager a big tip.

At this time, the United Nations Assembly was having sessions at the Palais de Chaillot in Paris. Helen told Mando that most of the guests at the reserved tables were delegates from different countries. Mando could recognize some Filipino delegates with their white female friends.

'Look at those people at the long table,' Helen told Mando. 'Seated together are the representatives of democracies and totalitarian countries. All of them are having so much fun, drinking champagne and eating caviar.'

'But when we read their statements in the papers, a Third World War seems about to break out,' observed Mando.

'That is called diplomacy,' said Helen, 'just a war of words. Better a battle of tongues than a battle of cannons.'

'But of course,' agreed Mando. 'That's the Cold War.'

Mando and Helen danced. After the cancan dance, which was the special attraction, Helen asked to leave, for she was to meet the playboy heir the next morning.

As they were leaving, Mando noticed a woman at a table. She was at the centre of a group of guests.

Mando stopped and looked. *Her face is familiar*, he thought.

He tried to remember, but the music was loud, and Helen was saying something. They went out, and Mando brought Helen to Normandy Hotel. He then returned to Bal Tabarin.

The woman and her companions were still there. He looked at her and tried to remember who she was. He was surprised to hear himself exclaim.

'Well, it's Dolly Montero!'

XXXIV

For a long while, Mando was rooted to the spot. He gazed at the olive-skinned woman, who was like a muse in the midst of the white women around her. He looked for further proof that she was, indeed, Dolly Montero. Memories flashed through his mind from the days before the war until the victory of the Japanese in the country.

Mando recalled that even when his parents were still alive, he was already working for the Monteros as a servant. His duty was to clean Dolly's room and to run errands for the family.

Mando saw the heartlessness of the family, their harshness in giving orders, and their lack of appreciation for service well done. Often, Don Segundo would hit Andoy's father for every shortcoming. Often, Doña Julia would hurl abuses at his mother when some clothes got torn while being washed or ironed. Dolly also insulted him or knocked him on his head if he had forgotten to clean her room or could not find what he was told to look for.

He felt hurt because of how his family was treated. It was easy to take the hardship, for they were used to work, but not the heaps of abuse and insults.

But he and his parents wanted him to finish his studies; otherwise, they would not have endured the cruelty of the Monteros.

His soul was bruised by the abusive words of Don Segundo when he was slapped by the Japanese at the headquarters because he had failed to salute a soldier. Instead of sympathizing and helping him explain, Don Segundo had just insulted and threatened Mando.

He also recalled the grave cause behind his leaving the Monteros and joining the outlaws. One day, Dolly found in a notebook of Andoy's a typewritten radio news report about the war outside the Philippines. Dolly gave this to Don Segundo, who confronted Andoy, hitting him and threatening to stop his studies. He also threatened to report Andoy to the Japanese military police.

That night, as Mando stood on one side of the renowned Parisian nightclub and gazed at the woman who had caught his eye, these memories rushed through him as if borne by dark wings. He was glad he was no longer the abused Andoy, a student-servant who cowered before the sharp voice of the master. He was now Mando Plaridel, a man with no master but himself, tested in the fires of war and by a thousand other dangers. He possessed a new personality with complete self-confidence—free, aware, intelligent and alert. He had a strong physique and a robust heart, and in his hands was entrusted wealth greater than the Monteros'. Mando knew this; now he could look anyone straight in the eye and not blink.

He wanted nothing from Dolly. True, she had grown lovelier, but in Paris and other cities, he had seen lovelier women. He had no wish to know this woman whom he used to serve, either to teach her a lesson, to seek revenge, or for any other reason. But despite his decision, he could not move nor draw his eyes from that alluring face that stood out among the other beautiful women around her.

Mando tried to get away from his memories. He went to the dimly lit bar and asked for a drink.

There were only a few guests at the bar.

His throat had hardly warmed from the whisky when she entered in the company of a white man. They sat near Mando, but they did not pay him any attention. The man asked for straight whisky and the woman, champagne.

Mando could hear their loud voices. The man had a French accent. 'Dolly, *mon chérie*,' said the man, so Mando was sure that she was, indeed, Dolly Montero, 'you are free, now that classes are over.'

Dolly pouted before answering, 'I told you that I don't plan to leave Paris during vacation. This is my only chance to go shopping. You know that I'll soon leave for Manila.'

'But just a week, my dear Dolly,' insisted the man. 'Ah, you have not seen the beach of Cannes, a paradise visited by famous stars and fashion models. We'll just stay there for a week. This is the ideal climate—spring. We'll go boating and swimming by day, and dancing and drinking at night. A carnival of joy, *mon chérie.*'

'Don't insist, Pierre,' Dolly said curtly. 'You may invite Yvonne or Odette and enjoy yourselves.'

'You are avoiding me,' the man said harshly. 'Is there someone else? The American?'

'No, no one,' she answered coldly.

The man stood up and tried to kiss Dolly. She turned her face away. Pierre, who was obviously drunk, persisted. Dolly stood up and started to leave, but Pierre stood in her way and tried to embrace her. She tried to free herself, pleading, 'No, please . . .'

But this scene did not bother the other guests. They were used to this and thought that the two were just lovers who had drunk too much. But to Mando, the incident could not be ignored. Here was a man molesting a woman; the man was a foreigner, and the woman was a Filipina.

Mando could not remain seated. He approached the two.

'Mister,' he addressed the man who would not loosen his grip on Dolly's arm.

'Mister' looked back and pushed Mando.

'This is none of your business,' he shouted and dragged Dolly away.

'Please, help me,' Dolly said to Mando.

So Mando intervened, but the man hit him and barely missed his eyeglasses. Mando returned with a left jab on the chin. The man let Dolly go and fell like timber on the carpet. Mando quickly took the girl out before any scandal could erupt.

'Please take me home,' Dolly said.

In the taxi, Dolly asked to be brought to her dormitory. Mando remained silent.

'Sir, are you Mexican?' Dolly asked.

Mando turned to the woman on his left, smiled, and courteously answered in Tagalog. 'I'm a Filipino. And you?'

'We are countrymen. I'm from Manila. Dolly Montero.'

'I'm Mando Plaridel.' He offered his hand. The name did not ring a bell with Dolly.

'I was lucky you were at the bar. Pierre is American-French, and he grew up in Paris. Impulsive and a bad drinker.'

'Why do you have such friends?'

'In Paris, choosing friends is just like buying goods—attractive but only in the display window. In Parisian society, you can't tell the prince from the pauper, the heiress from the dance-hall girl. But in Manila . . .'

'Ah, in Manila, one's true colour cannot be denied,' said Mando. 'There, the beggar can't pose as a prince, the dance-hall girl can't be mistaken for an heiress, as a crow can't be mistaken for a dove,' he added.

Dolly made no comment, thinking that Mando was just making a general remark.

'But perhaps, you have been away from the Philippines for a long time,' she said. 'From your appearance . . .'

'For a long time,' said Mando.

Dolly supposed he had been in Europe much longer than she had.

Mando told her that he had been to different cities, while travelling for a newspaper in Manila. Dolly said that she had finished a course in Paris and would soon return to the Philippines. She was not sure if she would go to the United States; perhaps, she would just pass by on her trip home.

At the door of her dormitory, Dolly thanked Mando profusely. She would not let him go until he promised to have lunch with her the next day. She chose a restaurant on Champs-Élysées.

Although it was almost dawn when Mando returned to his hotel, he still could not sleep, thinking about the strange coincidence. Who would have thought that he, a servant before the war, would now be regarded as a gentleman living in a grand hotel in Paris? And who could have guessed that the mean daughter of his master would be indebted to him and not recognize him? Truly, one reaps what he sows.

Had fate decided that Dolly should reap the abuses she had sown? Would Mando avenge his oppression at the hands of Dolly and the Monteros? He fell asleep with these thoughts.

The next day, he was awakened by a call from Helen, who said she was coming. When she came, Mando was already in the lobby and had just sent a cable to Manila.

'Let's go to your room,' she said. 'If I give you these 300,000 dollars in broad daylight, Hombre, the Paris gendarmes will rob you,' teased the lively Irish-Spanish Filipina.

'You sold it fast, huh?'

'And not in French money.'

Every dollar then was worth 340 francs and could easily buy 500 on the black market. During Mando's stay in Paris, the francs were spent like the Mickey Mouse money in Manila during the Japanese times. It was hard to exchange francs, whether Belgian francs or Swiss, especially for the English pound or the American dollar.

After Helen gave Mando the money for the jewels that had been bought by the playboy heir and had received her commission, she expected Mando to take her out to lunch.

'I'm sorry, Helen, but I have a date. In fact, I'm late now,' he said, glancing at his watch.

Helen laughed. 'I knew that after twenty-four hours, this poor chaperone would already be excess baggage.'

When Mando arrived at the restaurant, Dolly was already there. She looked even more beautiful in her light-blue dress.

'Did I keep you waiting, Miss Montero?' Mando asked as he sat beside her.

'Call me Dolly, and I'll call you Mando,' she suggested. 'I've been waiting since you left me at the dormitory,' she said in a teasing manner and looked straight at him.

Only then did she notice the scar on his left cheek, but she merely glanced at it and fixed her laughing eyes on his dark eyes. She did not ask how Mando got his scar.

Dolly related her experiences in Paris while studying at a finishing school. She also mentioned her life in Manila, her experiences during the war, and the liberation. Of course, she neglected the chapters about Colonel Moto and Lieutenant Whitey, her stay at a private hospital in Hong Kong and . . .

She asked Mando to talk about his adventures in the exciting cities where he stayed, his girlfriends, his preferences among the Spaniards, Italians, Belgians, English and Parisiennes.

'I don't have a girlfriend,' said Mando. 'Before you court a girl, you have to love her,' he said. 'I have met many beautiful white women, but not one made my heart beat faster.'

Dolly put down her fork and fixed her eyes on Mando's face.

'I salute you, Mando,' she said. 'But it's a surprise, if not a miracle, that during your long stay in Europe, you've had no girlfriend.'

Mando thought for a while and admitted that he did have a friend in Brussels.

'She is Flemish,' Mando recalled. 'Young, only twenty years old, but aged early by sorrow, with red hair and blue eyes. I was window-shopping at the Bon Marche in the foremost square of Brussels when I heard a cool voice. "Do you want to have fun?" she said in an inviting manner. When I turned, I saw in her beautiful face a mixture of shyness, fear and need. "How much?" I asked. "Not as dear as the goods you're looking at," she said, sneering. I was then looking at some pipes from London. I could see that she was hungry, so I brought her to a restaurant. She drank two glasses of beer and ate enough for two. Then she said, "I'm ready to do whatever you wish" and clung to my arm. The night was cool and inviting, but I didn't take her to my hotel. Instead, I hailed a taxi and brought her home. She lived in a hole of a cellar with her two small children. "I'm a widow of the war. I have to keep my children alive," she sighed. "There's no other way for me." While I was in Brussels, that unfortunate woman didn't have to roam the streets at night. With a little charity, she could rest early together with her children.'

Dolly was touched.

'Now, I don't only salute you,' she said with admiration. 'I want to kiss your hands. I feel like a Mary Magdalene before Jesus.' She threw Mando a meaningful look.

From the restaurant, they went to the different famous places in Paris, which Dolly said he had to see. They went to the Louvre, the largest and most famous museum in the world. Mando was eager, and Dolly did not tire of looking at the masterpieces and statues and paintings, murals and frames, marble, bronze, drawings, sketches without compare: Venus de Milo, Helen of Troy, Pallas of Velletri, Heras of Samos, Athena, *Mona Lisa, Maria de' Medici*. There were the works of Michelangelo, Cellini, Donatello, da Vinci, Raphael, El Greco, Murillo, Goya, Lautrec, Rembrandt, Titian, Tintoretto, Corregio, and many more that all cost a fortune. They visited Les Invalides, where lay the remains of Napoleon Bonaparte and other great men. Before dusk, they took a seat in the Notre Dame Cathedral where Dolly silently said the Angelus prayer.

They spent a half hour in the quietness of the park of Bois de Boulogne and watched the lighting of the countless lamps along the boulevard before Mando took Dolly to her dormitory.

'Please come back for me in two hours,' Dolly said.

'Aren't you tired?'

'In Paris, a contented heart doesn't know fatigue,' Dolly said happily. 'I'll expect you. We'll have dinner, then go dancing at a nightclub where no one will bother us.'

On his way back to his hotel, Mando thought that this seemed like a dream—the difference between his relationship with Dolly in Manila from 1940 to 1942 and their present relationship in Paris. Then, he was a miserable tool hardly noticed by Dolly; now, he was the idol of the haughty darling of the Monteros.

'Only lightning has no revenge . . .' Mando thought. Then he flicked his lighter and put a cigarette in his mouth.

XXXV

Mando and Dolly were both good-looking in their evening wear. The weather was fine, neither cold nor hot. At that hour, Paris was like a lovely but coquettish lover who was promising joy to all her suitors. All held their breath at its beauty, whether they were strolling under the trees on the grand boulevard or riding in the cars along the Champs-Élysées.

Dolly was elegant in her Christian Dior gown, but it was neither her dress nor her jewellery that first caught Mando's attention. The fragrance that she lightly sprayed on her hair and body was intoxicating. At first, he could not decide if it was a Lucien Lelong, a Caron Paris, or a Guerlain.

Dolly's necklace, earrings and ring were quite uncommon. But to Mando's eyes, which had been used to seeing the unique and fantastic gems in his collection, they all seemed like glass.

When Dolly came down, Mando greeted her in admiration, 'Who would notice the *Mona Lisa* at the Louvre?'

Dolly pretended to be displeased and reproached Mando for comparing her to a five-century-old painting.

'Oh, please forgive me,' said Mando. 'I meant that even Leonardo da Vinci's original can't compare to you.'

'Now that's better. Thank you,' Dolly said with a smile, 'but tell me, which do you like most, my hair, my dress, or my perfume?'

'I like everything,' he said. 'But I like you, above all. Even if you crumple your hair, or you're in a cheap dress.'

They got into the car in high spirits, and Mando told the driver where to go. The car stopped for a while at a flower shop. Mando got out and bought a corsage made of orchids so pale, they were almost white. Dolly asked him to pin it above her left breast. She broke off an orchid and placed it on the left lapel of his coat.

'Just tell the driver where we're going,' said Mando, 'I'm a novice in Paris.'

'Very well then. What do you want—French, American, or Spanish food?'

'Is there anyone who eats American food but the Yankees? Hotdog or pork chop?'

Dolly laughed and recalled the fishy canned sardines and tasteless sausage, which she always ate during the first days of liberation. Now she felt nauseated just thinking of them.

They went to a small restaurant on the banks of the River Seine, a place called the Forbidden Fruit. The small restaurants of Paris were unlike those in Manila, which were filled with flies. Those in Paris were small, indeed, but lacked nothing in elegance, luxury and service, including an orchestra and a show.

When their car stopped, they were welcomed courteously by the porter dressed in a uniform. He opened the door and led the two guests to the restaurant. Mando gave him a tip.

The head waiter bowed and ushered them to a reserved table. Two waiters immediately approached. Mando asked for scotch, and Dolly asked for sherry.

When they were seated, a girl brought a basket of fresh flowers. Mando gave a bouquet to Dolly. Then a cigarette girl approached Mando and he bought a pack of American cigarettes. The flower girl and the cigarette girl were both scantily dressed and looked like dolls.

As Mando and Dolly drank, the first violinist glided towards them, playing 'Hearts and Flowers.' He stood before Dolly.

Mando gave them several hundred francs.

When the orchestra played, Dolly asked Mando to dance. The waltz was sweet, and the lights began to dim. The partners became dancing shadows crisscrossing in the spotlight, which moved around the hall.

Like a petal attached to the wings of a butterfly, Dolly's slim waist was caught in Mando's right arm. She was as light as cotton. She rested her head on his shoulder, and he could smell the fragrance of her hair.

Dolly was inviting; Mando was trying to control himself.

To Dolly, whose heart was as playful as her eyes, the events were not surprising. Mando came into her life when she was in trouble, when the rash Pierre tried to force himself on her. Mando saved her. She did not know him then, but her heart began to beat faster.

When she met him the next day and had looked at him closely, and after they had talked on different topics, her utter fascination was complete. She noticed that his build and his height were unusual for a Filipino. Their conversations convinced her that he was witty and bright. And she saw that he was a gentleman, from his manners and his high regard for women.

Dolly made comparisons. She quickly decided that Mando was superior to any man she had known. Mando was different from Colonel Moto, who was like a coiled snake. He was different from Lieutenant Whitey, who was an opportunist. And certainly, he was much more different than the brash Pierre, who thought of nothing else but sex.

Dolly trusted Mando more than anyone else. In his arms, she felt like a bird, happy in the safety of her nest. As they danced, she would lightly press Mando's left hand, and she would brush her cheek lightly against his lips.

On the other hand, Mando felt like a house divided. He was aware of Dolly's invitation, perhaps as a sign of gratitude or of a daring and seductive heart. But Mando was hesitant. He could not decide whether to enter the open door—or to close it and turn his back.

Only a few days ago, he had told himself he wanted nothing from Dolly, and he did not even care if she would meet Mando Plaridel. There were many women in Paris far lovelier than Dolly, and in Paris, money was king—and Mando was richer than a king.

But despite his first impulse to avoid her, and because of unforeseen events that simply unravelled before them, Dolly was now here in his arms. He was intoxicated by the perfume in her hair, which felt like countless snares around his heart. He no longer hated her. The memory of a young girl who had shouted at him and ordered him around had turned into a shadow. That person could not be the same as this lovely girl smiling happily, with feet that seemed to float and a body smooth as silk, whose every word showed that she was in love.

Mando thought that even if Martin's treachery had left a permanent scar on his left cheek, the pain of oppression from the Monteros should have been healed by time. There is no curse without a corresponding blessing, just as there is no dark cloud without a silver lining. Because of the Monteros' cruelty, he had to leave. And how did this shape his life? If Don Segundo, Doña Julia and Dolly had been kind, he would not have thought of leaving. He would still be their servant, or would have been promoted to their clerk.

But because of what happened, he was now here in Paris, on top of the world, and he was gazing at Dolly. Should he wish to, he could make her pay dearly for what she and her family had done.

The music ended, and the two returned to their table. The waiter opened a bottle of champagne.

'Pierre called this afternoon and apologized,' Dolly said. 'Imagine, he had the nerve to ask for a date.'

'Making up is fun,' Mando said, baiting her. 'It's as delicious as this champagne.' He sipped from his glass.

'Do you want to know what I told him?' asked Dolly. '"I forgive you," I said. "But I don't want to see you again," I told him.'

'But why? Is there another one, the *"Americain"*?' Mando said, mimicking Pierre.

They burst into laughter. Dolly moved her face closer to him and said lovingly, 'Hoy, not "Americain", but Filipino. Let's celebrate,' she added.

She raised her glass and they drank.

After Mando had paid and given the two waiters and their captain a fat tip, they left the Forbidden Fruit.

They then went to La Puerta del Sol, a club with a Spanish motif. They drank, danced and watched a show *La Madrileña*. From La

Puerta del Sol, they went to the Crazy Horse. They did not stay long because it was crowded, and there were three noisy Americans whose eyes were like those of rotten fish. One was cursing angrily, insulting the French, who he said were at the mercy of the Germans during the war. He claimed that they owed their lives to the American marines who had landed at Normandy in May 1945. Otherwise . . .

'Crazy,' said one, as he stared at the neon lights of the Crazy Horse.

They instead went to a place called Naturalists. Here, they ate a special omelette while a starved-looking French artist made a crayon sketch of Dolly and Mando. By the time they finished eating, the sketch was finished. They admired the close likeness, and the artist kept on saying, 'Merci, Monsieur' after receiving 2,000 francs, which was equivalent to four American dollars on the black market.

It was already dawn when Mando and Dolly finished the last bottle of champagne at the Moulin Rouge. They were already drunk as they watched the special burlesque number. As they went out, Dolly could hardly walk. Mando had to help her in and out of the car. In the car, she reclined in his arms like a baby.

Earlier that night, Dolly had told Mando about a dormitory regulation against coming home after twelve midnight, even with a permit. Moreover, under no circumstances should they go home drunk.

'If we should stay after twelve and if I should get drunk,' she reminded Mando, 'don't bring me back. Take me anywhere. I'll just make up an alibi the next day.'

So they went to his suite at the Ritz Hotel. In Paris, a guest's room was his castle. Mando woke up the waiter, who had become his friend, and he asked for hot tea. Mando asked Dolly to drink a cup of tea. Then he made her lie down on a separate bed. After he changed his clothes, he lay on a couch in his receiving room.

But Mando could not sleep, for Dolly was moaning. Several times, he had to go to her, and the last time, she threw up. He led her to the bathroom. Then he brought out a robe, for her dress was already soiled.

Mando did not feel good, either. His head was already spinning, and he could hardly lift his feet. This was how he felt when he was wounded by Martin. He was not used to drinking heavily. A few glasses of champagne were enough. And he seldom went beyond three glasses. But that night, he let himself go. Dolly also did the same. They wanted to make merry, and both forgot themselves.

When Dolly returned from the bathroom, she saw Mando stretched on the bed. Feeling as weak as a wilted vegetable, she dropped on to the bed. Her head was on Mando's hard chest. They both slept soundly as if they had smoked opium.

The hot rays of the sun were already piercing the curtain of the open windows when Mando opened his eyes. The first sight he saw was Dolly embracing him, sleeping as if she did not want to wake up. On the floor was the robe; Dolly's breasts were exposed.

He thought he had been dreaming at dawn. But Dolly's appearance and his own made him recall that what happened between them was not a dream.

Mando brushed back Dolly's rumpled hair and kissed her. Her lips smelt of the acid of the champagne and the fragrance of Guerlain, and he went back to his disrupted dream.

XXXVI

It must be true that good fortune, just like misfortune, does not come alone. It is just like a guest who brings along others who were not invited.

Mando was merely selling his jewellery and storing knowledge, according to schedule. But on top of this, he also received an unexpected reward. With hardly any investment, the rare gem of Dolly's beauty fell into his hands. Since the wine had given way to their early intimacy a few weeks past, Dolly seemed to crave him. She was infatuated with Mando, but it would be hard to say that this was true love. Undeniably, she liked Mando more than any of her previous lovers. Like a new gown that she wanted to wear constantly, she sought Mando.

For an inexperienced girl, Dolly's feelings could be true love. But she was fickle and capricious. She would not rest until she got anything that caught her eye, or her heart. So no one could be sure, not even Dolly herself, whether what she felt was love. Only time could tell.

As for Mando, his heart beat fast and his blood was aflame when he was alone with Dolly. This happened often, for Dolly was persistent and impulsive. She had refused Pierre's invitation for a week at the beach, but it was she who persuaded Mando to stay for fourteen days in a private cottage. Nevertheless, Mando felt nothing but desire, which was natural for a healthy, lonely man in his prime.

In drinking from the cup of pleasure, neither the past nor the future mattered. For Dolly, it was best to shut the door of memory on her dark past. She would not spoil the present with worries about the future. True to her accustomed ways and her nature, she enjoyed the honeymoon of the happy night and never minded whether the sun would shine or not the next morning.

For his part, Mando had less need to look back, for his past always loomed in his present. In his mind, Dolly became a part of his stay in Paris, but she was not in his plans after Paris. Although he seldom took any step not related to his plan, and Dolly was indeed a gem of great value, still she was among the things he had consigned to time, or to chance. Unlike his cousin Puri.

Ah, Puri, a simple maiden, a meadow flower whose perfume filled even the very wind, although hidden within the folds of a leaf. What if Puri were in Paris instead of Dolly? But such musing came only fleetingly, like the streak of a comet in a dark sky.

Mando did not spend all his time in Paris on Dolly, nor in selling the jewels. He surely attended to his pleasure and his business, but he did not neglect his other important goals.

After seeing historical places, the old palaces which were being used by the present republic, the museums, the cathedrals, the parks, and other relics of the past and progress of the present, he observed the life of the people, especially the commoner.

As could be found anywhere, the common man in Paris, and especially in the rural areas, was industrious, loyal and quiet. More fond of work than pleasure, he knew how to have fun, but he attended to more worthwhile things. The French father and husband was loving, and few looked for happiness elsewhere.

But above all, the French loved freedom—of thought, of speech and of assembly. Only the boulevardiers added freedom in love. So in France, you could find almost all parties, organizations, churches and movements. All beliefs and doctrines enjoyed equal respect before the eyes of the law. The labourers, the intellectuals, even the anarchists and communists enjoyed the rights to form unions and spread their principles.

Strikes were ordinary happenings in disputes between capital and labour. During strikes, the police stayed neutral; they did not break pickets or serve as tools of the rich.

Even the free thinkers, the agnostics and the atheists had their own organizations and movements. No one accused them of being enemies of the law and society, just because they openly attacked fanaticism and belief in one Creator. The voice of the minority was not drowned out by persecution, although 97 per cent of the French were devout Catholics.

Mando saw a massive strike outside Paris when the workers in all factories of weapons and bullets stopped working, three years after the Second World War. The workers opposed the government policy, arguing that the country needed bread and butter, not guns and bullets. Both sides stood firm, but the government gave in a little and pursued its programme. It assured people of enough food and vowed to avoid provoking war and to move cautiously in the midst of the Cold War.

Mando observed the efficiency of the parliamentary system where the legislature, which was made up of the country's representatives, decided on important issues. The Parliament did not just sign laws; rather, it felt the pulse of the nation at all times. So that in deciding on any national issue, if the decision of the administration was nullified by the Parliament, the leaders immediately resigned to give others a chance. The advanced democracies in Europe considered the presidential system passé, finding it to be too slow and democratic only in name. Even if the party of the president lost in other elections and even if the country heaped curses on the mistakes and abuses of the administration, he and his assistants could not be replaced if the president did not wish it to be until the next national elections, or if the country was lucky, until death snatched him before his time.

One day, Mando's impatient American agent named Mike arrived in Paris. Mando spent the whole day and night with Mike, planning how to bring the jewels to the United States. According to Mike, although the giant Statue of Liberty stood on Staten Island in New York, nothing could freely enter the United States without paying the corresponding taxes. And if taxes would be levied on the remaining jewels that he wanted to sell in the US, Mando might have to withdraw all his deposits in Spain, Switzerland and England, and deposit all of them in the United States.

'Leave it to me; we can solve this problem,' Mike promised.

When Mando asked how, Mike's expression suggested an important secret, making it sound like the first hydrogen bomb in the Third World War. But all the American whispered was that he had a friend, an important member of the United Nations from a banana republic in Latin America.

'We shall invite him and you know . . . the unfailing prescription.'

'Money,' guessed Mando.

'Wine and women,' added Mike.

'If that's all, I'll give you a blank cheque; you write the amount.' According to Mike, said delegate was returning to Lake Success in New York after the session of the United Nations in Paris. He had a diplomatic passport, so his baggage and belongings were not opened at the port.

Mando recalled the wife of a Filipino ambassador whose baggage filled two trucks when she left Manila. The large crates were supposed to contain reports, papers, books and other documents. Actually, they were filled with expensive furnishings like rugs, chandeliers, silver dining sets, paintings, textiles, perfumes, wine and so many other items. How easy it was then for a diplomat to carry an ordinary valise like a portable typewriter.

Mike and Mando completed their plan. They would befriend the emissary of the banana republic, butter him up, and then ask him to bring the valise to New York. Of course, they would not tell him what it contained. Mando would keep the key. He would take the boat, while Mike and Mando would take the plane.

'See how easy?' Mike said when they had mapped out all the details.

Mando felt a twinge of conscience. Nevertheless, he thought of the importance of his purpose and plans in Manila for the welfare of his country. Thus, his anxiety vanished. His mind and his conscience were reconciled.

The next night, the two men met Colonel Mosca, Mike's diplomat friend. Mando offered him dinner, but they did not bring either Dolly or Helen. Instead, Mando invited three beautiful artists of the Carousel through their manager. He would reward the three artists with a month's pay; the manager was pleased with a traveller's cheque.

After supper, they spent several hours hopping from one club to another. The Carousel was the only club that they did not visit. Later, they agreed to go their separate ways. This was precisely as Mando had expected.

'*Hasta la vista*,' said the colonel, as he and his companion took a separate car.

Mando immediately brought his companion to her house, without reducing her fee. The beautiful woman was surprised but pleased.

The next day, the three men again met for lunch. By then, the colonel was practically promising the earth and sky. He had been so pleased the previous night.

'You can ask me for a favour, *amigo*,' he said. Mando saw his chance regarding the valise.

'The Filipino and the South American are the same in their ways and temperament,' said the soldier-diplomat. 'We're both gallant and we both like women. We seemed to have inherited these from Mother Spain.

Mando answered with a smile, 'But there is one thing on which we differ. We don't have your fondness for revolutions. For a slight thing, you revolt against a bad government.'

'And what is stopping you, amigo?' Mosca asked swiftly, but he took back his question. 'Let's set politics aside. I want you to know that that was some feast last night. A dish I won't tire of. If it were possible, I'd like an encore every night.'

'Your partner is the cancan star at the Carousel,' Mando said.

'I found out,' said Mosca, 'that she does the cancan better in bed.'

'And how was yours, Mike?'

'Like Goya's *The Naked Maja* in the flesh,' Mike said, clucking his tongue. 'If a Hollywood scout would discover her, she would surely be a star in a major film.'

The representative of the banana republic nodded, twirled his moustache, and spoke as if he were giving an interview.

'We should take our hats off to the French for their three specialities,' he said. 'They are number one in wine, perfume and beautiful women.'

'Maybe wine and perfume help a lot in making women beautiful,' Mike said.

'Of course, in our land, you'll also like the *señoritas*. I'd like you to go there someday, amigo,' he told Mando. 'Ah, our señoritas are also *hot tamales*. But compared to the Parisienne, they're like rice wine before champagne.'

'Why, they can't beat the American girls, especially in the shapeliness of the legs,' said Mike, who was from Texas.

'The American is a good sport, with beautiful legs, but doesn't offer much,' said Mosca. 'What I mean is that the American is cold, like a package from a refrigerator. I had a girlfriend in Washington. Every time we would go out on a date, if she wasn't chewing gum, she was reading a comic book.'

Colonel Mosca burst into laughter, followed by Mando and Mike.

'Amigo, tell us about you and your partner,' he asked Mando. 'She looks like a real spring chicken.'

'She looks tender as a pullet, but she's an old hen,' said Mando. 'Besides, I wasn't in the mood. When you left, I took her back to her apartment.'

'You should have asked her to join me,' the Latin diplomat said.

'That's easy,' said Mando. 'Here's her phone number.' He wrote her number on a napkin, which he gave to the colonel.

The next few days were the last meetings of the United Nations. Meanwhile, Mando finished his work in Paris. He then prepared for his trip to New York City.

Colonel Mosca took the second trip from the Paris station, accompanied by Mando and Mike. The colonel was bound for Cherbourg, from where he would take the boat for the United States.

Mando gave him a gold Swiss watch.

As they left the railroad station, Mando's fingers were playing with a small key inside his pants pocket.

On the eve of his departure, he and Dolly also had a farewell party, with only the two of them the whole night. They only stayed briefly at the clubs and lingered long on their private rendezvous. The lights in Mando's elegant suite at the Ritz Hotel burnt all night.

XXXVII

For a long time, Mando and Dolly had lived under the same roof in Manila, but on this night of intimacy, they were almost strangers to each other. Other than a sketchy narration of his past, Mando was unknown to Dolly. She was unaware that what she saw was the mask of a tourist, the disguise of a cosmopolitan man. Her former servant, Andoy, was hidden under the veil of time. The peasant roots were hidden under the handsome façade of a good-looking and cultured man.

Likewise, it could be said that Mando did not know Dolly, the real Dolores Montero, although she had surrendered to him her whole body. Was Dolly in love, or was she just amusing herself? Was she just whiling away her loneliness in a city known for its worldliness?

And Mando, how did he really feel about Dolly? Did he feel true love for the girl who had been the object of envy, attraction and admiration, but whom he secretly despised and avoided because of the gap between them? Or did he desire to possess her without marrying her? Did he wish to take advantage, to exact his vengeance?

These thoughts crossed Mando's mind during those moments with Dolly on the soft and wide bed of his suite at the Ritz Hotel. But he got no reassuring answer. It was the same with Dolly. She was not sure if Mando was to be the last man in her life.

On the other hand, they were both spellbound. They were sucked up by a force that they could neither fight nor evade. This was their last night in Paris. But it could also be their last night anywhere, forever. The lights were dim, their bed was soft and comfortable, the night breeze was balmy, and in the room floated a scent that seemed to blur their minds but sharpen their senses.

Mando turned to Dolly. She was in a sheer negligee. She had no more underclothes. Peeping through were her breasts, which were like ripe Spanish melons on a tree. Her smooth white legs were spread out, and Mando's hand would rub them or she would entwine them around his firm legs. Several times, Mando had seen the statue of the Venus de Milo at the Louvre. Dolly, at that moment, was a brown Venus indeed, but one made of flesh and bones.

'Are you thirsty, Dol?' Mando asked after a while. He stood up. His right hand rested on Dolly's breasts, and he would alternately rub and press them.

'I thirst for your love, darling,' she answered with a languid look and then she pulled his arm. He embraced her gently and kissed her lips. Dolly wound her arms around his shoulder until their bodies fused. Their kisses became fiery.

'I'm happy,' whispered Dolly. 'And how about you, my darling?'

'I'm happy as well, Dol,' whispered Mando.

Mando rose again, took Dolly and placed her on his lap. The belt of her negligee came loose, revealing the beauty of the Montero heiress. Mando rubbed its hidden treasures with his hands. Dolly did not protest; rather, she gasped, for the touch of Mando's fingers seemed to light small fires under her skin.

'I'm yours,' she said.

'Until when?'

'As long as you wish.'

'But I'm leaving.'

'Do you have to hurry? Why don't you wait for me, and we can go home together. Just a few more months . . . Then we'd have months of this. Don't you want this, darling?'

'I'm behind schedule on my mission,' answered Mando. 'My client in the US is already getting impatient.'

'Your mission is more important, is that it?'

'Come on. It just happens that I have to attend to it first.'

They stopped talking for a while. Dolly got up from Mando's lap and sat beside him. They leant back on the pillows. Like Delilah, she played with her fingers on the key to Samson's strength; her fingers played with Mando's manhood.

'I have a hunch that after Paris . . .' Dolly looked at Mando.

'Our Paris will not end . . .' he said. 'In Manila, in Baguio . . .' And he kissed her cheek. 'Let's have a drink.' Dolly nodded.

Mando got up after fixing his pyjamas. He poured martini into a glass. Dolly also got up, and they sat together in an easy chair. Both took the cold martini. Not just one glass, but two, three and . . .

'Next to your love, this gives me the most pleasure,' said Dolly, who seemed affected by the wine.

'I've to leave you in Paris,' Mando said.

'That's the sorrow of my life.'

'When I'm gone . . . you might be consoled by other friends,' he teased.

Dolly pouted and pulled his ear.

'Who . . . Pierre?' she laughed.

'The "Americain" . . .'

'Life is so busy, very busy, with Mr Plaridel,' the tipsy girl said, and then she laughed.

'Aren't you hungry, Dol?' he asked after a while.

'I've no other hunger except for you, oh, darling,' Dolly said. Then, she suddenly embraced him and buried her face in his chest.

That was neither the first nor the second time they had made love. What they had started had become customary and what was customary became a habit. If it did not bear any fruit, it was because Dolly had learnt to take care. She was given a lecture by the doctor in Hong Kong before she flew to Paris. And in her handbag, every time she had a date with Mando, and even before they met, she carried a bottle of pills.

It was already midnight. After they had finished the bottle of martini, she went to the bathroom. Mando had a hot shower. Dolly had a towel, and she bathed her hair and body with Guerlain.

'I get more drunk on your fragrance than on the strongest wine,' said Mando.

'That's the way it should be,' said Dolly.

They were like a real Adam and Eve when they returned to bed. When they were embracing, and their chests were pressed together and their legs entwined, Mando said: 'As the master of ceremonies of the Folies Bergère said, "This number is the last night in Paris."'

'"This is a night in paradise,"' Dolly corrected.

'Indeed.'

'Don't you want the lights out?'

'It's hard to find happiness, darling, so let's not allow it to escape in the dark.'

Their lips were sealed in an unending kiss. And their bodies and souls became one.

Morning still saw the bright lights in Mando's elegant suite at the Ritz Hotel.

XXXVIII

Mando was having snacks with Mike and Colonel Mosca five days after they left Paris. They met at the Athletic Club in New York City.

Everything went smoothly as planned. Colonel Mosca left Paris ahead, but Mando and Mike met the diplomat when he got off the boat at the port in New York.

Mosca handed the valise of 'souvenirs' to Mando. When Mando opened it at his hotel, the jewellery were intact.

That afternoon, Colonel Mosca was happy and even more good-looking. His wavy black hair was shiny, and his moustache looked like the horns of a black beetle. Mando noticed a gleaming pin on the tie of the elegant colonel. He did not have this in Paris. Mando was sure it was not among the jewels that he had sent through the colonel.

When Mando took notice of the pin, Mosca said he had good news, something that was related to the pin. Mando wondered if the colonel would sell his banana republic to Wall Street. He was wrong, but the news was truly sensational.

Colonel Mosca would marry an American widow, a multi-millionaire. Mike stood up and raised his hands.

'Mando,' he exclaimed, as if he had been robbed of his last dollar, 'our business is nothing compared to this Latin genius. Millions in a single transaction and, imagine, with no capital.'

'Hey! Mister, don't insult a friend,' said Mosca. 'Look at me, my bearing. What widow would regret giving up her millions?'

He met the woman at the dining hall of the luxury liner, *Ile de France*, on the first day it sailed on the Atlantic Ocean. He was introduced by a friend, who was an attaché at the State Department. They talked about the beautiful places in Latin America. The widow said she would travel there the following year. 'If you need an escort who knows Latin America as intimately as his fingers, I'm at your service,' the colonel said with gallantry.

Such gallantry was like Ali Baba's 'open sesame'. The widow put on her glasses and looked him over, from his glossy hair to his shiny shoes and back again. Mosca stood erect like a soldier about to be conferred a knighthood by his queen. She smiled and made room for him to sit beside her.

'But you're a married man, aren't you?' she asked directly.

'I'm divorced.'

'Aha.' He noticed the sudden lilt in her voice.

That night, he danced with the wealthy American in the ship's ballroom.

'You Latins are real experts at dancing,' said the merry widow.

'We're even better at love,' Mosca replied.

'Porfirio Rubirosa or Don Juan?' the widow asked in a teasing tone.

'Both,' he said. 'But *Señora*, please call me by my real name—Carlos.'

'Carlitos.'

From the ballroom, they went up to the deck. When she complained of the cold wind, Mosca took off his jacket and wrapped it around her shoulders.

The next night, Colonel Mosca was already sure of having landed the biggest catch in the Atlantic Ocean.

'She took this pin from her dress and put it on my necktie. And that's the whole story.'

'But you didn't mention how she looked,' Mike said.

'Well, I won't say she's as beautiful as the three artists of the Carousel,' Mosca said. 'But the figures speak. Forty-five years old, 200 pounds, and 14 million dollars.'

'Heavyweight in every way,' Mike said. He figured Mosca was only thirty-eight years old.

'She is a little older, but she looked younger than her years. Don't look for youth and beauty, for her beauty is in her bank book. Her late husband was a stockholder in several oil and steel corporations, and she inherited everything.'

'You're lucky, Colonel. Congratulations,' Mando said.

'When's the wedding?' asked Mike.

'In a week.'

It occurred to Mike that they should sell the jewels to the diplomat within the week, so he asked to meet her.

'When you're married, you can run for president of your republic. You'll have plenty of friends. It's in the bag.'

'Any position you like,' added Mando. 'In a capitalist democracy, an election is just an auction.'

Mosca looked at his friends and answered, 'Comrades, what for? When I'm married, goodbye politics. I don't know how it is in the Philippines, Mando. But in our country, a politician aims for a position to enrich himself. When he has amassed enough wealth, he resigns or is driven out by a coup d'état or a revolution. He seeks refuge in America or Europe, buys a villa and enjoys life. My future wife is a multi-millionaire. Why would I still need to be president? Why should I rob a poor republic?'

'What are your plans then?' asked Mando.

'Plans?' The word seemed new to Mosca. '*Mi amigo*, a man with money doesn't have many plans. To make merry, to amuse himself, to enjoy life. My future wife wants me to resign and help her manage her businesses. What more can you ask of life?' And he twirled his shiny moustache.

Before the wedding, the American multi-millionaire bought from Mike a set of jewels worth 400,000 dollars. Among them was a ring with three choice gems—ruby, diamond, sapphire—in the colours of the flag, costing 50,000. It was the widow's gift to her fiancé.

Mando was captivated by America, how huge and developed it was. He sought the secret of her greatness and saw that it was not a secret but a truth in modern history. America is the most powerful country today, although only one and a half centuries before, she was a poor English colony, a vast wilderness. Now, her railways and cemented roads stretch from the Atlantic shores in the East to the Pacific beaches in the West, from the Canadian border in the North to the Mexican border in the South. Her trains, ships, cars and aeroplanes, her skyscrapers, all kinds of industrial and factories, her mines, from black gold (carbon) to liquid gold (oil), her industries and agriculture, her arms for defence are greater than any other wonders known to history. To Mando, there was but one key to their wonderful success—sheer hard work.

Mando respected countries whose people worked hard day and night. They did not rest in the cities and farms, in the mountains and in the desert, on sea and on land, in the air and in the heart of the ocean. They also worked under the earth; in laboratories, in hospitals, in schools, in all places and on all occasions. There was no stopping, no respite from work, from discovery, from searching, from creating, from making new from the old; food, clothes, houses, wealth, everything that people needed. This world was too crowded and, Mando thought, in a few years, they would surely reach the moon.

And this was due to American manpower, to the American labourer, to the ordinary American citizen. Mando was filled with admiration as he rode the elevator to the top of the 102 storeys of the Empire State Building, or as he rode the subway hurtling through a tunnel under the Hudson River, or as he watched television at the Columbia Broadcasting at Radio City, or as he looked at the display windows on Fifth Avenue and gazed at the countless goods produced by American industry.

There's nothing that can't be bought in America and nothing that she can't afford to buy, said Mando to himself.

As if in answer to his thoughts, Mike came one day and told him of an offer of 5 million dollars for all his jewels from a noted jewellery store on Broadway.

'That's a good offer,' said Mando. 'Wholesale.'

'There's also a collector offering 1 million dollar for antique jewels that were made before Christ.'

'Then separate those, for a representative of the store is coming today.'

Mando sold the jewels for 5 million dollars, leaving only a few loose stones for his personal use. The store's representative said he was prepared to buy good jewels no matter how many they were and at any price. Mando remembered the jewels he had left with Tata Matias. They could bring in about 2.5 million dollars.

According to the Broadway store's representative, they also accepted pawning. In fact, they were keeping a dozen crowns from Europe as collaterals for loans. Some had been forfeited, for the owners had no hopes of returning to their thrones. Some former rulers in the old kingdoms had even become employees and mechanics in the United States.

The sale of the jewellery was over, and Mando thought of finishing his other business. He had been away for more than two years. In every city where he stayed, he had received a letter from Magat informing him of their newspaper and important news from the Philippines. Unemployment and disputes in the fields were worsening. Once, Magat visited the Montero Plantation, where the situation was critical in the face of the stubbornness of both Don Segundo and the tenants. Pastor had been removed as overseer, and he was now living with his daughter on a small farm outside the plantation. The two were doing fine. Pastor had joined the farmers' movement because of his anger at Don Segundo. Puri sent her regards and said she had received Mando's postcards. Tata Matias was well and was a devoted reader and critic of the *Kampilan*.

Magat also asked if Mando had already bought a rotary press to replace their old press. 'Even if you're enjoying yourself, please tell us when you're coming home,' Magat said in his postscript.

Actually, it was not pleasure that delayed his return. He did not waste any time at all. Except for the nights of pleasure in Paris, he had devoted all his time to his duties. Mando had tested his willpower. He had overcome many temptations in the cities of Europe and America. He realized why many Filipino students forgot their studies in America. Thousands of Filipino labourers who had emigrated to earn a living were not able to save any money and could not return home, like a misguided Ulysses. Government emissaries neglected their missions and attended only parties.

But Mando's good sense never deserted him. He deposited 6 million dollars in two New York banks and bought shares in a few solid stocks. He had already transferred the money in Spain and part of the money in England to the United States. Upon the advice of the multi-millionaire, the new Señora de Mosca, he had also invested 2 million dollars in steel and oil, where the money would earn more than in a bank.

Full of wonder at the limitless wealth of America, Mando went uptown one morning. He walked from the Commodore Hotel, instead of taking the streetcar, which connected Grand Central and Times Square, the heart of New York.

He happened to pass by the Bowery, which was within spitting distance from Fifth Avenue. Mando was shocked to see men in rags, unshaven and unwashed. All of them were pale and thin. Everyone had his palm outstretched . . .

'Please spare a dime for a cup of coffee. I haven't eaten breakfast.'

Mando was amazed that in New York City, with its Wall Street, where the richest banks and corporations could be found, beggars roamed the streets. Mando gave away more than a dollar for every outstretched hand.

With a few quick steps, he was on Fifth Avenue. He saw the grand matrons shopping at the ritzy department stores without any other care in the world.

XXXIX

Mando saw both sides of the silver and lead coins. Most pictures had two faces—smooth on the surface and rough inside.

Mando admired the greatness of America, but its weakness saddened him. Like the poverty exposed to him at the Bowery. Like the signs he read in many places: 'Off-limits to dogs and coloured people'.

After some months in New York, Mando took a train to Washington, DC, the country's capital. He planned to travel slowly from the East to the West of the United States and visit centres of education, science and research, law, art, industry and commerce, transportation, unionism and national organizations.

While New York was the show window of American financial power because of her great industries, Washington was the glass window of culture and civilization, government, and democracy. In New York could be seen and bought all the nation's products, cars fresh from Detroit and goods made of Pittsburgh steel, canned meat and food packed in crystal from Chicago, movies made in Hollywood, fruits and vegetables from Florida and California, beer from St. Louis, clothes, shoes, stockings, lipstick made in New York, Philadelphia and other cities on the Atlantic Coast, books on all topics, including technology, biography, history, religion. While in Washington, DC, the Capitol Building, its incomparable library, the White House with its famous rooms and garden, the museum and galleries of the Smithsonian

Institute, where one could see all the works of nature and man, animals, plants, minerals, stone, machines and art; the monuments and memorials of Washington, Jefferson, Lincoln, Lafayette, the Peace Monument where rested the bones of the heroes who had died in battle; the headquarters of different foundations, the organizations of various movements, culture, art, churches and cathedrals, and worship places of almost all faiths, almost as many as the number of nationalities in this great land.

Mando listened to the lively sessions of the two Congressional houses on Capitol Hill. Imprinted in his memory were the resounding speeches of some members about their pride in the land of freedom, the equality of men and nations, their inalienable right to pursue happiness.

He visited the Jefferson and Lincoln Memorials. He kept repeating what he had studied in his boyhood about their principles regarding men's freedom and equality. He went around the Arlington Cemetery on the other side of the Potomac River, including the former villa of General Robert E. Lee, commander-in-chief of the Confederates in the Civil War, and Mount Vernon, the personal estate of President Washington. These scenes only deepened Mando's admiration for America's glory.

But one day, in Washington, in the heart of American democracy, Mando's eyes were opened. He saw that few things did not have 'heads' and 'tails'.

He attended a meeting of former soldiers who had served in other lands during the last war. The purpose of the meeting was to take a stand on equal treatment for all American citizens—white, red, yellow or brown.

The organizers complained that while America was made up of all races, the whites were favoured above the coloured races. This was the situation before the war; it continued through the war and became worse with the return of peace.

This was seen in the army, in factories and business firms, unions, schools, vehicles and public amusements. The blacks were segregated. Many schools, hotels, restaurants, vehicles, shows and other institutions were off-limits to any coloured person. In many Southern states, where the blacks outnumbered the whites, they could not vote freely. If they were not killed, they were tarred and feathered if they voted for a candidate who was not supported by the powerful white men. Mando saw this bitter truth, and he was stunned.

They pointed out that of the millions of army men, a black very rarely rose in the ranks. It was usual for blacks to be carriers, waiters, dishwashers, drivers of heavy trucks and bulldozers, climbers of telegraph poles, diggers of tunnels and trenches, hunters in the forests, and fishers in the seas and rivers. The porters, servants, watchmen and laundrymen were all black.

Mando sat on one side of the theatre where the meeting was held. He noticed the announcement at the bottom, mentioning six hotels and restaurants in Washington, DC, some bars and movie houses where the delegates could go. Only these places were not off-limits to the blacks, while the others were closed to all coloured people. Mando was thinking of this problem when someone tapped his shoulder and sat beside him. It was a tall, lean black man.

'Hello, there. Remember me?'

Mando recognized him. How could he forget Steve? This black man was one of the first scouts who reached the mountains of Luzon before the Allied liberation forces. Everyone who knew Steve honoured his courage and his good heart. He was willing to help with his hands and shoulders, always supporting others in any hard task.

'How do?' Mando gripped the arm of the former soldier.

'Leading a dog's life,' Steve said with a dry smile and pain in his eyes.

Mando asked why. Steve was a real hero and should have had no cause to complain after his country had won the war.

'That may be true,' said Steve. 'I got a medal. But can a medal hide the colour of my skin? The same day I was awarded the medal by the Secretary of War, along with those cited for America's victory over the enemies of democracy. That same day, I went to a hotel for a good meal. I was stopped by a porter who courteously said, "Sorry, buddy, but your colour is no passport to this establishment." The porter was just following instructions. What could I do? I was wounded in the war and had very nearly died. But when I returned to the land for which

I made that sacrifice, with the medal still dangling from my chest, I could not eat in peace at a decent hotel in this impossible capital city of democracy.'

Steve said that he bought two bottles of whisky, went to the park and got drunk. He was arrested by a policeman and charged with vagrancy and disturbing peace and order. That night, the bed bugs in the police cell kept him awake.

According to Steve, he was jobless, and it was not his fault. His job before the war was already given to another man. Besides, he no longer had his old stamina or his skill from before he was wounded in battle. Now he was just surviving on a small pension.

'And to think that I'm not yet thirty,' Steve said with a sigh.

No, he was not married. His girlfriend, a mulatto, was gone when he returned. Now, what woman would be crazy enough to share his poverty?

Mando invited Steve to one of the restaurants listed in the programme. During lunch, he asked his friend to come back to the Philippines, where he would give his old friend a good job. He also offered free airfare to his old friend, who said he would think about the offer.

When they parted, Mando felt the pain and ugliness of what was happening in Washington and in other places in the US. Racial prejudice was its Achilles' heel, and it did not bode well for America's good name. For every three citizens in Washington, DC, one was black; therefore, in the very capital, one-third of the American citizens did not enjoy equality. It was said that Uncle Sam went to war twice for justice and democracy on behalf of the oppressed countries. But Mando could not reconcile this with the situation of Steve and the millions with his colour and his fate.

'What a contradiction,' thought Mando. He felt that soon, the blacks would rise, and the whites would regret their arrogance.

Mando also met an old Filipino who had lived long in America. He had come from the sugarcane and pineapple plantations of Hawaii, moved to the asparagus orchards in California, and ended up in the salmon fisheries of Oregon and Alaska. He had seen the oppression

of labourers who had emigrated to America during times of peace—
the Filipinos, Mexicans, Chinese and Japanese. He endured the term
'brown monkey', the ban against marrying white women, and was
resigned to the lowliest work for the smallest pay.

But this Filipino bore all of this in his desire to earn, save and study
somehow. Thank God for his strength, for he finished a course at the
university. But America's affection for the Philippines during the war
and the first years of peace had quickly vanished. The old loathing for
the coloured races returned. It really seemed hard to mix oil and water.

This Filipino thought his problem might be resolved by becoming
an American citizen. That way, he could claim the rights of a real
American. He expected this to open doors to a good job, to socializing
at parties, and to marriage. It would no longer be forbidden to
marry a blonde.

So he became an American citizen. He was happy and proud.

One day, he invited a friend, a Cuban mestizo, to a snack at a club.
He was then in Washington, DC. The Cuban was not an American
citizen, but he had a fair complexion because of his Spanish father.
At the door of the club, the Americanized Filipino received a hard
blow to his ego. He was not allowed to enter because he was brown,
but his companion was. The porter did not even pay attention to his
credentials, which he waved to show that he was already an 'American'.

He admitted sadly that what mattered was not the document or the
identity tag, but the colour of one's skin.

'A Filipino is a Filipino and can't ever become an American,'
Mando said after hearing the story of his countryman who had tried to
change his race by the stroke of a pen.

'Even in the Philippines,' Mando added, 'many of our countrymen
think it's good to become foreigners. They change their language,
clothes and manners. Even at home, they speak to their children only
in English, are ashamed to wear native clothes, don't care to watch their
own plays and movies, don't want to eat rice, and claim their stomachs
get upset when they smoke local cigarettes. But they only become the
laughing stock of those whom they imitate.'

The Filipino was dumbfounded. Then he asked for advice.

'But what should I do? I've become a man without a country. I spent half of my life in Hawaii and the United States. Even if I were to go back now, it would be hard . . .'

Mando looked with pity at the Filipino, then calmly said, 'What should you fear in coming home to the Philippines? That you would find many things unfamiliar? Didn't you encounter greater hardship and obstacles when you came here? Look back on your first year, the manual labour and the prejudice of the whites. Did you experience this in your own country before you left? It's not wrong to go to a foreign land to improve one's station in life. But when you've already prospered, you should come back to your country and use what you've gained. No foreign land can ever replace the land of your birth.'

Tears glistened in the eyes of the other man.

'Thank you for your advice,' he said. 'I'll think over what you have said. I have a profession and some savings. If I should return, it would not be in shame like many who bring nothing but disgrace to the Philippines.'

'The Philippines was destroyed by the war,' said Mando. 'Every good citizen can do something to help.'

Mando and his countryman met several times. At last, the latter realized that his being a Filipino was an indelible stamp of nature he could not disown. The last time he visited Mando, he brought other Filipinos.

'They also want to come home,' he told Mando. 'They won't be a burden to our country. They have some savings that they plan to invest in a business.'

'Mabuhay, then, to all of you. Welcome home,' Mando said, greatly pleased. He shook the hands of each of his countrymen with warmth.

XL

Mando sent home three letters, almost at the same time—for Magat, for Tata Matias and for Puri.

Mando and Magat often exchanged letters. He had also written to Dr Sabio. Mando's latest letter had been sent from Washington.

Dear Magat,

As I have told you, a book would not be enough for what I have learnt in the countries I have visited. I hope that you will also have the same chance to travel as I did.

Now I shall be content to discuss some ideas for our countrymen, including those who consider themselves well-informed because of our relationship with America.

The United States became free from England through the revolt of the thirteen states on 4 July 1776. They declared to the world, through the Declaration of Independence written by Thomas Jefferson, that 'all men are created equal, that they are endowed by their Creator with certain inalienable Rights, that among these are life, liberty, and the pursuit of happiness.'

At that time, this new country had only three million people and they did not know the vast forests, plains, mountains, and rivers that lay beyond the Mississippi River. But in one and a half centuries, they did miracles, and the land where people fled to escape persecution by their kings and from poverty in Europe is now the world's leader in wealth and progress. The three million have become 170 million, and the former forests and deserts have turned into industrial cities of plenty and of modern homes. These miracles were not due to nature or to God, but to man, to the brains and the industry of the American people. They started with nothing but their wits and honour. In the past, hardly any foreign country wanted to help or lend her aid, while her natural resources were not yet drawn from the womb of the earth and from the bottom of the seas. Nevertheless, they triumphed, for they resolved to work hard and succeed.

This was true for the progress of the United States. However, for the sake of accuracy, the Blacks from Guinea and Africa and the prisoners from Europe helped immeasurably in clearing the forests and levelling the mountains, in opening roads and ploughing the plantations. In the final analysis, the wealth of America came from her land and only its produce was finished and improved by industry. Therefore, the black and dirty hands of the first labourers sowed the seeds that blossomed into a new civilization.

The Philippines became independent from America on 4 July 1946. It had 30 million citizens, its natural resources were rich and untouched—an archipelago much bigger than its population. But the country is poor and does not profit as it should, because the people do not want to work hard. She depends on others, on God's will. But God does not help a person or nation that won't help itself.

In all branches of the government, foreign advisers tell us what to do, from the president to the army general to the head of education. Naturally, their first advice is that the nation cannot stand without the help of foreigners, foreign capital, foreign experts, foreign management. Like children without minds of their own, those in charge of our administration followed such advice, until the nation became like a plant without roots, like orchids hanging in the air. We became a caricature of a country, neither Western nor Eastern. While she is made a puppet by the West, which she imitates, she is ridiculed by the Easterners, whom she wishes to belittle. Only a Filipino whose sensibility is not in the heart but in his pockets will not abhor this situation.

The Philippines can copy many good things from America. Unfortunately, as Rizal feared, the first things that we pick up are the vices and weaknesses. Many Filipinos try to live like Americans in language, clothes, manners and customs, although that's impossible. The youth begin to forget their own music, songs and dances. They boast that they can copy the rough ways of the foreigners; that they don't want to watch anything but foreign games and amusements, nor read anything but that written by foreigners or published overseas. Where will the youth go with such a direction?

Even before the war, the Filipino had the highest standard of living in Asia. The basis is that the Philippines buys from the United States the greatest number of cars, cigarettes, preserved food, magazines, women's clothes, electric appliances, radios, movies and other things not used by other countries in this part of the world. But such comforts are not enjoyed by the whole country, only by some. And is this the right measure to determine the so-called high standard of living?

I think many Filipinos have a wrong concept of standard of living and cost of living. We pay dearly for our desire to have things that are not necessary; our tastes have become expensive. Our standard of living does not rise, but we become poorer in the long run.

Look at the cars. For every imported car, the Philippines continues to spend on gasoline and oil, tires and motor parts. Not one of these is made in the Philippines. Thus, so much money is thrown away every year just to maintain these flashy cars. A car is a sign of progress, but the Philippines should not remain an importer. Like Japan, Australia and other neighbouring countries, she should make her own cars.

In Manila, students, employees, and labourers smoke only American cigarettes. Do you know how much our country spends just on cigarettes? We are the world's biggest buyer of cigarettes. This is the saddest part. While the Manila cigar is said to be the best in the world, we don't buy any of it. This is why the distributors of American cigarettes get rich, our own factories close down, and our tobacco growers starve.

Let me go back to the standard of living. Here in the United States, if a labourer works for ten hours, he earns enough for a week's expenses. On the other hand, in the Philippines, one has to work a month to earn a week's expenses. Here, goods are cheap because they are produced locally, while there, goods are expensive because they are imported. Aside from that, the buyer pays for the cost of transportation, taxes, ads and the profit of the businessman.

An American worker who earns ten dollars a day spends thirty cents on a pack of cigarettes. A Filipino who earns four pesos a day or less spends a peso on American cigarettes. Think of the difference and see if you don't grit your teeth or shed tears.

I don't say that the Filipino worker should earn as much as his American cousin. Of course, this would be only right, at some future time, for how is a white man superior to a brown one? It is only right that the worker should be able to afford his daily needs. Why should a man work if the fruits of his labour are not enough for the basic needs of his family—food, clothes and a home? But how can this be expected of a country that imports its needs and whose businessmen are foreigners greedy for profit? They have become used to squeezing blood from a turnip. The leaders think only of their own welfare. So they allow the foreign exploiters to abuse the country, leading it to the poorhouse. The country grows thin and pale from hardship, yet the leaders and their kin are bloated like leeches bursting from sucking their victims' blood.

And this they do whenever they have the chance. I have seen the first rule of nepotism in our diplomatic offices. The diplomats' wives, children, in-laws, nephews, and relatives are appointed, although they are here just to have fun, to study, or to have a vacation. I know the wife of an important diplomat who does nothing but visit well-known dress shops and beauty parlours, and well-known places of amusement and relaxation. But she would never deign to visit the slums, hospitals, orphanages, schools, factories, libraries, or the independent theatres.

Many of our emissaries live like the maharajahs wherever they go. One American official in Washington said that we keep sending missions to get loans or aid, but our delegates vie with the sheikhs from the oil-producing countries of the Middle East. They stay in expensive hotels, their feet don't touch the ground and they don't attend to their duties here, but instead waste public funds on private matters.

One of our diplomats only cares for self-publicity. While he is known in many places, especially in private schools, for his lectures, giving interviews and issuing statements together with his pictures, many Americans have no idea about the Philippines, whether it is in South Africa, or whether its people have tails like that of monkeys or still live in trees, or whether it is an island of Guam. He promotes American interests, especially in the way the white people carry out their aims in the Philippines. If Philippine elections were to be directly influenced by Wall Street, the American Chamber of Commerce, the Rotary Club, the CIA, and the American Legion, you could bet that he would be the next president of the Philippines. And where would he bring the country? But don't they meddle not just in elections—but even afterwards?

I have observed that here and in Europe, many of our diplomats should be sent home for good, or if possible, we should have them live in the poor villages from time to time. Their indefinite stay in other lands is not good for them or for the country. One bad effect is that they care less about the welfare of the Philippines than of the country where they have been assigned. They forget that the life, welfare, policy and conditions of their own country are different from the country where they have been sent. I met a Filipino ambassador who seemed like a hired agent of the country where he had been staying for years.

Besides, it's a mistake to follow the example of rich countries like the United States, the Soviet Union, Britain, France and others that send to other countries their ambassadors, consuls and their respective employees, aides, chauffeurs and families. In our country, the appointment of ambassadors is mostly decided by the whims of our politicians, who are quick to give such positions to their kin and followers. At present, we only trade with a few countries. While it is desirable to increase them, it is stupid to imitate the big powers but do nothing else. We lack provincial roads and town schools. Is it not proper that we should first spend on this, instead of wasting money on diplomatic offices everywhere? There are many member nations of the United Nations who don't send representatives to some countries, but assign one of their citizens living there or ask to be represented by a friendly nation. This is the policy of many Latin American countries, and many of them are richer than the Philippines.

Don't think that there is no graft and corruption here. There is, my friend, and I'm inclined to think that this is one of our imports from the United States. There is theft in the government and outside of it. I'm quite sure that these diseases cannot be absent from a society that measures everything in terms of money. As in our country, the big thieves are seldom caught. It should be the reverse, for stealing is a habit to the mighty, while it is a necessity for the poor. What will you do to a person who steals because he has to, and one already has more than enough but steals just the same?

Be that as it may, I have not lost hope for the future of the Philippines. Our struggles during the Japanese times and the gradual awakening after the war show that our failures and mistakes are merely lessons in growth and progress. A mouse won't grow without falling on the ground. Every child learning to walk stumbles and hurts himself. The country makes mistakes because of its leaders, but the leader can be easily replaced, while the country moves on in its journey. Surely, she can be betrayed but not sold completely by traitors. In the long run, she will meet her destiny. Did we not experience this during the darkest days of the Japanese occupation?

On the whole, in the face of what I have seen, I am sad that I am a Filipino. My heart bleeds because after we were freed from one foreign power, many of our leaders began to act like slaves. The only way they can exploit the nation and remain in power is through the help of the former master.

Now, you might miss your deadline because of this long letter.

Always,
Mando

P.S. We have a new rotary press. It's not the best, but it will be good enough for our needs. It is not the machine but we, you, and your staff who make the newspaper. Don't be impatient; I'll be home sooner than this machine lands there.

The following was his letter addressed to Tata Matias:

Tatang, my trip has been good. According to plan. I'm glad you are well. I'm coming home soon.

Puri carefully folded and kept her letter, together with other things sent by Mando. This was the note she received:

My Dearest Puri,

During my entire trip, I have failed to meet a girl who could compare with you and your many virtues. And I am glad I failed. Don't think that I am flattering you.

Regards to Tata Pastor,
Mando

With Mando's long letter to Magat, he enclosed a clipping from a liberal paper in New York City. The article was written by a Filipino student in response to an American businessman who had attacked the 'ingratitude' of the Philippines in protesting against the Bell Trade Act, which gave many rights to Americans in the Philippines.

Wall Street Binds the Philippines

Manila, the capital city of the Philippines, remains a heap of ruins three years after American liberation. But the people, the ordinary citizens, have undergone a metamorphosis in mind and soul in such a short time.

Even during the darkest days of enemy occupation, the Filipino labourer knew that labour should use one language, that he had to overcome the handicaps of country and race. Because everywhere, labour is a struggle, and should move forward to its destination: the liberation of all from the chains of cruelty, fascism, and imperialism.

The Filipinos have long suffered. They bore the burden of imperialism for many centuries. They were abused and exploited by the conquerors and the Spanish friars for 333 years. During the last war, for three years under the Japanese, they were sucked to the bone, when the whole country of twenty million people was made into a giant prison camp.

The Filipinos are noted for their bravery and love of freedom. During the long years of Spanish colonization, a revolution would break out every five years. During the Second World War they stood in Bataan in an epic struggle against oppression. But more glorious was the fight of the people themselves, as moths against the flame. When the United States forces surrendered in Corregidor, the people continued on. From the fields, villages, meadows, mountains, slums and swamps, sprang the nation's army without weapons or bullets, but with a soul that would not bow.

This army of the people won the war for democracy, not only in the Philippines, but also everywhere else—in Europe, Africa, Asia, the South Pacific, America. Nevertheless, fascism is not yet crushed. It still lives, despite the death of Hitler, Mussolini and Tōjō. It still holds power in the Philippines.

Under the guise of altruism, the Yankee monopolists plotted to strengthen their grip on the Philippines in politics, economy, and the military. The return of independence on 4 July 1946 became a cruel joke. The prostrate country was threatened and blackmailed to pawn its heritage in exchange for a can of sardines and the excess junk of the US Army. The Filipinos had to amend their constitution to give parity or equal rights to the Americans and American big business. Their sovereignty hung in the air, with the islands to be placed under more than twenty military bases controlling land, sea and air, for ninety-nine years. In these bases, the Filipinos have no authority.

The government became a non-entity that merely followed the financial masters in Wall Street and the Pentagon. Seats in Congress were removed from the elected representatives of labourers and farmers. Strikes and pickets were forbidden. Labour leaders were persecuted, and some were even murdered by agents of the administration. Company unions and scabs were coddled. The freedom of the progressive elements was curtailed, while all help was given to spread the influence of the church and other enemies of democracy.

The National Federation of Farmers, with its half a million members, was banned. The Hukbalahap, the terror of the Japanese forces during the war, was outlawed. The Congress of Labour Organizations, with its hundered industrial unions and a stable base of democratic unionism, is being persecuted. These abuses and oppression have forced the nation to condemn the ways of the party in power, so that the fear spread that the poor might follow the stance of 'a tooth for a tooth'.

In spite of the excessive publicity about the American way of life, no one enjoys it except a few favoured ones led by politicians, landlords and puppets of Wall Street and other supporters of the status quo. Only they have palaces surrounded by walls, flashy cars and airconditioned offices. On the other hand, the Filipino worker, with five to six dependents, earns four pesos a day, which is worth about one American dollar. For three litres of rice a day, he spends two pesos, or half of his day's earnings.

Seventy-five out of one hundred farm workers have no land of their own. They are mere tenants. They serve under an antiquated system based on the economic needs of the United States; they are forced to produce sugar, tobacco, abaca, copra and timber, and to dig mines to support American industry. America buys these products by quotas and returns them finished from large factories without paying taxes. And yet the country is always short of rice and corn, its staple food.

Japan had promised reparations to the Philippines. But instead, the Supreme Commander of the Allied Powers, General Douglas MacArthur who was stationed in Tokyo, ordered the Philippines to send iron to Hirohito's revitalized factories. Then the materials were sold back to Manila as kitchen utensils, silverware, bicycles, hardware, and all kinds of toys.

You say you saved the Philippines from the hands of conquerors on two occasions—once from Spain, the second from Japan. Perhaps. But the Philippines was already free in 1898 when Admiral Dewey arrived in Manila Bay and, with a few cannon shots, sank three rotten Spanish ships. You might have us, but you stayed on for half a century, and aren't you there even now? In 1941, the Japanese attacked us because the US flag flew over Malacañang Palace. That was not our war, but we were forced to fight. You returned in 1945, after three years of untold sacrifices by the Filipino nation, and when the enemy was helpless and almost wiped out by the brave Filipino guerrillas. So the Japanese turned savagely on the people during liberation, and didn't spare even the women and children.

In the Philippines, you will not find an American shivering from the cold and begging for a cup of coffee that you see all over the Bowery in New York City. The ex-soldier and other adventurers go to the Philippines, and after some years, they become the managers of corporations or capitalists of mines. As in Hawaii in the beginning, the richest mines were the pockets of the Pinoy heiresses who, because of their studies in Europe and America, liked to marry white husbands.

Actually, the United States' generosity to Juan de la Cruz was not one-way traffic. It was mutual, a profitable exchange enforced by Uncle Sam. It was hard for the well-informed Filipino to believe the lie that a country should occupy another land for the good of the conquered and not for its own welfare. Such deceit is obsolete. It has always been the sales pitch of conquerors since Caesar and Napoleon. America gained a noble friend in the Far East in two world wars.

But the eyes of the Filipino people are opening to the bitter truth that they are neither regarded nor treated as friends and equals. The Filipino as 'a dear friend' is GI Joe's flattery for the gullible brown man. Perhaps they will not allow themselves to be used again as fodder for the cannon in times of danger and later, as beasts to pull the carts.

Never again in this generation of Filipinos, the spark of hope of their noble heroes.

XLI

The women writers of the society page ran out of words to describe the reception at the Monteros' for their housewarming. It also served as the welcome party for Dolly, who had just arrived after studying at a finishing school in Paris.

For some time, the expensive mansion had been standing on its two-hectare lot. But Doña Julia decided to postpone the inauguration until Dolly had returned from Europe.

When the mansion was finished, the architect Pong Tua-son offered a small dinner for some newspapermen and photographers. Doña Julia showed the guests the wide garden, the swimming pool, and the three floors of the house. Every room was built in a different style and had different furnishings and paintings. The mansion was set in the centre of the garden, and it combined old and modern architecture, the classic and the contemporary, because the Monteros wanted to give the impression that they belonged to the old families who could trace their roots to the first Spaniards who had settled along the shores of Maalat. However, they also wanted to prove that they were not behind the times. These wishes were given shape by the Chinese mestizo architect through this mansion with its Gothic-Renaissance framework, as well as its modern décor. In short, with the help of an unlimited budget, he combined beauty, function and durability.

The first who saw it were lavish in their praise. The walls of the living room were made of dark wood panelling. The ceiling was gold and the floor was covered with a thick red carpet from Persia. There was an arrangement of a few sofas and a set of antique chairs, as well as a small table of dark mahogany. Standing in some corners were large porcelain jars. Hanging on the walls were three or four paintings of the Old Masters. From the centre of the ceiling hung a blazing chandelier like the gaudy collar of a rich widow. At the end of the hall stood a large grand piano.

The rooms were just as grand. Señorita Dolly's room was called the Princess's Room. According to the architect-suitor, this could compare with the room of Princess Margaret in Buckingham Palace. Dolly herself did the main décor of her room when she arrived. Naturally, she wanted to try what she had learnt in interior decoration at the finishing school in Paris. She enrolled there, in addition to her studies allegedly at the Sorbonne, besides her observation in the cities she visited on her way home.

The three rooms and the living room were the main gems, but the whole mansion was a showcase of Philippine architecture. All four rooms were airconditioned. Each bed had a small radio at the foot and a lamp at the head.

A few days before the affair, the grounds were already decorated and looked like a small carnival. The carpet grass was mowed, the trees and the vines on the walls were trimmed, and the two-hectare grounds were swept clean. The servants, together with their relatives, were called to help. Doña Julia brought out the old clothes and had some bills changed to reward the hardworking helpers.

When everything was already spotless, they hung hundreds of Japanese and native lanterns from the low branches of the champak, evergreen and frangipani trees.

No less than three bars were set up, one near the swimming pool, one in the front yard, and one at the back, wherever the male guests would gather.

Round tables for twelve were set in the garden; three long tables were heaped with delicious dishes prepared by two well-known caterers.

Each guest could help himself or ask the waiters to serve any food to suit his taste—Chinese, French or Filipino dishes, including roasted pig.

Before dark, two famous orchestras began to play from their platforms, one under the trees across the swimming pool, another at the side of the terrace. The gleaming marble floor became a dance floor of many colours.

That night, the *crème de la crème* of Manila's high society arrived. Cars crowded around the estate. The road was temporarily closed by the police, and only those going to the Monteros' mansion were allowed to enter.

Policemen on duty could be seen chatting with the uniformed chauffeurs. They wondered whether they would be given their dinner outside, or allowed to enter and choose their food and drinks. The policemen had to drive away the dirty, curious children who came from the slums not far away from this palace.

Before seven that night, almost everyone who counted among the upper crust—in government, finance, politics and industry—had arrived. There were also some distinguished foreigners. Bishop Dumas, who was asked to officiate, came early. The archbishop was abroad, and the Papal Nuncio had been called to the Vatican. Beside the bishop, like an aide, was General Bayoneta wearing a gala uniform, with a medal pinned on his chest. No one could remember if the medal was given for helping the Japanese before Bataan had surrendered, or serving the Americans after Manila had been liberated.

Meanwhile, the Montero couple were getting uneasy over the delay of the president. He had the habit of coming late, even on national occasions. The couple had already been waiting for an hour at the main entrance and could not attend to their other guests. The bishop and the general joined a group in the garden. Among them were Senator Botin, Governor Doblado, Judge Pilato and their other associates. The waiters came carrying trays with drinks and *hors d'oeuvres*.

'We have a quorum,' said Senator Botin.

'For poker, yes, but not for a Senate session,' said the governor.

'What's the news, General?' Judge Pilato said to Bayoneta.

'Everything's peaceful.'

'If it is peaceful, then why does the army demand a large budget?' Botin said sharply.

'Because a small budget is the fuse of trouble,' said Bayoneta. 'Especially among the Army men who don't receive a raise amid the increased boldness of the outlaws.'

They were startled by a long siren followed by the sound of motorcycles.

'The president's here,' said the general and hurried to meet him. Right behind was Governor Doblado. The president shook hands with Montero and Doña Julia. The First Lady and Mrs Montero rubbed their cheeks against each other.

'Please come in, *compadre, comadre,*' loudly declared Montero as he led the honoured guests to the living room. Montero immediately claimed the right to call the First Couple comadre and compadre, because they would be his sponsors at the house blessing.

When the president had entered, the guests stood up and sat down only when he had gestured at them to do so. Those who were known to the president and his wife immediately came and paid their respects.

After a while, Dolly entered with Don Segundo leading her by the hand, followed by Doña Julia.

'Compadre, comadre,' said Don Segundo, 'here is my daughter Dolores. She just arrived from her studies at the Sorbonne.'

'Monte, so you have a Miss Philippines,' said the president.

The First Lady asked what Dolly studied in Paris. Upon learning that she had taken up interior design, she invited the girl to the palace at the first opportunity.

'The palace needs a new look,' the First Lady said, smiling. The president nodded, but after looking around at the numerous women guests in the wide hall, he added, laughing, 'But it seems to me that the whole New Look is here.' The First Lady looked to see what he meant—the clothes, jewellery, manner and hairstyles of the women, both married and unmarried.

The First Lady and a few others were in formal native wear, but most wore dresses of costly material fashioned according to the imagination of the designer—a battle among the chemise, sack and trapeze, although these styles were just being tried out by Christian Dior, Yves Saint Laurent, and other designers in Paris and New York.

Flocks of ageing but coquettish matrons were strutting about like peacocks; young matrons acted like hens who had just discovered a snake in their nests; and girls with pointed breasts, wide hips, and wriggling bodies restlessly sat or stood or posed about the grand mansion.

Someone greeted the mother–daughter pair Betty and Betsy Labajita, who looked like sisters. It was no secret that Betty, the mother, was widowed, and Betsy, the youngest of her three children, was sired by her latest catch, the wealthy Labajita. Both were dressed gaudily, coiffured like Audrey Hepburn, and had similar bags and shoes. Betty would laugh aloud when they were called the 'Labajita twins'.

Among the guests was Balbinitá Cuatrovientos, a former hostess in an expensive club, who married a Spanish athlete who played the pelota. The pelotari became a businessman after saving enough from his fixed games. Balbinitá was a veritable dragonfly flitting in the ballroom, perhaps because of her former occupation. She spoke in a mixture of English and pidgin Spanish. She was bragging that a daily massage and a tepid bath sprinkled with cologne helped her maintain her marvellous face and figure.

In one group, Blancanieve Cienfuegos was giving away another secret for keeping slim. No one could tell she had just come from the maternity ward. 'Of course, I always deliver babies by Caesarian,' she said. 'Let the nursemaid feed them.'

Meanwhile, in another group, Maggie Siemprejoven was telling her friends how to colour one's hair. 'Even after three weeks, the dye does not fade, and it still looks natural,' said Maggie, and she smoothed her hair and batted her eyelashes. Most of those listening were wives of cabinet members and senators who wanted to turn back the hands of time and the pages of the calendar.

A group of women made up of Mercy Mahabaguin, Conchita Pantoche and Doña Julia invited the First Lady to a benefit event for the city's poor.

The women were like goldfish in an aquarium. In fact, most of them flocked to such gatherings, not to please the host or see the house—and especially not to eat, for many had problems with keeping their weight—but to show off their colourful attire, their gaudy jewellery, their imported bags and shoes, and other trinkets dear to the hearts of the upper crust. Every gathering they attended became a fashion show of new and unusual clothes, all imported, that they had bought at fabulous prices.

In the midst of all these, Dolly still stood out. Her dress was unique. It was created expressly for her by the then-upcoming Saint Laurent, who had a shop at the Place de la Opera in Paris. It was made of cloth that seemed to have been woven using silk and fine glass, silver with a touch of sky blue, revealing her shapely figure. It was sleeveless and had a low neckline that dipped to her cleavage. Her beauty was enhanced by that dress with a simple ornament for accent—a ruby collar and a large red rose in her hair.

Everyone complimented Dolly. Architect Tua-son was like a tame Pekingese that kept on following her.

Dolly had become lovelier since she left Manila two years ago. Her stay in Europe and the culture of Paris had added to her innate sheen and polish. Her experience in the loveliest city in the world added to her colour, bearing and allure. She was no longer a young girl but a woman at her prime, no longer a bud smiling at the kiss of light but a fully opened flower exuding an intoxicating fragrance. If the president became a widower and decided to remarry, or if Bishop Dumas were freed from celibacy, the two men past their prime would likely be tempted by Dolly.

But Dolly was obviously not content in the midst of such adoration. One could see her listlessness, her forced smile and her pale cheeks. She would stop to listen to the sound of every car coming or the name of every guest being announced at the door.

The house-blessing rites were over; most had eaten and many were dancing.

But Dolly was waiting for her guest, Mando Plaridel. She had talked to Mando on the phone that afternoon and made him promise not to fail her. But it was already nine in the evening and he was not yet there.

Only Dolly was bored and lonely amid such joyous company filled with pomp and pleasure. Dancing with some guests like the architect Tua-son, Governor Doblado, General Bayoneta, made her more bored and impatient for Mando's arrival.

All were engrossed in watching a native dance on the terrace, including Bishop Dumas, who suggested that this be presented on stage instead of vaudeville and burlesque, where the female performers were almost naked.

'Art and morals are not enemies,' said Bishop Dumas. 'In fact, at first, the dance was a religious ceremony. But the devil makes everything his tool, so later, he used the dance the same way he quotes God's words from the Bible.'

'Even for commerce and propaganda,' answered Senator Botin, 'our native dances should be presented in our theatres. First, our artists would earn, and we would not have to import dancers from America and Japan; second, we would show the skill and the beauty of our native art.'

'It's unfortunate,' added Judge Pilato, 'that the foreigners are the first to appreciate our native dances in village fiesta-style gatherings and in expositions abroad. But here, the wealthy are crazy over ballet and the plebeians over jazz.'

The native dance of a thousand lights was rewarded with loud applause, but for Dolly, that applause was a welcome for Mando, who now stood at the entrance of the living room. No one noticed his arrival except Dolly, who hardly watched the show on the terrace.

'Am I not too late?' asked Mando, apologizing for his tardiness.

'I'll die waiting for you,' Dolly said to him. Her listlessness had vanished; her loneliness and paleness were replaced by the blush of roses on her cheeks.

Dolly introduced Mando to her father, the president, and some guests.

After the floor show, all eyes were on Mando and Dolly as they danced.

To those who did not notice the scar on Mando's left cheek and who saw only his bearing and elegance, he seemed like a foreigner.

'This is the first time I've seen or heard the name of that man,' the president said to Don Segundo.

'He stayed long in Europe,' replied the host. 'He met Dolly in Paris.'

'What does he do?'

'Dolly didn't say, but he is rich and bright. Which reminds me, it seems he is behind the newspaper, the *Kampilan*.'

'Oh, the radical paper,' said the president.

This was the same topic of interest for the others—Governor Doblado, General Bayoneta, and others who could not understand why the women considered Dolly's friend charming and attractive.

Architect Tua-son went to the bar to drown his sorrows.

XLII

Mando was pleased that no one recognized him, or even suspected his identity. He knew a number of those present at that fabulous party. They would surely remember him if given some reminders. Foremost among them were Don Segundo and Doña Julia; Governor Doblado who had been a constant visitor before the war; and General Bayoneta, who was a mere lieutenant or captain and aide to a high Japanese official during the last days of the Japanese in Manila.

Mando was not surprised that he was completely forgotten. Not only because of the change in his appearance but because Andoy, his former self, was not important enough to them to be remembered—a mere servant whose disappearance would hardly be noticed, or like a tool that could easily be replaced. Who would remember?

When he came down from the Sierra Madre mountains soon after the war, Mando had changed much. He had a long scar on his left cheek, which Tata Matias compared to a medal. Had he belonged to a gang in Manila, he would surely have been called 'Scarface'. He had grown taller and stood straight as a rod. His firm muscles strained beneath his clothes. He had grown older; gone was the youthfulness from his face and bearing. His lack of textbook knowledge was replaced by perseverance, by experience, by the marks of struggle.

And now, he had returned from a long journey across different lands, honed by the modern things he had experienced, filled with newfound knowledge. Who would even mistake him with the thin houseboy of the Monteros, the timid Andoy in khaki trousers and a faded polo shirt? Indeed, who would suspect that he was now this wealthy and elegant man with a magnetic personality, whose refined manners were like those of a nobleman?

Dolly, who used to shout and knock him on the head for every mistake—that haughty mistress had no inkling that the houseboy, whose disappearance she had hardly noticed, was the same man she met and became infatuated with in Paris. She had not noticed any resemblance even in their intimate moments in Mando's suite at the Ritz Hotel and other places of rendezvous. Despite the ugly scar, his attractive personality caught the attention of the president, who had asked Montero who he was.

But it was not Mando alone who had changed in appearance and outlook. Many things had changed, for what does not change with time? That house, which was obviously a rich man's house, was now an imposing mansion for a multi-millionaire. Even the surroundings were different. Gone was the small pre-war hut of Andoy and his parents; a large garage now stood there. Gone were the stones beside it and the faucet where his mother used to wash clothes all day long. But here remained Don Segundo and Doña Julia, who had not aged. And here was Dolly, the rising moon, now in her full glory.

Mando's thoughts were cut short when Dolly's head nestled against his chest.

'Don't tell me you're thinking of our nights in Paris,' she said. Mando laughed but said nothing.

'Don't you want to see my room?'

'Later, Dolly.' Mando was evasive. 'You have many guests.'

'Okay. Next time you'll come.'

When the orchestra stopped playing, Dolly invited Mando to the garden, which was lit with lanterns and fairy lights of many colours.

'I'm hungry,' she complained. 'Imagine, I've had nothing since this afternoon. But hunger is nothing compared to waiting for you.' She threw him a look of reproach.

Mando had not had supper either, for he was so engrossed in the meeting he was in, earlier. They went to a long table laden with food.

They got two plates, took some stewed beef, salad and bread. Then they sat at a table away from the crowd.

Only a few were dining. Many were dancing, some groups were chatting, and some men were drinking. All were making merry, as if there was no tomorrow.

'Now that we are in Manila,' Dolly said to Mando, 'you seem to have no more time for me.'

'Not really, Dolly. The truth is, I was away on a long trip, and I left much work, which I've to attend to right away.'

'In the daytime, yes, but how about at night? Since you've arrived, we haven't gone out.'

'I often work late at the office. Make allowance for my shortcomings. Believe me, this does not mean I'm cooling off.'

'Very well, then. I expect you'll find time for the picnic prepared by Papa's overseer.'

'Picnic? Where?'

'At our plantation. The overseer, a former army captain, came to invite us to the picnic which will be held in my honour. You'll come, won't you?'

'We'll see,' he answered lightly, but his thoughts were on Puri, Tata Pastor, the Montero Plantation, and the tenants. *The new overseer just wants to suck up to all of you,* he told himself.

'I won't take no for an answer,' Dolly said, noticing Mando's hesitation.

Before Mando could answer, Don Segundo came to tell them that the president was about to leave but had decided to stay for coffee. Don Segundo invited Mando to join them.

Tua-son was behind Don Segundo. When Mando stood up, he immediately sat beside Dolly.

The president was in Don Segundo's private office on the ground floor with Senator Botin. Both were seated on easy chairs. Don Segundo and Mando sat on the opposite sofa.

'I was going to ask Monsignor to join us, but he has already left,' said Montero.

'Why is it that for the weddings of the rich, the archbishop or the bishop officiates?' observed Botin. 'I have not heard them wed the poor.' The senator knew the answer but did not ask a follow-up question.

'As in the other professions, the archbishop and the bishop have their price,' said Montero, making the president and Mando smile. 'Aren't there doctors who will treat none but the rich? And lawyers who will appear in court only if paid their huge fees in advance?'

Two waiters brought the coffee. Montero poured.

'I've read your paper,' the president addressed Mando directly.

'I'm glad you did, sir,' the publisher said courteously. 'What is your impression?'

'I've a feeling that you're anti-administration,' said the president.

'And politicians,' added Senator Botin.

'And also against landlords and capitalists,' added Montero.

Mando cleared his throat and bit his lower lip before answering the three. 'No newspaper can exist if all it does is make enemies,' he said. 'The *Kampilan*'s mission is to find out and report the truth. If, in doing this, some are hurt, it's not because they are the targets of the paper. In supporting a policy, believe me, Honourable President, gentlemen, that we have never been moved by personal aims and feelings.'

'It's your duty to support the government,' declared the president, 'because the government represents the nation. The government has no other aim but the welfare of the nation.'

Then he took the cup and directly drank half of the strong, steaming coffee. When the president brought out a cigarette, Don Segundo quickly got the matches on the table and lit it.

'Tell me, is there anyone more concerned about the nation than its government?' the president asked, his gaze fixed directly on Mando.

'At first glance, so it seems,' Mando said, 'but in practice, it could be the opposite. If you'll pardon me for saying so.'

'Are you making an accusation?' quickly asked the president.

'I'm only citing actual happenings,' answered the publisher of the *Kampilan*. 'I shall explain, if you'll allow me.'

The president leant back in the lounging chair, while Senator Botin lit a cigar. Montero drank his coffee.

'I admit that your institution is good, your heart is pure, and your hands are clean,' said Mando. 'But on what issue did you win the

election? That you will get more aid from America. It's a mistake even
from the start.'

'Our country was destroyed, and our economy is in ruins,'
interrupted the president. 'It is America's responsibility to aid us, for
we were involved because of her. What can we do . . .'

'Please pardon me, Your Excellency,' quickly answered Mando.
'I was not against asking for aid or reparation, which is America's
responsibility. What I mean is that we should not be satisfied with aid
and charity. Many other American allies were laid waste by the war.
They, too, should receive aid, or even payment, if you wish. But above
all, we should depend on ourselves, our ability, our natural resources,
our brains, and our physical strength.'

Mando paused to give the others time to weigh his words. Then
he continued.

'I am still waiting, sir—if you'll pardon me, I wish to be frank,' he
said. 'I am still waiting for a leader who will tell our country that we
shall stand on our own feet, that we shall not be clinging vines, but
straight and firm like the molave tree atop the mountain, or amid the
lashing of the hurricane and wind. Either we remain conquered, or we
become independent. Frequently asking for doles like a beggar does
lessen one's worth. Who does not admire the ant that toils without
stopping, stores food, builds its houses, and dies fighting, even against
men, if it is harmed?'

The president lit another cigarette and answered with calmness,
'You are clearly an idealist. I began in politics with a vision just like
yours. A new Quixote. I thought I could tilt the windmills. Attacks
and optimism are good to hear from the opposition when they want to
wrest power. But the moment you assume office and you are swamped
with the many problems of the nation, with countless problems heaped
on your head, then you will see that doing is a lot different from mere
preaching. Who doesn't know that poverty is the country's number
one problem? Who doesn't know that this leads to unemployment,
discontent and disorder? Who doesn't know that we import more than
we export, so that the poor cannot afford necessities because they are
mostly imported? Both Filipinos and foreigners have suggested many
remedies—and many have been tried. You saw the frustrations of the

presidents before I came on board. I won't say that I have failed, but it makes me sad to admit that we're merely going in circles, ending where we started.'

The president took a deep breath, as if the said circle was a small ball that had been removed from his throat.

'That, sir, is a vicious circle,' Mando continued the analogy. 'I said our policy was wrong from the start; therefore, our plans must also be wrong. We should be free not only in name. We need to cut off all our strings. We should have our own goals in our economy, education and defence, agriculture and industry, in trade and foreign relations. Let's do what's best for the country, casting aside rumours and superstition. Let us be like the river flowing to the sea. Even in the wilderness, we can hear the sound of the river as it journeys to the sea.'

'You've an exceptional idea,' said the president, later on. 'But my friend, don't forget that theory is different from practice. I told you that I, too, was a dreamer. Now that I'm in this position, I realize that the problems of the nation can't be solved by the president right away.'

'Not even by two or three presidents, sir, if they don't learn to do right,' said Mando. 'Nevertheless, I believe where there's a will, there's a way. If the theory is right and it still fails, then the procedure must be wrong. The plan of the house may be good, but the architect is bad.'

'What do you think of the plan and execution of the house?' Don Segundo finally said.

'Excellent!' Senator Botin answered before Mando could reply.

'Let us be honest with the people,' Mando continued. 'Let them know the truth, the weaknesses, the sacrifice demanded of everyone. And may the leaders show the right example. The mistake of the politicians, if you'll pardon me, is to promise what they can't do.'

'How would you win an election then?' asked Senator Botin.

'That's the trouble. The politicians think that winning an election is enough. They do everything to win, promising even the moon and the stars to the people. But success should be measured by how satisfied the people are with the administration.'

The president disagreed. 'Pleasing the whole nation is a dream,' he said.

'That is why the goal is the contentment of the people,' Mando replied. 'For if a thing is easily obtained, where would a dream's beauty and nobility lie?'

After more than an hour of exchanging views, the president stood up and shook hands with Mando.

'Please give me a chance,' he pleaded. 'I'm not afraid of criticism. But perhaps, it would be good for all if you would help me instead of mudslinging.'

Mando nodded, but he made no comment. He felt that he could not sacrifice the truth, even for the president.

There were still many guests in the hall and on the terrace, but they started to leave after the president and the First Lady had left. Mando didn't stay long after Dolly walked with him to his car.

As Mando opened the front door of the car, Dolly held his arm and asked: 'Mister, aren't you going to kiss me?'

XLIII

Many raised their eyebrows at the sudden wealth of some Filipinos after 'liberation'. Their progress was not hard to see, however. They used the war to enrich themselves, often through sordid means.

Like Horatio Alger, were Segundo Montero and his Chinese friend Son Tua, now Tua-son, who started from scratch. Their origins still showed. True, both were already well-off before the war. Montero owned a plantation and some business enterprises. Son Tua cornered the trade in gambling and opium. Legitimate businessmen could not amass millions in such a short time. There was no doubt that the two were now multi-millionaires.

Montero himself said after the war that he would be like the saw, biting both ways, coming and going. He practised this with the Japanese and the Americans. Son Tua moved like a chess player, feeding pawns to corner a king. The Chinese millionaire had a limited Tagalog vocabulary, but he knew very well the ways of bribery, indeed.

It was unnecessary to look at a crystal ball to know the secrets of their sudden and astounding wealth. Manila had many such 'geniuses'.

One night, before nine, two guests arrived at the Montero mansion in a car with an important plate number. Montero met Governor Oscar Doblado and General Magno Bayoneta. They had earlier sent word of their arrival. They took the elevator to the third floor. The Chinese millionaire was already there, reclining on the lounge chair with his

back to the door. He didn't notice the new arrivals until General
Bayoneta kissed his hand.

'Have you been here long, sir?' asked the general, who had married
one of Son Tua's daughters.

Governor Doblado happily greeted the Chinese millionaire.

Montero got drinks from the bar, the waiter not being allowed at
such conferences.

'Well, let's drink first.' Montero poured the newly opened bottle
of scotch into two glasses. He poured brandy for himself. Son Tua
never drank.

'No, thank you, Monte,' the Chinese said.

After warming their throats, they sat facing each other. Son Tua
remained seated on his lounge chair.

'This is a meeting of our corporation,' began Montero, slowly.
Casting an affectionate glance at the Chinese, he went on. 'Our friend,
Son Tua, and I have decided to expand our operations. The dollar,
opium and jewellery businesses are doing very well, indeed. Also the
blue seal, rice and canned goods, as shown by your dividends. But now,
the greatest demand is for firearms. So we shall focus on them.'

Montero first cleared his throat. 'For every gun we buy at forty
pesos wholesale, we shall gain as much as 300, and in cold cash.'

The governor and the general exchanged glances, for other
contraband goods hardly netted 200 per cent. And this was going to
bring them a profit of 700 per cent!

'But arms are risks,' said Doblado. 'Diamonds and opium are easy
to hide, especially by a woman. Rice is easy to sell. But Thompsons,
Garands, machine guns!'

'How about the general? And the governor?' challenged Montero,
looking at Bayoneta as if asking for support. The general smiled. Son
Tua nodded.

'You take care to protect those who need to be protected,' Montero
answered his own question. 'The same tactics: meet and convey.
That's why, after deducting capital and expenses, the profit will be
divided by four.'

'What is the plan for the weapons?' Doblado asked.

'Very simple,' answered Montero. 'Just like drinking.' And he finished his brandy. 'Arms are in great demand in many places. The rebellion in Indonesia, the opposing camps in Indochina, the landlords in Thailand, in . . .'

'While trade in arms is that great, an agreement to reduce armaments is remote,' Doblado said.

'Also the end of the war, especially civil war,' Bayoneta surmised. 'If the army is increased, there will be fewer who are unemployed.'

'Business first, before the army,' Son Tua said to his son-in-law.

'As usual, Son Tua and I will provide the capital,' said Montero. 'And you two take care of operations and protection.'

'And the men?' asked Doblado.

'Get trustworthy ones. We have tested ones, haven't we?'

General Bayoneta explained that they had to choose the best sources at a low price. He mentioned some military bases with new and surplus arms in the warehouses, a few ships sailing to and from Manila, and installations outside the Philippines.

'As soon as you contact the officers in-charge, it is as easy as buying matches at the corner store,' Bayoneta said.

'The general is right,' agreed Montero. 'But the buyer's agents or the rival corporations should not know about this. We should just monopolize the transactions.'

'Just let them try to do anything behind my back, and we'll see where they'll land,' said Bayoneta, clenching his right fist. 'They can do that only if we allow it.'

'Good!' Montero said. 'As usual, Osky, you keep the arms until they are to be delivered. The warehouse has to be in your province where you're the king. General, you take care of the delivery. Is everything clear?'

'About the helpers, transactions, couriers, yes.'

'Just list down the expenses,' said Montero. 'Have I ever complained about my obligations? Son Tua and I understand. We have to spend more on public and private relations, representation, contacts and etcetera. The etcetera cost even more,' he said.

'Customs everywhere, right?' said Doblado.

'Too many checkpoints,' added Son Tua. 'Same as paying customs.'

'More, sometimes,' corrected Montero. 'If you pay taxes, you pay only taxes. Pay the fixed amount, and that's it. But here, there's no limit. As Son Tua said, too many checkpoints.'

'Going around the law is not only expensive but also risky,' said Bayoneta.

'Depends on the person,' the general's father-in-law disagreed.

'Why have many been forced to do this?' asked Montero. 'It's the government's fault. Isn't it, Son Tua?' Son Tua nodded.

'Is it not the government that's killing the initiative of business?' Montero asked. 'I have pointed this out to Senators Botin and Maliwanag. I have even mentioned this to the president. Taxes upon taxes and intricate layers of control, plus so much red tape. Not only are you overburdened, but your hands are also tied.'

'Control can be avoided, Montero, if there is a bribe,' Doblado said.

'Why not? In this country, money is king. But we businessmen want to help the government, if possible. Therefore, if one is forced into this kind of business, it's because we are protesting against its bad policy. If it wants to strangle legitimate business, then we should not be blamed if we try to survive through illegal means.'

'What happens then to the customs fees?' asked Son Tua.

'They just waste them in pleasure,' quickly said Montero. 'If they would only spend it for the country . . .'

Montero got a small notebook from a drawer at the bar and showed it to the three.

'Look at this month's expenses. If our business was legal, this money should go to the government treasury.'

Doblado and Bayoneta looked at the list.

'This is written Latin and therefore, indecipherable,' said the governor. 'This looks like MacArthur's cable that angered Truman— "top secret".'

'Of course, it's for me alone,' said Montero. 'Even if others should get it, in case of an investigation, no one would understand. But I need it to keep track of expenses. Or else how will I know how much I have paid for the advance expenses?'

At this remark, Son Tua cleared his throat.

'See who can guess the meaning of this,' said Montero and read the first entry: 'Chief, four.'

'I'm used to cables, but that's new,' said Bayoneta.

'See,' laughed Montero. 'Well, this is the chief of police who got 4,000 pesos.'

'There are many chiefs,' said the governor.

'Off the record, please,' said Montero, and then he whispered the name.

'But that one also asks extra from me,' said Son Tua. 'He's very greedy.'

'Don't give any more, Papa, unless it's me,' the general teased him.

Everyone laughed.

'Here's another: Secretary,' Montero read.

'Big potato, huh?' guessed Doblado. '7,000 for a secretary.'

'Surely not the secretary of a counsellor?' Bayoneta said.

Everyone laughed again.

Montero continued reading the list. 'Two Ham. Two.'

'Sounds like algebra,' chuckled Doblado. 'How do you read it, General?'

'I can make neither heads nor tails of it,' said Bayoneta.

'Wait,' said Doblado. 'Two hams at 1,000 each. What expensive hams these are, right, Monty?'

'I thought you were weak in algebra,' said Montero. 'These are the two heads of bases that helped us snag a juicy deal. They even asked for an additional blowout. So I asked for two white call girls. But, gentlemen, this is only just their down payments.'

'Those men are really expensive,' exclaimed Doblado. 'We are mere amateurs in this business.'

Governor Doblado gaped at the last entry for 'fifty' after a name which he could not read.

'Who's this beast?' he asked aloud. General Bayoneta looked at Montero's notebook.

Montero did not answer at once.

'Is it Mac or Wac?' asked Doblado with some envy. He couldn't believe anyone would receive more than him.

Montero grinned. 'Is there a Wac worth 50,000?'

'Then . . .' Doblado said, 'Tsk, tsk.'

'Yes, gentlemen,' said Montero without mentioning the name. 'You know the miracle, so you also know the saint.'

'Our corporation is really on top,' said Doblado and Bayoneta, and both of them laughed.

Son Tua's eyes narrowed into slits as he smiled. He had stood up to leave even before the laughter subsided. Bayoneta offered to drive his father-in-law home.

'Just a minute,' Montero held back Bayoneta, 'I'd like you to check out my plantation. Both of you know that I can't rest with what's happening. The troubles still continue, although I have already changed the overseer at your recommendation, General. I've told you about the agitators, right?'

'I know,' said Doblado.

'I want peace on the plantation,' said Montero.

'That can be done if the general and I put our heads together,' said the governor.

'What's aggravating is the alliance between the city labourers and the farmers,' General Bayoneta said. 'And they are being goaded by the *Kampilan*.'

'The backer of the *Kampilan* is a friend of your Dolly's,' Doblado said in a mocking tone.

'So, do everything possible,' said Montero, ignoring Doblado. 'I want to drive out all those who don't want to follow the old rules. Replace them with the meek ones. Captain Pugot says he can get replacements from the Ilocos. The Ilocanos are good, industrious and thrifty. If you just could drive away the troublemakers,' Montero whispered so that Son Tua wouldn't hear.

'Just leave it to the general and I,' the governor said. 'You may now sleep well. We know what to do.'

Montero handed Doblado a roll of paper bills. 'That's for the two of you. One roll for poker,' he said, smiling. 'And the other for the plantation.'

The clock was already striking eleven o'clock when two long cars left the gate. The mansion was like a giant suddenly wrapped in darkness.

XLIV

A charity benefit was on the agenda at a meeting of prominent women at the grand Manila Hotel.

It was already half an hour behind schedule, but not even the invitation committee had arrived. Right after lunch, Doña Julia rushed to get ready to attend the event. She opened her wide cabinet and looked over the dresses on the left. Then she looked at the clothes on the right. But she could not decide between a native wear and a dress. After a while, she got a dress with pastel colours; she thought that many would be wearing dresses. Actually, she wanted to wear something different, but she would run short of time if she wore a native dress. She would still have to have her hair and nails done as well.

After reminding Dolly to be ready at four o'clock, Doña Julia then went to her favourite beauty salon. After two hours, she returned looking ten years younger. Her hair was now newly set and shining. Her nails were trimmed and painted blood red. Her lips were as bright as her fingernails and toenails.

She started dressing at 3.30 p.m. and finished at 4.15 p.m. Dolly had been ready for some time. She was alluring in her red dress with prints of white *fleur-de-lis*. Both wore step-ins with glass heels.

Doña Julia came late, but she was still the first to arrive at the meeting. She saw the committee's secretary giving final instructions to the head waiter about the table arrangement. There would be a table for the First Lady, who was the special guest, and the members of the committee. Arrangements for food and decoration had been made several days before.

After another half hour, the guests began to arrive. All women, almost all had been guests at the blessing of the Monteros' mansion.

Arriving together were Mercy Mahabaguin and Mrs Conchita Pantoche, who had gone to fetch the First Lady. But the guest of honour could not attend the meeting. She had another urgent appointment. There was no explanation as to why both invitations had been accepted. Naturally, the absence of the honoured guest dampened their spirits. At such gatherings, the status of the guests was more important than the purpose. Mercy apologized to the group for the First Lady's absence. Everyone was disappointed; everyone had her own request to whisper to the president's wife. Now they had to wait for another rare opportunity.

Balbinitá Cuatrovientos, Blancanieve Cienfuegos and Maggie Siemprejoven were all dolled up, as if they were attending a grand fashion show. They had been planning hard where they would display themselves for the picture-taking. Balbinitá had asked Mercy to let her pin the orchids, while Blancanieve and Maggie had asked the photographer to take their picture with the guest of honour.

The committee decided to go on with the meeting as planned.

The first part of the programme was the food, of course. The guests grouped themselves at the tables spread out in the hall.

The waiters were used to such conversation that sounded like the humming of a thousand bumblebees. They were used to waiting on groups of women at such gatherings held on various pretexts.

At a group meeting of the wives of important officials, the "dessert" was the news of the separation of a department secretary and his wife.

'They have been separated for a long time,' said one.

'But they still lived under the same roof,' said another.

'Just for appearance's sake,' said the informant. 'Besides, their children are now all grown-up. But they don't eat or sleep together. They now have separate beds and even separate tables!' she said in English.

'Is that possible?' asked a third. 'That's hard. I think it's better to separate outright.'

'Hey, woman,' said an older one, 'if all estranged couples in Manila since liberation were to live apart, we would just worsen the housing shortage.'

The remark was met with loud laughter.

'Well, I have many vacant apartments for rent,' said one. 'There will be no scandal. Only we'll know what happens inside the house. If that should happen to common people, it would surely lead to a fight. And a bloody one, too.'

'Scandals are caused by gossip,' said the first. 'The rumour-mongers keep on talking about people who should separate. If we had divorce laws, the . . .'

'What for?' said the one who did not like the passage of a law on divorce. 'In Hollywood, where every three days someone changes their spouse, divorce is needed. But we are different here; couples who don't speak to each other still live together. Give the right medicine for the particular illness. Besides, we can manage without divorce. It was Quezon, I think, who said, "If you can eat it raw, why cook it?"'

Louder laughter again met the remark attributed to the late President Quezon.

On another table, talk floated about the merits of several Manila designers. Some complained of the few who did not meet their commitments, the lack of skill of some, wrong measurement and wrong style, and the greed of others who charged too high and asked for advanced payment.

'I have an easy solution for a bad dressmaker,' said a matron who looked like a bulldog despite her elegant clothes. Her nose was like a flattened cashew nut.

'What do you do?' asked the others.

'Why, I don't pay him. Let him try to collect.'

'Then you can't go back to him.'

'I certainly won't. Dressmakers are a dime a dozen.'

'Ah, I have no problem with our dressmakers,' said another who looked like a foreigner except for her rather dark skin colour. 'I don't have my clothes sewn here. I have a dressmaker in Hong Kong.'

'I thought it was Paris.'

'*Chica*, Hong Kong is the Paris of the East. You have no idea how many matrons from Manila fly to Hong Kong. Many go there just to play mah-jongg.'

'About dressmakers. Who is really better, a male or a female?'

'Men, of course,' chorused two in the group.

'Why?'

'Because women dress up for men. If there were no men in the world, women wouldn't even wear clothes. If fine clothes are for men, then it's better to have a male dressmaker. That's why Paris has a Christian Dior.'

'Then why aren't tailors women, following your line of reasoning?'

'Because of men's trousers. In taking the measurements, one always asks: does the family jewellery fall to the right or the left? Can a woman ask that?'

On the other table, the talk among the businesswomen was not so raucous. They were discussing the black market value of dollars and the peso, the smuggling of diamonds and blue-seal cigarettes, the many ways of squeezing money from government agencies.

'The lower our dollar resources, the lower the value of our peso,' said one. 'In Manila, the exchange is one to three, but it's higher in Hong Kong.'

'What about the wives of big shots? All expenses for trips, good times and purchases come from dollar profits. Even those without dollars earn by being dummies of foreigners, who control 80 per cent of our dollars.'

'The trade in diamonds has slowed down.'

'Why not, when there is an oversupply? At first, the smuggler brought in diamonds and sold them to the wealthy, to the wives and mistresses of sugar daddies. Now, it's the reverse. The wives of the big potatoes have become the smugglers and now sell diamonds to the wealthy Chinese.'

'Maybe the baggage of the big shots is not opened at the pier and the airport.'

'It's suicide for the customs agent to inspect the baggage of one with a diplomatic passport. And these people always travel with a special or diplomatic passport.'

'I read that even a maid was given a diplomatic passport.'

'You'd do the same if you were in their place, chica.'

'You can believe it. That's why my husband wants to run for senator.'

'On which ticket?'

'Any ticket. He's not choosy; just so he can squeeze in. If you're a senator, the party does not matter. It's easy to get a diplomatic passport later.'

At one table were Balbinitá, Blancanieve, Maggie, Betty and her daughter Betsy. Balbinitá told the waiter that she didn't care for the moist cake because it would ruin her figure. 'Just give me orange juice and a pack of Camels.'

For these five, the only worthwhile topic was how to stay young and beautiful, how to care for their complexion, stay slim and keep their hair black.

Maggie said that hair nowadays could be dyed with any colour. 'But it should match the colour of your eyes. Some just manage to look uglier because they don't match the colour of their skin.'

Betty Labajita passed around a picture of herself and her daughter to get the others' comments.

On another table could be heard the gripes of younger matrons about their housemaids. They ask for high pay, are choosy about their jobs, and even want the privileges of common employees.

'They now feel entitled,' said a young pregnant matron. 'Just because they have learnt to read and write, unlike their illiterate grandmothers. Now, they are imposing conditions on their masters and want to be the señoritas.'

She said that the maid who had just left them was from the north. She was being paid thirty pesos a month, free food, with no other work but to wash the dishes and clean the house, no laundry, no cooking, and yet, she wanted to be allowed to go to church on Fridays and see a movie on Sunday.

'They work as maids only to get to Manila,' answered another.

'And when they get here, they look for other jobs—waitress, vendor or salesgirl. But their real aim is to marry.'

'What should they come to Manila for? In their village also they can find husbands.'

'They want someone better. If they become waitresses or salesgirls, they might marry a Chinese.'

'Better a Chinese than a good-for-nothing Filipino.'

'A thousand times better. With a Chinese, you won't starve; with our countrymen, you will not only starve but might also get beaten up. So you can't blame the poor girls.'

'Well, the times have changed. I prefer the maids we were used to—no complaints about work. Just like members of the family, they don't think of leaving, and stay until their old age. They appreciate whatever you give them, no complaints, no questions. But the war has changed this attitude.'

'And the ones with the looks and figures become hostesses,' one said, pouting. 'And once a hostess, she might even become a congressman's mistress!'

The food was finished in less than two hours. Mercy stood up and said that the aim of their meeting, as stated in the invitation, was to hold a benefit for charity.

Several proposals for fundraising were given—mah-jongg, bingo, a dance, a movie, a fashion show, or a rummage sale, among others. The women didn't lack ideas but could not agree on one.

At last, they thought of asking for a sweepstakes lottery, but they did not reach a decision. When they adjourned, they resolved to hold another meeting, but they would make sure that the First Lady would join this time.

XLV

The new overseer's strictness at the Montero Plantation was the last straw that broke the camel's back. Don Segundo replaced Pastor with a former constabulary captain notorious for his ferocity and support for the Japanese.

The new overseer was not known by his real name, Caballero, but by the name Captain Pugot. According to Charles Darwin's theory of 'the origin of the species' in his book the *Descent of Man*, one could trace Caballero's ancestry not to the noble knight errant or an agile jockey, but to a donkey. He had a long face, a wide mouth, and an odd way of showing his teeth and kicking his feet. It was said that as a collaborator in Central Luzon, he surpassed even the Japanese military police in the number of people he had beheaded—both guerrillas and non-guerrillas. At the slightest suspicion that a peaceful citizen had worked with the bandits, refused to help the Japanese, or did not give what he asked for, he would be lucky if his head was not severed within seventy-two hours.

Just as lucky was Captain Pugot, who seemed to have been swallowed up by the earth during the two uncertain days between the departure of the Japanese and the arrival of the Americans. He was next heard from when he voluntarily surrendered to the Americans in Manila. Otherwise, the furious guerrillas would have given him a dose of his own medicine—his head clean separated from the rest of his body.

The tenants and sharecroppers at the Montero Plantation considered the hiring of Pugot a slap to all of them. It was obvious that Don Segundo would not only insist on the old system, but had no plan to even meet the farmers halfway.

Pastor, who was sympathetic because he was one of them, had already been replaced. Captain Pugot was a soldier who knew nothing about land and cared nothing about the tenants. All he cared for was his blind obedience to the Japanese, and now to Don Segundo. He was a good follower but certainly, a bad master.

The fears of the farmers soon came to pass. Their requests were turned down. All debts, even of those whose fields lay fallow during the war, were now being collected through force. Those who couldn't pay were given an ultimatum. Don Segundo also decided that the tenants should follow the old system of sharing expenses and harvest; he said that this was better than having no land to till.

The strict overseer announced this harsh decision. To prove that he wasn't joking, Captain Pugot built a strong fence around the yard of the plantation house left by Pastor and Puri. At the entrance stood an armed guard, a former soldier who had worked under Pugot during the Japanese occupation. He formed a troop of armed civilian guards, and he promised to lease to them all the farms that would be taken from the tenants. In addition, the new overseer contracted workers from Ilocos and Isabela, who were ready to accept the conditions rejected by the old tenants. They felt that the labourers' situation in their provinces was even worse.

Pastor and Puri had moved to their own land in a village not far from the plantation. Puri had inherited part of the land from her mother. Pastor had bought his brother-in-law's share.

Ever since he returned to farming, Pastor devoted his time to improving his farm and strengthening the farmers' union. The members often met at his place.

In answer to Captain Pugot's harshness, the tenants fought back. They stuck to their right to the land bought by Don Segundo's money, but in which they had invested their sweat and blood. Many of the tenants had been born on the plantation when Montero bought it from the first buyer of the friar land. The ancestors of many had been on the land when it was claimed by the friars who had asked them to clear it without pay, supposedly as a service to the church, and therefore, a service to God. The only payment was the granting of indulgences to those who cleared and ploughed the land should they commit sins, like not going to Mass on Sunday or to confession at least once a month, or slaughtering and eating meat on days of abstinence.

Mang Tomas and the parents of Danoy, both leaders of the farmers, grew up on the plantation along with the big trees around it. They didn't care to move to a new place. 'Our roots are buried here,' Mang Tomas told a gathering of people one night. 'This is where we will stay, no matter what happens. We respect the owner's right to his property, but he should also learn to respect our rights. For a long time, we have made the plantation and the Monteros rich, while we wallow in poverty. Who among you is without debts? Who among you has any savings at all? If you should die of hunger, who among you would have money for the Mass and the coffin? Tell me. Therefore, if we ask the landlord for new terms, if we ask the government to buy the plantation and divide it among those of us who have sacrificed for it, it's because we, too, have a right to live without misery. No matter how much Don Segundo paid for the plantation, he has been repaid many times over.'

Everyone felt the same way. Danoy added that they were not afraid of the civilian guards.

'We know Captain Pugot and his men,' Danoy said. 'They have not yet paid for their old crimes. Only lightning is safe from vengeance.'

'What happened to the petition we had sent to the governor?' asked a tenant.

'As expected,' said Mang Tomas. 'It was simply ignored.'

'The governor is two-faced,' accused Danoy. 'He gives us promises because he needs our votes. But in truth, he is tied to Don Segundo. I have no more faith in these political chameleons.'

The civilian guards and the farmers often had their near-skirmishes. There appeared a dividing line between them, the same line that had divided the collaborators from the guerrillas in the past, when courage and loyalty were tested between the opportunists and the nationalists.

The grass along the way to the plantation house had already grown tall. The fields lay fallow. The guns of the civilian guards were clean and shiny, while the farmer-guerrillas brought out their old weapons. They were prepared for any eventuality. Tension hung in the air.

Fortunately, Don Segundo sent word to postpone their picnic to the plantation because Doña Julia was ill. Montero was aware of his farmers' discontent, and he supported Pugot's move to hire civilian guards, thinking that this would maintain the peace.

'Everything is under control, sir.' This was the overseer's regular report to Don Segundo. In Pugot's mind, the situation was good whenever he stalled the farmers' petitions.

One day, Rubio and Iman went to the village. Rubio was the leader of a huge labour federation in the city, and Iman was a reporter at the *Kampilan*. The labour leader and the farmer had met several times since they joined forces the past year.

Pastor quickly sent for Mang Tomas, Danoy and the others.

When the rest arrived, Rubio told them that the labourers were already fed up with the widespread unemployment, with meagre wages, with the exploitation of thousands who work overtime but are underpaid, with the high cost of goods controlled by people who should enforce the law but who instead receive bribes, and the apathy of the politicians who care only for themselves.

'If those who control the nation's economy are like leeches and the government officials blind, then the people should act,' Rubio said.

'We also have serious troubles in the fields,' said Mang Tomas. 'You must have seen the guards at the plantation.'

'When conditions are bad in the city, they are also as bad in the fields and probably elsewhere else,' said Rubio. 'Prosperity can't be divided; at any rate, it shouldn't be. It is wrong to let a small part of the union live in comfort while the majority starve. This is not the fruit of our victory against the Japs. We did not spend lives and spill blood just to let the traitors gorge themselves again. My friends, in our hands, in the hands of the farmers and labourers, lies our salvation. Let us protest and fight . . .'

Rubio was carried away by his emotions. As if borne on swift wings, he remembered his own life, his sufferings when he was orphaned until he was blown by fortune like a leaf, as a newspaper boy, a driver, a cigarette vendor, until he was mauled by some Japanese soldiers who had left him almost dead while a thousand countrymen just watched in the square; his slaying of his betrayers, his hiding in Manila and in the provinces like a hunted animal, until he joined a band of guerrilla-outlaws, which he immediately left; his return to Manila at the end of the war, when he joined the many jobless and later led the workers' federations. These thoughts rose in Rubio's heart and mind and fired him up to seek relief for himself and others like him.

Rubio urged the farmers to attend a mass rally in Manila that would call for a general strike—the declaration of the nation's protest against the worsening conditions of the poor.

Iman brought Mando's message to Pastor and Puri to come early and drop by the *Kampilan* office.

Since his return, Mando had already visited them. He stayed almost the whole day and was alone with Puri while Pastor fetched the other leaders. So Mando knew the latest happenings at the plantation. Once more, he noted the difference between Dolly and Puri.

On their way back from the village to the national road, Rubio's group passed by the plantation. But they were stopped by two civilian guards who asked where they were coming from.

'Where are your passes?' one asked.

Iman explained that they went to visit someone and weren't going to the plantation.

'Even then,' the guard answered roughly, clutching his gun. 'Next time, ask for a pass there.' He pointed to the plantation house.

The newspaperman and the labour leader did not argue any more, but when the two civilian guards had turned their backs, Rubio said: 'But when we return, you might already be gone.'

The two hired guards of Captain Pugot looked back and fumed upon hearing the laughter of the two men in the departing Jeep.

XLVI

In all the villages and neighbouring towns of the Montero Plantation, the farmers prepared for the trip to Manila. They were excited to attend the meeting at Plaza Miranda. This was a hundred times more important than a fiesta. The oppressed now would decide whether or not to launch a general strike.

But when it was time to leave, not everyone could fit in the single bus that had been sent for them.

After lunch, the farmers gathered in front of Pastor's house, but only a hundred could be accommodated. Many decided to go by passenger bus instead.

Pastor and Danoy were chosen to be the farmers' spokesmen at the meeting. Pastor would relate the plantation's history, from the time it was taken by the friars and transferred to different owners, until it was bought by Segundo Montero before the war. Danoy would describe the farmers' oppression and relate how the present owner and the governor just blithely ignored their petitions.

The farmers were in high spirits as the bus reached Manila, not because they hoped for instant solutions, but because of their eagerness to meet their comrades in the city—the minor employees, the labourers and the jobless. Besides, thousands would hear their spokesmen talk about the injustice that cried to the heavens.

Puri, Pastor and Danoy sat together, with Pastor in the middle. After a while, they were silent, each occupied with his own thoughts.

302

Pastor was planning what he would say at the meeting. He had the history and conditions of the Montero Plantation down pat. For many years, he had served as a tenant, a sharecropper and an overseer there. But in his talk, he had to condense the whole into a clear and effective presentation. Pastor had often heard speeches which were so long that, like an unrolled string, they got the speaker entangled. Instead of capturing the goodwill of the listeners, the speaker became a dragonfly caught in a spider's web. He wanted to avoid this.

Puri's thoughts were riveted on her meeting with Mando. True, she was also concerned with the farmers' welfare. She was Pastor's sounding board regarding his ideas about the plantation. She had heard the tenants' discussions and served them food at home, or in the field. She was regarded as one of the plantation's brightest women.

But above this, she was also maiden in bloom. Like a budding flower living for the whisper of the bee and the kiss of the butterfly, both of whom offered the honey of dreams. Thus, her thoughts were more on Mando than on the farmers' concerns.

Puri had lost her former serenity since Mando wrote to her, 'I failed to see in my travels a woman who can compare with your virtues, and I rejoice in this failure.' In her heart, Puri was afraid that Mando was just flattering her, but it was such a sweet lie. Between a man and a woman, the truth often serves as an arrow that wounds the heart, but white lies are always sweet and they help heal the wounds of separation, so that love and joy can bloom.

Puri was pleased with Mando's words, although his hints went no further. She was not even sure if anything serious would happen between them. She hoped that when they met that night, they would have a chance to talk in a more intimate manner.

Danoy, who sat at Pastor's right, stole glances at Puri. He knew what he would say at the meeting and felt he also knew what was on Puri's mind.

Unlike Mando, Danoy had long gone beyond mere hints and told Puri about his love. Puri liked Danoy, but that was all. She felt no buzzing in her ears or fluttering in her heart when she was with Danoy. Perhaps if she had not met Mando, she would have been moved by Danoy's perseverance, but Puri was sure that such was not likely.

Danoy saw a certain smile and a gleam in her eyes only when Mando was around. Danoy was hurt, but he had learnt to accept his fate. He had enough experience to know that the pot could not clash with the jar and stay whole, even in love.

Besides, Danoy's respect for Pastor was as great as his love for Puri. He felt obliged to respect the girl's happiness even at a personal sacrifice. When Mando began to visit the plantation often, Danoy felt that it was not for the *Kampilan* alone. He saw where Puri's happiness lay, and accepted everything.

After two hours, they reached the capital city. The bus stopped before the *Kampilan* building. Mando came down to greet the guests. Many remained seated. Mang Tomas and Danoy said they would then go to their meeting place, the headquarters of Rubio's federation. They would see each other at the meeting that night.

Mando led Pastor and Puri to his office on the second floor. Magat greeted them and introduced Andres. The reporter Iman was out of the office.

Construction had begun on the new building, which was to be the permanent home of the media under Mando—a modern newspaper, as well as a radio and television station.

Mando proudly showed his guests the blueprint of the building and pictures of the rotary press that he had bought abroad. It would soon be installed in the basement.

'In three to four months, you won't recognize this place any more,' said Mando. He was sure that the work would be finished by then.

He said that the three branches of media—newspaper, radio and television—would bring the public accurate and honest news. They would also present wholesome entertainment on the air.

'Oh, that's a big task,' said Pastor, who was clearly awed.

'A big task and a big service to the people,' Mando said.

He explained that his organization did not aim to profit off its public service. He referred to other groups that often wore masks and pretended to be nationalistic, humane and godly. But despite such disguise, their real aim was to gain money, power and fame.

'One's sincerity can be seen in the result of one's action. You can count on this—the forge of the nation's sentiments will not be used as tools by politics, business, or even religion. These forces are too strong. While the country is weak and in want, we should search for one who will be the voice of truth.'

'You,' said Pastor.

'We,' said Mando.

Sometimes, Pastor wondered why Mando was concerned with the workers. He supposed this was because Mando was a man of principles, and the sterling virtues of truth and justice lay on the side of the poor.

Puri was more impressed by Mando. She listened to Mando and her father, hardly saying anything but savouring all the words that Mando said. She was convinced that Mando had no equal.

Pastor left the office and went to Andres's desk. Puri could hardly hear Mando's soft words as they looked at an album.

'Don't you want to live in Manila?' he asked.

Puri was taken aback.

'I didn't know Tatang had planned to leave the farm,' she answered coyly. 'With God's grace, we are living peacefully on our small parcel of land.'

But her heart was beating fast. She could not bring herself to ask Mando why he had asked that question. Mando's explanation did not calm her down.

'I was just asking,' he said in an evasive manner. 'No one can guess what will happen in the future.'

Puri replied, 'A person can adjust wherever fortune takes him. We saw this during the war. Thousands of families were uprooted. With God's grace, they survived.'

'Man knows how to adjust,' agreed Mando. He added, 'But just the same, the place where he is should also be adapted to his needs. This is only right.'

'Yes, that is ideal. But the farmers are used to adapting themselves. They are like the bamboo that bends with the wind so they won't break.'

'Tonight, we shall announce the beginning of the end of such humility,' he said. Puri noticed that his earlier gentleness had vanished.

'Tonight's meeting,' Mando continued, 'is the shout of the oppressed that they shall not always be forgiving.'

'Forgiveness is not a virtue, but neither is it cowardice,' said Puri. 'We peasants have a saying: if the rice is already full, then we should level it.'

Mando was pleased that Puri had not only the virtues of a village maiden but also a deep understanding of life. She had a deep concern for the problems of her fellow men. Clearly, Puri was not just a lovely gem to look at but a rare woman indeed.

Like her father, Puri also wondered about Mando's difference from the other rich men. She recalled Don Segundo's ways.

'Let's talk again about my question about your living in Manila,' Mando roused the girl, who seemed to have been lost in her thoughts. 'I'll explain why I asked you that question,' he added.

Puri did not answer, but her heart beat faster. Just then, Pastor peeped in through the door and reminded them that they might be late.

'Why, I didn't realize how late it had got,' Puri said.

Mando brought the two to dinner before they went to the meeting.

XLVII

It was a fifteen-minute drive from the *Kampilan*. Mando stopped the Jeep in a yard with an ordinary house.

'We're here,' said Mando, helping Puri alight. 'This is our home.'

It was only then that the guests realized where they were going. They thought they were going to a restaurant in the suburbs. Could this be the house of the wealthy publisher who was constructing a large building in Manila?

'This doesn't look like the house of a . . . Don,' Pastor teased.

Mando laughed and answered that he would rather be called anything but a Don.

'The best way to make Don Segundo mad is to remove "Don" before his name.'

'Tata Pastor, Don Segundo and I are opposites.' Mando smiled.

'Very few in your situation live in this kind of house,' said Pastor.

'This house is right for one person—a bachelor,' explained Mando, glancing at Puri, who quickly looked away. 'I remember that the philosopher Socrates once said when a friend asked him why he lived in a hut, "I am lucky if this small hut is filled with good friends". So, come in, my dear friends.' He stressed the word 'dear,' looking steadily at Puri.

The bungalow was in the middle of a lot surrounded by a low wall. Around were a few large acacia trees. It had two parts divided by a passageway that served as a garage. There was no other vehicle but the Jeep. The right was made up of the living room, dining room, library, two bedrooms, and a bathroom. The rooms were small. In this part lived Mando and Tata Matias. The second part on the left was the kitchen, the quarters of the two helpers, and a closet. Both helpers were male, a cook and the lad Kiko who had come to Manila with Mando and Tata Matias after the war. The cook bought the food, cooked, and did the other chores for Mando. Tata Matias hardly worked, except to tend a few plants and read. Kiko cleaned the house and the yard. Once in a while, he would drive Mando's Jeep, especially when he came home at night with him. Kiko went to night school and went to the *Kampilan* after his classes.

Mando asked the cook, Mang Simo, to serve dinner. Earlier, he had told him that he would have guests.

He introduced the guests to Tata Matias.

'He is my foster father,' said Mando. The old man knew the two by name, for Mando often talked about them. Mando had also told Tata Matias that Pastor was his mother's brother, but had asked him to keep this a secret. Mando kept nothing from Tata Matias.

Tata Matias and Pastor sat facing each other and were soon engaged in conversation. Mando showed Puri the various parts of the house of 'a bachelor'.

The library adjacent to the living room was small, but Puri was fascinated. She looked at the pictures and books, and some of Mando's precious mementoes. Mando showed her the old copies of *Noli Me Tángere* and *El Filibusterismo*, which had new binding. He told her that Tata Matias had kept these copies from the time of the revolution against Spain until the end of the Second World War. Also in the library were most of Rizal's writings, the complete collection of his letters in *Epistolario Rizalino*, the collection of the newspapers *La Solidaridad*, *El Renacimiento* and *Muling Pagsilang*. There were also some copies of the Bible in Tagalog, English and Spanish; books on world history; the histories of Europe, the United States, Britain, Spain, Japan, Mexico and Latin America; and the histories of the conquest of China, India and Africa. There were also three or four histories of the Philippines.

'Philippine history should be rewritten,' said Mando.

'Why?' asked Puri.

'Because it is full of errors and lies.'

'But is there a history which is not so?' asked Puri, repeating what she often heard from the farmers during the war.

'That's why Philippine history should be rewritten,' Mando repeated, this time with firmness. 'The one who should write it should not be one author but a committee of Filipino experts. The publisher should be the government. Many things should be changed,' he added, 'but not all at the same time.'

'Is that not the dream of all movements even before the birth of Christ?' Puri asked. 'Change and more change. What happens then to the leaders?'

'The blood of the martyrs glorifies the history of mankind,' said Mando. 'The story of our country should relate honestly the history of the Filipinos, their economic life, situation, society, civilization, culture and beliefs many centuries before the Spaniards came. Magellan and Villalobos did not only stumble upon a race of Negritos. The natives they met were elegant and civilized. But the Spaniards named these islands after their king. The history taught in schools during the last fifty years is the story of conquest by foreigners, their government and their deeds. These have to change.'

Puri understood, but at that moment, she would have been more pleased if he would explain what he had said about her, or about them. For example, why he was happy that in his travels he did not find a girl with Puri's qualities; his question of whether Puri would like to live in Manila someday . . . So when she sat on an easy chair in the library, she said that Mando's house was lovely because it was clean and peaceful.

'No one would say there was no woman to fix it,' she added.

'Are women the only—' But Mando cut himself short. Instead, he said, 'That is what this house lacks. That's why I asked if you wished to live in Manila.' Then he stopped abruptly.

'And I answered that I didn't know if Tatang had any such plans,' Puri replied. 'I don't see the connection between that and what this house lacks.'

'I'll tell you straight, Puri,' Mando finally took courage. 'What this house lacks is a woman; no, not just a woman, but you, Puri, only you. If you will agree to leave the farm.'

'Right away, you're already imposing a condition,' she said. 'That's putting the plow before the carabao.'

'The reason, Puri, is my timidity. I thought I was brave, with all my experience, but now I realize that I am faint-hearted. I am afraid to tell you that . . .'

'That you want me to be a maid in this house?'

'To be my queen.'

For a while, both were silent; both were at a loss for words while from each heart to the tiniest vein in their finger, ran a riot of emotions.

'Now, I have confessed to you,' Mando said, breaking the silence.

'When did you think of this?' Puri asked softly.

'Ever since I first visited the plantation and talked to you.'

'Years?'

'Centuries.'

'Then perhaps you will not expect an immediate reply.'

'Please don't prolong my suffering.'

'You placed the condition that I should live in Manila,' Puri said.

Mando felt the sting of her words.

'I have not placed any condition. I'm pleading.'

'That's why,' she said, 'my living in Manila will not just mean a change of address. I was born and brought up on a farm. Throughout my life, I have mixed with village folk, the poor like us who live in huts and know nothing except how to till the soil. I'm used to their ways, their relationship, their beliefs. You want me to move to the city. Shall I leave all that I'm used to? Can I change all those, my life, myself?'

Puri looked at Mando as if to read his answer in his eyes.

'You won't leave nor change anything,' Mando said. 'I shall be proud of everything you are, Puri. I shall not ask for any sacrifice or change. You will do nothing but love me as I love you.'

'That includes everything I have said,' said Puri. 'Your situation will force me to change. You are a publisher, an important person in society. I've read in the papers, and I've seen in pictures, the life and ways of society people, especially the women. I don't want to be a Cinderella or a mannequin of luxury, of the beauty parlour or of the fashion pages of the glossy magazines. I'm not afraid of change if this means progress.'

Mando could see that Puri was blushing. This made him admire and want her even more.

'You have nothing to fear,' Mando promised. 'I love you because you are you. You're different from the others. I don't want you to be like them in looks, manners and dress. Besides, I don't belong to the upper crust myself, Puri. The people's organization, the masses, are different from the society of the few.'

'Then, you are a fish out of water,' Puri said.

'What you see is only the surface,' Mando said. 'You don't see the real me, my origin. I was not always like this. I am also a farmer's son. I have known all kinds of hardship. I worked as a servant in order to study; I studied to be free from servitude. During the war, I joined the guerrillas. I lived in the mountains and fought. I gained good friends like Tata Matias and Dr Sabio. After the war, we pooled our resources together to establish a new life. You know the rest, Puri. That is my story.'

'It does not show, Mando. You have changed. Why should I not also change if it will help you?'

'Change is the first law of life,' Mando said. 'But we must change for the better. When I said you wouldn't change, I meant the inborn goodness of country folk. For example, who would want to replace modesty with immodesty, humility with arrogance, industry with useless activities, thrift with wastefulness? On the other hand, who would not want to learn the right way of living in the city, to gain knowledge, to do more good?'

Puri was about to answer when Mang Simo peeped into the library, reminding them that the dinner would grow cold.

Mando and Puri saw Tata Matias and Pastor still discussing the ills of the country.

'No one denies that our conquerors deceived us,' said Tata Matias. 'What we should do is return to the past. When I was a child, if I thought I had been misled by goblins, I turned my clothes inside out and retraced my footsteps. Sometimes, a child is wiser than many of our leaders.'

'In the field, a new idea is spreading,' said Pastor. 'You are right, sir, but many farmers feel that more is needed. They say that we should follow the water buffalo that breaks its rope and uses its sharp horns.'

'An empty sack can't stand alone,' said Mando. 'Let's continue our conversation at the table.' And they all went to the dining room together.

XLVIII

The meeting at Plaza Miranda began with the singing of the national anthem.

One couldn't even drop a needle through the thick crowd. Mando, Pastor and Puri had to inch their way to the stage on one side of the plaza.

The makeshift wooden stage was wide and well-built. It was also very well-lit. One could clearly read the posters emblazoned with the advocacy of the various groups.

There was a plan to have a preliminary demonstration in the afternoon on the city streets, passing by Congress and Malacañang Palace and ending at Plaza Miranda. But the officials did not give permission to the organizers. Even the meeting was only supposed to last until midnight.

Rubio was speaking when Mando arrived. Among those seated were Senator Maliwanag, Danoy and Mang Tomas, with the delegates from various groups. Rubio was just starting with his opening remarks. He said that the meeting was being held for the welfare of thousands of people from all walks of life. He wanted to ask the government and business leaders to halt the widespread poverty stalking the land. And should they fail to do so, a nationwide strike would follow.

'This crisis that is a burden on the poor is not caused by God,' Rubio said. 'It is the work of our skewed institutions, run by a group of greedy men. They are the people in power. Let us not blame Jesus of

312

Nazarene inside the Quiapo Church. Let us ask for an accounting from government leaders and big businessmen, because they caused these present crises. They are today's preying birds.'

The labour leader certainly did not mince his words. Like a boxer, he pleased the crowd with his short, straight jabs. He continued:

'Unemployment and high prices didn't come from heaven, I repeat. They are the means to enrich those who are already rich, and to further impoverish those who are already poor. They wallow in luxury while the nation starves. What do we ask for? The right to eat three times a day, to eat the food that comes from our own sweat. Only this. But we cannot have it. For the leaders are greedy to the bone and love only themselves. What shall we do? Speak up and tell us what we should do. Will we let them strangle the country? Let us strike and oppose this.'

Applause and shouts of 'Change! Change! Strike! Strike!'

But not everyone in the plaza had come to support the meeting. In truth, the meeting was teeming with spies and detectives from the government and business groups. They were in full force, listing down names and recording remarks, twisting the very meanings of the words. The detective listed down Rubio's words as, 'Let us confront the nation's leaders and big businessmen. The situation strangling the nation should be replaced with something better.'

Rubio knew about this, but he just blithely ignored them, for he was used to such tactics. He was known as a true labour leader. He knew that in the spy's vocabulary, any worker who could not be bribed was an enemy of peace and a friend of disorder. 'Rabble-rouser, Red, Communist' were the labels thrown at his face. But this shabby treatment was given only to the workers and their sympathizers. Businessmen, bankers and the politicians in power were not spied upon, no matter what they said or did.

At any rate, the majority of the crowd at Plaza Miranda was prepared to listen and support the growing movement. They ignored the detectives whom they considered similar to the fallen Japanese soldiers. In their veins flowed courage and pride in knowing that they were not just mute onlookers in the past, and nor would they be quiet in the future. Their nationalistic spirit remained aflame in their hearts.

Rubio introduced a student who started to speak in English. The crowd protested and told him to speak in Filipino.

'We don't need a foreigner here,' said a few who were standing near the stage.

'Speak in Tagalog so we can understand one another,' shouted the others.

'Our country is now free. Don't talk in the language of our former colonial master. The Americans have gone.'

The student apologized, explaining that he was from the Visayas. He tried to speak in Tagalog and was applauded heartily for doing so.

He said that the students could not just fold their arms indifferently in the face of alarming events. According to him, 90 per cent of students were the children of poor employees and labourers. A large number were working their way through college.

'If the cost of living is high, so are our school expenses,' he said. 'Then, who among the poor will have the chance to study? Is education like tinned food that is paid for in dollars? If the poor have to choose between rice and books, you know what the answer will be. Therefore, the coming generation will be an army of ignorant people.'

The detectives noted down the student's name and his school.

A delegate of the female workers in a cigarette factory faced the mic. She described the pitiful conditions of the workers.

'The best cigars are made in Manila,' she said. 'But the Filipino cigar makers are starving. Why? Because most of our countrymen smoke American cigarettes, the smuggled blue seal.'

'True! True!' said her listeners.

'Our product is excellent, yet we patronize those of others,' she continued. 'We think we are modern if we wear foreign clothes, eat foreign food, speak the language of foreigners, mimic their vices. But this only goes to show that we have no unity, no minds of our own. We have no self-respect.'

'Bravo!' many shouted.

The woman said that the mothers shoulder most of life's hardships. 'The woman holds the purse, but what can you do if the purse is full of holes?' she asked in a rhetorical manner.

Laughter swept through the crowd in the wake of her analogy.

She asked for a campaign against ostentation among the rich, especially the women.

'Actually,' she pointed out, 'wealth is not due to these extravagant orchids of society. They have no right to live like goldfish being displayed in an aquarium. Why should the workers who help in producing this wealth always remain in want? It is our right and our children's right to receive social justice.'

'That's our girl!' came the chorus from her fellow factory workers.

Puri shook hands with the woman and graciously moved to make room for her.

Rubio introduced Pastor, then Danoy.

The two showed with vividness the alarming conditions in the rural areas. Many were appalled upon hearing the dismal conditions at Montero Plantation. Pastor spoke with deliberate calmness and slowness, but his words were as sharp as the machete, and cut as deeply. Recalling the story of Cabesang Tales, Pastor said that the farmer who is robbed of his earnings is often branded as a bandit, a veritable enemy of the law.

'We till the soil, we harvest the rice, corn and sugarcane, but we always lack these very products. We have neither rice nor corn to eat, and the price of sugar is out of our reach. We just work in vain because of other people's bottomless greed. We must have change; we must fight for social justice,' Pastor said. 'Let them not force us to leave the plough for the machete.'

'Tatang!' Pastor overheard Puri's voice above the applause.

'I was calm,' said Pastor to his daughter when he had returned to his seat. He believed his speech was quite mild.

On the other hand, Danoy's speech was fiery. His words were fired like the staccato of a machine gun. He said that aside from oppressing them, the landlord used violence and gave guns to civilian guards. Danoy stressed that they were God-fearing, but they were not afraid of the sword.

'We bravely fought the Japanese after the American Armed Forces had surrendered,' Danoy said. 'If the farmers had helped the enemy, the course of the war would have been different; we are not only workers but also loyal Filipinos.'

The crowd applauded him.

'We did not fight the Japanese because of the colour of their skin, but because they promoted evil deeds,' Danoy went on. 'We shall not stop fighting evil. Pastor, who spoke before me, was right. We should ask for what is rightfully ours. We should ask for justice. Not only that. We shall also ask that the existing arrangements be stopped. We should not have equal share with the landlord who does nothing but grow layers of fat on his belly. It's time we owned our land, for ourselves and our children's sake, the fields that we enrich with our very own sweat and blood. Unless this is done, all talks of justice are but flowers of the tongue. They won't mean anything.'

There was a hearty applause. The detectives listed down the names of Pastor and Danoy and choice passages from their speeches.

There was also some commotion when two detectives roughly climbed the stage. They were stopped by three husky men assigned by Rubio at the stairs. The detectives wanted to ignore the reminders of Rubio's men and insisted on having their way.

Rubio intervened and allowed them to go up. They claimed that they were only after the safety of those on the stage. There was a report that there would be trouble brewing at the meeting.

'This is a meeting of the poor,' Rubio explained. 'There will be no trouble, unless the enemies of truth and justice have hired troublemakers.'

'We are just doing our duty,' said the two, and then they stayed behind. Rubio ignored them and introduced the next speaker: Mando Plaridel.

XLIX

The meeting became liveliest at ten in the evening. The sky was clear, and the stars competed in brightness with the lights ablaze in the plaza.

As the night deepened, the crowd also began to increase in number. It seemed as if everyone was prepared to stay the whole night long. The energy in the air was electric. Rubio introduced Mando as a 'friend of the oppressed.' He said that Mando was the publisher of the *Kampilan*, which defended the rights of the poor. Rubio said that a newspaper promptly folds up in a country where it is not a tool of the mighty. The birth of the *Kampilan* and the work of Mando Plaridel are forms of heroic sacrifices. Mando waited for the long applause to die down before he began.

Mando acknowledged that, indeed, he was the publisher of the *Kampilan*, which was owned by an association of men with noble principles. He said that the *Kampilan* was a defender not only of the poor, but also of truth and justice, which happened to be on the majority's side.

'The war has ended, and for years, the Philippines has been free,' Mando said. 'It makes me sad to say that until now, the lot of the common man has not improved. Our country gave everything for democracy. But do we enjoy the fruits of this democracy? Just look around us. The fortunate few are in their palaces, the many unfortunate ones in their hovels. The fortunate few are feasting; the many hungry pick trash cans for morsels of food. Is this the tomorrow that was promised during the war? Is this the reward for our many sacrifices?'

Mando explained what a free nation should enjoy. He said that without means, there is no freedom, for the slavery of poverty and hunger is the worst kind of slavery.

'Everyone should have means of livelihood, schools, hospitals and medicine for the sick,' said Mando. 'In short, there should be equal opportunity for all.'

Loud applause interrupted Mando. He waited for the thunderous applause to die down before he continued. He reminded the crowd that the country should depend on its people if they want to be freed from the terrible burdens of poverty.

'My brothers and sisters, the fruits of democracy are not tame doves that would just voluntarily alight on our hands. Not even a ripe guava falls by itself into the mouth of a lazy Juan. We have to work hard, and couple this with bravery, brains and unity. Under the present situation, it is a mistake to depend completely on scraps thrown by the government. The government is a tool of the people; what it cannot do should be done by the people themselves.'

Mando added that it is the people's duty to learn, to create their own means of livelihood if the administration is helpless.

'Our land is rich. You will not starve if you work hard,' he said.

Protest resounded through the crowd. Some shouted that the land was owned by the powerful.

'We have no land but the dirt on our body.' Everyone laughed.

'There is land,' Mando said. 'Land for those who are ready to move to new places and clear the forests. The Philippines is vast and won't lack land for hands willing to work on her lands.'

Mando pointed out the miseducation of the youth who flock to the city looking for office work.

'Instead of enjoying freedom and health in the fields, they want to work as employees. But we need more mechanics, electricians, carpenters, plumbers, technicians for radio, printing, factories and mines. But what kind of workers do we have? Clerks, messengers, stenographers, salesmen, agents and many other white-collar jobs.

Actually, we don't lack jobs, if the nation would only remember that we are just beginning to industrialize. We need skilled labourers and not those who are choosy about their work.'

Then Mando attacked party politics, whose candidates only focused on their rise to power or staying there. He pointed out that in the past fifty years, politics had become the opium of the masses.

'In all these, we are just going in circles. The nation seems to remain stationary. We know that our land is rich in natural resources, but then why are the Filipinos beggars? Two parties vie for power, but whoever wins quickly steals from the country. The nation has long been strangled by this two-headed monster. It's time the nation freed itself from these sharp claws, form a strong union, and wave its own banner of freedom.'

Mando's speech was followed by long applause. Rubio stood up, glanced at his watch, and said he would now introduce the last speaker.

Rubio had not yet mentioned his name, but the plaza was already astir. Everyone knew Senator Maliwanag as the lodestar of nationalism.

'He was orphaned as a child,' said Rubio. 'His grandfather was killed in the revolution against Spain, and his father fought bravely against the Americans. He was in the Death March after the fall of Bataan and imprisoned at Capas. One day, he escaped with a friend, who was later killed by the enemy. He joined politics and proved to be a courageous leader. My friends and comrades, I give you the poor man's candidate for President of the Philippines.'

Deafening applause and shouts of 'Mabuhay' and 'Long Live' greeted Senator Maliwanag. He stood for a long time in front of the microphone, before the crowd settled down.

The senator began with the story of the Arab and the camel.

'The Arab let the camel put his head inside the tent. This was followed by his whole body. In the end, he killed the Arab and got the tent for himself. That is our country and the foreigners who have sought shelter here . . . What should we do then with the camel?' asked Maliwanag.

The plaza echoed with angry suggestions.

'Lash him!'

'Drive him out!'

'Kill him.'

'That is only right,' answered the lawmaker. 'But until now, we have not decided to lash, drive away, or kill the camel. Until now, he is still inside the tent and we are outside. My countrymen, I do not want us to be like the camel, but neither do I want us to be like the Arab.'

Laughter followed this last remark.

'In Rizal's time, the patriot was either exiled or shot,' Maliwanag said. 'The slave was not allowed to ask for freedom. A Bonifacio and his Katipunan were needed to free the Philippines. As a result of our own weakness, we were conquered by the Americans. For half a century, Americanization was forced down our throats. The English language, clothes, products, vices, tastes, our ways of life. Then the unfortunate day came when the Filipino had forgotten his own and become a mere follower of his master. The Filipino now has only two ambitions: to be fluent in English and to have lots of dollars in his pocket.'

The senator stopped, drank from a glass water, and then he continued.

'Now that we are supposedly free, we should change many things. Let us leave behind the ugly uniform of a prisoner, of a slave. Let us aspire to be truly free, a real nation in our mind, in our economy, in the realities all around us.'

'If we have no bonds, then we can move freely,' Senator Maliwanag said with force. 'We are no longer blindfolded; our eyes can now see.'

'But our leaders are all blind,' shouted a shrill voice.

'It's up to you to change our blind leaders and drive away the shameless camel,' said the senator. 'When we revived the nationalist movement after Rizal and Bonifacio, many insulted us. Many of them were foreigners, but not a few were also Filipinos in complexion. It's shameful to admit, but in our midst, we still have Filipino slaves. But let us pity them. That is only to be expected; one only throws up what one eats.'

Senator Maliwanag then repeated some parts of the speech he had earlier delivered in Congress.

'The foreigners control the big banks, the rich mines, big trades and industries, transportation, electricity and communication services. Must we remain as mere carriers of water and hewers of wood?'

'No!' shouted the crowd.

'Then we should support Philippine nationalism with all our heart. Every powerful country is nationalistic. The United States, Britain, Japan, Germany. Look at their products. Made in the USA, made in England, made in Japan, made in Germany. They are proud of their own trademark, the name of their country. Look at the progressive movements of the independent countries in Asia and Africa after the last world war. China, India and Indonesia moved swiftly against the foreigners. Even Indonesia, Burma, Malaysia and Ceylon have already awakened. They no longer idolize the whites. Soon, the dividing line between the races will be gone, and each will enjoy his inherent right to live according to his own principles.'

'We should not be left behind by the sweep of history. Let us ride with the times, cast aside the slave's mentality. Let us keep studying and working. God does not favour any country or race. No race or country is more intelligent than another. Rizal was brown, but no white man of his time could compare with him in brains, courage and nobility.

'Nationalism is the key to our country's prosperity. If our natural resources are owned and developed by the Filipinos, all our riches— gold, iron, oil, pearls, rice, sugar, copra, tobacco, abaca—all our harvest and our finished products shall benefit everyone. I repeat what Quezon once said—that we do not need millionaires in the Philippines; what we need are millions of families living in comfort.

'It is obvious that if the country achieves economic independence through nationalism, vast armies of the unemployed and the hungry will disappear. Instead, we shall see a contented nation, one which is free.'

The applause was like the sound of a hundred rockets.

'Long live our candidate for President!' one part of the crowd shouted.

'Long live Philippine nationalism!' the other part of the crowd shouted back.

L

The distance from Plaza Miranda to the Montero Plantation was more than a hundred miles. While the people at Plaza Miranda were fired up by their ardour, a fire suddenly broke out in the farms of Central Luzon. The fire quickly spread to the warehouses and the granary, quicker than the shouts of a farmer.

There were only a few men at the plantation, since many of them were at the meeting in Manila. Even the overseer, Captain Pugot, was supposedly at the capital. He had left for the capital before dark.

The civilian guards came late. The women and old people were hesitant to control the fire. The people in the village prepared to safeguard their homes. The fire was controlled at the edge of the plantation.

After an hour, Captain Pugot arrived breathless, accompanied by soldiers. He quickly gathered the civilian guards, asked the sergeant for an immediate report, and then issued his orders. The fire started at the old warehouse, according to the sergeant. In a few seconds, the large granary was ablaze.

The granary was still smoking, and no one could give any clear testimony, but Captain Pugot was certain that the troublemakers had started the fire. His hunch could not be wrong, he said aloud.

'Those men won't stop until there is complete chaos,' he said. 'Let them hide behind their dead ancestors; they can't escape from here,' he said.

Captain Pugot knew who the 'troublemakers' were. In his vocabulary, they were the leaders of the farmers' movement and all their followers who had lost their marbles. He had a list of their names and identities, starting with Pastor, Danoy and Mang Tomas.

He ordered their arrest. He knew that these persons had gone to Manila, but in his mind, flight was proof of their guilt. When the sergeant reminded him that he had seen Pastor leaving, Pugot answered that he was aware of this.

'I know,' he said with a nod. 'They were not at the scene of the crime, but they were behind it. They may hide their hands, but their heads can be seen. Can there be better evidence than the fire itself?'

There was no doubt in Pugot's mind that the fire was intentional, that it was not due to carelessness, or may have been caused by others. He had not changed the old and petty ways he had when he worked for the Japanese Army. For him, it was enough that a person was suspected. The evidence did not matter; if there was none, then it could be planted.

He should have paid for his war crimes, for his brutality and savagery. But he was saved from the electric chair, or life imprisonment, by surrendering to the Americans until, along with many others, he was granted a general amnesty. The rural folk's hatred for him had somewhat subsided, but it was revived only when he reprised his brutal ways as overseer at Montero Plantation.

The soldiers and the men sent by Captain Pugot returned in high spirits. They had gathered some rifles at Pastor's house, documents at Mang Tomas's, and a kerosene can and rags at Danoy's.

'No doubt it's them,' Pugot said with glee as he examined the objects gathered by his men. They had gathered the evidence even if there was no court order to search.

'This would have been used to cause trouble at the plantation. If that had happened, blood would have flowed. For sure, they plan to kill me, perhaps Don Segundo and the others. And here,' he said, pointing with his rifle at a document. 'We can read about their evil plans.'

But when they read it, the document was nothing else but the printed constitution of the farmers' association.

Captain Pugot posted a hundred more guards near the entrance to the Montero Plantation to wait for the farmers who were coming back from Manila. He also placed guards at the suspects' houses. Meanwhile, he ordered the old people and the women at the plantation and the village to remain in their huts and not to leave without permission from the soldiers or civilian guards. He had ordered a real zoning to take place.

It was almost dawn when the guards heard the sounds of a vehicle coming. One looked out and saw two bright lights approaching. In a few minutes, a bus came speeding by.

The guards were sure this was the vehicle of those who had come back from the meeting in Manila. The passengers were talking and laughing noisily. The women were even singing. They thought nothing of it when the guard stopped the bus. But they got worried when the guard ordered the driver to stop in front of the headquarters of the civilian guards. All the passengers were told to get off.

Captain Pugot stood at the door. He threw away his lighted cigarette and threw a fierce look at the farmers. He immediately ordered a body search for all, except the women. Puri remained beside her father.

'Why, Captain?' Pastor asked.

Pastor and the civilian guards knew each other, as a collector knows a creditor. Pastor was the former overseer who was replaced because of his good dealings with the tenants.

'Don't pretend to be innocent,' Pugot said. 'Don't you know?'

'Know what?'

'The plantation had been burnt. You and your group planned it.'

Captain Pugot's words were like a grenade exploding before everyone's faces. Some of the men moved, ready to escape. But the door was already blocked by rifles.

'Captain, you are mistaken,' said Pastor.

'You can prove your innocence in court,' the captain shot back. 'Meanwhile, I'm arresting all of you in the name of the law.'

Upon hearing Pugot's words, a husky farmer grabbed a rifle, but a guard quickly hit him on the mouth. Trouble would have erupted had Pastor not calmed down the farmers.

'Please keep calm, comrades,' Pastor called out. 'There are women here.'

'Go on, dare us, fools! The bullets won't shy away from you.'

An uneasy peace was restored. Pugot separated the men on one side and the women on the other. In the dim light, he looked over the farmers. It was only then that he noticed Danoy's absence.

'Where is Danoy?' he said.

'He stayed behind in Manila,' a man said, 'at a friend's house.'

'Ah, he has deserted all of you. We found a kerosene can and rags similar to those used in the fire in his house,' Pugot said. 'He can't go far.'

After searching the men and asking the women to take out what they carried, the guards took down their names, ages and other information. The law enforcers took whatever the men carried—daggers, certificates of membership in the association, etc. The clothes taken from the bus were piled on one side.

The sun was high up when the women were released.

'Don't let them leave the houses,' Captain Pugot told his men.

Puri told Pastor that she was going to bring him food, but he told her not to do so. He could not eat alone, and it would be hard to prepare for a hundred people.

Puri saw a civilian guard on the stairs of their house. The furniture was all in shambles, and the dresser was open. The box of letters from Mando was missing.

Captain Pugot quizzed Pastor and Tomas, but the two eluded to the noose, which he tried to place around their necks. They knew that any talk with the captain, anywhere, at any time, would be used against them.

'Confess that you are the brains behind the arson,' Pugot said to Pastor and Mang Tomas.

The two leaders remained silent, pretending not to hear him.

'Where did you get the rifles found in your house?' he asked Pastor, who remained deaf.

'Where?' Pugot stamped his boots.

'There are no arms in my house,' Pastor said firmly.

'There they are.' Pugot pointed to the top of the table. 'You dare deny it?'

'They're not mine.'

'They were found in a room in your house.'

'If you say they were found in my house, maybe you put them there,' Pastor said angrily.

A slap hit his mouth, causing his face to jerk back. The women screamed. Mang Tomas made a move. Some farmers sprawled on the floor stood up.

Captain Pugot quickly drew his .45 and almost at the same time, the civilian guards raised their rifles. Some soldiers watched closely. The farmers gritted their teeth.

'Don't make any false move,' shouted Captain Pugot. 'Unless you want to be buried here.'

Not new to such a tight situation, Pugot breathed easily when he sensed that the farmers would cause no trouble despite their fury.

'You, Pastor.' Pugot faced the farmers' leader. 'You want to be known as tough. Let's see if you won't soften up. I have lost my patience with you.'

Pastor kept silent, but he looked steadily at the fiery eyes of the captain.

'Why do you keep these documents?' Pugot turned to Mang Tomas, shoving a pamphlet to his face.

'That is the constitution.'

'This is subversive. Anti-government.'

'It says nothing except how to unite the farmers.'

'It says that one of your aims is to remove the social classes. There should be no rich or poor.'

'The exploiters and the exploited,' said Mang Tomas. 'What's wrong with that?'

'That is communism,' Pugot said.

'It was Christ who spread such a principle—equality of men, improvement of the conditions of the oppressed.'

'Liar!'

Mang Tomas said no more, for he saw that Captain Pugot was at a loss. Because their exchange had reached such a point, he knew the captain would no longer use reason but force. Mang Tomas had no desire to taste what Pastor had in store for him. But the chief investigator would not leave him alone.

'Why did Danoy stay in Manila?'

'I don't know.'

'He won't stay for no reason.'

'Maybe.'

'What reason?'

'I don't know.'

Mang Tomas received the slap he was avoiding. The old man's face jerked back. Pastor made a move. Once more, the farmers got on their feet. But that was all. Pugot had a tight grip on his revolver.

'Never mind,' he sneered. 'Where would that Danoy hide anyway? If he does not come today, I will hunt for him myself and bring him back in chains.'

Pugot's threat was met by silence. He might as well have been talking to the wind.

Then he went out and signalled the sergeant of the civilian guards to follow. He said he would consult the governor and the Philippine Constabulary Commander at the capital. He instructed the sergeant to gather evidence.

'Don't allow any visitors,' he ordered. 'If someone brings food, accept it, but don't give it to the prisoners. Let them starve.'

'Yes, sir.'

It was morning, a morning different from the preceding night. The sun shone on the ashes of the fire at the plantation, but it did not brighten the fate of the farmers hunkered in the guards' quarters.

LI

Dolly was prettier when she returned to Manila and became once more the darling of the upper crust. She returned with an added sheen, a layer of glamour that the other women—young or old—envied. They felt that her charm was enhanced by her long stay in Paris, her experiences, and having all the luxuries she wanted.

But they were wrong to think that Dolly got everything she wanted. One thing she could not call her own was Mando's elusive heart. She often thought he didn't care any more, since he had no more time for her. Their affair in Paris was not rekindled in Manila. True, they met. Sometimes, he would take her to a nightclub, invite her to the movies or theatre, and escort her to some gatherings. But that was all. She wanted more.

Not once did he invite her to Baguio, where she longed to breathe the cool and clean air and watch the moon rise behind the tall pine trees. Once, she invited him to go with her to Zamboanga City. Couldn't Mando leave his office for a few days to fly with her to the famous pearl of Mindanao? But her boyfriend simply said that, perhaps, her only reason to visit the city was to prove what some Yankees had claimed: that 'monkeys in Zamboanga have no tails'.

Nevertheless, it was not Dolly's nature or upbringing to give way to frustrations. She just accepted that Mando was busy with the new building and with managing the newspaper. When Dolly looked at herself in her large bedroom mirror as she powdered her body after taking a bath, or putting on an elegant and expensive dress, she could not see how Mando could help wanting her. How many men, all distinguished—bachelors, widowers, or married—were crazy about her? Some gave hints; others openly declared their intentions; still others kept their desires to themselves. Pong Tua-Son was kept dangling on a thread of hope. She merely laughed at the proposal of the head of the Bachelors' Club. A wealthy widower, a congressman from the Visayas, was running after her, but she just made fun of him.

Dolly realized that she had fallen hard for Mando not because she had already given herself to him. This had also happened with Colonel Moto during the Japanese occupation and with Lieutenant Whitey during the American liberation. Surely, Dolly had other lovers, but this was different. Dolly felt her love for Mando was like an all-consuming flame. Her desire raged even more; she could feel it in every cell of her body, now that they both were in Manila.

Mando's seeming coldness only goaded Dolly's desire, which turned into a flame of impatience and jealousy. Dolly made sure that she was at her most beautiful when she got out of her car in front of the *Kampilan* building. She went to the office on the second floor. Mando was alone reading his mail.

He stood up and greeted Dolly. He was expecting her, for she had called up earlier.

'Please sit down, Dol,' said Mando, leading her to a chair. They sat facing each other.

Dolly said to him in a petulant tone. 'If I had not come, I wouldn't see you.'

'Dol, you know I'm very busy. Don't you know that . . .'

Dolly pouted. 'Maybe you're not too busy to give me a kiss . . . or don't you have time?'

Mando stood up but stopped when he heard her dry laughter.

'I came to invite you to lunch. We have to discuss something.'

'Where do you want to go?'

'Anywhere. Some place that's private. Papa spoke to me about Pong.'

'The little Chinese is persistent, isn't he?'

'He's ready to wage war just to have me.'

'And how do you feel?'

'As if you don't know.'

'If you can wait, I'll just finish my work. You read in the meantime.'

Mando got a women's magazine and gave it to Dolly. 'Care for a drink?'

'No, thanks.'

Mando returned to the table and Dolly started to leaf through the magazine. It was eleven o'clock in the morning.

Suddenly Magat entered, followed by Puri. Upon hearing Magat's voice, Mando raised his head and saw Puri.

'Puri,' he called quite loudly, standing up.

Dolly glanced back and saw the guest, a young girl who looked rather poor. Perhaps a factory worker or a fruit vendor? That was Dolly's first thought. So she turned her eyes again to the magazine in her hands.

'What brought you back, Puri? Or haven't you gone home?' Mando asked after Puri was seated. Magat remained standing behind a chair.

'There was a fire at the plantation. Tatang has been arrested.'

Although the two newspapermen were used to big events, the news startled both of them. It was only then that they noticed how different she looked. Her cheeks were pale and her eyes hollow, her hair was uncombed, and she had not changed her dress. Her hands and feet were also dirty. She looked bone-tired but seemed unmindful of her exhaustion. Worry creased her face.

Puri told them what had happened. How Captain Pugot stopped the bus upon their arrival and arrested the passengers, whom he blamed for the fire at the plantation. She was afraid of what might happen to her father, who had already been slapped by Captain Pugot.

She had escaped from the civilian guard by passing through the kitchen and the backyard. She crossed the field to reach the road, and took a bus bound for Manila.

Mando and Magat asked questions about the fire, Captain Pugot's behaviour, the arrest of Pastor and his companions, and the supposed evidence that led to their arrest. She mentioned the rifles that had been allegedly found in their house, the kerosene can and the rags in Danoy's house, and the documents in the house of Mang Tomas.

'Danoy is in Manila,' said Mando. 'He should know of this at once.' He told Magat to get in touch with the young leader.

'An old trick,' Mando said after a while.

'The usual tactics of ex-convicts,' answered Magat.

Mando and Magat concluded that the crime was not done by the farmers, but by their persecutors.

'I would know if father was hiding guns,' Puri said, 'for he would ask me to keep them. Just like during the Japanese times.'

'Don't worry, Puri,' said Mando. 'We won't let Tata Pastor and his group down.'

Mando looked at his watch.

'It's almost twelve o'clock now,' he said. 'Magat, better call Danoy at Rubio's office. Tell him to come right away. We have important matters to discuss.'

Magat went to his office.

Mando went to Dolly, who now appeared impatient.

'Shall we go?' she asked before Mando could speak.

'Dolly,' Mando said gently, 'may we postpone our date?'

'Postpone! And why?' she asked, surprised and annoyed at the same time.

'Something's happened. I should attend to it.'

'Why don't you postpone that? I've been waiting here for two hours.'

'This is urgent.'

'Is it because of the cigarette worker?' said Dolly, pointing with her lips at Puri.

'She's not a cigarette worker,' Mando said. 'She came from the province.'

'Oh, a provincial girl. And why should you care that much for her?'

Dolly had raised her voice, but Puri was not aware that Mando and the woman were talking about her. She seemed lost in her own world, for she was thinking of her father.

'Please, Dolly, I'll see you tonight,' Mando said.

'Now I'm sure of what I suspected all along,' she said in an accusing tone. 'I now mean nothing to you. That provincial girl is more important.'

'You're wrong, Dolly. She's my cousin.'

'Oh, your cousin,' she said. 'Who else then will receive all the pleasure?'

'Dolly!'

The phone rang. Mando left Dolly to answer it.

Dolly stood and went to Mando's desk. She glared at Puri, who was looking at the picture on the wall, taking no notice of Dolly who had sat facing her.

Dolly noticed the face and clothes of Mando's 'cousin'. A girl obviously from the province, but lovely, she grudgingly admitted. A pleasant face, smooth dark cheeks, soft eyes now clouded with grief, naturally wavy thick hair, rosy lips, firm breasts and shapely arms.

She wore a flattering native dress, but Dolly's sharp eyes saw that it needed to be washed. Miss Montero also noticed that the woman was younger than she was. She would not admit to herself that the younger woman was lovelier.

When Mando hung up, he left his office and went to Magat.

The two women were left facing each other.

When Puri noticed Dolly, she smiled in greeting. But Dolly gave her a suspicious look instead.

LII

Dolly was vexed not because of Puri's beauty or her youth. Many beautiful young women could be found everywhere. Dolly had been to the famous cities in the world, and she had seen much. Not everyone who was young and beautiful would be noticed.

A woman should have class, personality and the stamp of individuality. Like a diamond or any other precious gem, premium quality could not be faked. In Dolly's eyes, the girl quietly sitting opposite her had no class at all. One could tell this from her manner of dressing, her dirty fingernails and the cut of her hair. If Dolly had met Puri elsewhere, she would probably be sympathetic, instead of being simply annoyed.

However, the girl's arrival in that office had spoilt Dolly's plans with Mando. How could she possibly overlook that?

Even though Mando said that she was his cousin, Dolly could not bring herself to like her. If it had been someone else, she would probably try to be friends with Puri, a relative of the man she loved. Instead, Dolly could only think that Puri was the reason she could not have lunch with Mando and have a serious conversation. Nevertheless, she tried to contain the tempest brewing in her mind's teacup, for Mando's sake. Dolly decided to hide her usual coarseness in dealing with those who were inferior to her.

Instead, she wanted more information about Mando's cousin.

Without any pleasantries, she addressed the girl in a familiar tone. 'Your errand seems very important.' She was clearly fishing for information, for Dolly felt the girl could not have any other important purpose. She probably just wanted to borrow money or was looking for work, or a close relative had just died. But if that were so, then why should Mando postpone their date? Why did Mando say that this girl's business could not be put off? Why should Dolly give way? She was getting furious, and she waited for Puri's answer.

'I had to see Mr Plaridel, ma'am,' Puri said. She looked up and saw the frown on Dolly's face. Puri's eyes widened, for the face was familiar. Seeing the cold reaction to her words, Puri decided not to reveal her purpose of coming.

'Where did you come from?'

'From the village outside Montero Plantation.'

Dolly held her head higher when she heard Montero Plantation. So the girl was from that place. From the farm. It showed in her appearance. Probably the daughter of a sharecropper or a tenant of her father.

'Papa owns the Montero Plantation.'

'Don Segundo. Then you must be Señorita Dolly, ma'am?' Puri now realized why the face seemed familiar.

'Yes, and who are you?'

'Puri, Pastor's daughter.'

'Pastor? Does Papa know him?'

'He was the overseer of your plantation during the war, ma'am.'

'Ah, I remember now. He is no longer there, is he?'

'No, ma'am.'

'And you are his child?'

'His only child, ma'am.'

'Oh, are you the girl whom he brought along to the house? What are you doing now?'

'I help Tatang in the field.'

'Your father is foolish. Papa offered to take you in to live with us. You could have gone to school. Did you get any schooling?'

'Just a little,' Puri said humbly. 'But I know how to read and write.'

'Of course, that is enough in the village. But it's a pity. Like our houseboy, I can't remember his name. Papa sent him to school . . . But he was also foolish. He left suddenly during the war. That fool was already studying at the university.'

Puri realized that she was referring to Andoy. It did not occur to Montero's daughter that Pastor was the youngest brother of Andoy's mother. Therefore, Andoy was related to Puri. Those who lived in luxury naturally forgot the names and the services of their slaves.

'You, too. You should not be just a girl from the province.'

'But there is nothing wrong with being a *provinciana*.'

'What I mean is, you would have received a better education if you had lived with us, and got better opportunities.'

'Rural folk like us enjoy life on the farm.'

'Of course. To each his own. As the saying goes, each has his own destiny. With your looks, you could have lived in Manila and married an important man.'

'What do you mean?'

'Why, a professional, a lawyer, a director or one like Mando, or a wealthy merchant.'

'Village girls don't see what you call important men. For us, it is enough for a man to be good, to know how to make a living, and to love his family.'

'Then you would be content with a farmer, a labourer?'

'I would care for the person, not his occupation.'

'Even if he can't give you an easy life?'

'Rural folk are used to hard work. It is true we want to have better lives, but what's more important is the happiness that comes from faithful and peaceful relationships.'

'There can be no happiness and peace without life's necessities.'

'We have a saying—we must learn to curl up when the blanket is small.'

'That's why you rural folk won't progress,' said Dolly, getting bored. She stood up and looked at the door from where Mando had exited, a while ago. *What could be taking him so long?* she wondered.

But Puri would not let her mocking remarks pass and answered sharply, 'The village people don't progress through no fault of theirs. This is just what the landlord wants.'

Dolly was jolted by the pointed remark. She had thought the girl was stupid and timid.

'What do you mean?' the Montero heiress said, and then she frowned.

'Because they are not given the chance to have a life of comfort. In the landlord–farmer relations, only the landlord gets rich.'

'Why, is there a law against getting rich?'

'None, if the wealth does not come from another's blood.'

'Everyone has his capital—the landlord, his land; the tenant, his labour. The law is clear on the conditions and share of the harvest. Do you mean that the owner of the land and the money should have no share?'

'The farmers only ask for justice.'

'What justice? Isn't there a law that decides all these?'

'Laws made by the proprietors and landowners.'

'That's the trouble with peasants like you. You refuse to recognize the law. If you aren't satisfied, then work for changes. Change the lawmakers, if you can, since you can also vote. But use reasonable means, not violence.'

'Those who use force are the powerful. It is absurd to argue that the weak are the ones who use force.'

Dolly was not aware of the latest happenings at the Montero Plantation. Puri felt it best not to tell her. She could tell that Dolly's outlook was like a hard rock that could not be ploughed or nourish a plant.

'Even you women listen to bad advice,' Dolly said after a while. 'An unreasonable mother can only have insolent children.'

'Insolent because they have learnt to reason, because they now protest against oppression.' Puri raised her voice, and she also stood up. Dolly was standing behind a chair. 'The first lesson a village woman teaches her child is to live by the sweat of her brow and not to envy what belongs to others. We know that taking advantage of others is the cause of all troubles.'

'And who is taking advantage?' said Dolly.

'If there were no opportunists, the world would not be divided between the rich and the poor; there would be no mothers working the whole day in the fields, washing, doing heavy work, and lucky women who spend the whole day at social events, wallowing in pleasure and luxury.'

Dolly felt the sharpness of Puri's words and wanted to leave. It would be a shame to argue with a common woman. Dolly was now sorry she had bothered to talk to the lowly girl, who was now acting like an annoyed wasp. Nevertheless, she answered sternly.

'The trouble with you, common people,' she said like a snake spewing venom, 'is that you are a horde of envious persons. Just because you are ignorant, you envy the educated; because you are beggars, you envy the rich. It's impossible for all people to be alike.'

Puri could imagine Don Segundo Montero abusing his tenants. At that moment, she could no longer see the beauty of the popular society figure, but the ugliness of a Fury. Pastor's daughter denied that the worker's plea for justice was driven by envy.

'Your argument is farfetched,' she said, no longer giving deference to the haughty girl. 'Why should we envy you? What should we envy? Your greed, your coarse manners, wasting time and money on such useless things? The country women are real wives, real mothers; they work and care for the home, day and night. They raise their children and do not allow nursemaids to do their work. They prepare their families' food, not servants; they help and accompany their husbands, not their husbands' friends or their friends' wives. They are poor because they are cheated, but they are happy and peaceful in the midst of poverty. Why should they envy those whose fingers are covered with diamonds and whose bodies are wrapped in silk but who don't find happiness under their roofs and buy their pleasure in parties, nightclubs and gambling? We would never exchange our pure lives for the glitter of your society filled with hypocrisy.'

'You only see our faults, but you are blind to our virtues,' Dolly screamed. 'Our works for charity, religion, health . . . are those nothing to a stupid person like you?'

'Don't insult me.' Puri raised her right hand.

Dolly retreated.

Dolly was more experienced and better informed than Puri, but in that exchange, she was dumbfounded. She could insult her for her poverty, but Puri's arguments were like arrows hitting their mark. And she seemed ready to fight. Dolly told herself that she really is Pastor's daughter. And she remembered that this same Pastor had been removed as an overseer for being stubborn. He was more loyal to the outlaws than to the governor during the Japanese times and more sympathetic to the tenants than to the plantation owner.

Dolly decided it would be useless to argue with the girl whose mind had been filled with such ideas. So, after throwing her a dagger look, she went to the door without a word.

Near the door, she met Mando. 'Are you leaving?' he asked.

Dolly left without answering. Puri was standing by the desk, just looking at the two.

LIII

Mando was caught in a bind. Of course, he was used to being caught between a wall and a dagger, between the devil and the deep blue sea. How many times did he encounter Japanese soldiers and fake guerrillas during the Second World War? The big shark when he and Karyo dove into the Pacific Ocean for Simoun's wealth? Other dangers also lay in wait in the mountains and on the plains. And in the glittering foreign cities, during his travels. But he lacked experience being caught between two women who both loved him and needed him at that moment, demanding his time and attention. Mando was not used to the wily chessboard of the heart. So he hesitated when Dolly left in a huff, while Puri anxiously waited.

Nevertheless, Mando overcame his confusion. He asked Puri to sit down, and then he followed Dolly. He caught up with her on the stairs.

'Dolly, wait a moment,' Mando called after her.

She stopped, looking vexed. Her pride was hurt by Mando's neglect and Puri's discourtesy.

'Please forgive me,' he said.

'Is that all you have to say?' Dolly made a move to go down.

'I admit I neglected you because of an urgent reason.'

'Yes, your cousin's business is important.'

'I'll go to your place tonight.'

'Never mind, don't trouble yourself.'

Mando went with her to the car and helped her get in.

'Tonight, Dol?' he repeated.

'I've to go. Goodbye!'

When Mando returned to his office, he told Puri, who had just left. 'That's Dolly, Don Segundo's daughter.'

'Yes, we had a talk,' Puri said. 'She seemed offended by my answers.'

'She came to invite me to lunch. But how could I go?'

'So, that's why she seemed annoyed with me.'

'Your business is many times more important than her invitation.' After arranging the papers on his desk, they left.

'Come along, Gat,' Mando invited Magat when they passed by his desk.

'I'll wait for Danoy. We'll go together,' Magat said.

When Mando and Puri reached his house, Dr Sabio was already there, talking to Tata Matias. From Mando's phone call, the professor already had an inkling about what had happened.

Soon, Magat and Danoy arrived. Danoy asked Puri what the civilian guards did to her father, Mang Tomas and the rest of the men. Puri told him that they were hunting for him, and Captain Pugot had threatened to come to Manila if he didn't return to the plantation within twenty-four hours.

After lunch, Dr Sabio asked Puri to relate to him all the events at the Montero Plantation since they had returned from Manila. The girl repeated everything that she had already said earlier, adding some details she had overlooked. She also answered the queries of Danoy and Dr Sabio.

Puri narrated how Captain Pugot had slapped her father when he would not admit that he had anything to do with the fire. Her father also accused the captain's men of planting the guns found in his house as evidence. Puri said that were it not for the farmers' concern for the women, blood would have flowed. The farmers who had been hurt were all sporting for a fight.

'They are in danger,' she said. 'Captain Pugot threatened to kill anyone who made a false move. He shouted at Tatang and threatened to soften him up.'

Mando calmed down Puri's fears and said that the tenant could no longer be treated like a water buffalo. Now there were laws that recognized every person's rights. One could sue a landlord or chief who has committed abuses.

'But many laws are as worthless as wet paper,' Danoy said. 'Often, the law is applied according to the place and the person involved. In our experience, justice has always eluded the plantation's tenants.'

'Because you have accepted such conditions,' said Mando. 'The law should be given life, not only by the officers but also by the affected citizens. A child who does not cry won't be fed.'

'In our government offices, the small fish will always be the small fish.' Danoy said. 'In our courts, justice is on the side of the rich.'

'For an even match, both sides should have the same weapons,' Mando said. 'I said there are laws, and anyone who commits abuses should be made to answer for them, because the small fish are no longer alone. You saw their strength at the meeting last night; they have unions, a mouthpiece like the *Kampilan*, friends like Senator Maliwanag, Dr Sabio . . .'

The president of Freedom University nodded. Then he looked into the legal aspects of Pastor's case, Captain Pugot's use of physical force and illegal detention, and the steps they should take to free the detained men as soon as possible.

'Captain Pugot is not alone in this,' Magat said. 'Pugot is only a tool. Who gave him the orders? Who would profit most from such a plot?'

'The answer is obvious,' said Danoy. 'But besides Don Segundo, I'm sure Governor Doblado and General Bayoneta are also involved.'

'Captain Pugot was supposed to be at the capital during the fire. When he returned to the plantation, he was accompanied by soldiers,' Puri told them.

'See?' exclaimed Danoy, for Puri's statement seemed to confirm his suspicions.

'Now they have met their match,' Mando said.

Then he asked Dr Sabio to tell Puri and Danoy about his plan to buy the Montero Plantation and other lands with tenancy problems.

'As you know,' began the professor, 'the farmers have long been asking the government to buy the land and sell it on instalment to the tenants.'

'That's what we ask,' Danoy said, 'but this request just fell through a basket full of holes.'

'Either will be hard for our government at present,' Dr Sabio said. 'First, there is no money in the treasury. Second, it does not want to have any more white elephants. There is hardly a government corporation that is not losing money because of poor and corrupt management. These administrators have no management skills at all; they were usually chosen because of their political clout. Besides, many big politicians are landlords. Will they agree to a sale where they won't make huge profits?'

'In other Asian countries, the tenancy problem has been solved,' Mando answered, 'because the government knew that peace was impossible until this problem was solved.'

'True,' Dr Sabio said. 'But before that happened,' he added with a slight smile, 'the former government of landlords and businessmen were overthrown by revolution. The new government took over the lands held by foreigners and their tools. This happened in China, Egypt, Burma, Indonesia and Cuba.'

'There are no signs that we will see this here in our lifetime,' Mando answered drily.

Tata Matias then spoke for the first time. 'That was one of the aims of Supremo Bonifacio,' the former revolutionary said gently, 'but he was killed by the revolution that he founded, and this revolution passed into the hands of the bourgeois. When the republic was set up in Malolos, Aguinaldo was already surrounded by the slimy tentacles of the status quo. Their only concern was their own welfare. They swiftly became the first to help the Americans, the new colonizers.'

After saying this, Tata Matias remained silent. But what he said clarified Dr Sabio's views.

'I've talked to Segundo Montero,' Dr Sabio continued. 'I told him that Freedom University wanted to buy the plantation. At first, he said that it was not for sale. Then he mentioned an offer from a foreign millionaire. He would not reveal the name, although I think it came from his friend, Son Tua. I reminded him that a foreigner could not own land unless he used a dummy. I also said it was better for Freedom University to own the plantation, for it would not be used for profit.'

Don Segundo was annoyed and asked what was wrong if the land should yield profit when it involved a large capital. He wondered why Dr Sabio, a scientist, was such an idealist, whereas he, Montero, was a practical businessman. Dr Sabio corrected him about his wrong conception of Freedom University's aims.

'There are many gains other than money,' said the professor. 'For example, the farmers' additional knowledge.'

Finally, Don Segundo said he would sell the plantation at the current market price. Dr Sabio offered to add 30 per cent to the assessed value.

'It would be good if we were to buy your land,' Dr Sabio added. 'You will have no more headaches arising from the conflicts. Don't you get tired from the trouble in the fields?'

According to Dr Sabio, Segundo Montero then stood up and banged his fist on the table.

'That is the main reason why I don't want to sell,' he shouted. 'Those shameless farmers might say I'm afraid of them. Let's see who is stronger.' Dr Sabio's associates were more bent on buying the Montero Plantation because they felt that the attitude of the present owner hindered peace and progress.

'It's sad that we still have the likes of Montero,' Dr Sabio said with a sigh. 'His way of thinking dates back to the days before the coming of the printing press.'

Dr Sabio made an apt comparison between progress and the people who enjoyed its benefits.

'It's been 150 years since the first steamship arrived,' recalled the wise old man of Freedom University. 'We have had electricity for half a century. There are many railroads and streets crowded with cars. Planes now crisscross the air. In a minute, the radio can bring the latest news around the world. Atomic force has been harnessed, no longer to destroy, but to serve humankind, to explore the moon and the planets, and to promote civilization and happiness.'

Dr Sabio rubbed his forehead with one hand, then he continued.

'But what has not changed is man's bottomless greed, his blind self-love. Montero as an example.'

Puri served hot coffee. Mando asked Dr Sabio to allow Puri to stay temporarily in the girls' dormitory at Freedom University. Danoy would stay at Mando's house.

'But I can't rest until Tatang is free,' said Puri.

'He will be free by hook or by crook,' said Danoy with heat.

'We shall do all we can,' Mando said calmly.

They all finished their coffee.

LIV

The farmers endured fatigue, hunger and anxiety in the civilian guards' quarters at the Montero Plantation. The guards closed the windows and doors after Captain Pugot rushed to the capital. They were no better than sacks of rice bran dumped in a small and airless warehouse.

His men followed the captain's orders and more. No visitors were allowed. Food brought by the relatives was accepted, but then eaten by the guards themselves.

They were stingy even with water, bringing in only one pail from the brook before noon. How could this suffice for twenty-five men who had neither eaten nor slept?

Puri had planned to bring food, but her father had told her not to bother. No food would have reached him anyway.

Many sat on the floor and leaned against the walls. Many dozed off. Pastor, Mang Tomas and two or three others remained awake. Pastor urged Mang Tomas to rest, but the latter said he could not sleep. When the guards left, they spoke softly about their grave situation.

'They did this because of last night's meeting,' said one.

'No, they had already planned this for a long time,' said Mang Tomas. 'Those people have nothing in their brains except gunpowder.'

'And they blame us for their crime,' answered another.

'That has always been the exploiters' tactic since the time of Christ,' said Mang Tomas. 'May the news reach our friends in Manila.'

'For sure,' said Pastor. 'They have not captured everyone in our village and the other towns. Puri is neither ignorant nor a coward.'

'Puri and the others have guards,' said the first speaker.

'They can place daggers in her path, but I know my daughter. She will find a way,' Pastor said with pride in his voice. 'Puri has the heart of a woman warrior.'

'It's a good thing Danoy had stayed behind,' said Mang Tomas. 'I'm worried about his rashness. When he learns of the plot against us, there's no telling what he might do.'

'He often says, "Only lightning can't hit back,"' said Pastor.

The captives barely noticed that the day had already passed. It was dusk. They did not complain. Hunger was not new to them, although they tried to avoid it like an unwelcome relative. Several times, they asked for water, but the door remained locked.

Only the echo of their own voices answered them.

It was already seven in the evening when Captain Pugot returned. He did not tell his men about his mission at the capital. He usually kept such secrets to himself. That day, he had met Governor Doblado and the prosecutor, made arrangements with the commander of the military police headquarters at the capital, and reported to Don Segundo and General Bayoneta via long-distance telephone calls.

'How's everything?' Pugot asked the sergeant of the guards on his return.

'Okay, sir.'

'No visitors?'

'None, sir.'

'No one was fed?'

'No one, sir.'

'Good. We shall transfer them to the capital tonight.'

The captain thought a while, then told the sergeant to prepare rice gruel.

'Yes, sir.'

Then Captain Pugot ordered the opening of the headquarters' door. He entered, followed by the sergeant and some guards. He looked haughtily at the captives.

'Why aren't you sleeping, Tomas?' he asked the old leader sitting next to Pastor.

'And you, Pastor,' he sneered. 'You are tough, huh?'

He got no answer and decided to go out.

After an hour, the guards brought in a large can of thin, plain gruel which was still steaming.

'Eat your fill,' mocked the sergeant and locked the door again.

There was no ladle, cup or plate, but after an hour, the sergeant saw that the can was clean. He could not imagine what the captives had done with the boiling gruel. He looked at the floor, but nothing had been spilt. He didn't show his amazement. Pastor and Mang Tomas laughed secretly over their small victory.

Out of revenge, the sergeant ordered the guard not to give them water.

That night, the farmers charged with burning the plantation and planning trouble were transferred to the capital. Pastor and his companions were loaded in a covered military police truck. The truck sped from the headquarters of the civilian guards accompanied by a weapons carrier loaded with guards and soldiers. They firmly gripped their rifles, showing their fingers were itching to press the trigger.

The two vehicles entered the fenced military police headquarters. It was past nine in the evening.

Upon reaching the yard, Captain Pugot went ahead in his Jeep, motioning the truck driver to follow him. He stepped before a low building shaped like a granary. It was made of wood and stone, with a galvanized iron roof.

He told the farmers to get off and enter the granary, which stood 200 yards away from the barracks and the office of the commander. It was obviously a prison for special captives.

The granary, which was like an inverted tortoise shell, had several parts. At the entrance was the office of the sergeant of the guards. Beyond this was the prison, and behind that, a secret room with no opening. The narrow door was permanently closed. Opposite it was a combined toilet and bathroom. There was a guard at the door between the sergeant's office and the prison, with another guard at the door that led to the secret room with thick walls. The bathroom had no water. Water had to be fetched from a well outside.

The dark prison was fifty square yards with no light, except for a small bulb. The dusty cement was cold, a strange coldness that could cause rheumatism. A swarm of hungry mosquitoes buzzed, and cockroaches crawled all over. Under the roof, without a ceiling, hung a tangle of cobwebs, adding to the gloom of the place.

The twenty-five farmers were dumped like lifeless objects. On Captain Pugot's list, they were supporting a dangerous movement; these people were his enemies. They would show him no mercy if their positions had been reversed, so his conscience didn't bother him for his cruelty.

The sergeant told the farmers to keep quiet.

'You are in jail, not at a meeting,' he said.

Mang Tomas found an old sack in a corner and mopped the dirty floor. There was no sleeping cot or boards to place on the cold floor; no mats or mosquito nets.

Nevertheless, many fell asleep from sheer exhaustion. They had had no rest for almost forty-eight hours. Their bodies were weary and their minds confused.

Pastor and Mang Tomas lay down side by side without speaking.

When many were already snoring, and Pastor was dozing off, he felt the end of a hard object on his neck. He opened his eyes and saw the small mouth of a rifle. A guard was rousing him from his sleep.

Pastor got up. Mang Tomas pretended to be asleep. He opened one eye to see what was happening.

Mang Tomas saw Pastor being taken by the guard to the end of the prison beyond the door. The old farmer was sure his friend was not being taken to the bathroom, for he had not called out to the guard.

Mang Tomas imagined what could happen in the secret room. He knew that the investigation did not end at the quarters in the plantation. He had heard Captain Pugot's threat to soften up Pastor and the other similarly tough men. Pastor was firm and was known for his fearlessness. But Mang Tomas also knew that there were limits to human endurance. There were no limits to the cruelty of their enemies' tools.

Mang Tomas listened intently, cupping his hands over his ear. He thought he could hear thuds and groans, but these were only in his thoughts. The strange silence of that night disturbed old Tomas.

There was no light in the hidden room where Pastor was brought. The only light, the guard's flashlight, fell on the face of the farmer's leader. He felt blinded. Two strange men kept on grilling Pastor. He could not see their faces, but they seemed as young as Danoy. He had not met these men before. They seemed to be investigators from the intelligence branch of the armed forces.

At first, they tempted Pastor with the siren's song, praising him, his war record, and his loyalty to the workers' cause. Then, they reminded him that if he had not been 'lost,' he would now be enjoying a good life. If he would only help the landlord or the officials, he would receive what he wanted at once—land or money, even both.

But Pastor answered with defiance. He said that he could not be an exploiter's tool. The guard's hand swiftly hit his mouth. Then he was told by the two investigators to choose between prison and freedom. The evidence against him would surely put him behind bars if he did not help them.

'Choose!'

Pastor didn't even wipe the blood from his lips.

Finally, they tried to make Pastor admit that he owned the guns found in his house, that he was the brains behind the burning of the plantation, that he threatened to start a bloody uprising in the fields. But he would not admit to any of their lies.

Pastor again received hard blows from the husky guard. He staggered and fell. For two hours, the two detectives left Puri's father at the mercy of the guard, a real executioner who played his role to the hilt. When the two returned to the hidden room, Pastor was already sprawled in a corner, lying unconscious and bathed in his own blood.

LV

The two detectives were not concerned about Pastor's condition after they had beaten him up.

'He is really tough,' said the guard as the two looked at Pastor, who was like a crumpled bag in the middle of the room.

'I'm getting tired of that devil,' said one detective, shaking his head.

'He won't listen to reason,' said the other.

'He can't get away with his foolishness,' said the guard. 'He will rot here.'

'Don't give him all; he might not wake up any more.'

They had asked the guard to fetch water, which they poured on Pastor's face. The blood flowed through his veins. He regained consciousness and sighed. Then he opened his eyes. His eyes lit up, a sign that he recalled what had happened.

Pastor tried to get up, but all his bones ached. He remained seated on the floor.

'You only want to get hurt,' one investigator said.

'If this had been another time or place, you'd be already dead,' added the other.

Pastor felt it was useless to argue with these men. They were men only in appearance and were worse than destructive machines fixed on their targets.

Meanwhile, Mang Tomas was uneasy as he lay. He was attacked by mosquitoes, but he ignored them. He was afraid his companion would be killed. After several hours, which seemed like a year, he could make out two shadows coming out of the door at the prison's end. He recognized Pastor being led by the same guard who had taken him out. He could not bear to look at his companion's face. Pastor could not walk without help. Mang Tomas was sure Pastor must have broken some bones during his stay in that cell.

'We're not through yet,' Mang Tomas heard the guard say.

Pastor sat down without a word, but he could hardly lie down. Mang Tomas got up and helped him lie on the cold cement floor. The old man asked in a whisper what was hurting. Pastor complained that his whole body felt like a swollen boil. Mang Tomas gently rubbed Pastor's hips and arms. His tears fell out of pity for his friend.

Dawn had broken. Other than the whispers of the two farmers, nothing broke the tomb-like silence of the dark prison. Even the guard outside seemed to have dozed off in his wooden chair.

Soon, Pastor's soft groans stopped. To Mang Tomas, they seemed to come not from his lips but from the very depths of his soul. These were not ordinary groans from physical pain, but the recoiling of the soul against cruelty.

Perhaps Mang Tomas was the only one who had not slept. He thought of Pastor and the guard, their similarities, their differences, their goals, the reason why Pastor was a prisoner who was abused and why the guard became the henchman.

Mang Tomas found only one answer—the desire for a livelihood. They had the same goal but different means. Pastor was a farmer living off his own sweat and fighting to live a better life. The guard also lived on wages paid for fulfilling his duty to keep Pastor from reaching his goal. He even bore the attractive title of a 'law enforcer'. But if he analysed the events just past, the guard was the enemy of the law, and Pastor its victim.

Mang Tomas figured that the guard was only a hireling. Indeed, evil was not inborn. This man also just wanted to make a living, even by a means contrary to his conscience. If the guard shed his uniform and joined a group of farmers, he would appear to be one of them, thought Mang Tomas. Perhaps he was even a farmer's son.

If Pastor wore the uniform, he would appear to be the guard. The dividing line between Pastor and the guard was very thin, but the gap was very wide in their actions.

The hands of the clock might be slow, but time moved inexorably.

Several loud whistles roused the farmers. It was already six o'clock. The morning was hot and humid.

Most had been awake for some time, but they didn't stir. They remained lying down, alert to every sound. Each was thinking of the past two nights when they had been locked up at the quarters at the Montero Plantation, and now in this prison at the military police headquarters in the capital.

What would happen to them? How are their families? What was in store for them on this day? They could foresee that they would again be subjected to questions and more cruelty from the guards and soldiers.

They felt intense hunger and thirst. But the wounds in their souls were even more painful.

Pastor was awakened by the whistle. He had fallen asleep after he had been brought back from the cell. He opened his eyes and turned to Mang Tomas, but he was not there. He had slept with Mang Tomas on his left, but he was not there now.

Pastor looked at the others, but Mang Tomas wasn't there, either. In their situation, a moment's separation caused anxiety. Pastor tried to calm himself, thinking that Mang Tomas must have answered a call of nature. He thought that Mang Tomas must be suffering most from the hardships, because of his age.

When the guard saw that the new sergeant had entered, he ordered them to fall in line.

'One line,' he hollered.

In the sergeant's hand was a list of the detainees' names. He was short and squat, with dark skin, and seemed ill at ease in his clothes. Surely, his parents must have come from their dwelling place in the trees and forests to buy dogs to eat. Unlike his ancestors, the sergeant was learning to walk upright; in fact, the heels of his boots were six inches tall.

He threw the row of farmers a sharp glance and looked at his list. But before starting, he gave them another dirty look and delivered a short speech.

'You are prisoners,' the sergeant began, although no charges had been filed against them. 'You have been jailed because you are enemies of the government. But even if you are bad men, we shall treat you well. You will not starve, for you will have food twice a day—at ten in the morning and at five in the evening. Here, you won't be hurt unless you lie. Here, your life is safe, unless you try to escape. You know that a bullet is faster than your feet. Now, perhaps that is clear?'

Then he read the names, which were in alphabetical order. Everyone called answered, 'Hep!'

Several times, he stammered and was forced to spell the name that he could not pronounce. The detainees kept quiet every time the sergeant read a name more than three syllables long. He was like an unskilled acrobat on a flying trapeze. After reading Pastor's name and casting him a furtive look, he said, 'So you are their leader, huh?'

'I am a farmer,' answered Pastor, who could hardly stand straight.

'It's too bad we did not meet earlier. I heard of you during the Japanese times,' said the sergeant.

'Because I was with the other Filipinos,' said Pastor.

When the sergeant approached Pastor, all eyes were on them, but he did not raise his right hand.

'You are a hero; that's why you're here,' he said with a sneer. 'Just wait, I'll pin a medal on you.' And he turned away abruptly.

Pastor just looked on and said nothing. The sergeant went on calling the other names. Up to the end, he didn't read the name of Mang Tomas. Pastor thought the old man's name must not be on the list.

The sergeant went around the jail, went to the hidden cell, then returned and went out the front door. His chin was raised, and his shoulder twitched with every step.

When the door closed after the sergeants and the guard, the farmers immediately rushed to Pastor. Mang Tomas was not the only witness to Pastor's trip and return from the cell. A part of Pastor's face was swollen. Both sides were black and blue, and he felt that his ribs had been broken. The guard had hurt even his most sensitive parts.

The farmers were hurt and very angry.

Some recalled the cruelty of the soldier-collaborators and the civilian guards during the last war. They were worse than the enemy in torturing the guerrillas, the townsfolk and the farmers.

'Just thinking of it makes my blood boil,' said a farmer. 'When a guerrilla was captured by those beasts, his tongue would be cut off, along with his ears, his fingers and his genitals, before he was beheaded. I saw this with my own eyes, and I barely escaped.'

'Not only that,' said another. 'Sometimes, they would slice off the flesh on the thigh or arm of a fellow Filipino, roast it and make him eat it. If he refused, they would knock out all his teeth. It was terrible.'

They became more worried when they could not find Mang Tomas. They asked each other, but no one had seen him taken out. They were all sound asleep. Pastor thought that this must have happened when he had slept. No one could tell if Mang Tomas had been taken to the torture cell or outside the jail.

Before ten o'clock, some soldiers brought a can of boiled bran with some small fried fish and hot ginger tea. That was the first real food tasted by Pastor and his companions in three days. The grumbling of their stomachs stopped.

LVI

Mando and his associates took the necessary steps right away. After leaving his house that afternoon, each did his own part. They could not take their time because the situation was urgent.

Dr Sabio brought Puri to the female dormitory.

When Mando reached his office, he immediately met with Iman, his reporter, and asked him to gather all information about the events at the Montero Plantation. He asked Iman to rush to the plantation and take photographs, providing him with a car and money.

After bringing Puri to the female dormitory, Dr Sabio asked the law officers of the university to take steps to free the farmers and file charges against Pugot and his men.

Andres and Rubio joined Mando, Magat, Dr Sabio and Danoy at the professor's office, the following night.

They discussed the workers' other problems, aside from the case at the Montero Plantation. Andres was well-informed about the troubles in the city.

'To succeed, any progressive programme should be supported by the labour force,' said Magat. 'So the blow against unionism is also an attack on progress itself.'

Rubio said that the foreign capitalists and their tools always hinder the growth of company unions. He said it was easy to spot the company unions and their leaders because, while the members suffered oppression, their leaders lived in grand houses and rode in flashy cars.

'It is treachery for the leader to wallow in wealth while the union is poor,' said Rubio. 'The union should provide a living for the leader, or he will be bribed by the capitalists. But neither should he live in poverty nor in luxury.'

Danoy said that the union leaders were lucky because they enjoyed a more strict security than the farmers' leader.

'There, we are always hounded by the landowners and their hirelings.' Danoy said. 'We always have one foot in jail, or in the cemetery.'

Magat pointed out, 'In this country, there is no difference between the landlord and the factory owner. They have but one capital and one viewpoint. Both will dare to do anything and oppose any movement that will reduce their profit.'

After this exchange of views, Dr Sabio brought the discussion back to Pastor.

'Are you sure, Danoy,' he asked the young leader, 'that you don't own the kerosene can, and the rags said to have been taken from your house?'

'Do you have any doubts, Dr Sabio?' asked Danoy.

'None, but I wanted to hear it from you.'

'It's also certain that the guns don't belong to Tata Pastor,' added Danoy. 'Regarding the papers found in Mang Tomas's house, if there was anything other than the constitution of our association and the list of members, it must have been planted by the civilian guards.'

'They have been jailed in the camp of the military police for two days now,' Dr Sabio said. 'I wonder if they are safe.'

'As safe as a canary guarded by a cat,' Danoy answered, clenching his fist. 'Oh, if only it were the Japanese times and our guerrilla troops were intact,' he said with a sigh.

'If it were the Japanese times, Tata Pastor would not be in jail because Captain Pugot would be in hiding,' Magat said with bitterness. 'Now, we former guerrillas obey the law, and the collaborators are holding the reins of power.'

'While they are detained, we should not rest,' Danoy said.

'That's why we are working overtime,' answered Mando, who had been listening silently. 'This is being done without even suspending *habeas corpus*.'

Then he asked Dr Sabio about Puri. The professor said she was settled at the dormitory. 'But she insists on going back to the plantation or the town. She is worried about her father.'

'If she is at the plantation, there's no telling what could happen to her,' Danoy said. 'The men are mauled by the civilian guards; the women are raped. It was lucky Puri escaped.'

'Puri has a presence of mind and does not easily panic,' Dr Sabio said.

'From childhood, Puri has been used to hardship,' Danoy said with admiration. He looked at Mando as if to say, 'There's a lucky guy.'

They were about to end their discussion when the phone rang. Iman wanted to talk to either Mando or Magat.

'Big news!' The reporter's voice was loud.

Mando asked him to come right away.

In a few minutes, Iman rushed in.

'Mang Tomas and another farmer were slain,' he blurted out. The news hit them like a grenade. Danoy stood up, waved his fists in the air, slumped into his seat, and covered his face with his hands. He cried as Iman related the latest news.

According to the military police's report, the two had tried to escape. This report was based on Captain Pugot's account. Mang Tomas and his companion were said to have escaped, but were caught and fired upon when they refused to halt. Both had wounds in their backs.

'And Tata Pastor?' asked Mando.

'Tata Pastor is in jail, incommunicado. We could not go near the detained farmers,' Iman reported. 'But I have pictures of the corpses, which are now in the village outside the plantation.'

According to Iman, the civilian guards had forbidden them from taking pictures and even tried to confiscate their cameras, but the lieutenant intervened. The lieutenant said that there was no need to be afraid that the public would see the pictures of the slain men. Was it not the practice of the constabulary and some officials to parade the corpses of the 'outlaws', some of whom were headless, with their arms tied at the elbows? Some used to be nailed on the cross or hung upside down on bamboo stakes in the plaza as a warning.

So the sergeant agreed and posed with other guards who were looking at the corpse of the old farmers' leader.

'The situation at the plantation is serious,' said Iman. Soldiers and civilian guards swarmed like ants all over the place, as if the villages were now under military rule. The people appeared calm, but they were seething inside like a boiling cauldron.

'No one we talked to could believe Mang Tomas was killed while he was escaping,' Iman continued. 'He was killed, pure and simple, they said. Old Tomas was tough, but he would not try to escape. If it had been Danoy, maybe. Many fear that they will do the same to Tata Pastor. He is also tough, according to the village folk.'

'Did you talk to Captain Pugot?' asked Magat.

'Captain Pugot was away,' said Iman. 'He did not appear at the plantation. Nor in the town. Some said that Segundo Montero had asked him to go to Baguio.'

'He can't hide forever,' Danoy said.

Andres left after hearing Iman's report. He hurried back to the *Kampilan* to prepare the latest edition of the newspaper, which would come out at the first hour of the morning.

'Use the pictures on the front page,' Magat said. 'The corpses of Mang Tomas and the other farmer.'

After Andres had left, Magat said that long after the war with the Japanese, conditions remained similar. He asked who should answer for this reality.

'That's the major cause of the conflict that's dividing people,' Dr Sabio said. 'Many want to start where the war had left off, which is as it should be. Those in power want to restore everything and fix the world again, but from their point of view.'

He said that almost everywhere, especially in formerly colonized countries, the social revolution had won and changes had taken place to equalize opportunities among the people.

'Except in our country,' said the professor, 'which goes on kissing the boots that kick it. As the Spanish saying goes, "*El mismo perro con distinto collar*". Same dog, but with a different collar.'

'There is unrest in the villages, but what can be done?' asked Rubio. 'Will they be content to weep over their dead and bury them?'

'And how can we teach and establish the correct philosophy, beliefs and system . . ?'

'By struggle.'

'By the power of the tongue or the sword, Doctor?' asked Danoy.

'Whichever is effective at the proper time,' Dr Sabio said with a smile. 'At times, the mouth and the pen are effective; at other times, the sword. But at all times, they should be guided by the clearest mind.'

Even the hotheads, Danoy and Rubio, agreed with the professor.

'Very well, then.' Mando stood up and suggested, 'It's time we take a rest, because we have much to do tomorrow.'

The first rays of a new day were beginning to tinge the horizon.

LVII

Everyone complained of the intense heat of early summer, as if the rays of the sun had burrowed inside the skin. The cars of Manila's 100 richest families competed with each other in raising dust along the road from the capital to the cold mountain city of Baguio.

Among the earliest to reach the summer capital was the Montero family. They opened their new bungalow along the row of vacation cottages in an exclusive place near the Mansion House.

From the latter part of February until the first weeks of June, when the winds signalled the coming rains, Baguio was more exclusive than the Little Baguio in Quezon City or even the grand Forbes Park in Makati. Here gathered Manila's crème de la crème; hence, the latest fashion, ostentatious parties, costly pleasures and also vices were put on full display. The festivities at the Mansion House, popular amusements, the Pines Hotel, and even the churches that were crowded with saints—all became veritable shows for clothes, jewellery and cars of the elite from Manila, the small and tight circle of those who held power in their hands.

Like crows, the usual cronies had gathered after supper in the poker room of the Monteros' bungalow. But that night, they were not thinking of either poker or drinks. Don Segundo had invited them to discuss more serious problems.

Seated at a round table were Son Tua; his son-in-law General Magno Bayoneta; Senator Botin, Governor Oscar Doblado; and Montero himself.

They were joined at dinner by Captain Pugot, who had been summoned by Don Segundo to report on the latest incidents that had flared up at the plantation. Later, the head of the civilian guards left and didn't join them in the poker room.

Doña Julia and Dolly had been invited by the architect Pong Tua-son to a grand party at Pines Hotel. Ever since Dolly had left the *Kampilan* office in a huff, Pong noticed that she no longer avoided him, or answered him crossly. The Chinese mestizo's ardour only became more fervent at these displays of encouragement.

When Don Segundo's guests had settled down, sipped their drinks and lit their Sumatras, the host announced that they needed the help of Senator Botin very badly. The lawmaker was the angel of the mysterious Montero–Son Tua corporation, a client who never rejected his wishes. During his whole stay in the Senate, Botin had proved that influence-peddling was indeed a rich source of unimaginable wealth. A senator's salary was not enough for the expenses of his office. Montero said that the pulse of the public railing against graft and corruption and the rise of nationalism would harm their corporation. The noise of the *Kampilan*'s campaign and the bigger noise of the unions and other national movements would lead to strictness at the port, investigations and the filing of anti-smuggling bills. Their illegal businesses would not prosper under such conditions.

He asked Senator Botin to oppose all the radical measures and policies that would be filed in the legislative mill. He considered 'radical' any change in the status quo that would cut the profits of 'free enterprise'. The free enterprise of the Monteros and Son Tuas was not freedom of capital and honourable business, but greed and license to amass blood money through deceit.

Senator Botin was a professional politician who only wanted to remain in office by fair means or foul. For him, faithful service to the nation was not the key to strength, but skill in manipulation along with a sharp mind, a smooth tongue, and an agile political stance. He tried to get along with everyone. He offered candles alternately to God and to Satan. But every minute, he did not neglect to serve himself. Montero knew the senator's weakness, and this was the glue in their relationship.

However, Senator Botin hesitated regarding Montero's suggestion. Times had already changed—it was now difficult to go against the rising tide of nationalism. He admitted that the likes of Senator Maliwanag could now do a lot, together with men like Mando Plaridel, to lift the ignorance that had long shrouded the land.

'Let us admit that they can light up people's minds like a flashlight in a dark room,' the lawmaker said.

'Such dangerous people,' said Montero.

'We Chinese have a way of handling dangerous people,' said Son Tua, and cast a meaningful look at everyone around him.

'Our army solution never fails,' said Bayoneta.

Montero and Doblado smiled, but Senator Botin disagreed.

'The silken gloved hand is more effective with these people,' he said.

'An iron hand in a silk glove,' Bayoneta said to correct him.

'There are many ways to kill a chicken,' said Don Segundo. 'What we want to know, Senator, is if you're still with us.'

'Did I say otherwise?' the lawmaker answered swiftly.

'Can you stop the radical proposals in the session?' Montero suddenly asked the senator, who was caught unawares.

'Surely. For a fee.' The senator pursed his lips, then tilted his nose upward.

'Of course,' said Son Tua. 'When have we ever said no? How much?'

'Very well, then. I shall ask around and let you know.'

'You take care of it,' agreed Son Tua.

After another glass of whiskey, Senator Botin left. As a parting gift, Montero gave him a sealed white envelope bulging with cash.

When the four stockholders of the corporation were left alone, Montero reported that the situation was alarming.

'You know this without my saying so,' he said. 'You, Magno, as general, and you, Osky, as governor.'

'A storm is brewing,' Doblado said.

Montero continued, 'These are bad signs. The workers' meeting at Plaza Miranda and the fire at the plantation.'

'The fire?' Governor Doblado asked.

'We just beat them to it,' answered Montero, 'or else, worse things could have happened.'

'Aren't things bad enough as they are?'

'We are still on top of the situation,' Montero said with confidence.

'Until when?'

'As long as those in power like you don't lose heart and while those with money know how to pay.'

'We are not afraid, and we have no complaints against you,' said Bayoneta. 'But Senator Botin was right; times have indeed changed. Before, a general was like a king; now an officer can be shot by a mere soldier. Before, a millionaire could buy anything; now, the millionaire is afraid of a newspaper's front pages and the Senate's investigation.'

Son Tua agreed with his son-in-law and recalled how in the past, he could walk on a red carpet wherever he went because of his money. How many times did he travel around Asia in his flashy car? Then he would buy diamonds and other precious gems in Hong Kong, Bangkok, Singapore and other cities, and contraband goods worth hundreds of thousands. He would hide them in the gasoline tank of his car. This was why he brought it on his trip. Upon his return, his car would just zoom out of the pier. Who would suspect that his gasoline tank was full of diamonds? In Manila, the jewels cost five times as much without taxes.

'Where would the department stores in Escolta get their diamonds?' he said.

He paused for a while and then rubbed his hand over his face.

'Now, you give bribes left and right, but still, there's much fuss,' Son Tua said. 'Men are very bad these days, very greedy.'

And the Chinese multi-millionaire reclined once more in silence on the soft cushion of the easy chair.

On the other hand, Segundo Montero recalled the happy days soon after the war, when his orders were brought by an American official who made frequent trips overseas. When he and his wife travelled, they were met at the pier by the wife of a Malacañang Palace official. Thus, no one could touch their hand-carried valises filled with contraband goods. Often, their influential friends even asked the customs examiner to put their baggage in their car.

'A pat on the shoulder or a small gift was enough then,' said Don Segundo. 'Now they are too strict and want a very big share. The examiners get rich faster than the smuggler who invested his capital.'

'As long as they accept bribes, that's not too bad,' said Doblado. 'Those that can't be bribed are harder to deal with.'

'Like the *Kampilan* and Senator Maliwanag,' Son Tua said.

'But there is no pot without its matching stand,' said Bayoneta. 'If I'm not mistaken, the *Kampilan*'s publisher is a friend of Miss Montero's.'

'What?' Don Segundo was taken aback. 'What do you mean, General?'

'Is it wrong for Miss Dolly to use her influence on Mando Plaridel?' asked General Bayoneta.

'Bad, very bad,' Son Tua swiftly answered. The general remembered that his brother-in-law, Architect Pong, was courting Montero's daughter. He took back his first suggestion and said that if Mando would not listen to reason, then one should try other means.

'I still believe that every pot has its match,' he repeated and drank his whiskey.

They agreed to push through their operations despite the present hurdles.

'We're still on the side of those in power,' Montero said. 'And we should not waste this chance.'

'The more risk and expense in business,' said Son Tua, 'the greater the profit.'

They all decided to go ahead with the transactions on arms, jewellery and other contraband; increase bribes to the government; get more helpers; shadow the enemy, the radicals in the administration and outside; and prepare for any eventuality. In short, the corporation was prepared to wage war against those who favoured change.

When Pong brought home Doña Julia and Dolly from the party at the Pines Hotel, Don Segundo's guests had left.

It was very late. From the heights where the bungalow stood, they could see the mellow lights around Burnham Park. They could also smell the fresh pine-scented air which, like delicious wine, boosted both body and soul.

LVIII

The next morning, Don Segundo had finished breakfast and was reading the newspapers on the terrace. Doña Julia had gone shopping in one of their cars. Don Segundo was waiting for Dolly because he wanted to talk to her.

As he read the front page, his mind was on General Bayoneta's suggestion. 'Is it wrong for Miss Dolly to use her influence on Mando Plaridel?' Bayoneta had asked. Don Segundo had rejected such an idea, but this morning, he gave it a second thought. After thinking it over, he asked himself, 'What's wrong with it? Why not?'

Dolly was a good friend of Mando Plaridel's. Of course, he could not refuse her. Mando's newspaper had rapidly gained many readers because of its editorial policy of truth without fear or favour. The newspaper exposed the many anomalies in politics, business or society. It launched relentless attacks against the enemies of nationalism, against smuggling, graft and corruption, influence-peddling, and other dirty deals. One word from Dolly would be like a red light on the speeding *Kampilan*, which, if not stopped, might run roughshod over the Montero–Son Tua Corporation.

Don Segundo was aware that Dolly was no neophyte in using her charms on a man's heart. During the Japanese times, the strict Colonel Moto turned into putty in her hands. After liberation, the elusive Lieutenant Whitey was caught in the spider web of her charm. In terms of silver, the greedy father counted his gains from urging Dolly to become friends with the two foreigners. He could not measure the loss for Dolly, who was a hundred times more precious than any material thing. He had no idea that the very room of his daughter in their old house saw the colonel collecting debts from Dolly, in exchange for the favours given to Montero. He had no idea why Doña Julia and Dolly took a vacation to Hong Kong before she went to Paris to study at the Sorbonne. Also unknown to Montero was the extent of Dolly's intimate relationship with Mando in Paris.

The father thought his child was still a virgin, although mischievous as a butterfly and as elusive as a moonbeam. He thought the playful Dolly was just amusing herself with her suitors. He thought Dolly's relationships with the other men were similar to Pong, that Colonel Moto's and Whitey's kisses meant nothing at all. Kisses could be washed away with soap and water. What girl during these times did not kiss her boyfriend?

But Moto's and Whitey's days had passed. Don Segundo saw nothing wrong with Mando. He looked honourable, after all. Also, he knew that Dolly could make Pong sit in a corner. So he thought Mando would not reject Dolly.

Dolly came out on the terrace in high spirits. Upon seeing her father, she hooked an arm around his neck. Then after looking at the society pages, she sat down. The maid served them their breakfast at the terrace.

'Pa, where's Mama?' Dolly asked.

'She left a while ago to go shopping.'

'Why didn't she take me? I said I'd come along with her,' the girl sulked.

'She didn't want to disturb your sleep,' the father said with fondness. 'Don't you have a date, *hija*?'

'Pong asked me to a banquet for architects.'

'It looks like Pong can't stay away from you,' said Don Segundo.

'Here in Baguio, it's convenient for a girl to have a regular escort.'

'And how is your publisher friend?'

'Him? Always busy. It's annoying.'

'Isn't he coming here?'

'I wouldn't know.'

'Why don't you ask him to come up here for a few days?'

'What do you want from him, Papa?' Dolly became curious.

'Nothing. I just want to get to know him better.'

'What for?' Dolly said.

'Isn't he courting you? It's only natural for a father to want to know the man interested in his only child.'

'You've already met him, Papa. Didn't you talk to him at my party and other gatherings? Before that, I've already mentioned him in my letters from Paris.'

'But I don't know his character, his ways and likes, his . . .'

'What for? He's not courting you.'

'But you are my child.'

'Even then, Papa. You're not me. Suppose you find fault with him, but I like him. What then?'

'I would advise you.'

'And if I don't listen?'

'You are the queen of your feelings, Dolly. But then, I would have done my duty as a parent. Anyway, you are of age now.'

'Thanks, Papa.' The girl was pleased. 'Okay. I'll invite him, but I can't promise he'll accept my invitation.'

'Can he refuse you?'

'You really don't know that man.'

After breakfast, Dolly called Mando long distance. Luckily, he was at the *Kampilan*. This was the first time he'd heard her voice since she had left his office in anger.

'How's Baguio?' Mando asked.

'Cold and shivering.'

'Isn't that what people go there for?'

'I want to feel heat amid the cold,' the girl teased him. 'If you come, Mando, then I shall find the heat amid the cold.'

He gave a low whistle.

'It's really hot in Manila,' he answered in an evasive manner.

'When will you . . . find the time to come?'

'Is that an invitation?'

'Why do I even bother calling you?' Dolly whispered. Then she added, 'I'm always doing the calling.'

'Let's see. There will be a meeting of editors there,' said Mando, ignoring her reproach. 'Maybe Magat and I will go there.'

'I know you won't come because of me,' Dolly said. 'But thank you for coming up here. Maybe when you are here, you'll remember to visit me.'

'For sure, Dol.'

'Can I count on it?'

'Not only a visit, but . . . we'll go out and have fun.'

Dolly's was happy once more, her voice tinkling like a bell. Mando could imagine her smiling at the other end of the line.

'Is Magat your only companion?' she asked.

'Who else?'

'Won't you bring your cousin . . .the village maiden?'

'Now, Dolly . . .'

A restrained laugh came from the other end of the line.

LIX

After two days, Mando and Magat arrived at the Pines Hotel. The next few days would be the national conference of all the newspaper editors.

The publisher and editor of the *Kampilan* attended the conference to disseminate to everyone their aims. First, their stand on free and fair reportage. Then, respect for the citizens' constitutional rights without fear or favour.

Above all, the *Kampilan* staff agreed to launch the move for the Filipinization of newspapers in the Philippines. They wanted Congress to pass a definite policy. Not a few lawmakers agreed with it. Senator Maliwanag had once discussed it in a speech he delivered at the Senate.

A newspaper is a powerful tool, shaping the national sentiment through its news, editorials, opinions and feature articles, pointed out Senator Maliwanag. It was not right that this democratic force should be entrusted into the hands of foreigners. A newspaper is different from any other ordinary business that is open to non-natives. Rather, a newspaper is a strong influence on the mind and heart of a nation; it is actually being used by a few foreign publishers against the nation itself, especially on political and international issues. This is not only a grave insult but also a treachery of a guest against the host. Such anomalies go on unnoticed under the guise of freedom of speech and of the press. These freedoms are provided to the Filipinos by the nation's constitution, but should these also be enjoyed by foreigners who use them to betray their host country, which has shown them hospitality and goodwill?

370

Mando and Magat discussed the pros and cons at length with the *Kampilan* staff before they went to Baguio. They firmly believed in the Filipinization of newspapers, some of which are controlled by foreign capitalists. On the other hand, high government officials often hindered the free flow of information, opposed access to records and official documents, refused to give information, especially about scandals, and denied accurate news if they were involved.

Moreover, those in power often committed abuse in investigations, searches, arrests and detentions. Their illegal acts were often accompanied by threats, violence, and brutality—especially in far-flung areas, where the people were ignorant and poor.

'The newspapers should take a united stand against these evils,' said Mando. 'I can almost see the many editors who will lose their tongues when this resolution is brought up.'

'Of course. The more money goes to the publisher, the more he will lick the boots of the mighty. Those who pose as the nation's newspaper fool no one but themselves,' said Magat.

'I bet this resolution won't pass,' Mando said.

'If the Filipinization of retail trade is still pending in Congress, how can this one on journalism be approved by the editors of papers owned by foreigners? They'll be afraid to lose their jobs.'

'Have you ever thought that the newspapers themselves are strangling a free press?'

Magat agreed. 'Look at the bias of some papers for their advertisers, who are their gods; news of strikes at large companies, demonstrations, pickets and the like are either censored or not published at all. As long as it is against the advertiser, or a bad product like harmful medicine, the readers don't learn about it.'

'It's no surprise that some newspapers and journalists should lose their reputation,' added Mando. 'Often, the rotten politicians and the crooked newspapers are compared because both get rich suddenly without apparent sources. So, it is the duty of the press to cleanse itself. Some are used to throwing stones while they themselves wallow in the mud.'

'Let us make the *Kampilan* a model, then,' said Magat. He felt that if he could not cleanse a vast coral, he could keep at least keep his own house clean. 'We should be honest and courageous.'

'Honesty and courage used for good ends,' Mando said.

Magat was sure that the nation would hear their voices loud and clear because the *Kampilan*'s circulation was growing by leaps and bounds.

'We sell more than a hundred thousand copies every day,' he said with pride.

'But that's still too small,' Mando said. 'I won't be satisfied with less than a million . . . I'm not kidding. A million copies are not enough for 23 million people. Look at the newspaper circulation in Japan, England, the United States, Russia and Germany.'

'As long as the nation is only used to reading news about crime and the comics,' Mando went on, 'but not about the economy, science and world events, that nation will remain ignorant. It will remain a victim of fake news. The reader should know that the atomic force is now many thousand times more horrible than the bomb that the Americans had dropped on Hiroshima and Nagasaki. They should know about the Cold War, and why countries burn wheat and cotton, while millions of people in poor countries die of hunger and cold every year. They should join the campaign for peace, the disarmament of nations, raising the standard of living, eradicating disease, and saving mothers and infants from early death.'

'Mando, we need a hundred years for such a campaign to bear fruit,' Magat said. 'Besides, we should not deny or forget that society makes the government.'

'That's right,' said Mando. 'Changes cannot be done in one generation alone, but in several. True, we shall not enjoy its fruits, but we should support the movement for our children's future.'

Mando paused as their car reached a narrow wooden bridge. Then he continued, 'In our own time, it's a sin to be indifferent. Have you heard the story of the ignorant old man in China who hewed down two mountains that stood in his path?'

Mando related the story. The old man who was called a fool was blessed by God because of his strong determination. Mando explained his plan to develop a taste for reading. They would send free copies of their newspaper to the schools, public libraries, clubs, national organizations for language, social and charitable organizations.

'If we send them free copies, yes, we can develop their love for reading, but are we not teaching them the bad habit of not spending for their own good?' Magat said.

'If they have no money for rice, how can they buy newspapers? Up to now, a newspaper is still a luxury for thousands of poor families.'

'The *Kampilan* will then go bankrupt.'

'The country will benefit,' Mando faced Magat before going on. 'The *Kampilan* was not established for profit. Besides, the free copies are only temporary.'

Both lit cigarettes, each in his own thoughts. It was soon time for lunch.

After lunch, they had time to tour the popular places in the mountain city. They passed by the Mansion House but did not enter its elegant gardens, went up Dominican Hill and tested their legs on the long stairway to the shrine of the Blessed Virgin Mary, and then went to Camp Allen to see the campus and buildings of the Philippine Military Academy. Before dusk, they alighted before the big marketplace. Mando and Magat were fascinated by the Igorot handicrafts—wooden images, brass implements and objects made of stone. They bought a few items.

'This is a wonderful city,' said Magat, 'but it is sad that the beauty, climate and joys of Baguio belong only to the rich and are denied to the poor.'

'What do you want,' asked Mando with a smile, 'bring Baguio to Central Luzon?'

'I would like the law to help the poor and enable them to spend a few days every year in Baguio. Or Los Baños, Tagaytay, or other resorts,' Magat said.

'I have read it is hard to change the world all at once,' said Mando. 'But we should not shirk the responsibility of working for change.'

'That's what we have begun, isn't it? And we found out right away how few we are.'

When they returned to the hotel, many editors and reporters from Manila were already on the patio, in the lounge, and the dining room. A big group sat around the bar.

They joined their colleagues in the usual conversation—about the VIPs in Baguio, which meetings of professionals, businessmen and officials were scheduled for summer, and what pompous gatherings of the upper crust were being planned. The two did not hear of any plans to launch the timely Filipinization of mass media, freedom of the press and respect for the rights of the citizen as provided for by the constitution. Or that someone would notice the condition of the Igorots, who were deprived of land and driven to remote places in the name of civilization.

'Just think,' Mando pointed out to Magat, 'the Igorots are the race that made the rice terraces, which are considered one of the seven wonders of the world. The pharaohs used millions of slaves to build the pyramids, which symbolize their pride. But the Igorots built the rice terraces for their food. They are admirable.'

Before getting dressed, Mando called up Dolly.

'Please have dinner here,' the girl said.

'Alone?' asked Mando.

'I want to see you.'

'Really?'

'And I want to be alone with you,' Dolly said.

Dolly was worried about her relationship with Mando. Until now, the lovely Montero heiress could not tell if the *Kampilan* publisher was her sweetheart, her fiancé, or just a boyfriend. Because they had no definite agreement, and she could not blame him for it because he had always been elusive about such commitments.

But now, Dolly longed for Mando and was anxious to be clear on their relationship. Time was passing her by, and many matrons were now younger than her.

Dolly realized that their affair in Paris was mostly because of her. First, she was annoyed with the foreigners who hovered around her, especially when they learnt that she was the only child of a millionaire. Second, she was eager to have the exceptional Filipino bachelor who was the object of glances and sighs of the white women in the famous city. In Manila, it was common for society girls to boast of escorts with aquiline noses and cat's eyes. But in Paris, Dolly saw that a man was not judged by the colour of his skin, but by his manliness and personality. No Westerner could surpass Mando in the eyes of the hard-to-please Manila girl.

Now that they were both in Baguio, Dolly expected to feel Mando's love. She looked forward to their moments of happiness.

In the face of the wavering attention of the man she loved, she would be obliged to accept Pong. She didn't care for Pong at all, and often brusquely answered the coaxing of Doña Julia. She would say she would rather be an old maid than take the Chinese mestizo seriously. But she said this only because Mando Plaridel was there. Actually, Pong was not bad-looking and was educated as well. He was a favourite at the Bachelors' Club, distinguished in his profession, the son of the millionaire partner of her father. Pong was also wealthy in his own right.

'Let fate decide,' Dolly told herself, thinking of Mando's coldness.

She thought of all their circle, men and women, who got married without love. Name, money, love of luxuries and other factors were considered more important than love.

Fickle by nature and without firm convictions, Dolly was tired of such thoughts. What she planned was not because she didn't love Mando, nor did she care for Pong. Rather, it was her hurt pride for which she sought a remedy, a revenge in which she would be the first to get hurt. She would see how her conversation with Mando would turn out tonight.

On the other hand, Don Segundo looked forward to a serious conversation with the publisher. He wanted to come to an understanding with Mando, whom he had heard of as being a man of principles. Don Segundo could not understand how a man with such opportunities could turn out to be a radical. The landlord was afraid that neither his money nor Dolly's beauty could change his mind. He felt that he and Mando were worlds apart and could not be reconciled. Mando would not shy away from issues contrary to Montero's interests. For their part, Montero and his colleagues were not prepared to change, or to retreat.

It would be good enough, Don Segundo thought, *if he and Mando could agree to disagree.*

Like Dolly, he was eager to meet Mando at dinner tonight.

LX

From the window in his room at Pines Hotel, Mando looked at the famous zigzag road, which was coated with a silver sheen of moonlight. He could see the seemingly endless road shaped like a horseshoe, and later shaped like a series of intestines, at the height of 5,000 feet. At first glance, this wonderful road, a feat of modern engineering, was like a giant snake coiled on the breast of the mountain, with its head hanging over the mouth of the ravine. Mando recalled stories he had read as a child. Such paths, caves and hills were supposed to be crossed by a knight-errant before he could reach the castle of a beautiful princess atop the mountain.

Mando smiled to think that he had only to take a car below at the hotel. In a few minutes, he would reach the house of the girl waiting for him. The doors of her home and of her heart would be open. So after fixing his tie and putting on a woollen suit, Mando went down with energy. He talked a while to Magat in the lounge and said he would not be back for dinner.

'A night in Paris,' Magat teased him upon learning that Dolly had invited his friend.

Mando left without making any comment. He was thinking of other things.

Dolly greeted Mando at the door of their beautiful bungalow. She pressed his arm.

'I'm glad you had time tonight.'

'I had to come and see you.'

'So you have not completely forgotten about me.'

'We didn't quarrel, Dol.'

The girl led Mando to the living room. Don Segundo was seated in an easy chair.

'Papa, Mando is here,' said Dolly.

The old man stood up and shook hands with the guest. Doña Julia came in and also shook hands with the publisher.

'When did you arrive?' asked Don Segundo when they were seated.

'At noon, sir.'

'Will you be staying long?'

'The newspaper editors will meet for two days starting tomorrow. Today's Friday, so I shall leave Monday morning.'

'You seem to be in a hurry.'

'It's hard to stay away from Manila for too long,' said Mando. 'The new rotary press is being installed. Soon, we shall inaugurate a radio station.'

'Oh . . .'

'I hope you and your family will come.'

'Let me know, and I'll attend.'

Doña Julia announced that dinner was ready. They all went to the dining room. There was no other guest.

'It seems very quiet here,' Mando said.

'Not really,' answered Doña Julia. 'Pong Tua-son often comes,' she added, casting a glance at Dolly. 'The other night, the governor and the general were here. Also Senator Botin. Dolly here keeps on receiving invitations.'

'I often decline because it's tiring. I came here for a vacation, didn't I, Papa?'

'But Baguio is not a place for rest,' Don Segundo corrected her. 'During summer, it replaces Manila. Here are the government, business and society. How can you rest?'

'In fact, expenses in Baguio are double,' Doña Julia said.

'Of course, because everyone is here,' said her husband. 'The capacity of public services is limited. They are meant for a small group of special guests, but now who does not come for a vacation in Baguio? Imagine! One day, Burnham Park was filled with buses of excursionists—salesmen and salesgirls of the Chinese bazaars in Manila. Each had his bundle of food, too. So, after lunch, the food wrappings of leaves and cartons were scattered everywhere. I don't know why people who do nothing but throw garbage are allowed here. They bring along their bad manners.' Doña Julia said with a sneer.

Mando made no comment on Doña Julia's complaints or on Don Segundo's harsh words against the lowly employees who had come to see Baguio. He did not remind them that the government had spent the people's money on the City of Pines, and no one had the right to consider it their private preserve. But Mando was already used to the haughty ways of the Monteros. Once more, he saw that the glitter of gold and diamonds could not cover up their bad behaviour, but it had made them even prouder. Mando wondered how they would react should they know who he was. Would they insult him as Andoy, the houseboy, or would they fear him as the formidable Mando Plaridel? He thought this might be a good chance to find out.

After supper, they returned to the living room. Don Segundo removed a wrapper from a Corona cigar. Mando and Dolly lit cigarettes. Doña Julia stayed behind to give instructions to servants. Then Dolly went to her room.

'I read in your newspaper about the incident at my plantation,' Montero began, when he and Mando were alone.

'The news in the *Kampilan* is a result of our investigation,' Mando said.

'But often, that result follows the intention of the one investigating, isn't it?'

'Our only interest in the issue, sir, is to print the truth. We take no sides on this issue.'

'Has it ever occurred to you, Mr Plaridel, that truth has many shapes, and that reason has two or more sides? Who can have complete certainty about anything?'

'Philosophically, what you say holds true in many cases,' Mando said. 'But on what's happening at the plantation, some facts can't be denied. First, those accused did not light the fire. Second, revenge is the only motivation for the farmers' arrest and detention. Third, under your management and that of your overseer, peace would be impossible on your plantation.'

Don Segundo lighted his cigar again. Then he said calmly, 'You judge hastily. Do I have any arrangements that other landlords don't follow? Whether for tenants or sharecroppers, I ask nothing except what the law provides. If the law is wrong, then we should change it first. But I won't be the first to change it. I invested money in my businesses. Is it wrong to profit from my capital?'

'No one is saying that,' Mando answered. 'But if you know that the law is biased, a law that had been signed and made by the powerful, why don't you take the initiative to improve your tenants' lives? They are always in want, while you . . .'

'My wealth didn't come from them. Since the war, I have been losing a lot of money on that plantation. The farmers are poor because they're stupid. They prefer to loaf around rather than work, and what they should save, they throw away on their many vices.'

The landlord puffed his cigar, and after inhaling the grey smoke, he added. 'Perhaps, you don't know the farmers' ways. What do they do between planting and harvesting? What do they do with their share of the harvest? What should be spent in a year is finished in a month. Don't blame the landlord if the tenants who don't know any better should live from hand to mouth, instead of having plenty of rice, chicken, eggs and vegetables. They are their own enemies.' The grey smoke from the cigarette floated and almost blurred his face.

Mando let Don Segundo recite the farmer's weaknesses, because he knew that some of them were true, but not for all. Many had tried their best and worked day and night to support their families, but they were still in difficult straits. Mando felt that arguing with Montero would only lead to rancour between them.

'I hear you, Don Segundo. But one fact will remain: that the landowner and the tenants are like oil and water. The fire and the farmers' arrest had burnt whatever bridge still lay between them. I believe that you are now losing money. It is also true that your tenants are unhappy. But the land is big, and it's a waste to keep it idle. The land will remain even if you are no longer the owner and even if it is tilled by other hands. Does a corporation want to buy your plantation, Don Segundo?'

'I've had offers. The government itself . . . The Chinese multi-millionaire Son Tua. To get rid of my headache, I have thought of giving up that plantation. But only if those who wish to buy are ready to pay my price.'

'If it is reasonable . . .'

'A reasonable price is the market price. The land will not grow stale or rot.'

'Perhaps Dr Sabio had talked to you in the name of Freedom University, which will manage the plantation if he buys it?'

'Yes, we have talked about it,' Don Segundo said. 'He mentioned his plans for the university, the research and experiments and the supposed advantages for the students and the farmers. But his offer was low. So my answer was like that of the archbishop to some Catholics who were working doing some business: "I am happy that you are Catholics, good Catholics, I hope," said the archbishop. "But in this transaction, religion is out. This is business, and as the American saying goes—business is business." That was the end of the discussion.'

'You are a good businessman, and it's not for me to advise you that it is better to sell and convert into cash the land that is causing you losses—as well as headaches.'

'That's true, I guess. But some losses become gains.'

'How can that be, sir?' The publisher was surprised.

Don Segundo saw his chance and followed with a barbed answer.

'For example, your newspaper. You can't deny that the *Kampilan* is losing money. But you continue to finance and print it.'

'But the newspaper is not a business; it's a form of service,' said Mando.

'Don't fool yourselves.'

'Don Segundo, I'm sure the *Kampilan* is not a business. We're not here to make money.'

'Well, if you insist, then I won't argue with you,' the Don said. Then he added, 'But your newspaper is rather . . . unusual.'

'What is your basis for comparing the *Kampilan* and the Montero Plantation?'

'I invested in the Montero Plantation to help produce food for the country,' Don Segundo said. 'You invested capital in the *Kampilan* to offer services, as you see it. Is that not so?'

'Yes, in a way . . .'

'So your newspaper is a harsh critic of what happened at the plantation.'

'A critic of anomalies,' Mando corrected. 'Of graft and corruption, smuggling, cheating—'

'Very well, then,' the landlord cut him short. 'You fan blind nationalism and radicalism. You goad the poor, so they'll turn against the rich.'

'Mr Montero.' Mando was put on the defensive.

'Your friends want to buy my plantation,' Don Segundo went back to their topic. 'Well, I have a proposition for you.'

'I am listening, sir.'

'If someone wants to buy the *Kampilan* at a good price, will you sell it?'

'Certainly not.'

'Would you agree to an exchange?'

'With what?'

'My plantation for your newspaper.' The landlord said each word slowly and distinctly.

Mando stood up, surprised. But he quickly saw that Don was baiting him. The wily old man was not serious about his offer.

'And what will you do with the newspaper?'

'A newspaper is a powerful weapon in anyone's hands.' Montero's answered. His lips were tight, like a line slashing across his face.

'Oh, you will reverse the policy of the *Kampilan* if you own it.' Mando's face turned with anger.

'A newspaper is just a property like any other,' Montero declared.

'Not the *Kampilan*.' Mando stood up. He was disgusted. 'Never.'

When the discussion was already getting heated, Dolly entered the room. She was followed by a servant carrying a tray with a coffee pot, sugar, cream and bone-white cups.

Dolly poured coffee and served her father and her boyfriend. Her perfume overcame the aroma rising from the brewed coffee. Mando suddenly recalled their happy nights in Paris.

Dolly told Don Segundo. 'Papa, it's already past ten o'clock. You should now rest. Besides, I didn't invite Mando to debate with you the whole night long.'

Then Dolly left, after whispering to Mando that she would watch the moonlight from the terrace.

The old man stood up.

'Mr Plaridel, I feel I have come to know you.'

'That's good, sir, but you could be mistaken.'

'I have learnt we don't have the same beliefs,' he said.

'Perhaps so, sir.'

'And you don't wish to come to terms with me.'

'Even if I wished for it, I think that would be rather difficult.'

'Even if you like my daughter?'

Mando was taken aback, like an actor when someone did not follow the script. Nevertheless, he spoke with calmness.

'It seems, sir, that there's no connection.'

'Really? And why not?'

It was the perfect moment. *It's now or never*, Mando told himself. It could no longer be avoided. He faced Segundo Montero.

'Because if you would know who I am, either you would curse me—or you would curse yourself.'

Don Segundo was surprised. His eyes widened, and he moved back a few steps. It seemed to him that Mando Plaridel had changed appearance before his very eyes. 'Who are you?'

'Don't you remember me?'

'Who are you?' repeated the landlord.

'Then you will know a few hours before I leave Baguio.'

Segundo Montero tried to control himself. He was filled with a mixture of anger and fear upon hearing Mando Plaridel. He stared at the young man, the ugly scar on his left cheek, his dark glasses, his body that seemed to possess unusual strength. As when he first saw this man, Don Segundo once more searched his memory: who was this mysterious man standing before him?

He left the room without saying goodbye, as if he were fleeing from the devil. Mando was left standing beside a table.

Then, he went to the terrace. A cool and strong breeze met him, wafting the perfume of the woman waiting for him. Dolly went to him and clung to his arm. The moon was round and full, and the stars glittered like diamonds in the sky. Some stars were like lights flowing from the branches of the tall pine trees on the hills. Mando expected that his conversation with Montero's daughter would not be different from his talk with Don Segundo.

'Did you fight with Papa?' she asked.

'We never got along well. *Never.*' Mando's harsh words sliced cleanly through the cold air. Dolly could not imagine what he meant by 'never'.

'Mando!' The girl was puzzled.

'Dolly, perhaps, after tonight, you won't wish to see me again.'

The girl was even more astounded.

'Mando, what's wrong?' She guessed that her boyfriend had indeed fought with her father.

'I shall repeat what I told your father—that if you knew me, you would either curse me or curse yourself.'

'Who are you?'

Mando removed his dark glasses and covered the scar on his left cheek with his three fingers. Dolly stared at him, but she could not remember anything. She took two steps nearer and looked closer. She removed the hand covering the scar, and her eyes almost touched the face that she had kissed a thousand times, the face that had pressed against her breasts and rested on her lap, the face that in the midst of happiness, she did not want to let go of, as if it were a dream that might suddenly vanish.

Then she moved back and asked, filled with anguish.

'Who are you?' Dolly said.

Mando put on his dark glasses and held Dolly tightly by the shoulders.

'Have you forgotten your servant, your slave before the war? The one often beaten up by your father and mother, the one you often insulted and rapped on the head, the one who, in your father's desire to please the Japs, was betrayed to the Japanese military police? Don't you remember?'

Dolly seemed rooted to the spot, then . . .

'Andoy!' she shouted, ashamed and afraid. It was as if she had seen a ghost.

'Yes, Andoy.'

'You . . . traitor! Cheat!' Dolly was filled with great shame and frustration that she had given her honour—everything—not to the exceptional Mando, but to the servant Andoy, the peasant and vagabond. She could never forgive herself. She would never forgive this snake that had fooled her.

Then she sank to the floor, covered her face with her hands, and wailed. When Mando moved towards her, she turned, and like a fierce lioness, she screamed: 'Leave me alone. I don't want to see your shadow. Traitor! Slave!'

It was not the lowly Andoy who left quietly but the honourable Mando Plaridel. For a long while, Dolly remained on the floor, unmindful that the moon had already descended and the cold felt like pricks of needles on her skin.

LXI

The country recoiled in horror at the atrocities that erupted on the plantation and in the nearby village. When the public read the news and saw the photographs in the *Kampilan*, everyone talked about it. Senator Maliwanag delivered a fiery speech at the Senate, asking for an immediate investigation of the terrorism stalking the farms. Rubio also called for a resolution of the protest supported by the vast army of labourers in the city.

Meanwhile, Dr Sabio and some lawyers continued with the court battle. They asked for the release of Pastor and the others detained at the military police headquarters.

On the other hand, Pastor and his group were charged by the military police with arson, possession of deadly weapons, and conspiring to commit rebellion. They invented evidence to justify the farmers' detention.

Nevertheless, at the first court hearing, the farmers were granted bail. The court declared that they had cause to sue those who had illegally detained them.

Captain Pugot was charged with the killing of Mang Tomas and another farmer. But what justice could the old man hope for, now that he was already in his coffin?

Mang Tomas was not buried at once. The farmers had his remains embalmed and laid him at the union house in the village. They felt it best to wait for Pastor and the other detainees to arrive. They wanted to pay proper homage to Mang Tomas, who had become a martyr to their cause.

What Mang Tomas used to say had come to pass. Whenever he talked of an oppressed worker, he would ask, 'Who among you, if you should die of hunger, could afford a Mass and a coffin?' His death proved it was true.

But Mang Tomas' poverty didn't deprive him of an expensive coffin. Day and night, the union house was filled with people attending the wake, and there was a lot of food.

Despite the rumours that Mando was paying for all of the funeral expenses, the farmers also wanted to help. They passed around a collection hat. Those who had no cash contributed rice, food and drinks. Many volunteered to do any of the chores. His relatives wailed when they first saw the face of the dead man, but an old man calmed them down.

'We should not weep over the death of Tomas,' he said. 'He died with honour. He just seems to be asleep.'

Others said he had never looked more serene. His thin silver hair was combed back; his lips and cheeks were coloured from the slight rouge used by the embalmer. He seemed to have just taken a nap after speaking at a meeting. He wore white native formal wear, white pants and black socks. The old man said he had known Tomas since childhood, but he couldn't remember seeing him wearing socks. His socks were the mud from the fields.

Two tenants noticed that Tomas' clasped hands held the small cross of a rosary, which was like a small chain tying his hands. It had been placed there by Tomas' female cousin, with whom he had never got along.

Among the wreaths, which were already starting to wither at the foot of the coffin, stood out the names of Pastor, Puri and Mando. The two wreaths had been sent from Manila.

'Tomas is fortunate; he is now at peace,' said an old woman.

'My husband is still detained with Pastor,' said another, but she was relieved because her husband was still alive.

'We shall all die,' the old man said. 'What matters is how we live. Tomas led a noble life. In death, his is nobler than Segundo Montero, who has not even begun to pay for his many debts to the people.'

Unlike in the usual wake, there was no cheerful playing of the ukulele or the guitar. There was no gambling, either, and no teenagers drank and fought.

The various groups were just talking quietly. There was no loud laughter or improper behaviour. They talked of the dead man's life and deeds, his beliefs and loyalty to the farmers' cause. They exchanged views on nationalism, the rising prices and widespread unemployment, the filth of politics, the exploiters among government bigwigs and their many schemes.

'We are also to blame,' said one. 'In a democracy, the majority should be followed. The poor are the majority, but we are just ignored. We allow what's happening. Whom should we blame?'

'The leaders are at fault,' another said.

'Who chose the leaders?'

'Many leaders rise to power through money, threats, cheating.'

'Truly, we never learn our lesson.'

'But if you oppose them, you'll end up like Mang Tomas or Pastor.'

'Sometimes, the dead are better off.'

'I prefer to be alive,' said a woman. 'You manage to eat, somehow. When you're dead, you'll just be eaten up by worms.'

It was a day before the funeral when Pastor and Puri arrived at the village. The detainees had been freed by a court order. Pastor had picked Puri up from the dormitory and brought her home in a car provided by Mando. Mando had planned to attend the funeral, but he had to attend an editors' conference that Saturday. Nevertheless, he had paid for all the expenses and asked Andres to take his place.

A long and solemn procession carried Mang Tomas to his resting place. The farmers' union took charge. As ordered by Governor Doblado, the military police and civilian guards did not interfere; neither did they watch the long cortege of mourners. The Governor, the Commander, and Captain Pugot had all left. It was learnt that they went up to Baguio.

The funeral procession was more than a mile long. The mourners were farmers, labourers, common folk not only from the plantation and the villages but also from the towns and Manila. Senator Maliwanag, Rubio and Danoy came. Andres was also there, with Pastor and Puri.

Before the funeral, Danoy clung to the coffin of Mang Tomas for a long time. He did not shed tears but in the veins of his clenched fists flowed boiling lead instead of blood. Danoy was closest to Mang Tomas, and was trained by the old man to be a leader of the farmers.

Danoy was sure Captain Pugot was behind the killing of Mang Tomas. Pastor had told him about the mysterious disappearance of Mang Tomas from their room after his own harsh treatment in the secret cell.

'I wonder why they killed Mang Tomas instead of me,' Pastor said.

'If I had not stayed behind, for sure, you would also be burying me,' said Danoy.

Both were sure of the dark and dreary days to come, as long as the problems of the plantation remained unsolved, and the civilian guards stayed.

'Will you return to Manila after the funeral?' Danoy asked.

'That is the advice of Mando and Dr Sabio. They want Puri to stay at the dormitory and study at the university. What are your plans?'

'I shall not be far from here, but the enemy shall not get me. We cannot abandon the tenants and the barrio people.'

'Danoy, my staying in Manila for a while does not mean I'm neglecting them. Only . . .'

'I know, Tata Pastor, I know . . .'

Some touching eulogies were delivered at Mang Tomas's graveyard. Danoy, Rubio, Andres and Senator Maliwanag spoke. They compared the life and martyrdom of Mang Tomas to a fertile seed from which would sprout a luxuriant, healthy plant bearing delicious fruits.

Senator Maliwanag vowed that he would want to realize the wishes of the killed leader, to transfer the plantation's ownership to the present tenants or to a corporation that would promote social justice. However, the senator could not make the promise in the name of the administration.

It was already dusk when the people left. Senator Maliwanag rode in his car together with Rubio. Andres led Puri to their car, which was parked on the narrow road.

But Pastor and Danoy remained standing beside Mang Tomas's grave, speaking quietly.

'They have killed Mang Tomas, but his beliefs will spread,' Pastor said. 'It is our duty . . .'

'It's not enough to spread his teachings,' Danoy said. 'The criminals who killed him must pay.'

'As soon as possible.'

'I shall not rest, I swear . . . even if I'm alone.'

'Then you shall not be alone,' Pastor said. 'Many oppressed people will join you . . . Let's go.'

Pastor walked towards the waiting car. He looked back and watched Danoy moving away until his shadow was completely lost in the dark that now shrouded the whole graveyard.

LXII

The soil had hardly settled on Mang Tomas' grave when blood flowed again at the plantation's border. One night, two of Captain Pugot's civilian guards, who were noted for their ferocity, were ambushed on the wild path between the plantation and the next village. The unknown assailants vanished in the night.

Someone who had answered the cries for help found the two guards with deep machete wounds on their necks. They were dead on arrival at the town hospital. The investigators only got a few clues, since the victims could hardly talk before they finally died.

Nevertheless, they said that six to seven men stopped them. Upon learning that they were civilian guards, the men raised their arms. The leader then told them to repent for their sins.

One of the assailants suggested they shoot the civilian guards with their own rifles, but the leader decided to save on the bullets.

'Just cut off the heads of the beasts,' he said.

'Let the dogs tear their bodies apart,' added another.

After hearing the snatches of stories from the two civilian guards, the investigators asked a few questions.

'Was Pastor the leader?'

'His face was covered.'

'Was it Danoy?'

The dying guards could not tell, but they could identify them if they should see them again. But they died on the way to the hospital.

The next day, an uneasy silence reigned over the whole plantation and the nearby villages. There were no group gatherings, no discussions—and only a few people walked on the streets.

Civilian guards patrolled in threes, with a military police sergeant or a private. They went from house to house, asking the residents to come out.

New checkpoints were set up between the plantation and the villages. Guards were added at the entrance to the plantation. All the guards carried rifles and steel helmets, as if they were geared up for a real battle.

The civilian guards and the soldiers queried all the villagers and farm folk. They were asked if they had seen Pastor or Danoy within the last twenty-four hours. Each one said 'no'. Some said they had seen Pastor and Danoy at Mang Tomas's funeral on Sunday afternoon. But that was the last time they were seen in public. They probably went to Manila after the funeral. Pastor and Puri were in the *Kampilan*'s car. Rubio rode with Senator Maliwanag.

During the interrogation, the village seemed to have been turned into a locked chest. The people said they had seen nothing, heard nothing and knew nothing. Yes, sir, they were ready to help the authorities. Yes, sir, they would help catch the criminals. Yes, they would report any news to the law enforcers. But that was all, and the blanket of silence covered all of them again.

Captain Pugot returned from Baguio. He could be seen in his Jeep, going back and forth between the plantation and the village. His Jeep was full of his armed men, and they were always in a hurry, as if being hounded by something they could not see.

Curfew was imposed throughout the troubled areas. From eight o'clock at night, no one could go out without a pass. Lights were turned off by nine o'clock. Nothing disturbed the silence and the darkness, but the sound of the boots of the civilian guards patrolling in groups. It seemed like the Japanese occupation times all over again.

Captain Pugot's suspicion was right. His two men were killed not by the plantation's tenants or by the village farmers. Nor did he suspect the farmers whom he had detained, except for Pastor and Danoy.

This was the work of the outlaws, Captain Pugot told himself. His eyes flashed, and he gritted his teeth as if grinding the bones of a skeleton.

After the war, many guerrillas did not return to their towns. They kept their distance for various reasons. Some were not willing to return to the conditions before the war; some were evading punishment for their crimes; some decided that they would be happier living the free life in the forest, with no masters but themselves and not bound by laws made by those in power.

Sometimes, the outlaws came to the town when they needed something. They allied themselves with the radical farmers, who supported them in return for protection. This began during the Japanese occupation and had continued after the war. That was why the farmers had the courage to defy the landlords and government officials. The tough warriors in the forest were on their side.

Captain Pugot had no doubt that the killing of the two civilian guards was connected with Mang Tomas's death. The two incidents were certainly linked. His men killed Mang Tomas, and they were made to pay. The captain was filled with rage. In his bones, he knew that either Pastor or Danoy and their associates were behind the latest killing.

Without a doubt, they had given the word and goaded the others to avenge Mang Tomas.

'The devils are asking for trouble!' Captain Pugot said. He was vexed with his guards, who did not arrest anyone or make a definite report about the investigator. The report coming from the military police was also vague.

'Why didn't you arrest anyone?' Captain Pugot snarled at the head of the civilian guards. 'He will confess when he is full of bruises.'

The sergeant reminded him of the court order to release the detained farmers. Besides, those who detained them were also warned. Captain Pugot and his men were charged with Mang Tomas's death, despite their report that the old man was trying to escape.

'You're a bunch of cowards!' Captain Pugot said. 'You are easily scared. Two of your companions were beheaded, and you have not even avenged them. What runs in your veins? Coca-Cola?'

That night, the people in the village retired early. They took their dinner before dusk so they would no longer need a light. They did not stay downstairs after their meals and exchange views about the day just past. They were thinking of the curfew and knew the consequences of breaking it, even if they did not have the intention to do so. They had no wish to give an excuse for the enforcers to punish them. So they spread their woven mats early and tried to sleep, acting as if they had heard ghost stories.

It was already midnight when the village was shaken by the continuous shooting. Shouts, curses, groans and weeping answered the firing of the guns. Some thatched huts burst into flames. Some fleeing shadows suddenly stopped, staggered, and were swallowed up by the thick darkness.

The confusion lasted for hours. People just huddled inside their small hovels. It was almost morning when silence returned. The sun shone brightly on the corpses of men, women, and children lying on the ground. Around them were the ashes of burnt houses. Many of the wounded could not walk. Instead of being given first aid, they were arrested by the soldiers and civilian guards.

The civilian guards were the first to report what had happened the previous night. They claimed that a group of armed bandits had attacked, but they were repulsed by law enforcers and suffered many casualties. Some citizens were allegedly caught in the crossfire and killed.

But some farmers who had stayed awake had seen what happened. No outlaws raided the village. There was no encounter at all. The shots came only from one side—the civilian guards and soldiers. It was a deliberate killing of the farmers who were asleep, unarmed and defenceless.

And the farmers knew who had plotted it. This was Captain Pugot's vengeance for the death of two of his men. He did not take it out on the outlaws, but on the poor families of the innocent farmers.

'That is my answer to the bandits' challenge,' Pugot said. 'If you leave a lash on the water buffalo, then I'll leave a welt on the horse.' His loud laughter startled some of the guards.

LXIII

On their trip back to Manila from Baguio, Mando told Magat to give free copies of the *Kampilan* to institutions and national organizations. Mando learnt from the circulation department that they might have to double the number of copies. They would surely lose money, according to Magat. But Mando said that publishing being a cultural industry that served the nation, this should not be considered a loss.

However, Mando was aware that it was not the volume of the newspapers that was important but the contents—news, pictures, columns and public opinion. Different groups also published several reading materials. They were filled with propaganda and favoured vested interests. They often reported the opposite of facts.

On the other hand, the *Kampilan* was full of features that could not be seen in popular commercial newspapers. Their only concern was spreading awareness about the truth.

After the editors' conference in Baguio, the *Kampilan* became even bolder and more militant. It seemed to have assumed a new lease on life. With vigour, it attacked the abuses, graft, greed and callousness of the very people who should serve as role models, because they had high positions in government, industry and society.

The *Kampilan* unmasked the officials on the blacklist and published their names.

It published a long 'White Paper', which listed these names along with the ways and means by which they enriched themselves overnight.

It pointed to the sharks, the crocodiles, and other monsters in and out of the government. It proclaimed that if the county should desire to prosper, these people should be put behind bars.

Naturally, the articles led to a storm of furore, anonymous letters and open threats. Many hired lawyers who looked for charges that could be filed against the *Kampilan*, its publisher and its editor.

'Don't go out without bodyguards,' Senator Maliwanag warned Mando while they were having snacks, one afternoon.

But Mando merely shrugged his shoulders, saying that although he didn't wish to die, he could not do his work if he was afraid.

Then the *Kampilan* followed up with an exposé of the abuses in the farms and demanded that the leaders responsible for the farmers' deaths be punished. It published news of the actual incidents, contradicting the reports of the military police and the civilian guards. The paper published concise analyses of why the farmers remained poor. They were always the victims of unjust systems—of usury and a meagre share of the harvest. It also pointed out why there could be no peace in the plantation under the present owner, who clung to unjust laws. Finally, it suggested remedies: sell the farms and turn them into cooperatives managed by the administration or by a corporation, with safeguards for implementing social justice.

The newspaper also featured the declaration of the farmers' union, which included the signatures of Pastor and Danoy. The latest incident at the plantation was blamed squarely on the landowner and the law enforcers.

What is the farmers' union? After the last war, the tillers of the soil began to unite. They had to, because otherwise they would remain oppressed. They formed their union following the law. Their activities on behalf of the workers were legal.

We challenge those who are sworn enemies of the poor to prove that we are the enemies of order and peace. The charge that we are communists following a foreign ideology is an old tune that dates back to Jesus Christ. Did not the scribes and pharisees also call the Nazareth a rabble-rouser, a violator of the laws of the temple and of Rome, a destroyer of peace and order? Jesus, who was meek as a lamb, was sentenced by Pilate and nailed to the cross between two outlaws. On the other hand, the murderer Barabas was set free.

The fake gods of politics and business know that we cannot be bought. We are free Filipino citizens who present our ideas on national issues. This country was enslaved for four centuries by foreigners, but we are descendants of Filipinos who strove to be free. In our veins flow the blood of our heroes, of Lapu-Lapu, Rajah Soliman, Dagohoy, Diego Silang, Burgos, Gomez and Zamora, Rizal, Bonifacio, del Pilar, Luna Jacinto, Jose Abad Santos, Crisanto Evangelista, and many others who chose prison, death or exile over an easy life within a master's cage.

We are behind the independence movement. We want our Constitution to be amended so that our Republic shall have complete independence and erase the ugly marks left by our colonial masters. We are against wasting the lives of Filipino soldiers in other lands to keep foreign dictators on their thrones. We are against raising and adding new taxes while jobs vanish and the black market exists. We want a living wage for our workers in the factories and the farmers in the fields. We are not against cooperation between labour and capital in a just manner, but we do not like the cooperation between the rig driver and his horse.

Inside us flames the spirit of sacrifice and courage, because we believe that the nation, justice and God are on our side. A wise man said that one may hold back the waves of the sea, but not justice for the common person.

The union of labour under one confederation, one society and someday, under a real political party, is part of the spread of a shared brotherhood. It should be encouraged. It is better that the poor use the ballot rather than the bullet. But it is sad that in the eyes of a blind administration, even asking for a clean election is already a crime.

Those in power often say that the people should be loyal to the government. But these people forget themselves. They think we have a dictatorship or a monarchy, and not a democracy. In a real democracy, one does not have to ask who has the first duty to be loyal—the people or the government. If the latter is true, how little is the disobedience of a citizen to the administration compared to the treachery of a whole administration against the people!

Our sacrifices are only an example of the untold sacrifices of the many. Thousands, millions all over the country; farmers like us, labourers, employees, soldiers, ordinary citizens, the old, women and children, live in poverty. They live in eternal darkness, without the hope of any tomorrow. They feel like orphans inside a dazzling, noisy city; they are hungry in a land of plenty.

If our voices are heard now, it's because we are part of the many who are oppressed, abused and persecuted, not because we are criminals, but loyal Filipinos defending our four freedoms. For this noble principle, we are ready to suffer. And the sorrows and poverty of our lives will not weaken our resolve but will only add courage for us to continue, heads held high, until our motherland becomes free and prosperous—now and in the next generations.

The *Kampilan* was praised when common people gathered together, but not in the higher councils.

'This is sedition; it urges rebellion! That Mando Plaridel is a dangerous man,' said an influence-peddler.

'Well, he is just digging his own grave,' said a fat politician. 'We shall see.'

LXIV

The new moon rose early, like a golden bow across a grey violin. The night was bright, and the diamonds were aglitter in the thick hair of the sky.

Mando was leisurely driving his car. But the wheels of his car were slow compared to the furious beating of his heart. Mando was visiting Puri at the girls' dormitory of Freedom University. He had called ahead, so he knew that Puri was already waiting for him. They had not seen each other for more than a week. They had seen each other only two or three times since Puri had rushed to Manila, until Mando went to Baguio. They had talked on the phone, but only for a short while. Both were eager for their meeting that night.

Puri stood up when Mando showed up at the door of the visitors' hall on the ground floor of the dormitory. She wore a white dress with blue trimmings on the neckline, sleeves, and hem.

Mando's eyes showed his surprise and admiration.

'I came to see a village maiden, but a college student met me.'

Puri was embarrassed. She quickened her steps as she led Mando to their seats.

The hall was wide, with a high ceiling. Some girls were with their guests, talking quietly and laughing once in a while.

'I think you are getting along well here,' Mando said when he and Puri were already seated.

'What makes you say that?'

'It shows. You seem healthier—and even lovelier.'

'Can my appearance still change? I still look like a village girl even if I'm dressed like a college student.'

'You are more beautiful than all of them.'

'Oh, no. You're too kind.'

Mando was not flattering her. There were many young women at Freedom University who had come from different provinces, and many of them were gorgeous. But surely none could surpass the pristine beauty of the girl from the village beside the Montero Plantation.

When Mando and Magat first saw Puri a few years ago, Magat said that she was a rare, pink-petalled orchid hidden among the vines of a forest. Mando said that she was like a pure, round pearl whose whiteness was made more dazzling because it had been kept in Simoun's treasure chest, with only the waves at the bottom of the sea as sentinels. Puri's dreamy eyes met Mando's gaze. Her dimples bloomed on her light olive cheeks as she smiled sweetly.

'Do you have any news?' she asked.

Mando didn't answer at once, but continued to look at her loveliness. He remembered Dolly, who was like sparkling champagne in an amber cup, tempting one to drink it in one gulp. But Puri's beauty was different; it was enchanting in its purity and modesty. Her beauty was not intoxicating; rather, it grew on the beholder.

'What's new?' Puri asked her guest again, who was simply staring at her.

Mando appeared to hear her for the first time. He shielded his embarrassment by laughing softly. He recalled Ulysses, who had asked to be tied to the post of a ship as he sailed near the island of the sirens. Then, he told her the latest news.

'After the massacre of the farmers, the situation at the plantation only took a turn for the worse,' Mando said. 'This is not the end of the issue. The government officials like the governor and some military police officials are washing their hands off it. It's hard to expect justice. The president should step in to prevent more bloodshed.'

'Tatang wants to return to the village,' Puri said, worry creasing her face.

'I told him not to do that,' Mando said. 'He said he could not let down his companions and Danoy. I told him it would be suicide to do so. He and Danoy are being hunted at the plantation. The civilian guards won't go easy on them.'

'I've asked him to stay,' said Puri. 'But if he insists, I shall go with him.'

'You, too?'

'Why should I hide here?'

'But this is your place now,' Mando said with emphasis. 'You are not hiding here, just waiting for the storm to pass. In times like these, the plantation and the village are not for a beautiful girl, the daughter of Pastor, at that. Dr Sabio and I want you to stay. We are not mere observers in this fight. We are involved, and we are with you. And Puri, you are important to us. I need you. When peace returns, I want . . . to . . .'

'That makes me more afraid,' Puri whispered.

'About my intentions?'

'Your safety.'

'Thank you, Puri.' Mando was delighted. 'I know you have some regard for me. But I won't come to any harm. No. Fate has saved me from the Japanese bullets. Good fortune shall spare me now for the sake of the country—and for you.'

'I am frightened, at times,' Puri said. 'I don't know if I'm becoming a coward. I don't understand. I'm used to the struggle. During the Japanese times, although I was still a teenager, I surprised many with my bravery. I was a guerrilla courier. I brought food and medicine to their hiding places. I gave first aid to the wounded. When I grew up, I helped in the campaign of the union. I spoke at meetings. But now, Mando, I can't sleep well at night . . .'

'Puri, you're not a coward. Your resolve has not weakened, but . . .'

'But what . . .' Puri searched his eyes for the answer.

'Your heart feels a new emotion.'

'Mando!'

'Yes, Puri, my love for you is not a stone flung into the desert.'

'Not a stone flung into the desert,' Puri repeated softly to herself.

'Is it not true, Puri?'

Puri bowed her head, then she raised her face. Mando held her gaze.
Mando took Puri's hand, and its warmth gave him all the courage, all
the energy he needed.

Later, she asked what Mando thought of Dr Sabio's suggestion that
she should take up domestic science as a special student.

'Good. Of course, you have graduated from political science.'

'You're mocking me,' Puri said.

'I mean, you know much about housekeeping and earning a
living, also about citizenship. You will attend classes because you're
here anyway, and to supplement your knowledge. You have learnt
political science from your experiences in the farmers' movement,
their teachings, goals and strategies in the struggle, whether against the
Japanese or the landlord. For example, the relationship between politics
and economy. Because while their lives influence the decisions of the
policymakers, their decisions also shape the economy. We see this every
day, everywhere. We see it at the plantation, in the rice bowl that is
Central Luzon, in the teeming cities, in the mostly useless Congress . . .'

'I have ideas about political science, about the government and its
branches and its relation to the people and the country. I have heard
of modern political economy, of capital and labour, wages and profit.
About domestic science, I know how to sew and mend, cook rice,
sour tamarind soup and chicken stewed in soy sauce and vinegar . . .
Isn't that enough?' Puri smiled and raised her eyebrows, waiting for
Mando's answer.

'Very good,' he said heartily. 'You'll be not only a good wife, but
an ideal mother.'

'And how about Dolly Montero?' Puri shot the unexpected question.

'I don't remember that name any more,' Mando. 'In my heart are
written only four letters: P-U-R-I.'

LXV

Mando's and Puri's hearts were full of joy when they separated at the girls' dormitory. More than at any of their other earlier meetings, Puri got clear answers to her doubts and worries. Mando loved only her. Although he did not get a categorical answer because of her inborn modesty, Puri showed her feelings in various ways. A girl's love cannot be hidden. As the saying goes, 'One does not have to declare or announce what can be seen from one's actions and looks.'

Of the two, it was Puri who was unsure that Mando would be faithful. Mando was confident, because only Danoy was his serious rival. Even Danoy had waved the white flag when he saw that the bright and handsome Mando Plaridel seemed to be the prince who would awaken the sleeping princess of the fields.

Puri was happy to hear Mando say that Dolly Montero had been erased from his memory. Nothing was engraved in his heart but only Puri's name and image.

As he had done earlier, Mando drove leisurely on his way home. It was only ten in the evening. He was still full from the heavy dinner, and he had no other urgent business to attend to.

He would pass by the *Kampilan* and probably see Magat and Andres about their paper's campaign and the disorder in Central Luzon. Mando was aware that in addition to the threats, the *Kampilan* had been the talk of the town. The usual question was: 'Have you read the

402

Kampilan?' This happened in coffee shops, barber shops, marketplaces, offices and schools.

Mando smiled when he overheard this. He knew that they were just beginning. As soon as the radio and TV stations were inaugurated, things would really jump. Then they would see how thick the hides of the enemies of truth were.

Mando's car was moving slowly when he reached a dark section. The moon seemed to have closed her sleepy eyes. The road became darker because of the shadows of the big trees on both sides.

Suddenly, Mando almost hit a vehicle that was parked in the middle of the road. Had he not quickly swerved and stepped on the brakes, he would have met with a serious accident.

Mando stopped and got out. He saw that the stalled vehicle was a Jeep. Two men were bent over the motor, which was exposed, and were tinkering with something. A third man walked towards him.

'It stopped, Maestro,' he greeted Mando.

'That was close,' Mando answered.

'It stopped in the middle, Maestro,' the man repeated. 'Can you help me?'

The man looked intently at Mando and his car and stared at the number.

Mando went over the Jeep. The two men looked up.

'What's the trouble?' asked Mando.

'I don't know; the connection seems to have been cut off.'

'Don't you have a flashlight?' Mando asked, bending toward the motor.

'Here.' One of the men held a flashlight. However, instead of pointing the flashlight towards the motor, he hit Mando's head with it.

But Mando had not come to the Jeep like an innocent child. He was already suspicious from the start. The Jeep stopping in the middle of the road at that time and place while he was passing was not just a coincidence. Those men were after something. But just the same, he stopped and got off instead of remaining in his car and driving off.

But his eyes were open and his senses were alert. He didn't like the faces and looks of the three strangers. Although their action didn't give them away at first, Mando's intuition had warned him.

Senator Maliwanag's reminder flashed through his mind.

'Bring a bodyguard whenever you go out.' He had just shrugged his shoulders, but he knew it was not a joke.

Now it had come to fruition. And he was alone.

But Mando was always ready. He had a purpose in asking for a flashlight. Mando quickly dodged so that the man missed his mark. The flashlight broke on the motor. There was no time to explain. Quickly, Mando turned and hit the man with the flashlight, hitting him squarely on the jaw. The flashlight was flung afar.

Mando turned to the next man. The man tried to wrestle with Mando. He was shorter but well-built. But using his skill in judo and karate, Mando pressed the shorter man's Adam's apple. When he was about to push him, Mando looked back. The third man, the one who had approached him first, was carrying a gun. He seemed to be just waiting for Mando to be free of his companion, who he was wrestling with him.

'Coward,' Mando shouted so that the man would lose his cool.

As he wrestled with the second man, the third man pulled the trigger. Mando felt a fire blaze by his side. Suddenly, the second man's vice-like grip loosened, and his body sagged. The bullet, which had whizzed by Mando, had gone cleanly through the other man's chest and got embedded in his heart. The man's eyes stared lifelessly when Mando let go. Both of them had blood on their bodies.

The gunman was dumbfounded. Mando took advantage of this and went for him. But the man got over his surprise and fear. His trembling fingers pulled the Colt's trigger. Once more, a gunshot roared. Mando grabbed the gunman and pinned him down like a nail caught in a wrench.

Mando was as strong as he was in his younger days in the Sierra Madre mountains, not afraid of the Japanese, the shark, the criminal Martin, and others against whom he had pitted his strength. He tightened his grip until the man's skin turned black and blue and became swollen. The gun fell, and the man tottered, as if he had been squeezed by a python.

The man who was hit by Mando's fist regained consciousness and tried to crawl away. But before he could get far, Mando ordered him to lie face down, or get shot. Mando held the Colt that the third man had dropped.

Mando fired two shots upwards to get other people's attention. Meanwhile, the new moon shone again on the bloody view of a corpse, another man sprawled, and a third one lying face down with his hands clasped on his nape. The last two were alive.

Mando lit a cigarette as he looked at the scene. He thought that if he had just been a bold publisher and not an experienced fighter, he would surely now be the corpse, instead of this unfortunate gangster.

Two police patrol cars rushed to the scene. They found Mando sitting, pressing a handkerchief on a bleeding wound on his right shoulder, a newly lit cigarette between his lips, and a revolver in his right hand. The loss of blood had weakened him, but he did not take his eyes off the two prostrate men.

The law enforcers helped Mando into the police car. While Mando was being rushed to the hospital, the two gangsters were taken by the other car to the police headquarters, and the dead man to the morgue.

LXVI

Mando's wound was not fatal, but he had to undergo surgery for it. The bullet was embedded in his shoulder blade. The wound on his side could easily be treated.

That same night, Magat and Andres rushed to the hospital. Dr Sabio came as soon as he heard the news. After learning that the publisher was out of danger, Andres returned to the office. The morning edition of the *Kampilan* should banner the news about the attempt on Mando's life.

Magat and Dr Sabio stayed in the hospital's lobby during the operation. They waited until Mando was brought back to his room. According to the doctor, he should stay in the hospital for about two weeks.

The professor and Magat analysed the root cause of the violence against Mando.

'He has no personal enemies,' Magat said. 'For sure, this attack was not personal.'

'There's no doubt about that,' Dr Sabio said. 'His enemies are all those people whom the *Kampilan* had written about. But those who tried to kill him were only hired men.'

'As long as evil is widespread, those who do good are in danger,' Magat said.

'This is true,' said the professor. 'Mando, you, Senator Maliwanag— you are all playing with fire.'

'And you too, Dr Sabio,' Magat added.

'Hasn't Mang Tomas already paid with his life? The fight will just turn out to be more violent.'

'We won't stop until they're defeated,' Magat said with force.

'And while those in the wrong do not retreat,' said Dr Sabio.

'What's the use of living in a society where evil reigns?' said the former guerrilla leader. 'We had driven away the Japanese, but evil remained. Now, Filipinos themselves are fighting against each other, doing evil unto each other.'

Then they pinpointed who would gain from Mando's death. Who had reason to hate him enough to have him killed?

Magat told Dr Sabio about the heated argument between Don Segundo Montero and Mando. The millionaire landlord and head of the smuggling syndicate learnt that neither his gold nor the beauty of his daughter could change Mando's mind. Mando had let Dolly's father know that he would go on supporting the campaign, which went against Montero's interests. This must have convinced him that if Mando would not listen to reason, then it was up to him . . . There were other, more effective means.

'That group will stop at nothing to remove any obstacle,' said Dr Sabio, after hearing Magat's story.

'They are even worse than criminals,' Magat said, clenching his fists.

'To think that those people are thought of as honourable and regarded highly in society,' said the president of Freedom University. He added, 'They are the worst birds of prey.'

'Idols with feet of clay,' Magat added. 'But their days are numbered.'

'I wonder until when they can do these dark deeds,' Dr Sabio said.

They stopped only when they saw Mando being wheeled out of the operating room. A doctor and two nurses transferred him to his bed in a private room.

The patient was awake but not allowed to move or talk. After a while, Dr Sabio made a sign that he was leaving. Magat stayed to watch Mando. A private nurse had been assigned, but Magat decided not to leave his friend. He knew that the plotters would not rest if they learnt that Mando had survived.

Mando had a fever and was restless the whole night. Magat didn't sleep a wink.

The next morning, Dr Sabio returned with Puri and Pastor. It was only that morning when the professor had told Puri about the incident. She insisted on going to the hospital right away. They fetched Pastor. Tata Matias was already told what had happened, but he was only going to be brought to the hospital once Mando could talk. They reassured the old man that his foster son was not in critical condition.

Puri had already forgotten her shyness. When she entered Mando's room, she sat on the side of the bed and held his hand. The young man opened his eyes, and his pale lips smiled slightly. He saw that her eyes glistened with tears.

Andres came with Iman. He brought a copy of the *Kampilan* with news of the attempt on the publisher's life. Because of the printing deadline, they were unable to include the more explosive report from the police that the incident was a plot to kill Mando Plaridel. The investigation showed that the slain man and two captured men were civilian guards at the Montero Plantation. They had also revealed the name of the mastermind!

'Our suspicions were correct,' Dr Sabio told Magat after Andres told them about the investigation done by the Manila police. Later, two members of the police department went to the hospital. They confirmed that the two men who had shot Mando signed a confession.

Senator Maliwanag came visiting that day, together with Rubio and some other friends. Old Matias also came, but Pastor later brought him home, after he had seen Mando and had been assured that he would be fine. The old man was very mad, but he just gritted his teeth.

'Lord, please don't let anything happen to him,' he whispered.

Senator Maliwanag shook his head and reminded the patient of his advice to have bodyguards.

'Perhaps, when I go home,' Mando said softly and secretly motioned towards Puri and winked. The senator smiled. Puri, who was talking to a nurse, was unaware of the situation.

'If you need bodyguards, just tell me,' Rubio said. 'If it's force they want, then we are ready for them.'

On the other hand, Mando did not receive any message from Dolly, not even a telephone call or a letter. She had not yet returned from Baguio.

Puri asked her father's permission to stay at the hospital to help Mando's private nurse. Pastor agreed, but Mando would not hear of it. He said he would be happy to have Puri visit him every day, but he didn't want her to waste the time meant for her studies. Mando was pleased with this new proof of Puri's love, but he felt she should not stay. Anyway, there were doctors and nurses assigned to him.

'Thanks, Puri. If I were seriously ill . . . but I'm not. Use your time for your studies, because you're pressed for time.'

She did not insist any more. She wanted to show Mando that she was ready to look after him. She forgot that they were not yet engaged. She didn't care any more what others would say about her offer.

Nevertheless, as Puri was leaving after the others had already gone, she showed some reproach.

'Are you coming tomorrow?' asked Mando.

'Didn't I want to stay? But you don't want me to. Of course, your nurse works hard and is pretty, too.'

'Do you really love me?' Mando asked, ignoring Puri's words. 'You're not answering . . . Do you really love me?'

'Do you still have doubts?' The girl smiled and bowed her head, then she walked out.

At that moment, Mando felt completely well. He wanted to get up and run after her. But the nurse took his temperature and observed that it had risen.

'You are tired because you have too many visitors,' said his doctor when he saw the nurse's report.

But only Mando knew why his temperature had suddenly risen.

That night, after dinner, when Mando was alone, an unexpected guest came.

'Danoy!'

It was Danoy, the missing leader of the farmers. Danoy said that he was staying in a remote village outside the planation and was just observing everything. He said he had joined forces with the outlaws.

They had heard of the attack on Mando. So he secretly came to find out how he was. He was relieved to see that Mando was fine.

Danoy would return to the village that night.

'We shall settle our accounts with them,' he said grimly. 'I am just biding my time.'

When the nurse returned to Mando's room, the mysterious caller was gone.

LXVII

Within a few days of hearing the news about the failed attempt on Mando's life, the small circle of prominent people fled Manila almost simultaneously. Only recently, the group had met at the Baguio cottage of the Monteros. Was it only a coincidence, or were they hiding something? This coincidence did not escape the eyes of the publisher's friends. Magat and Dr Sabio discussed it.

Senator Botin flew overseas. The congressional session was over. It had really become the bad habit of congressmen to follow up the hundred days of idle meetings in Congress with a junket overseas. Thus they travelled at the government's expense with some kind of excuse. But Senator Botin was not considered among the distinguished lawmakers who were sent to represent the country at international conferences. Just the same, he left and said he would be gone for several months.

Governor Doblado took a vacation in Hong Kong. His invalid wife had died, which brought him two good fortunes: money and freedom. They were childless. Since he became a widower, Doblado seldom went home to his house in Quezon City. He just stayed two or three times a week in the town next to the capital.

Doblado was not a stranger to the house of Tindeng and her two children. When Doña Ninay was still alive, he used to have lunch and rest there after office hours. The youthful Tindeng was said to be related to Doña Ninay. But her neighbours, especially those who

411

hung around the nearby store, said that the relationship between the playboy governor and the middle-aged woman was not that between an uncle and his niece. The two children, they were sure, were born from this affair. And when the governor was released from his marriage, whom would he fear? Now he could expose everything, for all the world to see.

But when Doblado went to Hong Kong, he didn't take Tindeng along. Among the passengers on his plane were Doña Julia and Dolly. Was this just a mere coincidence? For the new widower and the youthful matron, this was a rare chance. Before Doña Julia married Don Segundo Montero, her boyfriend was Oscar Doblado. The only obstacles were Oscar's parents, who had wanted him to finish his studies first. Montero saw his chance. He won over Julia's father, and so she married the man who became Dolly's father.

'Oscar and I had gone the whole way, Dolly,' Doña Julia had said when she discovered her daughter's affair with Lieutenant Whitey. Dolly had developed a fondness for unripe fruits when the American pilot was assigned to Iwo Jima. To console her daughter, the mother revealed a similar thing she had done when she was young.

To make Dolly feel better, Doña Julia added: 'I told you of my experience to show you that what fate does not mean to be, won't be. You weren't meant for Colonel Moto, or for Lieutenant Whitey. Why should you crack your head over this? Are they the only men in this world? You are young and beautiful. You won't lack suitors.'

And the two had gone to Hong Kong without any noise. But their present trip was for a different reason. Now they were going on a tour and also to do some shopping. Although Dolly was hurt by her break-up with Mando, her earlier experience had given her strength. She had taken pills so she would not become pregnant. In Paris, the City of Lights, a girl could learn anything she wished to know.

From Baguio, Pong Tua-Son went to Manila and then flew to Hong Kong to supervise the construction of a modern building. He invited Doña Julia and Dolly to show off his newest architectural masterpiece. The two women would be guests of the Chinese mestizo who had long been lighting candles to the gods so that the Montero heiress would agree to his proposal. From the coquettish glances of Doña Julia to Governor Doblado and their exchange of private jokes, especially when Dolly was not around, it was clear that they would not be lonely in Hong Kong.

Their earlier affair would likely have a sequel.

Meanwhile, General Bayoneta suddenly went to the Visayas and Mindanao to 'investigate rampant smuggling in the south'. Sea traffic was supposed to be open from the ports between Jolo in southern Philippines and Borneo in northern Malaysia. From Jolo, the smuggled goods were then distributed in Zamboanga, Cebu and Iloilo, among other southern cities. Naturally, they also reached Metro Manila.

Although his real aim was to avoid the troubles in Manila, he also wanted to know the new groups of smugglers who were lording it over in the south. For a long time, the syndicate ran by his father-in-law, Son Tua, and Montero, almost monopolized the field. Now, everything was finished. Therefore, there were now other officials—both political and military—who were helping themselves to the pot. There was no news about Montero and Son Tua. They could not be found either in Manila or in Baguio. It was said that they were just resting. But word got around that, actually, they had gone into hiding.

The newspapers, including the *Kampilan*, did not mention it, but Magat and Dr Sabio observed that the group took flight because of the failed attempt to kill Mando. Perhaps, they would not be so uneasy if Mando had been killed, and his attackers had not been caught. After all, the dead don't talk. But Mando was alive and safe, and their hired killers sang everything to the police.

Mando was out of danger. He might not have to stay for two weeks in the hospital, as the doctor had earlier said. After a few days, he could already sit up, propped by pillows, and have the nurse read to him. Sometimes, he would listen to music on the radio.

But he often had visitors. Every day, Magat and Dr Sabio never failed to see him. Rubio and Tata Pastor also came. Mando knew the latest events, the progress of the investigation on his assailants, the flight of Montero's syndicate, the disappearance of Son Tua and Don Segundo.

He showed no signs of being hurt by his complete break-up with Dolly, not even to his confidant, Magat.

Only a sigh escaped his lips.

But when Puri came every afternoon, he could not hide the glow of joy in his eyes, and the colour that came to his pallid cheeks. He was bored when Puri was away. It was not the skill of his special nurse or the doctor that healed him. It was the girl's presence, like a sheen of light in his room. When Puri came, Mando seemed well. He asked to be propped up on the pillows and would talk lovingly to Puri. He asked about her studies, her life at the dormitory, her needs and problems. Puri would sweetly remind him that she was the visitor and not the patient.

For his part, Dr Sabio brought some books and Andres, some magazines. On the small table beside Mando's bed were copies of *Reflections of the Revolution of our Time* by Harold J. Laski, *The Atomic Age* by Bertrand Russell, *Toward Freedom* by Jawaharlal Nehru, *The Good Society* by Walter Lippmann, *Residencia en la Tierra* by Pablo Neruda, some works by Jean-Paul Sartre, and the latest editions of *Science and Society* and *Dissent*.

Mando looked at the books and smiled at Puri.

'How can a sick man read all of those?' He shook his head.

'Perhaps Dr Sabio wants you to read them when you get well . . .'

'Maybe. The truth is I lack time to read. What can I do? I have to work day and night.'

'Do you want me to read to you?' said Puri. She was about to get up from the side of Mando's bed.

'No, let's just talk.'

'Aren't you tired of talking to me? I'm here every day, and we have been talking all the time.'

'Please call me "dear",' the patient asked.

'Answer my question first. Don't you get fed up?'

'If I were a poet, Puri, I would tell you that the butterfly would tire of sipping the flower's nectar, the stars would tire of shining in the sky, but I would not tire of talking to you.'

'But what shall we talk about now?'

'Many things, Puri. There are many things I have not told you about my life.'

'Would they change my feelings for you?'

'I don't know. Maybe not, but I don't want to have any secrets from you.'

Mando was thinking of telling Puri who he was before everything changed, and he became Mando Plaridel.

LXVIII

One late afternoon, Puri was pushing a wheelchair on the hospital grounds. Then, she stopped before a wooden bench under a shady tree.

'Let's stay here,' the girl said, looking at the patient. 'Aren't you tired?' she asked with love in her eyes.

Mando smiled. This was the first time he had left his room. They brought him down from his room by elevator, and the nurse and Puri brought out the wheelchair to the garden.

'You're the one who might be tired. Even if I have lost weight, I'm still heavy.'

Puri rubbed her arm and smiled.

'I'm used to hard work. Don't forget, you're with a country girl.'

Then she helped Mando on to the wooden bench. She cleaned the seat, and they sat side by side.

The golden breeze was cool and gentle.

For some moments, they were silent. Mando was watching two birds chasing each other on the branches of a tree while Puri was looking at the golden rays of the afternoon sun, blending in radiance with the green of the grass. Mando was thinking that he and Puri would be like the lovebirds, not only playing among the branches but also building a special nest and living there happily. On the other hand, Puri was thinking that the breeze, combined with the colour of the grass, created a new loveliness like their love. She felt like a new person—a being pure, filled with sweetness and joy.

Puri was eager to hear Mando's secret, which he had mentioned the day before. But Puri felt it was not right to ask him about it. Anyway, Mando did not keep her in suspense any more.

'Puri, it's time you knew this,' said Mando, breaking the silence. 'You should know who I really am.'

Puri quickly looked up and stared at his face. She could see no one but Mando Plaridel. Her lips parted slightly, but she said nothing. Her eyes showed her bewilderment.

'I am Andoy,' Mando said.

Puri was startled, although at first the name meant nothing. 'Andoy?'

'Yes, Andoy, the son of Tata Pastor's sister.'

'My cousin!' she said. 'Can this be true?'

Mando placed his right hand on hers, then told her all his experiences.

He recalled his family's difficult life under the Monteros, his life as an orphan, and a servant whom Don Segundo sent to school. He narrated his escape when the Japanese occupied Manila, his flight to the mountains, the dangers and hardships he encountered among the guerrillas, his meeting old Tata Matias and his finding of Simoun's treasures. Puri already knew about his experiences since he first went to the Montero Plantation and about his travels in foreign lands.

Puri withdrew her hand and said with hesitation, 'I should be happy to know you, the real you, because Tatang and I have no other relative except you, but . . .' She stopped.

'We are first cousins,' Mando finished for her.

'Why did you keep it a secret for so long?' There was a trace of reproach in her sad voice. She felt that if only she had known about this earlier, she would not have fallen love with the only child of her father's sister.

'For two reasons, Puri,' said Mando. 'First, because my story had to be kept a secret until I had finished my mission; and second, because I fell in love with you the first time I saw you.'

'But . . .'

'Are you changing your mind, my dearest?' Mando took her hand again.

Puri looked into the distance. The two birds playing among the branches were gone, and the golden glow had disappeared from the grass. Instead, the green had turned to grey as darkness began to fall all round them.

Puri was sure that her feelings would never change even with what she had just learnt. If Mando was Andoy, what then? To her, Mando was Mando and no other man. This was the man she had known from the start, the man she would continue to love.

'But how about Tatang?' Puri said, not knowing what to answer.

'I shall tell him everything.'

When Pastor learnt that Mando was his only sister's son, he embraced him and thanked God for the young man's good fortune.

'No wonder I felt drawn to you at once,' he said, very delighted indeed.

'That's why I called you Tata Pastor right away.'

When Mando mentioned his love for Puri, the face of the old man changed. He thought for a long time.

'What will happen to both of you if you should be separated?' he asked after a while.

'It would be a punishment we could not bear.'

'Of course,' Pastor said. 'Who else would care for each other?'

Mando's eyes showed his gratitude to the older man.

'Don't worry, I shall talk to Puri,' Pastor added. 'I can't give her happiness.'

After a few more days, Mando left the hospital.

* * *

When he was stronger, he invited Pastor and Puri, Dr Sabio, Magat, and Andres to a gathering. He told his guests that the gathering was not only to celebrate his recovery but also to plan a programme that had been his goal since he came down from the Sierra Madre mountains after the war.

'Tata Matias knows about this,' said Mando, looking at the old man seated in one part of the living room.

Mando then told them of a comprehensive programme for education, the press and information, research and agriculture, and other branches of knowledge to help society.

'We have funds for all of these. We shall not use these for business or politics but for humanitarianism. We shall not work singly or by twos or tens. We shall form a corporation that shall manage and implement our programme through several branches.'

Mando said that money used selfishly was like a monster that preyed on animals and fish, but did not nourish life. He recalled what the immensely wealthy steel magnate Andrew Carnegie once said—that the time would come when one would be ashamed to die a rich man.

Included under the extensive corporation were the *Kampilan*, the radio-TV station, Freedom University, and the plantation, which they planned to buy.

He asked Dr Sabio to explain the long-range programme of the university on studies related to common welfare. It pledged to develop intelligent and nationalistic young people who are educated and prepared to succeed in the scientific age.

'The university will never become a diploma mill,' said Dr Sabio. 'We shall support students who will become the pillars of the nation.'

Mando told them the findings of the last investigation by a congressional committee headed by Senator Maliwanag. It was discovered that Montero Plantation and other vast agricultural lands had been bought by the government from the Mitras and other former owners. But after some years and because of schemes of the greedy and the ignorance of the farmers who had been given the land, the partitioned lands were recovered by the rich.

This case would be brought to court. Based on strong evidence, the government was expected to confiscate these lands. Although Don Segundo had bought Montero Plantation, the sale was illegal. He didn't have to be repaid, but he would likely be taxed for his excessive profits from the plantation under his management.

At this point, Dr Sabio explained why he did not follow through with his university's plan to buy the plantation from Segundo Montero. Senator Maliwanag had mentioned the congressional investigation of the former friar lands to him. Mando and Dr Sabio had agreed to wait until the property had been reclaimed by the government.

'Therefore,' Mando concluded, 'we might buy the land from the government itself, supervise it for the tenants, and contribute to the boon of agriculture in our country.'

Everyone approved the plan that Mando presented.

Before they began their dinner, Pastor asked permission to make an announcement.

'I am honoured to announce that my only daughter, Puri, and Mando Plaridel will be married soon.'

The guests received the news happily and they shook hands with the betrothed. Tata Matias went to Puri and affectionately kissed her on the cheek.

'I have no doubt you and Mando will be very happy,' he told the radiant girl.

After the other guests had already left, Mando gave Maria Clara's medallion to his fiancée. Mando told her the story and value of the jewel. 'It was supposed to have brought bad luck to its first owners,' he said. 'But I'm not superstitious. Take care of it because it is precious and because of its link to the history of Maria Clara, Huli, Simoun and Cabesang Tales.'

'I shall value this as a token of a past that should always live in our memory and as a symbol of our love,' Puri said. Her face seemed to glow.

LXIX

Early one morning, two children who had been gathering wood were horrified to see a corpse hanging upside down from the branch of an ancient tree. The sun's rays had hardly pierced through the thick woods between the Montero Plantation and the village.

The frightened children ran back to town and told the first person they met about what they had seen. Right away, many farmers rushed to the spot. They exclaimed when they saw the corpse. Although the man's face was black, his red eyes staring, the tongue caught between his teeth and his jaws rigid, they could still identify him.

'Captain Pugot!' one of them shouted.

'Yes, it's Captain Pugot,' confirmed the others.

Some sighed deeply, while others made the sign of the cross. The women offered prayers.

A farmer hurried back to town to report to the village lieutenant, who would then report the incident to the authorities.

One wanted to cut off the rope binding the feet and tied to a branch, but he was stopped from doing so. They decided to let the law enforcers take over.

The corpse wore a khaki uniform and had boots on and a crew cut, Japanese-style. Instead of his former ferocity and usual sneer, now pain and grief were frozen on his face.

'At last,s he has paid for his sins,' said one of the older farmers.

There was no need to explain the fate of the overseer. If the people had anyone in mind, they just kept their mouths closed. No one dared offer an opinion on who drew the curtain on the bloody story of the notorious Japanese spy, who had earned a frightful reputation. His record as a collaborator was reiterated when he became the overseer of the Montero Plantation.

But in life as well as in death, Pugot was just a small fish. The noise over his death was drowned out by the sensational exposé of the powerful smuggling syndicate, which included many of the big fish in politics, business and society. The *Kampilan* splashed their names and photographs on the front page—Don Segundo Montero, General Bayoneta, Governor Doblado, Son Tua. There was also an insinuation that Senator Botin, who was travelling overseas, might also be involved.

The charges against the syndicate were rather serious. Some were also charged with individual offences. Montero was charged for the plot to kill Mando Plaridel. Also involved were Captain Pugot and the hired men who had to turn state witnesses. Son Tua faced possible deportation for his illegal businesses.

The *Kampilan* published a hard-hitting editorial on the sudden fall of these people.

> Like Antaeus, the preying birds have a hidden weakness. The moment they are separated from their perch of deceit, they can be hit by the bullets of truth, and their beaks and claws can no longer tear apart their hapless victims.
>
> Once, we said in this editorial: Gone is the cursed creature using the disguise of the Eagle, the Vulture, the Owl, and the Vampire Bat. He has left his descendants and those of his tools and accomplices. They can be found not only in the mountains, but also on the plains, in the fields, at sea, in towns and cities, in large buildings, among high government officials, in important enterprises where their sharp beaks, teeth, and claws gobble up lives and suck their victims' blood.
>
> But one day, no longer the mysterious hand of fate will be writing on the wall, as with Belshazzar, but the hands of the oppressed will give them justice. We shall live to witness that day.

Who knows if the editorial of the courageous *Kampilan* might have been prophetic? Its warnings swiftly came to pass.

One night, as the millionaire Son Tua was returning to Manila from Baguio, his car was stopped by a group of armed men in a secluded spot in Central Luzon. They kidnapped the wealthy Chinese, but let his driver go. The driver reported this to the authorities.

'They didn't look like bandits,' said the driver to the Philippine Constabulary. 'They looked more like farmers than criminals. They didn't know me but they took my master. I heard their leader say, "Son Tua, you have many sins against this country."'

The Philippine Constabulary suspected that the ones who had killed Captain Pugot were also behind the kidnapping of Son Tua.

After a few days, three famous Manila doctors rushed to Baguio. They had been fetched to examine Don Segundo Montero, who had become paralysed. He was unconscious, but his life was not in danger because his heartbeat was normal. But should he live, he would just be a vegetable, according to the doctors' diagnosis.

It was learnt that Don Segundo was on the phone when he had had his attack. He was talking to his lawyer in Manila about the cases that had piled up against him. The most serious were the unsuccessful attempt on Mando Plaridel's life and his being the head of the smuggling syndicate of arms, jewellery and blue-seal cigarettes. He also wanted to know if the *Kampilan* could be charged with libel.

'Why wasn't that beast killed?' were Don Segundo's last words before he suddenly collapsed.

Aboard the first flight to Manila from Hong Kong were Doña Julia, Dolly and Pong, the architect. They returned as soon as they received the cable about Son Tua's kidnapping and Don Segundo's heart attack.

Meanwhile, there was no respite from the troubles at the Montero Plantation and the nearby villages. The conflict was worse than during the war. The Filipino soldiers and civilian guards seemed to be more cruel than the Japanese. The bloody abuses were links in a long chain starting from the day Captain Pugot took over as the overseer. A fire broke out at the Montero Plantation at about the same time as the workers' meeting at Plaza Miranda. Then the farmers and their leaders were arrested, jailed and starved for several days. Mang Tomas, a veteran farmer's leader, was killed. To avenge his death, two civilian guards were beheaded. But the revenge of Captain Pugot was more brutal: a raid on a whole village where even women and children were not spared, and the innocent and defenceless were shot. Finally, the cruel Captain Pugot paid with his life. He was found hanging upside down from the branch of an old tree in the forest, like a new Judas who died not by his own bloody hands but at the hands of those whom he had sinned against.

Like a fire in the heat of summer, the flames did not stop after burning down a group of houses at its source, but spread, devouring the whole area because of the strong wind. The flames could not be stopped until everything had turned to coal and ashes.

The death of Captain Pugot did not restore peace. Those who sought justice did not believe that he was the root cause of all the troubles at the plantation. There were other skirmishes between the civilian guards and the farmers, and casualties piled up on both sides. The farmers resorted to their guerrilla tactics of surprise attack, attack-retreat. Thus, they were able to collect weapons and sow fear in the hearts of their oppressors.

Later on, the farmers joined forces with the outlaws, and they occupied the Montero Plantation. By then, the plantation had lain almost idle, because Captain Pugot had been killed, and his notorious troops had fled. Don Segundo could no longer appoint a new overseer, because he had wilted to a vegetable on his bed.

'Let us look after the plantation so that it won't revert to a wilderness,' said Danoy. 'The land should be used to serve those who till and care for it.'

A large group of farmers now prepared to work on the vast plantation and the nearby villages—former tenants, people who used to be peaceful and obedient, but had been driven to the forests and mountains by the landowners and officials. Now they got ready to defend their right to work and live by the sweat of their brow.

The armed troops were alarmed at the report of the provincial commander.

'The rebellion of the dissidents in Central Luzon has spread,' came the report from the provincial capital, which was quickly picked up by the newspapers and the radio.

'Banditry and anarchy reign,' said an additional news piece.

It was worse than the signal for an impending tropical storm.

'This kind of propaganda is an omen that the Army intends to solve the social problem with an iron fist,' Mando said, as he and Magat were having coffee at the *Kampilan*'s canteen.

LXX

Mando's fears were not unfounded. The next day, he received a telegram from the president, inviting him to a meeting at the palace. He learnt that Senator Maliwanag and Dr Sabio had also been summoned. The telegram did not state the agenda.

They guessed that it was connected with the latest news from the army in Central Luzon.

More than once, the president had warned against so-called instigators of the farmers. Although no names were mentioned, the three instigators were called radical leaders.

Several times, the palace had attacked the activities of an 'ambitious senator' and his allies, 'a university professor' and a publisher of a radical newspaper.

The three men agreed to meet in Mando's office on the same day. Senator Maliwanag and Dr Sabio arrived together late in the afternoon.

'The president's telegram is an ultimatum,' the senator began.

'What shall we do?' asked Mando.

'We have to face the lion in his den,' answered Maliwanag.

'First, let's analyse the president's intentions,' Dr Sabio said, 'and let us give a tentative answer, an analysis of a serious problem, and the steps the administration should take to solve these problems peacefully.'

'Good,' said the legislator. 'We shall not be accused of criticizing without proposing a remedy. Perhaps no one wants trouble, except General Bayoneta.'

The three brought a prepared statement when they went to the office of the president that day.

When they were already seated, the chief executive spoke. 'I invited you, gentlemen, because the situation is critical. If you don't help me, what I wish to avoid might happen.'

He glanced at the *Spoliarium* by the painter Juan Luna on the wall of the office. The painting showed gladiators dragging corpses in the Roman arena.

'I don't want trouble and I don't want to use an iron fist.' The president looked at each of his three guests. 'That is why I called you. Here is the army's report.'

He handed the report to Senator Maliwanag, who looked at it and passed it on to Mando and Dr Sabio. The confidential report stated that serious trouble would erupt at any time. At the end, their names were mentioned as instigators.

'This report is biased, Mr President,' the lawmaker said.

'My aim is peace and order,' the president said, ignoring Maliwanag's protest. 'If the army would have its way, you know its solution. The authority of the government should be obeyed. I don't want it to reach that point, so I invited you.'

'On that point, Mr President,' said Senator Maliwanag, 'perhaps we have no quarrel. Every good Filipino is against disorder. We want to help, because we know that in every disorder, the first to be hurt is the nation and the government. We are the nation, and the government is us. So it is everyone's duty to be concerned with peace and order.'

The senator presented their paper to the president.

'This is a short paper that we prepared,' he said. 'Sir, here is a list of problems, the grievances and petitions of the farmers and labourers, and, according to our studies, effective solutions, if you will agree and accept them.'

The president scanned the pages.

'Some petitions are reasonable,' he conceded. 'But most cannot be granted right away. They are neither in our hands nor in the hands of the government.' Then he re-read a page. 'Besides, it includes a warning, a threat. The government cannot be threatened, gentlemen . . .'

'We have done nothing but let you know the feelings of the oppressed,' Mando said. 'No more, no less. It is different from the army's report, sir.'

'Very well, then. This village school is okay.' And he slowly looked over the petitions. 'This one, construct roads in the villages, okay. This one, put up a hospital, later; we shall look for funds.'

He stopped and stared at his guests.

'This one, ban civilian guards,' he continued. 'On the one hand, the landowners' rights should be protected. This one, remove the Philippine Constabulary from the vicinity of the plantation. Gentlemen, it is the government's duty to keep peace and order. And this, take the plantation, expropriate, and divide it among the farmers. Our government is democratic, not authoritarian; here, the landlord and the tenant have equal rights. The law does not forbid a citizen from owning a piece of land, or a whole plantation.'

'Then, sir,' Dr Sabio tried to cut in.

'I advise you to go to the villages in Central Luzon, especially the Montero Plantation. Many will listen to you. They are ready to obey. Talk to the farmers. Advise them. Tell them to be more patient, because my administration is not sleeping on the job. I am doing everything under the law. I care for them; my heart is with the poor, because they are among the five million who had elected me to this high office, but I am not God, nor a dictator . . .'

'They have been forgiving and sacrificing for too long,' said Senator Maliwanag. 'They are on a plantation that has amassed and is still amassing wealth for the landowner. But they are starving, their wives are sickly, and their children can't go to school.'

'Don't forget that the war has just ended.' The president was evasive. 'The Japanese robbed us for three years, and the returning Americans destroyed everything . . . Don't expect me to restore all of these in two years. Especially without your cooperation.'

'The oppression of the farmers is older than two wars, sir,' Dr Sabio pointed out.

'If they are still disappointed in your administration, no one can say if—' Mando was unable to finish, because the president cut him short.

'I know what you mean,' he said with some heat. 'If the farmers lose their trust in the government, they will take matters into their own hands. That, my administration cannot allow. Mark my words. I don't want to follow the army's advice, but if they don't respect the law . . .'

'Sir, they are fed up with the ways of those in power,' Senator Maliwanag said. 'Promises, threats, more promises, threats, violence. Please change the tune, Mr President. This is a chance to be different from the earlier leaders. Please help the country by acting on its problems. Come down from the palace, go out into the fields and villages; look at their lives and their conditions first-hand; let your feet get muddy on the potholed roads; let the tears of the mothers and children wet your hands . . .'

The senator continued: 'You are said to be surrounded by a *cordon sanitaire* by your staff, by the favoured elite who are only after wealth, position, and personal power. They get you drunk with feast and pomp, they burn incense, they praise your mistakes and shield your eyes from the sad truth.'

The president reluctantly calmed down after the successive arguments from Senator Maliwanag and Mando Plaridel. He rubbed his right hand over his closed eyes before speaking.

'We shall see,' he said slowly, as if talking to himself. 'It appears that the president of a country is the most powerful leader. It appears that he has the power to do whatever he wishes. Ah, sometimes, I want to exchange places with a professor or a publisher.'

He paused a while, ran his hand over the thick pile of papers on his table, then continued. 'But gentlemen, I confess my hands are often tied. You can't imagine the pressure of the various forces and the varied interests. The politicians, the foreigners through their embassies, the newspapers and other mass media, and the citizens themselves. There is also nepotism, the temptation to give jobs to relatives and friends. You know I am not rich, nor am I enriching myself even though I could become a millionaire within twenty-four hours. Oh, Maliwanag, put yourself in my place.' He hit the arm of his tall chair with his right hand in frustration.

'What you said, Mr President,' Mando answered in a sympathetic tone, 'are problems that come with the position. For one who is weak-willed, these are reasons for drawing away from the people. The common people don't come to this palace, and you have not gone to them except during election campaigns. Forgive me, Honourable President, but since we are talking heart-to-heart, your image among the people won't please you, sir.'

'What image?' The chief executive frowned.

'If you'll pardon me, sir, your image is different and far from how your followers have painted you.'

'But my image is good in our press and in the American press.'

'They are using glasses of a different colour,' said Mando.

'Certainly different from the glasses of the *Kampilan* publisher,' the president said mockingly.

'Sir, the *Kampilan* is committed to the truth, not to profit by pleasing those in power. Look at the business enterprises of some foreign publishers. The *Kampilan* does not claim to be the paper of the nation, nor the clarion of freedom and truth. It is known for its daily publication.'

'You were the first to report a planned coup d'état against my administration, weren't you?'

'It's my honour, sir, whereas the other newspapers were mute,' said Mando.

'You'd also heard about the planned coup d'état, Senator Maliwanag, before it was published, didn't you?' the president asked.

'Like a man whose house is burning, Mr President, you are the last to know,' the senator answered enigmatically.

'And where did these traitors come from?' the president gloated. 'Those men said the same thing. My image was ugly. The people were angry with my administration, the nation whose 5 million elected me to this position.' He took a deep breath after repeating his favourite statement about his election. 'What is the suggestion of those close to me? That I should establish a dictatorship. If I were a dictator, many heads would roll in the mud.'

'Maybe the nation will not allow the president to become a dictator,' said Dr Sabio, an expert in political science.

'Even to save the republic?'

'Not for any reason, sir. The aborted coup d'état was plotted by ambitious military men who were instigated by foreign agents. This is common in Latin America. They are easily prodded and bought, but just as easily stopped.'

Mando added, 'When the executive loses his patience because of democracy's problems, he might be tempted to become a dictator. Just like Hitler. For sure, the nation will resist—and revolution will break out. Such a revolution can't be stopped because it is a general uprising of the people and not a coup d'état of a few traitors. The aim of a revolution against you, for example, Mr President, is not only to remove you from office but also to destroy a termite-eaten building and change a system that harbours evil. It aims to establish a new government structure that answers the hopes of the whole nation.'

'You speak boldly, Mr Plaridel,' the president said.

'I want you to feel the gravity of the situation.' Their eyes met.

'You think you are always writing an editorial,' the president said more heatedly.

The dialogue ended. Mando did not answer the insult.

'Señores.' The president broke the silence. He no longer bothered to conceal his anger. 'I called you not to ask for lectures on how I should perform my duties. No one can teach me this. I see that it will be difficult for us to understand each other, because you don't want to help in keeping peace and order. That's up to you. You have read the confidential army report. So don't blame me.'

'Mr President!' protested the three visitors.

The chief executive brushed aside their protest with a wave of his hand.

'Let us put our cards on the table,' he said. 'Either you stop your followers, or accept the consequences.'

'Whose duty is it to stop disorder, ours or yours here in this palace?' asked Senator Maliwanag.

'Are you challenging me?' asked the chief executive.

'Or are you threatening us?' answered the legislator.

'Señores, I wish to avoid bloodshed, but if you . . .' And he stood up, the anger clear in his hard-set jaw.

The three also stood up, red-faced in contrast to the president, whose lips were pale and whose eyes were ablaze. Like a final blow, Senator Maliwanag said these words: 'Honourable President, you're the one who will make the decision. Nevertheless, remember this: the three of us can be killed, a hundred or a thousand farmers can die, but the nation can never be destroyed by those who betray her.'

'I hold the list of traitors to the country and to the government.' The chief executive's voice trembled. 'I am sure they will not escape the punishment of the law. Good morning, Señores.'

His aide entered and was told to lead the guests downstairs. But before Senator Maliwanag left, he said some words in parting.

'Mr President, remember that King Belshazzar did not heed the handwriting on the wall.'

'The moment there is disorder in Central Luzon, I shall suspend the writ of habeas corpus,' shouted the president.

'Stop the waves of the sea first.'

Without a word, the three got into Mando's car and asked to be brought to a restaurant outside Manila.

'Let us eat first before we get arrested,' said the young publisher.

At that moment, on the Montero Plantation and in the neighbouring villages, the farmers were already uneasy. They were talking about the tense situation, so taut like a rubber band stretched from end to end. Many recalled their experiences of fighting with the Japanese during the occupation. They were confident they would not be defeated, and could defend themselves against those who ran roughshod over their rights.

Rubio arrived at the Montero Plantation with a letter from the labourers in Manila and other cities. They said they would not allow their brother farmers to be oppressed and would offer men, money and other needs.

'We are free farmers and labourers who have the right to live as human beings,' said the declaration in part.

Early that afternoon, crowds of farmers and village folk had already gone to the plantation. Pastor lit a torch and set fire to three large effigies, which looked like scarecrows. The faces were those of

Don Segundo Montero, Governor Doblado and General Bayoneta. Being made of rags and straw, the three replicas were soon ablaze and devoured by fire, amid the cheers of the village folk.

'Death to the beasts. May they die like the executioner, Captain Pugot,' shouted the crowd.

'Long live social justice!' echoed the answer.

'Long live the Filipino people!' The chorus was like a country speaking as one.

But their joy was short-lived. Everyone fell silent when they saw what was coming. Without warning, two trucks dashed towards them, filled with soldiers and civilian guards. Close behind rumbled a tank with a long cannon. The feet of the soldiers hardly touched the ground before they rained bullets on the farmers. The three burnt effigies were still smoking.

Like chicks scattered by the gunshots, the surprised farmers and village folk ran at the soldiers' attack. Some sought cover. The few who had weapons were forced to fight—that was better than being killed without defending oneself.

The zealous soldiers who jumped from the two trucks were like tigers chasing mountain cats. The scene simply reenacted similar acts of cruelty in different places in Central Luzon during the Japanese occupation.

The captain, the leader of the soldiers, held a .45 revolver in his right hand and looked fiercely at the dead and wounded farmers lying around him. He counted twenty-seven.

Not one of his soldiers had a scratch.

He went to a prostrate body, turned the head with his boot so it faced upward. He saw that the dead man was Pastor.

The captain was pleased and said, 'Now, it's you, Pastor. Yesterday it was Tomas. Tomorrow, it will be Danoy. Not one of you will remain. Our bullets will wipe out all of you.'

Meanwhile, the earth was stained with the blood of the wounded. Moans filled the very air. But no one came to their aid.

In a secret place outside the city, Mando and Magat met with Rubio and Danoy, the whole night. The first two were brave fighters against the Japanese. The last two were labour leaders in Metro Manila and of the farmers in Central Luzon.

Before they separated at dawn, Mando said, 'Now we shall use all our strength and do everything we can so our nation will be free, and our people will be the masters of their own land. A just democracy, equality before the eyes of law and in opportunities in life. These are our noble goals, and we are ready to offer our lives for them.'

The End

References

Efren R. Abueg, 'Ang Sosyalismo sa Nobelang Tagalog', *In Sampaksaan ng Mga Nobelistang Tagalog* (Quezon City: Ang Aklatan, University of the Philippines, 1974).

Teodoro A. Agoncillo, *A History of the Filipino People* (Quezon City: R.P. Garcia Publishing, 1970).

Aurora E. Batnag (ed.), *Panunuring Pampanitikan: Mga Nagwagi sa Gawad Surian sa Sanaysay* (Manila: Surian ng Wikang Pambansa, 1984).

Andres Cristobal Cruz, *Panata sa Kalayaan ni Ka Amado* (Manila: Keystone Press, 1970).

Jun Cruz Reyes, *Ka Amado* (Quezon City: University of the Philippines Press, 2015).

Alice Guillermo and Charlie Samuya Veric (eds.), *Suri at Sipat: Araling Ka Amado* (Manila: Amado V. Hernandez Resource Center, 2004).

Amado V. Hernandez, *Philippine Labour Demand Justice* (New York: Far East Publishing, 1979).

Caroline S. Hau, *Necessary Fictions: Philippine Literature and the Nation, 1946–1980* (Quezon City: Ateneo de Manila University Press, 2000).

Patricia May B. Jurilla, *Tagalog Bestsellers of the Twentieth Century: A History of the Book in the Philippines* (Quezon City: Ateneo de Manila University Press, 2008).

Thelma B. Kintanar, 'Tracing the Rizal Tradition in the Filipino Novel', *Tenggara*, 25, pp. 80–91.

Eduardo Lachica, *Huk: Philippine Agrarian Society in Revolt* (Manila: Solidaridad Publishing House, 1971).

Bienvenido Lumbera, 'Rehabilitation and New Beginnings: Tagalog Literature Since World War II', *Brown Heritage: Essays on Philippine Cultural Traditions and Literature*, ed. Antonio G. Manuud (Quezon City: Ateneo de Manila University, 1967).

—*Revaluation: Essays on Philippine Literature, Cinema and Popular Culture* (Manila: University of Santo Tomas Press, 1997).

Mallari, *From Domicile to Domain: The Formation of Malay and Tagalog Masterpiece Novels in Post-Independence Malaysia and the Philippines* (Bangi, Malaysia: Penerbit Universiti Kebangsaan Malaysia, 2002).

Edgardo B. Maranan, 'Ang Usapin sa Lupa sa Mga Nobela nina Amado V. Hernandez, Rogelio Sikat at Dominador Mirasol', *Galian 6*, 1985.

Patricia M. Melendrez, 'A Monomythic Reading of Amado V. Hernandez's *Mga Ibong Mandaragit*', *University College Journal*, 7 (First Semester), 1964–65.

Resil Mojares, *Origins and Rise of the Filipino Novel: A Generic Study of the Novel Until 1940* (Quezon City: University of the Philippines Press, 1983).

Soledad S. Reyes, *Nobelang Tagalog 1905-1975: Tradisyon at Modernismo* (Quezon City: Ateneo de Manila University Press, 1982).

Jose Rizal, *Noli Me Tangere* (Translated by Soledad Lacson-Locsin) (Manila, Bookmark, 1996).

—*El Filibusterismo*, trans. by Soledad Lacson-Locsin (Manila. Bookmark, 1997).

Epifanio Jr. San Juan, Epilogue to *Mga Ibong Mandaragit* (Las Pinas City: M&L Licudine Enterprises, 1969).

John Schumacher, *The Propaganda Movement, 1880-1895: The Creators of a Filipino Consciousness, the Makers of a Revolution* (Manila: Solidaridad Publishing House, 1973).

—*The Making of a Nation: Essays on Nineteenth-Century Filipino Nationalism* (Quezon City: Ateneo de Manila University Press, 1991).

Rosario Torres Yu (ed.), *Magkabilang Mukha ng Isang Bagol at Iba Pang Akda ni Amado V. Hernandez* (Quezon City: University of the Philippines Press, 1997).